DEFEAT AT STALINGRAD

What his eyes saw was the effect of a shell explosion within the closed interior of a tank. The driver still sat at his place, but he was headless. The force of the explosion had sheared off the flesh of the chest and biceps. A skeleton sat there, with lungs and heart visible. The other three men of the crew had vanished; there was left of them only a bloody scum pasted to the walls of the tank . . .

* * * * * * *

An entire army writhed in agony. The army was breaking up; the center of the huge organism was numbed, its communications no longer functioned, its peripheral parts were paralyzed. Men died and the dead were no longer buried. In the streets of Stalingrad corpses lay like logs of wood and snow piled up on them until they resembled fallen birch logs . . . Here was the scene of the lost battle, of the lost war, of the zenith of German power and the most crushing defeat in German military history . . .

STALINGRAD

Theodor Plievier

Translated from the German by
Richard and Clara Winston

A BERKLEY MEDALLION BOOK
published by
BERKLEY PUBLISHING CORPORATION

STALINGRAD

FIRST THERE WAS GNOTKE.

It was a gray November day and August Gnotke carried a spade. Eight yards long, two wide, and one and a half deep was the pit that Gnotke, Aslang, Hubbe, Dinger, and Gimpf had just finished. Sergeant Gnotke, Technical Sergeant Aslang, Corporals Hubbe and Dinger, and Private Gimpf outwardly did not differ at all from one another. They wore neither shoulder straps nor insignia, and their hands and faces were as grimed with dirt as their uniforms. Once, long ago, they might have been the hands and faces and uniforms of men.

The last shovelful had been dug. Hubbe and Dinger picked up a stretcher, Gnotke and Gimpf another one. They moved slowly, without pausing, without looking up. They had stuck their spades into the pile of earth beside the pit; now they trotted off with the stretchers and disappeared into the mist.

This was happening in the region to the east of Kletskaya, in the loop of the Don River between Kletskaya and Vertiachi, in the area of the 376th Infantry Division. To the west, the great river rolled downstream under its winter coat of gray ice; to the rear, two days' march eastward, was the Don again, for here it swings around in a great arc. Beyond the Don and another two days' march to the east lay the Volga and Stalingrad. This was the northern flank of the division, along the Don. Ahead and behind, underfoot and in the air was the front.

It was a good post for the disciplinary battalion. The orders read: "The term of punishment is to be served in the farthermost front line. The punishment shall consist of the most difficult and dangerous work, such as mine clearance, burial of the dead, etc., under enemy fire, etc. . . ."

The regulations further specified:

"Pay: to be curtailed. *Uniform:* to hinder desertion—uniforms without insignia. Insignia of rank, collar tabs, and shoulder straps to be removed. *Shelter:* less comfortable than that of the other troops. *Mail:* at discretion of the officer in charge.

Packages will not be distributed, but will be held by the unit delivering mail. Association with other units or civilians is forbidden unless in line of duty. *Lighting:* none to be supplied. *Privileges:* will be granted in special cases only by the officer in charge."

Gnotke had been in the disciplinary battalion for ten months. The campaign of the previous winter and the march on Moscow had "corrupted" him; his "refusal before assembled troops to obey orders" had earned him a stiff sentence. The case of Private Matthias Gimpf was also an "inevitable" result of the last winter campaign. In a trench behind the frozen Shisdra—on a day when trees cracked with the cold and the wind whipped fine powdered snow into the men's faces—Gimpf had stood in a thin overcoat and torn boots, and like all the rest had kept his hands in his pockets while the regimental commander was inspecting the positions. When spoken to about his unsoldierly attitude, he had responded with an uncomprehending smile, he had not removed his hands from his pockets and as the adjutant had put it in his report, "had not even clicked his heels." Thus he had provided a dreadful example of the "low morale," of the troops, and his sentence had been correspondingly severe. Sergeant Aslang had not been with the squad long, and the two corporals, Hubbe and Dinger, had been sent up with transport from the rear quite recently, to fill out the ranks.

Gnotke and Gimpf had formerly been attached to the Fourth Panzer Army and with it had crossed the Kursk Steppes. While the engineers cleared narrow paths through the minefields, the "chaff" of the winter campaign—soldiers like Gnotke and Gimpf, sometimes aided by local villagers, women and adolescents, and evacuated Jews from Warsaw, Budapest, and Hamburg—cleared away the rest of the mines. These groups of "chaff" worked on either side of the lanes when the army had broken through, their numbers constantly diminished by casualties and replenished by more Jews and more natives. They were as much a part of the army and of the eastward offensive as the armored divisions, the shock troops, and the infantry attached to the Panzer Army.

More than once Gnotke and Gimpf had been knocked flat by exploding mines; they had been bruised and their skins flayed. Sometimes they had even had to wipe pieces of flesh or entrails from their faces—all that remained of the man or woman blown to bits next to them. But they themselves had not become casualties. Then their sector had been taken over by Italian and Hungarian troops. For this reason, or perhaps

8

because the southern front was already beginning to consume men more rapidly and therefore had greater need of human chaff, with a whole truckload of their kind, they had been attached to a regiment on the march. But they had not gone far; they had been unloaded again in Valuiki and once more assigned to an engineer company. They went on working their way across minefields and clearing barbed-wire entanglements under shellfire, this time attached to the Sixth Army, following it across the Don Steppes and deep into the bend of the river. Here they lost many: sailors from Norway, men who had stolen army property, psychoneurotics from the Luftwaffe, former truck drivers who had suddenly been thrown into combat and whose morale had cracked under fire. But Gnotke and Gimpf, these two grains of sand, were again spared and were transferred to another squad.

In the northern loop of the Don were troops of "chaff" who kept to their foxholes by day, and emerged at night, moving like ghosts over the river lowlands as they laid log roads. Once more it was those who were exhausted and unnerved, the men who were the last remnants of shattered regiments, who perished here from artillery fire or from fever and exhaustion. Between Kletskaya and Vertiachi the German advance had ground to a stop. At Keltskaya the Red Army had driven a bridgehead over the Don, a key post for future operations. Farther south, at Kalach, the Sixth Army's drive advanced across the Don and over the plain between Don and Volga until it reached Stalingrad, where it came to a halt in the labyrinth of ruins. But here, in the Don noose, positional fighting went on for a long time and men marked time, fought and died on one spot. A great mass of German and Rumanian troops were assembled opposite the Russian bridgehead at Kletskaya, which represented a severe threat to the Stalingrad northern front. Corduroy roads and pontoon bridges were set up again and again, and as often hacked to pieces by the Russian artillery. For weeks the corpses of German soldiers floated down the Don. On the plain and in the hilly terrain to the east and north of Kletskaya there were many dead, too. Gnotke and Gimpf were put to work burying them.

By October they had buried almost the entire battalion to which they belonged, including three company commanders and the battalion commander. Commanders of battalions were to be provided with coffins of rough boards, company commanders to be wrapped in shelter halves, and the enlisted men of the tank divisions in blankets. Such, at least, were the instructions to the graves registration officers, and perhaps these

9

instructions had once been carried out. But no longer. Nor were ceremonial volleys fired over the graves, even when entire half companies were interred. Divisional chaplains held hasty services in the presence of any medical aides, truck drivers, and stray supply-service men whom they stopped on the road and hailed over to the grave. This more solemn part of the interment took place without benefit of Gimpf's and Gnotke's attendance; they observed it only from a distance as they dug the next grave.

Grave upon grave they dug. October came and went, and it was November. Snow in the air, the ground frozen, crevices and hollows filled with drifted snow that was often coated with a thin layer of ice. From the bottom lands and the Don, clouds of vapor billowed up, as from a vast laundry, and rolled over the landscape. Now and then there was a distant flash like lightning in the upper layers of mist. Then the roar of cannon would be heard, and somewhere in the mist a fountain of snow and frozen clods of earth would jet up. The soldiers in their dugouts and trenches crouched underground. The ammunition was brought up each morning toward dawn, and rations were not brought up until it was dark. Hardly a man ventured to lift his head above ground during the day.

Only the burial squads walked about freely.

Today more than ever they resembled phantoms floating through the mist. One in front, one behind, they melted into a single shape with the laden stretcher. The mist distorted all forms. A man on horseback who suddenly appeared looked as if he were riding a dog. And Hubbe and Dinger, with their load between them, Gnotke and Gimpf with theirs, looked exactly like heavily-loaded barges moving slowly down a river.

The pit, dug originally by Russian women and old men, and widened by Aslang, Hubbe, Dinger, Gnotke, and Gimpf, had been intended as a mass grave for the scattered dead of the last few days. They had been given provisional burial and were now to be disinterred and placed in a common grave as a memorial to Hitler's triumphal march to the East. But an attack two days ago by twenty-eight tanks and an infantry battalion had been beaten off with heavy losses by the Russians and the burial crews had been forced to revise their plans. Now, in addition to the week-old corpses who belonged here, the grave had to be enlarged to receive the dead of the tank division and the assault battalion. All the signs indicated hasty interment; here would undoubtedly be yet another "forgotten grave." The "death men," as the members of the penal battalion were called, had been the only witnesses of such services before, had stood by the new grave they were digging and watched the overworked chaplain and the graves registration officer suddenly appear, mumble some words into the mist, and vanish as swiftly as they had come. Then the death men would return to cover the mass grave with earth.

As for shrouds, it was the middle of November and the army had already been through an initial period of sharp frosts. Where, when winter equipment was being supplied to the living in scanty quantities or not at all, were they to get shelter halves and blankets for the dead? Wrapping was necessary only when the burial crew had to carry dismembered bodies, and then only on the brief path to the grave. One blood-soaked shelter half had to serve again and again, and at night the burial squad often spread it out on the damp ground and slept upon it.

Hubbe and Dinger returned to the pit, set down their stretcher, tipped it, and let their burden fall. It struck the bottom of the grave like a filled grain sack; it was one of the disinterred corpses, like a mummy covered with a layer of frozen mud. Hubbe and Dinger picked up the stretcher again without pausing or looking up, and vanished into the mist. And Gnotke and Gimpf came up in their turn and performed the same routine. When it was a dead tank driver or a rifleman, half of the dogtag, the belt, leather straps, and contents of the man's pockets were placed on the ground next to Technical Sergeant Aslang, who stood silent as a post, making a short vertical mark on a sheet of paper each time Hubbe and Dinger or Gnotke and Gimpf came up. After every fourth stroke he made a cross stroke. They did not speak, though lost here in the mist they were not under strict surveillance; they had lost the habit of talking, just as they had ceased to expect warmth or light in the holes where they spent their nights.

While Gnotke and Gimpf were making their third or fourth trip, an artillery shell burst near by. Splinters howled through the air and clods of earth thudded back to the ground. Although the blast scarcely touched them, thick streamers of smoke drifted by their heads like a warm breath before dissolving into the whitish mist. The two men paid no attention. One in front, one behind, they continued on, dumped their burden, went off again and again returned. Sixteen cubic yards of human flesh were required to fill the grave, and not all the corpses could be transported in one piece; where the infantry battalion had fought they had to pluck fragments of flesh and rose-red entrails from the frost-whitened underbrush.

Once, for several days, Gnotke had been the recipient of one of those rare privileges granted "at the discretion of the officer in charge." He had been relieved of the duty of carrying the bodies and instead had taken up the position held by Aslang today, standing by from morning to night, watching as the grave gradually filled with mud-coated figures, with contorted faces, insanely staring eyes, severed legs, arms, torsos, and unrecognizable fragments of flesh.

"*Dearest Sepp . . .*" "*My poor dear Karl . . .*" "*Darling sweetheart . . .*" "*My dear son . . .*" "*Dear brother and brother-in-law . . .*" "*My darling . . .*" "*My sweetest, most beloved Max . . .*" So began the letters he had collected and, in the evening, placed with the other possessions that had been picked up. Then he would draw up a list of names for the graves registration officer. "*Darling sweetheart . . .*" "*My dear husband and papa . . .*" These were voices from a far distant shore; they had faded to a whisper that could not reach Gnotke. He knew that those to whom the letters were addressed, in September when the sun was hot and the earth dry, had lain on the steppes like dry wood and had been gathered like dry wood. And he knew that, after time had passed, they had lain without withering, with all their juices intact, and had been somewhat heavier; and that when more time had passed (there had already been days when the temperature was as low as thirteen and even twenty-two below zero Fahrenheit) they had lain hard and heavy as stone on the stretcher, frozen in sitting positions or into spread-eagled St. Andrew's crosses that made them even more difficult to carry and took up a disproportionate amount of room in the pit.

"*My darlingest boy . . .*" and: "*Take good care of yourself . . .*" and: "*Don't volunteer for anything; don't push yourself forward . . .*" and: "*Be sure your feet don't get cold—pad your shoes with cardboard . . .*" and all the other phrases in the letters couldn't possibly apply to the withered summer corpses or the fresh autumn corpses or the refractory frozen corpses. These were indifferent, meaningless, silly phrases, as Gnotke knew. The other things in the letters, the hopes, fears, geographical or military observations, meant nothing at all to Gnotke. He had reached the point where hope no longer exists.

". . . *Am waiting with longing for the end, and with still greater longing for your first letter after the battle, so that I'll be certain you. . . .*" What kind of end could there be, and what kind of battle could be followed by letters?

". . . *Alas, there is still no end in sight to the fighting around Stalingrad. When this city is taken it will more or less finish this year's offensive. At most, operations in the Caucasus will continue, if we should succeed in taking the Klukhov, Mammissov, and Cross Passes, since a winter campaign is possible*

*south of the Caucasus, and then we might at least take the
Baku oilfields before the year is out."*

*". . . The struggle for Stalingrad still goes on. Today we saw
it again in the newsreels. I'm so excited. When will the place
fall? Perhaps tomorrow, Sunday, as a Sabbath gift, we shall
hear that the city is entirely in our hands."*

Again and again in these letters "Stalingrad," "Stalingrad."
But the oft-repeated word meant little to Gnotke. His past (he
never thought about it) had been cut off sharply ten months
before, and his present was without reality, without even geographical reality.

Wet, cold, sand, graves. Even at night water dripped; even
at night sand trickled into his face. On this autumn day it grew
dark soon after three in the afternoon and the mist settled like
a blanket over the system of bunkers, pits, trenches, and
barbed-wire, concealing everything beneath it. The land was
cloaked in darkness, and it was gloomiest in those flimsily-
covered trenches where the outcasts of the disciplinary battalion lay waiting for the night upon rotting straw and muddy,
stained shelter halves, under guard.

In that damp, spectral night Gnotke sat up once and brought
his face close to that of Gimpf, with whom he had been together for so long. "Matt . . ." he whispered.

Gimpf stared at him and said nothing.

AND THERE WAS VILSHOFEN.

But Vilshofen stood for more than the face and personality of a single man; he signified the new world that was to arise out of blood and tears; he embodied a society convulsively taking new forms, revising boundaries, and changing governments. It had begun with a dense cloud of dust rolling down from the Carpathians, and crossing the Pruth, the Dniester, the Bug, and the Dnieper in the course of the summer, then raging like a prairie fire over the Ukraine. Vilshofen, who had been assigned to the Moscow front, in the second year had taken command of a panzer regiment. Vilshofen embodied the might that sought to shatter and crush the independence and will of other nations. He symbolized, too, worry over pitted cylinders, over carburetors that failed to keep out the fine sand of the steppes and the desert, so the motors wore out faster than they could be replaced. He was concerned with reserves of machines and men and often—two thousand miles away from his own land—he was momentarily stunned by the vastness of the operation and the way the goal receded. Vilshofen had stood with his tanks on the northern rim of Stalingrad. After a hundred days of indecisive fighting, he and his group had been pulled out and sent across the Don to be thrown into the fighting west of Kletskaya. He had been ordered to take a roundabout route through Vertiachi, but instead he had sent his smoking, mud-slinging line of tanks hurtling down the Gumrak-Rossoshka road and through idyllic Peskovatka, the corps headquarters. The staffs had set up shop there and closed the highway to the passage of troops, but Vilshofen drove on. He would just as defiantly have rolled through the place if Army Headquarters had been located there.

That evening Colonel Vilshofen, accompanied by his adjutant, stood by the edge of the road watching his tanks return. He had sent out twenty-eight, and twenty had already rolled past him. He was waiting for the rest.

14

The assault troops of the armored division were going by. The last truck stopped.

"Hello there, Tomas!" called Vilshofen.

A man stepped down and approached through the mist—Captain Tomas, the company commander. He confirmed what his chief had already learned from the tank drivers. After an initial success and the silencing of a Russian battery, the attack had broken down under fire from the adjacent battery. Some two hundred dead men were the sole results of this attack. Four tanks had been left burning, four more were being towed back and would be along soon. Colonel Vilshofen waited until the rattle of caterpillar treads began again. Like a tug in a foggy harbor, one tank towing another damaged one made its appearance. It was followed by a second, a third, and a fourth. The first was not damaged badly; Vilshofen judged it might be ready for battle again by tomorrow or the next day. The same was true of the second; the third had lost only a tread. And then the fourth came along, stripped of treads, moving very slowly on its bare rollers, its hull rent open by a direct hit. Why bother with it, thought Vilshofen. It was no time to collect scrap.

Vilshofen signalled for it to stop and went up to make an inspection. He switched on his flashlight and peered through a jagged hole into the interior. The white light of the headlights fell full upon his face—the face of a man of fifty with a big, jutting nose and clear, large eyes. What those eyes saw was the effect of a shell explosion within the closed interior of a tank. The driver still sat at his place, but he was headless. The force of the explosion had sheared off the flesh of the chest and biceps. A skeleton sat there, with lungs and heart visible. The undamaged hands, still gripping the steering wheel, looked like gloves on the ends of the bare armbones. The other three men of the crew had vanished; there was left of them only a bloody scum pasted to the walls of the tank.

The colonel knew their names, knew too where they had come from. "Burstedt of Wuppertal, a toolmaker's son; Hofmann and Redemacher, both from the same village on the Eder, and Sergeant Elmenreich of Schwerin," he murmured, and the words were like an epitaph.

Tomorrow would be November 19th.

From the Russian bridgehead in the west the no-man's-land extended northward down to the river. It was swampy lowland thickly overgrown with brush, dotted with ponds and tiny lakes and quicksands. Along the front line, down to the eastern part of the Don loop, was hilly terrain gashed by ravines,

15

fought over for weeks by the Russian artillery and infantry. Here and there the Russians had broken through, and ever since the Luftwaffe had bombed these areas daily and the Germans had launched numerous counterattacks. On the night of November 18th, however, a deathly silence had settled over this unquiet sector.

There are ship captains who suddenly start up out of sound sleep at a change in weather. Without having consulted the barometer or glanced at the state of the sky or the leaden sea, they sense an impending storm, feel it in the air they breathe. In the same way, Colonel Vilshofen sat up in the middle of the night, huddled on his cot, and listened tensely. What was there to hear? Only the breathing of his host, the commander of a flak battery who had offered him a bed. The thick walls of the bunker excluded outside noises. Colonel Vilshofen stood up, crossed the anteroom, and stood for a moment looking down at the youthful face of Latte, his adjutant, who was sleeping there. He went up the steps. Outside there was nothing —a vaporous sky, snow and dampness in the air, the black earth below. Except for a rocket flare far off on the northern horizon, there would have been nothing to indicate that two armies were engaged in a life-and-death struggle here. A dark, a sleeping landscape—that was all, apparently. But Vilshofen was uneasy. He picked his way through the cluster of dugouts, found the hole he sought, switched on his flashlight, and went down the mud steps.

A heavy atmosphere of huddled sleepers and the smell of damp, oily clothing wafted toward him. These were his repair crew's quarters. Vilshofen beckoned to the sentry and had the man show him the cot where Private Wilsdruff was sleeping.

"Hey there, Wilsdruff!"

A broad-faced man with a drooping mustache opened his eyes.

"What's the story on those two tanks, Wilsdruff?"

"Tanks . . ." Then the soldier, fully awake, recognized his regimental commander. "The tanks, sir?"

"How long will the repairs take?"

"Two days, probably, sir."

"Probably. But how long will it actually take? I want them tomorrow."

"Well, then we'll have to start work now."

"Yes, at once. It's urgent."

The colonel left without waiting for Wilsdruff to wake the others. When he re-entered his own bunker he found that the flak commander was awake too. He was sitting at the table looking at a map that Vilshofen had sketched.

"It's beginning—and before the twenty-third," Vilshofen said, as he came in. A Russian offensive had been expected around November 23rd.

"It's never stopped over here, Colonel," the flak major replied. "At any rate we've been expecting it, and are ready for anything."

"We might be if we had enough heavy artillery over here and on Hill 120. As it is, I'm afraid we're in for a surprise—it will be a big one."

"May I ask one question, Colonel?"

"Ask away, Buchner."

Flak Commander Buchner again looked down at Vilshofen's sketch. Vilshofen had something of a reputation for his rough sketch maps and plans, drawn with charcoal or even a soot-blackened finger. Real interest and argument were roused by the black marks he habitually made on them with his thumb to indicate weak spots.

The major put his question. "This black spot here—I don't understand it at all, sir. It seems to me that's where we're the strongest."

"Where we ought to be strongest."

The 48th Panzer Corps was there, the 23rd and 14th Panzer Divisions, and the Royal Rumanian First Panzer Division—a considerable force of armor. But in reality, as Vilshofen had discovered on an inspection tour, a good part of the tanks were scattered over the length and breadth of the Don Bend, many of them in the repair shops. Tanks and men too had been worn out during the unceasing summer advance and the constant battles around Stalingrad. They had no business in the front lines; they belonged in the rear echelons for thorough overhauling and weeks of rest, to be followed by training and largescale maneuvers. That was true of the German troops, and still more of the Rumanian tank division, which was equipped with matériel scraped up from meager German resources and from booty taken in the French campaign. This division had not yet been in action and needed training badly.

Vilshofen heard his adjutant stirring and called out, "Latte, I still have a supply of cigarettes; please take a few packs out to the repair crew and see how the work is getting on."

He turned to Buchner again. "Yes, as I was saying, if only we had enough heavy artillery here and on the flanking heights. But I saw nothing up there but some flak and chemical companies and a few horse-drawn field guns."

17

The door above opened and shut. A gust of snowy air entered the bunker, followed by silence, the utter silence of the night. Twenty tanks, Vilshofen thought, and two more will be repaired. That makes twenty-two fit for action.

The unusual silence was also felt in the disciplinary battalion's dugout. Gnotke could have counted the drops of water that dripped from the ceiling prop. Perhaps they were actually being counted by the sentry. With his steel helmet and fixed bayonet he stood like a gloomy statue, blocking the entrance. Gnotke had long since given up counting the drops, but he felt the silence, keenly, like a man who suddenly becomes aware that a clock in his room is no longer ticking. He looked down the row of stretched-out sleepers. Nearly fifty lay hunched up there in their wretchedness. At his side lay Gimpf, sleeping with open mouth.

Gnotke lay awake until reveille. Breakfast was a bit of bread and a cupful of ersatz coffee. Then—it was not yet dawn—they set out for their place of work. Aslang, Hubbe, and Dinger looked around uneasily. To the north, where the Russian batteries were usually active, and toward the swamplands beyond the rolling mist in the direction of the Don, where for weeks the clatter and noise of battle had been heard, silence now lurked like an omnivorous maw.

They picked up their stretchers and began their usual monotonous routine. And yet everything was unusual. It was dreamlike, and as Gnotke walked with dangling arms into the mist, a dream actually took shape in his mind. Where did it come from? It was a hand, a woman's hand—a recumbent figure, the limbs and face shrouded, the shape obscured like the half-buried body of a soldier. But the shroud was not mud and earth; it was a fluff of soft blankets. And she was not alone; she was lying with a man, although only her hand could be seen. And Gnotke knew this hand. But what . . .

The earth shook, trembled underground, belched upward. Where—where did this hand come from. . . . Pauline? The earth, the sky! The sky flamed, in the north and above the Don too. The sky above the swamps and the river was no longer white as milk, but red like spurting blood.

Artillery. Mortars. Roaring cannon. Thousands of tons of explosives. For hours it went on, hours that were not hours at all, that were spewed-out fragments beyond time.

On the morning of November 19th the Soviet troops to the northwest of Stalingrad broke through the German front. Gnotke's position at the time was on the northern flank of the front, where it was supported by the Don Bend; he was precisely at the break-through point, in fact. Gnotke had taken part in the march on Moscow, and under Russian artillery fire he had fallen back sixty miles. He had been in the dash across the Kursk Steppe, and had cleared mines in the Don plains. But all that his eyes and ears had seen and heard in the way of attacks, bombings, and mine explosions had been mere preludes to this. This was the culmination or—it is the same thing —the very nadir of his experience.

But all the screams and shocks, the flashes and explosions that burst on his eyes and ears had long since ceased to touch his consciousness. His inner self had long since walled itself in. That core of being where will, emotion, sympathy, love, and fear have their source could scarcely be reached by anything any longer; over it lay earth, snow, many things. But his eyes were still clear and his hearing keen. It was mechanical, automatic, but he saw and heard.

He saw and heard everything that was going on in the air and on the ground—all the roaring tumult around him. But for him, too, time was no measurable unit; it was beyond all possibility of measurement. He could not have said where the stretcher lay or what force had wrenched it from his hands, nor how he had come to be lying in a hollow in the ground, nor how and when he had made his way back to the grave pit only to find that it no longer existed.

He lay there. Within the bloodstained mist a thousand gaping muzzles howled and screeched. Ahead of him lay the German pillboxes and batteries, and beyond them the Russian positions, swathed in a pall of smoke in which rust-red dots flared. The red dots expanded, devoured the smoke, clawed at the sky, rose into a steep cliff of red fire. The German batteries fought back, fired as fast as they could. But it was like throwing glowing coals into a racing prairie fire, and they did not fight long.

Beyond the German line there, the shellfire was landing. Exploding charges of powder sent the metal—cannon in flat, mortar shells in steep trajectories—hurtling down to detonate and rend the earth. Had there been a forest there, the trees would have been mowed down like grass under the strokes of a mighty scythe. But there was no forest; it was flat, treeless terrain and looked now like the surface of a lake beaten by plump raindrops. Only here it was not rain but glowing metal tearing into the earth, and what was thrown up was not spray but sand and mud; what remained were yawning shell holes. Where snow had lain, the fierce heat laid bare the scarred grass, and a moment later grass and topsoil as well disappeared. A landscape like the mountains of the moon was created; it drew closer and closer to the German lines and took over a terrain where there was not only sand and mud, but bunkers and corridors, and pillboxes with built-in battery positions, machine-gun nests, and mortars; a terrain where munitions dumps, command posts with map tables, stables, bedrooms and living rooms were embedded under heavy layers of soil, and where the crowded German crews fought—eyes glued to sights, hands on firing levers, dragging up shells and mortar ammunition. The muzzles of the guns flashed; shell after shell shot up out of the mortars. Brown smoke rolled over the earthworks. Where machine guns and riflemen began firing, it was a sign of incipient panic, for there were as yet no recognizable targets.

Along the whole front death stalked the German positions.

Foreground and background were a billowing mass of smoke, dust, and fiery vapors bursting toward the sky and sinking down again. A hill spitting fire appeared—a heavy battery had blown up in the shape of an inverted pyramid. The dark fragments in the glare were pieces of metal and bodies. Black, cloudy masses spurted upward. Darts of fire, balls of smoke. Beams and props clattering to earth. A horse falling from the sky, legs and hoofs pointed upward. A barbed-wire entanglement with posts attached floated through the air. An infantry regiment with its divisional artillery was blown up, fell back to earth, and was again thrown up, turned over, and reduced to dust.

The human figures that bounded out of a crater and moved over the ground like dry leaves swept before the wind, that stumbled over one another, fell and remained on the ground or stood up again, struggled on a little farther, only to fall again and run again—these figures were no longer members of a regiment; they were "chaff." The tall lieutenant who emerged from the zone of smoke staggering and gesticulating like a drunkard, and suddenly breaking out into peals of laughter—this was no longer a platoon commander; it was a madman. A figure crawled over the snow like a worm, leaving a trail of blood behind him, and finally tumbled into a hollow. He was the commander of a company of panzer grenadiers, Captain Tomas of Vilshofen's regiment. The cloud of mud and spurting snow that moved down toward the highway from Hill 127 was Major Buchner with a group of automatic flak guns; he was fleeing from his mangled positions, leaving behind guns, searchlights, direction finder, and other apparatus.

At the exit to a village of connecting dugouts a man stood

20

like a towering pillar, stopping all the bewildered engineers, infantrymen, and anti-tank crews who came his way and gathering them around himself. Then, making use of a ravine that led to the rear, he marched off with this group toward a wrecked farmhouse where he had sent his remaining six tanks, all that were left of his twenty-two. This was Vilshofen.

The artillery attack reached a new phase.

A few isolated shells continued to fall forward, gouging out new craters. But the concentrated fire of the Russian batteries had lifted. It still roared through the air, a cataract arching high above, but the cutting, slashing, smashing metal now rained down upon the rear positions and struck into the retreating columns of infantry and ordnance.

On the left flank, under cover of the mist, something else was taking place. The Rumanians in the swamplands, where they had received the full force of the main assault, had been routed. And now thousands of Russian hands and thousands of Russian bodies, chest deep in the icy water, were busy laying pontoons and log roads over the river and over the swamp and quicksands.

That was the situation when Gnotke reeled to his feet, retraced his course, and reached the place where the last grave had been dug and almost filled. The pit was no longer there. Beside it was a crater so large that a peasant hut, roof and all, could have been fitted into it. The sixteen cubic yards of human flesh had been blasted into the air and had fallen back again, and now dangled over the edge of the crater. There Gnotke sat down, recognizing a familiar corpse. He might have lain down at the bottom of the shell hole, as did Gimpf, who had stayed close beside him all along. There was room enough there, and it would have afforded some cover. But if Gnotke thought anything at all at this moment, it was that he preferred to be buried nearer the sky, not so deep in the earth. He sat down beside the mud-covered heap of corpses, and beside him sat Sergeant Aslang. Aslang's face was completely black, and his teeth were bared as if he were laughing. Gnotke noticed it, or perhaps he did not notice. Aslang dead seemed more natural to him than Aslang alive, and he did not even wonder where Hubbe and Dinger might be. Sitting there, filthy and smeared, staring with popping eyes into space, he looked more dead than the grinning Aslang and the high pile of frozen corpses.

The pile at his back shielded him from the icy wind that was rising in the east. But after a while Aslang's body no longer imparted any warmth. Gnotke moved somewhat away and leaned against the still warm body of a horse that had collapsed and

21

died near the other dead things. There he sat without moving again, while drifting smoke and mist narrowed his field of vision. Daylight faded; the hours passed in a hazy twilight. The German front had been penetrated, the troops in the foremost lines killed or scattered, taken prisoner or cut down while fleeing. Through the breach poured a never-ending torrent of Russian infantry, tank, and assault units.

Everything that lay within Gnotke's direct line of vision, he saw, but nothing of what went on to right or left. For no matter what happened, whether the caterpillar tread of a tank rolled close to him, whether rifle shots whistled into the ground beside him, or sabers whipped through the air and wild cries resounded, Gnotke did not turn his head. He saw tanks moving across the cratered terrain, bobbing up and down amid the floating streamers of smoke and fog like boats on a choppy sea; he saw the flashes of their guns; and he saw dark forms rising up out of the swamps. These were the Rumanians running for their lives. Horses and riders leaped into the mist of the fleeing mass. The horses reared up on their hind legs, and the riders slashed and hacked around them.

The pile of corpses on the edge of the shell hole seemed to form the watershed of the shattered front. Again and again the tanks came up and turned south there toward Kalach. And the mobs fleeing up from the Don scarcely ever got beyond this monument to death. There, and all around the grave, they were cut down by sabers, and then the Russian cavalry also swung south toward Kalach. But the earth-encrusted, sweetishly redolent heap attracted no attention; a tank driver who saw it suddenly looming before him steered his vehicle away, and the Cossacks also rode around it. The Russians were no longer firing at invisible targets, and this heap of corpses of which Gnotke was a part was no target for a tank, nor for a rifleman, nor for a saber stroke.

Evening fell. The wind from the east rent the overhanging clouds. A patch of frosty winter sky was laid bare, and the moon emerged. A weird light shone down upon the land. Gnotke's glance was attracted to a clump of brush that still stood, waist-high. The bursh alone remained—bare flat land beyond, and then another clump of woody brush; then bare flat land covered by tracked snow under the uncanny moon. It was a drear landscape, full of roaring, like the sea.

But it was the roaring of the void.

The German army retreated eastward, beyond the Don. Russian tank and cavalry forces had broken the front and gone on toward Kalach, where they met a second spearhead driven over the Volga south of Stalingrad and joined it to form a firm ring around the German divisions. The army retreated through Golubaya.

One of the last persons to see the Golubaya highway in its normal state, as a supply road, and the village of Verkhnaya Golubaya before the confusion of retreat struck it, was Colonel Vilshofen. The first time had been on his drive to Kletskaya. The second time was when he came down again to obtain rations, ammunition, and fuel for the combat unit he had gathered around him. The first visit was one week and the second a few minutes before the general collapse of the front.

The first time had been on a foggy morning. The village street with its peaceful huts, here and there a shutter being thrown open, and the villagers coming out to sweep the street with brooms, had reminded him of a beautiful woman rubbing her eyes as she awakens from sleep. A gate had opened and a rider had appeared for his morning constitutional, his prancing horse flaunting a glistening hide. Down the street a second and a third rider had appeared, the neighing of their mounts filling the morning air. Vilshofen had just come from the factories of Stalingrad, and could not resist saying to Latte, his adjutant, "You know, Latte, it's a long time since we saw anything like that."

Afterward he had breakfasted with the officers of the staff, who were wearing neat undress uniforms; then he had discussed the situation with the corps commander and the artillery officer, Lieutenant Colonel Unschlicht and General Vennekohl. He had been much amazed by the optimism of these well-rested officers.

That first time he had passed through with his twenty-eight tanks (the others were being repaired at Stalingrad). The second time he had broken in upon Lieutenant Colonel Unschlicht's morning gymnastics. When Vilshofen informed him of the break-through, Unschlicht had been much impressed. However—and as a member of the General Staff he was probably right in this—he did not jump to conclusions on the basis of Vilshofen's report. He thought that the Golubaya Hills, where were the obvious next line of resistance, would be held; the 16th and 24th Tank Divisions were already on their way as a relief force, and he felt sure they would prove more than sufficient to seal the breach. Vennekohl, the artillery commander, held the same opinion. In his thickest Berlinese he had said, "Why, man, those Russians'll be smashed to pieces when the boys from the Sixteenth and Twenty-fourth get there."

23

Vilshofen had expressed disagreement, but of more immediate importance was the fact that he had obtained neither rations nor fuel for his makeshift unit; he returned empty-handed. On his way back everything he saw made him realize that it was the last chance, the eleventh hour and later, as far as the collapse in the Don Bend was concerned. Returning to his six tanks and his ragged troops, he witnessed scenes like a Napoleonic retreat. Rumanians with and without weapons, on foot and mounted, mixed with German infantrymen, engineers, construction units, remnants of ambulance companies, leaderless hordes of fleeing stragglers. This mob washed down from the Golubaya Hills into the valley and crossed and mingled with the retreating supply columns. Groups, individuals, and masses of men emerged from every road and every ravine, and before many hours had passed a dense jam of horse-drawn peasant carts, armored cars, artillery and infantry was squeezing through the narrow pass. It was impossible to move against the stream. Vilshofen had to abandon his vehicle and cover the last few miles on foot with Latte.

One of the men in the human river moving sluggishly through the Golubaya valley was Prisoner August Gnotke, with Prisoner Gimpf at his side.

In a vision, the day before a hand had appeared to August Gnotke. The hand had been Pauline's, of course, and the white nest was Pauline's bed. He knew it well enough, knew the alcove in Klein-Stepenitz where the bed stood. But what did it matter to him now? Surely by now she must have married the other fellow. Still and all, he could remember a woman as he groped through the mist, and that meant there was still 'something to live for'; there was still hope, and he had taken his first steps back into life.

He had dragged Gimpf out of the crater and set out with him. Gimpf, however, was utterly passive; Gnotke could get nothing out of him. "Sergeant Aslang!" he said to Gimpf. "Hubbe, Dinger," he said. But he had been unable to get a sound out of Gimpf. The man had merely looked at him with dead fish eyes and had remained silent. Aslang, Hubbe, and Dinger had remained behind and were probably dead—so what did they matter to him now?

The two men wandered silently over the moonlit field. Once they had flung themselves down, until some passing Cossacks had vanished again in the snow and the thud of hoofs could no longer be heard. Another time they had discerned a group of men marching in the darkness, and since Gnotke did not know

24

whether they were Germans or Russians he had pulled Gimpf to the ground beside him. This had been repeated several times until at last they found a dugout and crawled into it. There they had fallen into so deep a sleep that they had not noticed how the hole gradually filled with other stragglers.

"The Russians are coming!" Gnotke and Gimpf had slept until the cry rang out and men suddenly started up all around them and ran. They, however, remained where they were. By the gleam of a pair of glasses slowly approaching his face in the darkness, after a while Gnotke saw that there was another in the dugout who had also not run away.

"I suppose you don't give a damn either?" the man said to Gnotke.

"Not exactly . . . no, right now I do. . . ." Gnotke replied.

"Right now," meant little to the man, who made out only the vaguest outlines of Gnotke's face and the shadow of Gimpf crouched against the wall, with nothing to mark the two as convicts.

"I still care," the man said. "I want to get back home some-time, don't you?"

"Home . . ." repeated Gnotke. The word was as painful as his recent dream. Home. What did it mean? "There is such a place?" he said.

"Of course there is. I've got a wife and a little girl—she's five now. . . ." He changed the subject. "Our whole battalion is *kaputt*. You're from the Fifth?"

"No, from the penal battalion."

"Oh, I see. Well, it doesn't matter much now."

The man with the glasses was from Cologne, and no longer young. He was about Gnotke's age. In his pack he still had a portion of sausage and some bread which he shared with Gnotke and Gimpf. There was no sign of the Russians, but more stragglers continually descended into the dugout. As soon as dawn broke, Gnotke and Gimpf set out with these men, fol-lowing the tracks left by others who had fled before them. Down a slope they caught a glimpse of the deep gash of the Golubaya valley and the moving stream of trucks, horses, and men. They descended a gulley, and the man from Cologne met two men from his own platoon, two of his friends from whom he had been separated during the night. One of them was also from Cologne and was named Schorsch; the other was Hans Kettler of Crefeld. They addressed the man with glasses as Tünnes. These three, with Gnotke and Gimpf, stuck together for a while.

Now they were on the valley road to Verkhnaya Golubaya.

The pace was slow; again and again wheels stood still and the columns choked to a halt. On the hillside houses were burning.

An explosion, a second and a third. Shouts of "Russian tanks!" In the narrow pass, with wheel jammed up against wheel and man against man, there was no chance for dispersion. Gnotke saw faces turn gray under their crust of dirt. Gimpf's watery blue eyes continued to stare into space as usual. Tünnes remarked that there couldn't possibly be so many tanks there.

There was another detonation, but no sign of tanks. Ahead, smoke puffed up. When they finally reached the place, they saw that the German tank crews, stalled by the road for lack of gasoline, were blowing up their vehicles. The five smoking wrecks were the remains of a proud panzer regiment.

The column moved on all through the day. Gnotke kept Gimpf going, made him stay with their group. This blank face that had been with him through mine clearing on the Kursk Steppe and the Don Steppe, through the collapse at Kletskaya, that had never changed its indifferent expression amid smoke and death, was too precious to lose.

Night fell before they reached Verkhnaya Golubaya. Here too was snow, here too was the endless, slowly-moving ribbon of wheels . . . howitzers, field guns, infantry columns, groups of dispersed Rumanians. Over the snow there flickered a delicate flamingo pink, reflected from burning houses. The village was burning at both ends. Passing horses and vehicles cast gigantic shadows. In the middle of the village square a huge bonfire was burning. Gnotke, Gimpf, the two men from Cologne, and the one from Crefeld stopped to warm themselves. Here a top sergeant took them in hand, led them into a hut, handed each of them some bread and sausage, and set them to work cleaning out some bunkers.

The place had been a corps headquarters. Tünnes and Schorsch and Gnotke and Gimpf lugged out to the street all the things that the sergeant, a provost marshal, an administrative secretary, and others saw fit to hand them. To Gnotke and Gimpf, who had come straight from a mass grave to this hurly-burly of filing cases, boxes, frightened clerks, screaming civil employees, and white-faced officers, it was a fantastic business. And in point of fact, what was going on was the height of fantasy. Since May of that year, from Belgorod to the Don, this organization of civilians, officers, and attached personnel had been on the move. In command cars and busses, followed by a caravan of trucks, they had traveled from base to base and from village to village over four hundred and fifty miles of conquered territory. While the troops had bled and died as they marched, to the staff the corpses, sore feet, and shirts stiff with sweat had remained abstract concepts; to the members of the staff the drive to the Don had been a triumphal parade. They had settled in houses and bunkers, and when the fighting continued for weeks and the advance halted in Stalingrad and degenerated to skirmishing in the streets and in underground mazes, when the attempt to cross the Don in a northeasterly direction had resulted only in more and more bodies drifting downstream—they had passed their hours off duty reading books, playing cards, furnishing their bunkers, exercising their horses, and waiting impatiently to move forward. Soon, they kept hoping, the new marching orders would come and would read "Right face, march, toward Baku and the Caspian Sea," or: "Left face, march, toward Saratov, Kazan, and Moscow." So the weeks passed and the second winter of the campaign in the east—began. Even this morning they had not thought of flight as a possibility. A setback—that was possible and tolerable. But that morning they had been certain the Golubaya Hills and the valley would be held.

This night, this night was sheer fantasy!

Regiments were no longer regiments. Panzer regiments reported: Orders carried out; last five tanks blown up. The motorized artillery had to be abandoned—there was no more gasoline for the tractors. There was scarcely enough fuel for the trucks assigned to the various staffs in the retreat. But the alarming report that the Russians had broken through to Kalach meant that they must escape as fast as possible beyond the Don. Could it be done without gasoline, without the horses, which were far away in remount depots? That meant many things would have to be left behind. And that meant hasty orders, munitions dumps blown up, pale faces and wild eyes. A frenzy of destruction seized the members of the staffs. In the midst of it all stood Gnotke, his arms outstretched while the sallow-faced administrative secretary loaded him with files full of documents and ordered him to pile them on the truck drawn up in front of the house. Near by stood Gimpf, who was being loaded down with brand-new boots by the sergeant. Tünnes had his arms full of sweaters, Schorsch carried laundry, Kettler uniforms, and so on. Outside by the truck, however, all this stuff was refused; a lieutenant sent them on, and documents, sweaters, laundry, uniforms, books, and a thousand other objects were thrown into the mountainous bonfire. The flames leaped higher and higher.

The secretary came out and looked around wild-eyed. "Lieutenant, the regulations—I can't burn all this. Don't you have any more room on your truck?"

"You want me to . . . for Christ's sake, man, you want me to take all your damfool regulations? Are you crazy? Regulations —at a time like this!"

A lieutenant colonel suddenly appeared, his ascetic features more haggard than usual, hollow shadows in his cheeks. "What's going on here?"

"The regulations, *Herr Oberstleutnant* . . ."

"Clear out that truck! Throw everything into the fire. Only ammunition and rations in the trucks. It's a matter of life or death!"

The administrative secretary slunk off, arms hanging loosely, and vanished inside the house. Sparks shot upward. In the red glare the slowly rolling wheels of vehicles and the feet of marching men could be distinguished.

"The Russians are in Kalach!"

"Army H.Q. has fled from Golubinskaya, flown out in a Stork," was the next alarm that spread among the staff and was picked up by Gnotke, Tünnes, and the others. The lieutenant in front of the house had loaded his truck with food and small-arms ammunition. The driver was helping him into his coat when a sergeant, his face chalk-white, rushed up to him. "Sir —he's lying there—in the office—good God. . . ."

"What? Who? Pull yourself together, man."

"In the office—the secretary—he's shot himself."

Three bridges led across the Don.

The one at Perepolni was under Russian artillery fire from the north; the one at Luchenski was threatened from the south by the Russian armor and cavalry; the third, at Akimovski, lay between the two others and had been badly damaged. The middle of it had collapsed, but the engineers had repaired it with pontoons and planking.

Gnotke, Gimpf, and their companions had watched the corps staff leave Verkhnaya Golubaya, and then they themselves had resumed their march. The moon was still high in the sky when they arrived at the bridge. They saw dawn rise over the ice-crusted, snowy surface of the river—an expanse of moving wasteland. Across the river were swamps and quicksands and flat, open terrain. Vertiachi, Peskovatka, and Sokarevka, the villages on the other bank, were wide open to any attack.

On both sides of the bridge, along the sloping shore and on the flat land to the east, the gray mass waited—men, horses, vehicles, and guns. The only sign of movement was in a narrow lane up to the bridge and away from it on the other side, but even in this slender channel progress was by fits and starts. The ice on the river was still so thin that it would scarcely have supported a child. Trucks that had ventured out over it had almost immediately sunk in, and men who had tried to cross alone had broken through farther out and vanished under the ice. Officers and M.P.'s—unshaven, unwashed, unfed—were directing traffic, shouting, gesticulating—from time to time bracing themselves against the press of men and horses in order to speed through a staff car, a tank, or sometimes a bus in which rode a group of higher officers, or divisional staffs, or officers and civilian employees of some supply depot.

On flowed the stream, infantry, artillery, tanks, anti-aircraft units, cavalrymen in high lambskin caps—these last officers of the Fourth and Fifth Rumanian Corps. As a general rule the infantry from the area of the break-through arrived in disorganized hordes, with artillerymen and tank crews on foot. They had abandoned their guns and tanks, after blowing them up or failing to do so. Others, after dragging their weapons with them for days, were forced to leave them at the bridge or in the nearby assembly area where they blocked traffic. The crews moved across to the other bank without tanks and cannon. Bumper to bumper, horse after horse, long trains of ammunition, rations, field kitchens, and ambulances moved across the bridge. Then another jeep, followed by an entourage of big eight-ton trucks.

In the jeep sat the commanding general of an infantry division. With the main body of his troops he had passed through Perekopka. Scattered remnants of his division were now straggling down the Golubaya highway; others had been left behind. The car with the general rolled along. Ahead was a bottleneck of men and vehicles, behind a bottleneck of men and vehicles, on either side a lane of gray soldiers' faces. Some of them knew the general, had seen him at inspection, heard about him. Gnotke and Gimpf knew him as a supplier of many corpses.

General!

The way was long and the pack heavy. Hand grenades at the belt, spade on the hip, pockets full of ammunition . . . the way led through Flanders, through Arras, Bailleul, Hazebrouck, Poperinghe; it led in the east through swamps, through rivers, through smoke, over steppes, and there was no end to it. Faces begrimed, cheeks hollow, boots worn and sockless.

Today a king, tomorrow a dead man!

The way led through two wars, general. The Iron Cross on

your chest is a token of the first war, the bar and the Golden Cross betoken a second war. The first war was lost; will the second be lost too, and shall the great sacrifices we made at Shebekino, at the crossing of the Oskol, the victims of Klets-kaya, all go for nothing? For what are we dying, general?

Will our wives, our children, dry their tears on the banners of victory or must they weep forever? Was this war a just war, and for a great and sacred goal? Must we defend the father-land on the Oskol, on the Don, on the Volga?

What will you answer the mothers when they ask: where is my son? Where is the father of my children?

Where is your division, general? Part of it drowned, part blown to bits at Kletskaya, part of it lost in the Golubaya Hills, part of it hopelessly scattered. Seventeen thousand of us marched out; now there is only a handful left on the wooden bridge between Akimovski and Vertchiatchi.

Where are you leading us, general?

Across the Don: retreat to the East!

But in reality no soldier could speak in this fashion.

The men stood silent along the railing of the bridge and watched as the general in the jeep with his retinue of eight-ton trucks rolled past. The sky hung low over the land. The wind whipped snow across the surface of the river, drifted waves of snow against the bridge, tossed handfuls of snow into the men's faces, powdered the horses' manes with snow. The soldiers stood there until the staff cars had passed; then they formed in line again and followed. But they did not get far. As they came down off the bridge they were stopped at a control point. "Halt. What unit?" And when they had replied: "On your way. Route step, march!"

The endless procession moved on.

Again the military police with their tin badges stepped forward; again they cleared a space for another general and commander of an infantry division in his armored car. The general in the jeep had been of medium height, with pale eyes and reddish hair. His face, half hidden by his turned-up fur collar and the broad visor of his cap, appeared ravaged by many nights of wild excess. Certainly the past few nights to the east of Kletskaya—alarms, no orders or contradictory orders, re-ports of enemy tank break-throughs, abandonment of depots and destruction of guns—had left their mark. But the general in the armored car was a small, thick-set man, his face a weather-beaten brown, gnarled as a dwarf's. The first was well known for his daring; he disliked long-winded calculation, was a practical man and a realist. The other, transferred to active

30

service from the Historical Section of the War Ministry, was circumspect, a careful reckoner, a theorist and believer in ideologies. The first was a hearty eater, fond of women, liked his friends around him, and managed to live his usual life even in combat. The other could get along by himself and had continued his studies and literary work even during the campaign. He had done articles on Central Europe, on the problems and difficulties on the blitzkrieg, and had written chatty columns and military analyses for magazines and the radio. From the collapse east of Kletskaya the first man had salvaged a few thousand cigars, the second a voluminous manuscript entitled, *On the Northern Route to the Caspian Sea*. (The southern route was that via Cairo, the Suez Canal, and Asia Minor.)

The first was Major General Damme, the second Brigadier General Gönnern. Whenever Damme's pale eyes lit upon one of the figures along the road, he observed with precision every detail—the gray face, the filthy overcoat, the battered boots, the missing small arms, or blanket, or mess kit. On the lapels of a group of soldiers he saw the insignia of a heavy anti-aircraft unit and looked around for the guns, but found none; he noticed the uniforms of artillerymen, motorcyclists, and signal corps men, but there were no signs of the howitzers, the motorcycles, or the radio trucks. A stinking mess! was the conclusion he came to.

When the other officer, Brigadier General Gönnern, glanced around, he scarcely noted details at all and no individual face was impressed on his mind. He did not observe evidences of disorder in a uniform, but he saw a mass of infantry, artillery, signal corps men, a remount depot, bakery companies, butchers, repair crews, all intermingled in one grand confusion. He heard ten thousand shuffling footsteps, heard the clank and clatter of wheels from long columns of light and heavy vehicles; and it was not the full-throated roar of an advance. He saw more than a pair of eyes could grasp at a glance; he envisioned the whole of the gray mass flowing like a thick gruel down the Golubaya valley, pouring down from the height and flooding Perekopka, thinning out where it crossed the wooden bridge, and then forking out again on the opposite bank and continuing eastward. He saw the leaden sky above and imagined the masses of snow which would soon settle upon man and beast. This vast panorama he perceived, and the multitude of sounds, of audible and visible phenomena, swept past him like the wind over the sea. Crunch of footsteps, battalions slogging through the snow, shouts, curses, scraps of conversation, a message, smoke from a field kitchen, antiseptic

31

smells from an ambulance, a horse dying in harness—all the sights and sounds were repeated a thousand times. It was a vast monotone of mist and drifting snow and sweat and blood and screams and bent backs and lashing whips and white foam on horses' legs and the endless procession of weary soldier faces.

The two generals rode down the same highway, the one a few miles behind the other, and the sights they saw were both the same and not the same. Gönnern in his armored car rolled off the plank bridge onto the eastern bank. In front a truck had bogged down in the swampy ground. The heavy truck, the bent backs, the groaning bodies, the hands wrapped in rags, and hands like rags, gripping the wheels and sides of the truck (fifty prisoners of war were trying to push the mired truck along)—all this was a part of a great total movement, a line in the vast panorama to Gönnern. And since General Gönnern was not only the commander of an infantry division, but a military historian also, he saw not only Russian backs bent; he saw Carthaginian, Macedonian, Ethiopian backs, and it seemed to him quite in order that the road that led his new Occidental Empire to the shores of the Caspian and on into Asia should be cemented with the bones of conquered slaves. However, at this particular time and place the prisoners of war were not pushing a triumphantly *advancing* car through the mire. This constituted a distortion of the picture, a jarring note. But he thrust this disquieting notion aside. "Come on, get moving," he said to his driver.

Damme, too, had passed by the bogged truck and the laboring Russian column, but no historical parallels had occurred to him; he had thought neither of the old Roman Empire nor the new "Greater Germany," nor of the "Great-German" road to Asia. His gaze lingered on a pock-marked face and a pair of gray eyes and he thought: that chap must be about thirty, probably has played around a bit and acted as if he owned the earth—and now he'll never have a schnapps or his Masha again. In a few weeks he'll be flat on his face and done for. It's tough, of course, and no wonder he's got that icy glare in his eyes.

Damme's car stopped, blocked by a jam of horses, wagons, men, and sleds. The general got out, ordered his driver to follow him later to the headquarters of the infantry division in the village, and continued on his way on foot. To one enlisted man he snapped, "What's your name? Regiment? Can't you stand up like a soldier? Don't you know how to salute an officer?"

On the road he caught sight of a captain limping along with the aid of a cane. "Hello there, Tomas! Where have you come from?"

32

"The same place as you, general."

"What's the matter with your leg?"

"The Russians got me. It's not bad; I just have to get the metal out." Tomas was not alone. With him was a young lieutenant, Vilshofen's adjutant. Tomas presented him: "Lieutenant Latte."

"And where is Vilshofen?" the general asked.

"The colonel is still over there with his men." Lieutenant Latte looked back across the Don. "And I am looking for corps. I must find the chief of staff, Lieutenant Colonel Unschlicht. Perhaps the general has some idea where he is?"

"In my opinion he'll be here or in Peskovatka. Yes, it's a hell of a mess. What does Vilshofen say about it?"

"The colonel thinks we ought to be moving the other way, the army ought to turn west and try to re-establish contact with the German front, even if it means giving up Stalingrad!"

"Give up Stalingrad!" Tomas exclaimed.

"Yes, strong medicine," Damme said. "But that's the way Vilshofen is—always goes to extremes."

"The colonel says there's hardly anything else for us to do in this situation."

"Strong medicine," General Damme repeated, and went off. Soon afterward he saw another familiar face before him, that of his divisional chaplain whom he had sent ahead some days earlier.

"Hello, chaplain. Well, what's new and what are you doing in all this mess?"

"I held services in Vertiachi this morning, general, and then went to Peskovatka. But when I got out of the car I saw that it wouldn't be possible to hold services in all that confusion. The yard of the field hospital was jammed full of ambulances and there was a regular mass migration going on. They were coming in from the south and also over the bridge at Luchenski. . . ."

"There too?"

"Our lovely Peskovatka is unrecognizable, general. You remember Peskovatka, don't you, sir?"

Of course Damme remembered it. He had been there for a conference of divisional commanders and had seen what a luxurious set-up they had had there. It wasn't anything like his own staff headquarters across the Don, or like Vertiachi, where the houses were still standing but seemed to be set in open fields because all the barns, outbuildings, and fences had been torn down and carried up front for construction of bunkers and combat posts. Peskovatka, on the other hand, with its corps and divisional staffs, its offices, inspection stations, field hospitals, rest camp, casino with billiard rooms and card tables, gardens behind the houses, and trees and shrubs in the streets —Pestkovatka seemed a thousand miles behind the lines. Everything was still in its place; not an outbuilding, not a barn had been removed; even the wattled fences still stood. And since the village was out of bounds for marching troops, it was an area of profound peace. "Really, changed, eh?"

"Fugitives everywhere, from across the river, some from Kalach too. Officers, mounted and in vehicles with Rumanians among them. You can scarcely get through by car."

"And what kind of gypsy camp is this?" The general pointed to a farmyard ringed in by a wall of vehicles—peasant carts, sledges, trucks. Even the entrance was blocked by ambulances and masses of soldiers with bandaged heads and stumps of limbs wrapped in rags.

"This is the field hospital, general."

In passing, Damme heard moans from the trucks and a few words: "Kletskaya . . . Perelasovsky . . . bread . . . no food for three days."

Someone called out, "Take him away, take him away, he's in my lap."

"What's that? What about him?" Damme asked the soldier.

"He's dead, died hours ago."

Damme called several of the soldiers standing around. "Here, lift that corpse out."

"There are more here," voices called from the back of the truck.

"Isn't there a medic here?"

The chaplain came up with a doctor.

"Doctor, these men have come all the way from Perelasovsky. They've been on the way for days and say they've had no rations."

"We can do nothing, general. This unexpected deluge of wounded—it's simply impossible to take care of them all here."

"But you can't let the men die right at the door of the field hospital. . . ."

"The building, the yard, the corridors, every square inch of space is full, sir."

"Well, what's to be done about it?"

"We have orders to set up clearing stations farther to the east. As yet it hasn't been decided whether most of the wounded are to be sent on to Dmitrevka, Novo-Alexeyevka, or somewhere else, sir."

"You're from the Rhineland, aren't you?"

"*Jawohl, Herr General.* From Aachen."

"Been with this division long?"

"No, I was in a rest camp. I just arrived here."

"Well, tell me, why aren't all these men, the dangerously wounded cases anyway, being flown out immediately?"

"Army order: only wounded who can sit up are to be flown out."

"What about the others?"

The doctor made no reply. He merely looked at the general. Damme grasped the situation. He decided to hurry on to divisional headquarters and stop asking about things that didn't concern him and weren't in his province.

Soon afterwards he came across a number of women and again stopped. They were German women—looked like a flock of swallows, he thought. Their faces were all young, all disheveled, all exhausted, as if they had just been pulled out of water. They wore the uniform of Red Cross nurses.

"Is there anything I can do for you, ladies? Where are you bound, where are you from?"

They wanted to get to Pitomnik airdrome and had come from Kalach, had fled when Russian tanks were already rolling through the streets. On the way their truck had run out of gas and here they were now, on foot, in their blue-and-white striped uniforms, coatless, frozen, and tired out. Damme looked around for the chaplain, but he had remained behind at the field hospital. So Damme had to take the women along to the headquarters of the infantry division.

Staff headquarters of this division, which fronted northeastward, resembled more than anything else an insane asylum. So, at least, the commander and his staff officers affirmed. Trucks and wagons drove up continually and drove away again; the place was swamped with lost officers from the half dozen routed divisions that were pouring over the bridges and spreading out over the countryside. A number of commanders and higher officers from across the Don had made themselves at home in the office of General Geest, the divisional commander. General Gönnern and General Damme were there; also General Vennekohl, the artillery commander. All these officers wanted some kind of help, wanted telephonic communication with their corps (which in most cases could not be found, since the corps too were on the move), or communication with Army (likewise impossible, since the location of the new Army H.Q. was not yet known). They needed supplies, medical care for their wounded, shelter, gasoline for their vehicles. In sum, they needed everything and they were refused everything. The division itself had supplies for only ten days; fuel was even scarcer; and both the field hospital and the clearing station were filled to capacity. In only a few cases could quarters be provided, and then only for staffs. General Vennekohl and his whole staff were quartered on a pig farm to the east of the town. For General Gönnern and his staff two rooms belonging to the administrative staff of the prisoner-of-war camp and one of the guards' barracks were cleared. The guards in their turn had to clear the prisoners out of some of their shelters. When Damme arrived later and also demanded quarters, Gönnern had to surrender one room to him, and the second guards' barracks in the camp was evacuated. Finally an order was issued to clear out even the sickroom at the PW camp.

Besides this problem of quarters, Geest, the commander, and his staff were over their heads in other work. Their division's own situation required extreme care. Behind all these retreating divisions were the advancing Russians. And in their own sector there were sharp attacks and break-throughs at some points. They had to be blocked; almost hourly new measures were necessary. A Russian tank attack had been beaten back that same day, but a few tanks had broken through as far as the houses of Vertiachi and into the village streets. The west, which only yesterday had been the peaceful rear, had become the front overnight. Across the Don, at Perepolni, the adjacent division, retreating too, was still holding a switch line toward the north, and at Luchenski, Geest's own division was maintaining a bridgehead against enemy cavalry attacking from the south. Only as long as this position and bridgehead held would the crossing of the Don remain open for the defeated troops.

To the northeast there were penetrations, in the west the front had reversed itself; across the Don a construction battalion and some makeshift troops were combatting tanks and cavalry; still farther west were improvised combat groups like that of Colonel Vilshofen, who insisted that the dam would burst if he disengaged and ceased fighting. Vilshofen's adjutant was at the moment trying to obtain gasoline, munitions, supplies, and help from the nearest infantry division. On top of it all were the fugitives from the south who were telling wild tales of Russian tanks in the streets of Kalach. Such was the situation as the commander saw it.

A few rooms away the chief of the staff company, Captain von Hollwitz, was also thinking about the fugitives' stories of Kalach. Contradictory orders by the dozen, he thought. And those stories of the civilian population joining in the fighting with axes, kitchen knives, and boiling water—the stuff sounded almost like Göbbels' propaganda. Still, anything could happen now. And it's time to move out, anyway. It was advisable to travel light at a time like this.

The intendant, a civilian administrative official, came in. He was looking for the mess officer, but stopped a moment and said, "Now the flour's gone, captain. Sixty tons, think of that!"

Captain von Hollwitz thought of nothing at all. The intendant, the civilian official in charge of supplies, realized this and called in Sergeant Pöhls. "Tell the captain how it happened. You see, captain, the flour was stored across the Don."

"I was just coming along with a train of sleds and the camp was burning. Flames were already shooting up out of the roof; a lieutenant gave the order to set the storehouse on fire. That's all I could find out." Sergeant Pöhls spoke briskly.

"You see, that's the way it goes, all our good flour," the intendant said, and went his way.

Captain von Hollwitz was not alone for long. This time his visitor was the chaplain of the 376th, who had been staying for some days as a guest of the division. His entrance disturbed the captain in what appeared to be extremely urgent business.

"What's new, Herr von Hollwitz?" the chaplain asked. "Do we stay here or move on?" Von Hollwitz shrugged; he wanted to get his business done. His hands kept riffling through papers, personal letters, and snapshots. The chaplain took note of the open stove door. He realized that Hollwitz was going through and burning his personal correspondence; he also realized that at the moment he was not wanted. However, those hands nervously leafing through papers were, in a way, the answer to his question about the military situation.

The chaplain left. He had made himself useful while staying with the division and now needed an order from the adjutant for a work detachment to dig mass graves. He also wanted a requisition for bread, to be distributed among the wounded lying in the trucks in front of the field hospital. In the hall he encountered a corporal of the staff company whom he already knew by name; the man was now a courier with the hastily-assembled combat group on the other side of the Don.

"Well, Riess, how do things look across the river?"

"Cossacks are attacking us," the corporal replied. "We need reinforcements; otherwise we're all right. But at our rear where some tank colonel's combat group is fighting—all hell is loose there."

The chaplain went into the office of the adjutant, a Major

von Bauske. With Baron von Bauske he found the divisional commander, who along with Gönnern, Damme, and Vennekohl, had fled from his own room to escape the ceaseless coming and going there.

Baron von Bauske was holding the floor. The subject: suicide in a hopeless predicament. He was telling a story about his native town, Rakwere in Courland, where in 1625 a group of Germans besieged by Russians had blown themselves up with their wives and children. He knew a number of other cheery stories in a similar vein.

The telephone rang—it rang, in fact, incessantly. A regiment that had just crossed the Don was looking for its commander and the adjutant wanted to know where he could find quarters for his troops. "Not another man can be quartered in Vertiachi, not another man, I can't help it," Bauske replied and immediately hung up. He was about to continue the interrupted conversation and had said, "Well, what else can we do . . ." when the telephone rang again. This time it was the commandant of the PW camp. Bauske replied, "Look here, those are the orders; the Russian bunkers have to be cleared. . . . No, not in the stable; it's needed too. Well, what can I do? I can't help it. Yes, as soon as you can have them shipped off."

Von Bauske turned to the others again. He looked at his superior, General Geest. "There you are. What else can we do if the Russians surround us here?"

Geest had nothing to say. Gönnern looked as if he were thinking hard about a difficult problem. Damme stared at the ashes at the end of his slowly-burning cigar. Vennekohl thought of his wife and his eight-year-old daughter, whose picture he carried in his breast pocket. "Yes," he said, "that's a fine idea —blowing yourself up with your wife and child."

Bauske stated in a tone of authority: "In any struggle between Slavs and Teutons the losers always kill themselves."

"Well, chaplain, what d'you think of that?" Vennekohl asked. The chaplain had plenty of ready arguments against suicide. However, they evoked no more than a charitable smile from Bauske, and not just from him. All of them were relieved when the conversation was interrupted. The operations officer came in with reports from the front for the commander. After Geest had read them, he said, "It's tough, but we're holding. The situation across the river, though, is not good. If that tank colonel Vilshofen weren't making a stand on the Golubaya, our bridgehead would collapse."

The G-3 also had a radio message from Army Headquarters. Geest read it and silently passed the sheet of paper on to the others. The content of this message made them forget for a moment the danger looming across the Don. After reading it, Vennekohl carefully polished his monocle, fixed it in his eye, and looked in turn at Gönnern, Damme, the G-3, Bauske, and the chaplain.

"Gönnern, you're the history guy around here," he said, falling into slang. "Ever heard of anything as crazy as this?"

"Yes, Valdai and Kholm."

"D'you mean when we got stuck there last winter? Well, that wasn't so hot either. But I mean way back, in military history."

"No, there are no parallels, aside from a few cases in siege warfare."

"That's what I thought. Seems to me the idea always has been to get out when you're surrounded."

"Yes, the idea is to get out of the trap—that's self-evident," Damme agreed, forgetting that only an hour ago, when he had heard that Vilshofen had recommended these tactics, he had called them "strong medicine."

"Come in, Unschlicht," Geest called to Lieutenant Colonel Unschlicht, chief of staff of the corps on the other side of the Don, who had opened the door and, murmuring an apology, had been about to withdraw. "We're to hedgehog, dig in, and hold tight. What do you say to that, Unschlicht?"

Lieutenant Colonel Unschlicht was a man who always formulated things very carefully. He replied: "I am informed that the commander in chief has taken into consideration the difficulties involved in establishing a hedgehog position. First, no prepared defense works exist where the west and south fronts would have to be formed, and secondly it would be impossible to supply so large an army by air. The commanding generals have supported this estimate of the situation and a report giving their opinion has been radioed to the Führer."

"Here is the reply," General Geest said, handing the lieutenant colonel the message from the Army H.Q. in which, on the basis of the order to dig in, the new defence lines were defined.

"There must have been weighty reasons in favor of hedgehogging," Unschlicht said after he had read the message.

"After all, the boys up top must have something special in mind," Vennekohl observed.

"It's possible, even probable, that the relief army is already on the march," Gönnern suggested.

While this conversation was going on, a jeep rolled into the yard. Colonel Vilshofen jumped out. In less than a minute he was in the adjutant's room, standing before the assembled officers.

"Gentlemen, the 384th is no longer holding; the bridgehead at Perepolni is collapsing. Troops must be assembled here, whatever can be scraped up, and led back across the river at once. I beg your pardon, general." He introduced himself to Geest, whom he did not know. "Vilshofen." Geest nodded.

"As far as my group is concerned," Vilshofen reported to Unschlicht, the corps chief of staff to whom he had been assigned, "we've retreated through Verkhnaya Golubaya as far as the dairy and are now making a stand with some other troops—whose complement is extremely low—between Luchenski and Perepolni. We urgently need ammunition."

Unschlicht looked at Vennekohl. When the general said nothing, he explained: "On orders we have blown up all stores of munitions which were not transportable."

"Blown them up . . . but gentlemen!" Vilshofen examined their faces more carefully. Had they altogether lost their heads? he asked himself, and he began to wonder about the conversation he had interrupted on entering. Hedgehog—what did they mean?

"Gentlemen, as I came in I heard you say 'hedgehog.' What does that involve? Is it a careful, previously planned operation, provided with quantities of ammunition, gas, rations, and heavy weapons and so on? Obviously not, and nothing of the kind was expected. On the contrary, the possibility of our digging in was never even considered; our supplies are exceptionly low and part of what we had being left behind in retreat or thrown away or blown up. Where will it lead? Hedgehogging means—let us call a spade a spade—that we're encircled; it's something that has been forced upon us, a predicament from which we ought to try to escape as fast as possible."

"Before you go on, read this!" Geest handed Vilshofen the radio message from Army Headquarters.

"What does it mean?"

"It means that the Führer has ordered us to hedgehog."

"I see . . . well, then here I have the parallel order—the only one, incidentally, that I've received from my superiors. It says that from today on the troops are to be placed on half-rations.

"That's how hedgehogging begins, is it?"

"Yes, that's the way it begins and it may end in one hell of a mess," Vennekohl said.

"Well, in any case, I've got to get back across the river. And I must have 3.7 cm. anti-tank and 5 cm. mortar shells and machine-gun ammunition, and some troops must be scared up over here at once, as I've said."

General Geest conferred with his G-3, and Vilshofen received his anti-tank and machine-gun ammunition. He sent his jeep to the depot, had it loaded, and then rode off with his adjutant. Geest did still more. From the staff company, the supply service troops, and collected stragglers, General Geest also organized an emergency company and sent it across the river under the command of his staff captain, von Hollwitz. When Geest returned to the adjutant's room to bid good-bye to Gönnern, Damme, and the others, night was already darkening the windows of the small frame house.

Vennekohl and Unschlicht set out together toward the eastern end of the village. Gönnern and Damme were going toward the northern part and also got into one car together. There was mist and snow in the air. The roads were still jammed with masses of soldiers. The two generals rode along the highway that flanked the river. To their right orchards lined the road. The trunks of the apple trees, whitewashed the preceding year, flitted past like gray phantoms. To the left the swampland ran down to the river and to the Perepolni bridge.

Ahead of them was movement—the clatter of metal, cooking pots, mess kits and spades—a marching troop of soldiers. It was Captain von Hollwitz's scratch company on its way to the bridge. Among those in the ranks of this company, stragglers whom the M.P.'s had picked up, were the two metal workers from Cologne, Schorsch and Tünnes, Ketteler the cutler from Remscheid, and Sergeant Gnotke and Private Gimpf.

Gönnern and Damme drove past them. The marching column faded like smoke behind them. A mile and a quarter on, they found sentries and a long barbed-wire fence. Behind the fence, lying together in heaps or standing around, were Russian prisoners of war who had been evacuated from the shelters they had dug.

The car drove on further, then stopped in front of the headquarters barracks. As Gönnern and Damme got out and glanced around at the bleak heaps of earth, an explosion boomed up from the Don. The Russian artillery, which had been intermittently firing away at the Perepolni bridge, had scored a hit.

"Well, we won't be here long, anyway," Damme said.

Lieutenant Viktor Huth of the medical corps had been convalescing in a rest area beyond the Don. Far from the roar of the front, in a lonely farmhouse in the Golubaya valley, he had

41

looked up into the autumn sky, watched the winter drawing closer, and thought many things about the war and what he had done in it. Naturally the army couldn't always go on like this, yesterday crossing the Don, tomorrow the Volga, then across the Ural and someday, perhaps, the Indus. Always, he and his medical company had come trotting along behind, handing the men laxatives or, as the case might be, anti-diarrhetics, and Nitigal for the itch and Cuprex for crab lice, and inoculations against smallpox, dysentery, typhoid fever, and parathyphus, patching them up and classifying them as fit for service again, or preparing them for transportation to the rear, or turning them over to the chaplain who also "took care" of them in his own fashion, setting up one cemetery after the other, each one a few miles farther to the east, until he could look back upon a respectable number of forest, desert, and steppe cemeteries. . . . No, it certainly couldn't go on forever that way; sooner or later something would have to give. Medical Lieutenant Huth had been expecting disaster, a breach in the dike, but he had not thought it could come so soon nor from the rear; he had never imagined the flood would pour from the west and float him still further eastward. Then, in rest quarters, suddenly the order had come for him to report to the division surgeon at the field hospital in Vertiachi. No transportation was provided, and on the Golubaya road he had been unable to obtain a ride on a passing truck. Consequently, he had left his own baggage behind and walked, becoming one of the thousands of figures in the gray mass of humanity that moved across the Don bridge.

He had spent only a day and a night in the Vertiachi hospital. The very next day he was assigned to a medical company under Captain Bäumler, and they had set out for a motor transport depot south of Vertiachi to set up a clearing station there. When they arrived at the farm they found throngs of wounded already present. As at Vertiachi, they were still lying in the trucks; there was no place to put them. The house and the tractor sheds were already filled and overflowing with soldiers. It was evening before another order arrived to move the clearing station still farther to the rear, on the outskirts of a tiny village named Otorvanovka.

On the following day Captain Bäumler and Lieutenant Huth, with their medical company, moved on in horse-drawn peasant carts. Aside from Huth, these men were remnants of a medical company that had been shattered and scattered in the Don Bend. There were thirty men altogether.

The road led down into the Peskovatka ravine and on to the

highway from Peskovatka. After they reached the highway, they were no longer alone; they became one small group in a steady stream of infantry, ambulances, ammunition trucks, baggage transports, staff cars, vehicles from ration and clothing depots—all of them coming from Peskovatka and Vertiachi and some of them from even farther away. Above the marching columns and the long lines of vehicles hovered a low gray sky, strewing wet snow on man and beast and machine.

Huth and Bäumler marched side by side. Both had sleepless nights behind them, and their conversation—it concerned where they had come from, the preliminaries of acquaintanceship—soon ebbed away. Bäumler was twenty-nine years old, Huth thirty-four. Bäumler had attended the Academy of Military Medicine and had planned on the career of a military physician from the start. Huth, however, had not become a medical officer until the war. The little Bäumler heard of Huth's career sounded distinctly odd to him.

Bäumler thought of the work that lay before them in setting up their clearing station. He brooded about the scanty inventory of equipment they had saved from across the Don, the small quantity of medicine, the limited personnel (the medical company had formerly consisted of six doctors, a pharmacist, a paymaster, and one hundred and sixty-five men). Well, they would manage somehow; they would scrape along on what they had. He looked around at his colleague Huth. Huth had lingered behind, let the procession of peasant carts roll past, and slumped down on a sledge which, because of the sparse snow, was carrying the lightest load. Bäumler noted this with dissatisfaction, and his thought shifted instantly from his medical colleague to his military subordinate, Lieutenant Huth. Of course the man was tired, but who was not? No reason for such slackness; he really ought to order Huth off the sled. However, Captain Bäumler said nothing; he tramped crossly on through the soft snow and mud.

Huth was not thinking at all about the impending work. He sat and dozed. When he looked up he would see a heavily-laden truck, the feet of mud-spattered marching soldiers and, once, a herd of cattle that belonged to a corps headquarters. What strange things he was doing now that the war had taken on this new aspect, so different from anything imaginable a few days ago. Strange ways, he mused as he rode along breathing the damp, cold, snow-filled air. And that general yesterday, or had it been the day before yesterday: "But you can't let the men . . . why aren't all these men being flown out. . . ." Of course you couldn't, but they weren't, and you did. And if someone lay on the table with an abdominal wound and you knew he needed an operation that would take an hour and a half, you took a minute to stick a bandage on the wound and the case was laid aside, finished—finished forever. You couldn't and yet you did, because if you didn't, twenty or thirty others who needed treatment would wait for an hour and a half, and some of them were just as bad as the abdominal case. You did what you could, so that things could keep going the way they were going. Strange ways, and here he was now on the road from Peskovatka to Otorvanovka.

And Lucia too was traversing strange ways, Lucia in Berlin. Now she was a member of the National Socialist Women. Africa belonged to Europe geographically and climatically, she wrote. And there were other things in her letters, geopolitical terms like "field of force" and "key position," phrases like "our unique Führer," "every man a fortress." "The Jew is to blame," seemed to be the indicated next step, but she probably couldn't go that far—not with a Jewish father. Lucky for her that she was an illegitimate child, her origins not disclosed in her papers. But now she was beginning to write about the scarcity of tobacco, about soybeans, "stoopies" (so called because the storekeeper stooped under the counter to get goods for favored customers), the high price of poultry, and the flourishing black market. Also, of course, about the staunch fighters on the home front. Evidently she had remained (like High Command communiqués) flexible and elastic. Ah, those had been the days, when they lived together in the attic room with their home-made plywood furniture and played a game of dominoes at night to decide who would get up first in the morning and go down to fetch breakfast. Those were the days, and if Hitler had not kicked the Jews out of the universities and hospitals, so that young doctors were urgently needed and nobody could fail the examination, he might not have passed to this day, and if his allowance from home had kept coming he might have gone on living like that forever.

Those were the days. Medical Student Viktor Huth had been interested in many other things besides medicine—not only in literature, painting, music, politics, and sports, but in those who practiced them. He had made efforts to meet the writers, painters, musicians, athletes, and politicians in cafés, in their studios, at their desks, wherever he could find them. And among the politicians he had been just as interested in the men of the Left as in those of the Right. He tried to understand the basic nature of all of them and to grasp their significance to society as a whole. It was no wonder that living human beings,

44

acting, talking, suffering, involved in intrigues and affairs, took up more of his time than the corpse of a suicide stretched out on the board in the anatomy room. The semesters were too short for him to get any proper grounding in all these fields. Finally Hitler had come, and with some special credit given for Huth's achievements in boxing and gymnastics he had passed his medical examination. He had spent a year in the army and afterward (to the great relief of his family) gone through his interneship. He had not broken with Lucia (in this disappointing his family), but stayed on with her. For a time he had been a resident physician in a large Berlin hospital, and then the war had come. And now . . . now . . . now, a peasant sled dragged by a slow-moving pony with a hide like a sheep dog's and he himself sitting on it, on his way to Otorvanovka.

It was twilight by the time the column reached Dmitrevka. They entered a long, straight street with many gaps. Some houses had been carried off whole; others were without barns, without fences, with porches torn off; still others lacked roofs. For a while they went on across an open field, and it was quite dark by the time they reached their destination. On one side of the road were five frame houses, on the other three mud hovels. Such was Otorvanovka, where they were to set up a clearing station. The casualties from Vertiachi, Peskovatka, and the new front that was being formed on the Don were presumably to be taken in here and cared for. But they could hardly be said to be "setting up" anything, for they had to go to work at once to take care of the throng already there. Hundreds had come or been brought to this place on the strength of the rumor that a dressing station was to be established. In ambulance busses, trucks, carts, sleds, and on foot they had poured in; the hovels were already occupied to the very last place.

The medical company truck with the generator arrived. A room in one of the peasant houses was cleared of wounded, two huge operating lamps were hung over the tables, and immediately Captain Bäumler and Lieutenant Huth bent over the first of a long row of wounded and began unwrapping the filthy, blood-soaked rags that served as dressings. The work began, and the man with the saw in his hand ceased to be a military doctor accustomed in winter at his Bavarian garrison to go skiing when off duty and in summer to swimming and sailing and acquiring a tan, who in the evenings went to his favorite café table and played cards with his cronies. The other doctor ceased to be a bohemian who played dominoes with a girl named Lucia or chess at his café, and who spent his free evenings at political meetings, concerts, athletic events, and dis-

45

cussions on Chinese lyric poetry, psychoanalysis, or the newest thing in Aryan art. The two men in rubber aprons, with rolled-up shirtsleeves, were no longer doctors in the ordinary sense of the word, no longer medical practitioners, no longer surgeons. They were laborers with scalpel and saw, applying tourniquets, hacking through bones. The medical aides assisted, loosening bandages, rebandaging, anesthetizing the patients, sterilizing the instruments, holding an arm or leg in a particular position while the surgeon sawed and cut. Bäumler's aide was familiar with his chief's every movement and obeyed the slightest hint. Huth's was not yet broken in. The air became stale, laden with the smell of wounds. A fierce heat came from the sterilizer and the big lamps overhead. Windows could not be opened. Sweat dripped from doctors and assistants. The assembly line of shattered bodies continued. One was carried away, another laid on the table. Blood covered the boards.

No time to look up. Dawn came and Bäumler was standing in a pool of blood; Huth was standing in a pool of blood. An orderly came in with a cup of black coffee. Bäumler reached for it and drank without sitting down. Huth did the same. For a moment he closed his eyes, then bent again over a torn human limb. A thigh wound, a splinter to be removed. Anti-tetanus shot, dressing. The next: shot through the buttock. The man lay on his face with his nose in the ether cone, his jacket over his head, trousers pulled down, feet in heavy, mud-encrusted boots. The rags were cut off the wound, the edges cleaned, a drain inserted. Next. Abdominal wound, hopeless. A scrap of bandage on the wound and laid aside.

Next!

Then there were the sick. Where does it hurt?—Head, stomach, feet swollen, ankles swollen, pain in the side. And the malingerers—everything hurt them, from head to foot, inside and out. What regiment? Regiment so-and-so. Very well, return to your regiment. Wounded, sick, malingerers. Two doctors and thirty medical aides sifted through the mass of them, "worked" them. In the evening there had been several hundred; in the morning there were still several hundred. Loaded ambulances drove in constantly from Vertiachi, from Peskovatka.

The next, the next . . .

"Doctor, sir, there's no more room in the huts."

"Get them moving. They can stop a truck on the road, get on somehow. The ambulants will have to walk, the sitters can sit. Next!"

No more room in the houses. Munitions trucks loaded with wounded arrived from the front; ambulances loaded with wounded arrived from Peskovatka. The drivers laid the men on the ground in front of the house and drove off. In the hovels those who could sit up sat along the walls—as well as those who were only propped up. The hopelessly wounded lay on the floor, on the wooden floorboards, or in the mud huts on the bare, trodden earth.

Four hundred, the sergeant counted, and the procession still went on.

Near the operating house a horse was slaughtered for the field kitchen. Behind the house a pit was dug for the dead, a second pit for the blood, scraps of flesh, and pus that were constantly being carried out by the pailful.

Next...

The soldier showed swollen feet that looked blue. First degree frostbite. "Frost salve. Fit for service." A medical aide handed the soldier brown salve and a length of fine bandage—thin stuff so that he could bandage his feet and still get his shoes on. He was turned over to a sergeant who was assembling men fit for action. Still others, who had glanced into the huts and decided they would rather not stay, reported of their own volition. A corporal took command and the mob moved off in loose formation into the twilight, toward Peskovatka and the front.

Next...

Mud-smeared, blood-stained rags, encrusted wounds, open wounds. Blood spurting freshly under the scalpel. Doors closed, windows closed, vapors of a hundred suppurating wounds. The thermometer reading one hundred and a second icy night falling outside. Black coffee. Collodion. Next. Sift them out. An ambulance from Vertiachi—tank-gun wounds and bomb fragments. Tanks and bombers at Vertiachi, at Peskovatka too; the front approaching, moving across the Don.

Bäumler's aide sagged. Down Bäumler's bare arms, down his blood-spattered body, sweat ran in streams. "Bäumler, take off for a while—go ahead and lie down. I'll go on until you're rested."

Bäumler removed his apron, hung it on a nail, and went into the adjoining room. Huth went on, worked with forceps, scalpel, scissors, saw. He removed the bullets, plucked splinters out of ripped masses of flesh, trimmed the edges of wounds, sawed off legs, sawed off arms. In that one night he made up for all the times his father, his sister, and his other relations had worried about how he would turn out; he put to shame all the things that had ever been said about him as an "eternal student" and as a doctor who was interested in everything but

47

medicine. In that one night he passed his test; with hands that had once dreamed of painting and that had longed to produce living beauty and perfection. With nervous but steady hands, like those of a master surgeon, he worked against the stream of bloody and battered bodies that poured in on foot and in every variety of vehicle. He worked until Bäumler started up out of a deathlike sleep, returned, took his apron from the nail and relieved him.

Forty-two hours had passed since the first of the wounded had been placed on the table.

And the front moved farther eastward. Geest's division was forced out of its comfortable dugouts and had to take up quarters in shallow foxholes hacked into the hard ground, each with room enough for three men. Geest had hurriedly had these dug by Russian PW's. The men of the other retreating divisions did not even have such holes; they found themselves shelterless in open fields. Not rifles but spades became their most vital weapons. The land was flat, the terrain marked only by an occasional hill, by the gorges on the way to the Rossoshka heights, by ravines descending to the little Karpovka River and by the beds or runnels formed by melting snow in the spring. It snowed and the temperature fell from four to thirteen and then to eighteen below zero Fahrenheit.

Such was the line west of the Rossoshka valley which had been fixed by the High Command and the Führer: the line that was to be held "under all circumstances and at all costs." The steppe settlements of Bolshaya Rossoshka, Baburkin, Novo-Alexeyevka, and Karpovka (west of which lay Dmitrevka and the five frame houses and three mud huts of Otorvanovka) were now headquarters for the various staffs.

Snow, cold, a waist-deep hole in the ground with a shelter half spread over it. The soldiers who had carried stoves with them found no wood for heating. One such hole was occupied by Sergeant Gnotke, Private Gimpf, and a boy from Ottakring. A few yards away, in another hole, lay Evald Stüve who was a mechanic. The second man in his hole was Georg Ketteler, the cutler from Remscheid, and the third Erich Urbas; in the next hole lay a farm boy from the Sudetenland, a soldier from Billerbeck in Westphalia, a farmer from Mecklenburg. All along the "line" soldiers lay or crouched in similar holes. Such were the conditions in Captain von Hollwitz's emergency company. The sole dream of all these men was for a dugout, a real dugout with a stove in it, and they occupied their off-duty hours digging one. Their sole hope was General Hooth who was moving up from the south with a tank army to break the ring—or so they said.

They talked little about this. The snow and the cold kept them tight-lipped. As for Gimpf, there was something else that made him taciturn. What was it? Gnotke mused about it as he drove his spade into the earth and lifted the frozen earth in order to deepen the hole. He knew little about Gimpf, but he did know some things. Matt was a farm boy from Alten-Affeln in Sauerland; as a second son he could not inherit under the new farm law and so his father had sent him to high school in the near-by town of Hagen. During the war Gimpf, then a corporal, had been ordered to Munich to attend an officer candidates' school. There he had had a love affair with another soldier's wife. The husband had found a military blanket and a shelter half belonging to Gimpf in his apartment and had denounced him for theft of military property and, incidentally, for adultery. Gimpf was sent to the front and during the winter campaign, in the vicinity of Shisdra, he had got into trouble. But that was only half the story and the less important part of it; for even before Shisdra something had happened in or near Vyazma. What it was Gnotke did not know; he could never get it out of Gimpf. Gimpf refused to talk about it. In any case, he scarcely ever talked; usually he uttered only brief exclamations relating to hunger or cold or some other physical state.

"What was her name, the one in Munich?" Gnotke asked him once more. Gimpf merely looked at him out of absent blue eyes and again bent to his work.

"Liese, wasn't it?"

"Yes, Liese."

"And then her husband suddenly came home on furlough ..."

"Yes, came home."

"Then he saw the pictures of the two of you, the snapshots you had on the wall."

"He did."

"He hounded you for money, didn't he? He must have been a bastard...."

"Yes, I even gave him my watch."

"You did, and he fooled you anyway?"

"Yes."

"And you were shipped off to the front and that was the end of your officer's career."

"That's right."

"And then you were in Vyazma. ..."

That was the point in which Gimpf fell silent; Gnotke could

not get another syllable out of him. Gnotke began talking about his own affairs. "At home there was a girl, her name was Pauline . . . we grew up next door to each other. . . ." No doubt about it, by now Pauline must be married to his old SA pal, Sergeant Riederheim, the one who'd sent him to the penal battalion. It was a long, involved story. But Gimpf was evidently not interested. Gnotke saw that the other man was not listening and broke off his tale in the middle. Hooth and his advancing tank army also did not interest Gimpf. He paid no attention to the boy from Ottakring who had to let down his pants every few minutes and squat over his spade. To Gimpf nothing mattered at all. He hardly cared when the first corporal returned from Dmitrevka bringing only half their rations. That meant hunger, but hunger too was everywhere, and what else could be expected? That was Gimpf; he was like a cracked bell that would not ring.

Not only the boy from Ottakring but many others had diarrhea and headaches and stomach aches and were so feeble they could scarcely move. Ketteler was worst of all that day. He crouched against the wall and was in the way of the two others, Evald Stüve and Corporal Urbas, who were trying to deepen the hole.

Stüve tried to cheer him up.

"If old Hooth breaks through, we'll get out of this mess," he said. Ketteler did not even raise his head. "Then we'll all have furloughs and get back to Cologne just in time for the carnival." This time Ketteler raised his head and essayed a smile. It was such a wretched grimace that Stüve understood; for Ketteler carnivals were over forever.

Later in the day Stüve watched Ketteler as he tramped slowly toward the rear, arms dangling, and finally vanished in the white field. Together with him Stüve had marched from the borders deep into Russia. Once they had gone on furlough together and come back together. Side by side (with Schorsch who now lay across the Don) they had marched up to this point. Stüve continued looking across the field for some time after his comrade had disappeared. "Spit and pass on," Corporal Urbas said. "We won't see him again."

Ketteler, along with other sick soldiers, was led to Dmitrevka. Since there was no room there, they had to march to the clearing station at Otorvanovka. There too everything was overcrowded, and a mob of soldiers sat in front of the reception house. Ketteler sat down in the snow beside the others. He sat until the mud huts sank into the earth and in their places appeared the row of one-family houses that lined the street in distant Remscheid, and he did not know that hours had passed before he awoke from his trancelike doze.

"Next," he heard the medical aide repeat irritably, and the man next to him nudged him vigorously.

He stood before a lieutenant of the medical corps.

"Dysentery too?" the doctor asked.

Ketteler merely opened his eyes wide—big blue eyes that were clouded now and looked very mournful.

"Room Five," the doctor said.

Then Ketteler awoke fully. "You mean I'm going to have a roof over my head again. Thank you, doc."

"You're from Remscheid?" Huth asked, recognizing his accent.

"Yes, sir."

"Well, go in there and warm yourself up a bit, Ketteler."

Ketteler was led into one of the mud huts where he had not only a roof over his head, but warmth; the crush of bodies in the room was an excellent substitute for a stove.

Doctors Bäumler and Huth were now having a relatively easy time of it. Into December they had stood over the operating table fifteen and twenty hours a day, the blood underfoot never drying. From the tattered bandages they unwound from the wounded men lice had crawled in gray lines over their aprons and their bare arms. But now the clearing station was fully set up; the field kitchen was operating; the new arrivals were taken care of fairly promptly—if the little that could be done for them might be considered "care." Ambulatory cases were sent to the nearest local headquarters where they would wait for a truck going toward Stalingrad to take them to the Gumrak hospital. Bäumler and Huth had no idea what was being done there with the swarm of patients coming in from all parts of the pocket; they could not imagine. It was not their affair. Men who could sit up were taken on sledges to Pitomnik airport where they were to be flown out. The critically wounded simply lay in the huts, for the most part, and with the limited facilities for treatment their fate was usually sealed right there.

In the middle of December food became scarcer and rations shrank. The clearing station often received only half the quantities that were distributed to the combat troops, and so one sled-horse after the other had to be slaughtered. Few wounded were arriving these days, and there were scarcely any splinter wounds from tank and rocket guns. Bäumler once remarked: "Perhaps after all there's something to the story that the Russians are about at the end of their rope." Huth thought there was probably another reason for the diminishing tank and

51

artillery attacks. "The Russians are busy elsewhere," he said. "Something's going on at Kotelnikovo with Hooth's tank army." That was as far as he would go with his hints. Evenings he sat with Bäumler in the bunker (which had meanwhile been built by Russian prisoners of war), picking lice and listening to the army radio. More than once he felt inclined, in spite of Bäumler's presence, to listen in on Moscow or London, but each time he refrained.

Although there were few wounded during this period, there were a large number of sick to be sorted out every day. However, close examinations were scarcely needed. It was enough merely to look at the men—pale men with sunken faces, their bodies skin and bone, expression only in their sad, dilated eyes. The shame expressed in their eyes and their weak, weepy voices were additional symptoms of dysentery. It was not necessary to take their pulses; the pulse was always rapid and shallow. The question, "Have you dysentery?" was unnecessary; you smelled it. There was nothing to examine. And the men themselves wanted only to crawl into a hole; fine if they had a little warmth too. And warmth could be given them—not heated rooms, but the warm vapors of other men in like state.

Clean quarters, decent ventilation, careful disinfection, clean linen—those were the things that were needed. But these men lived up front in holes scooped in the snow, and those that had dugouts lay one on top of the other like sardines. And these enfeebled men who populated the clearing station, these skin-covered skeletons, did not even lie down; they squatted in the huts, often feverish, often delirious, mostly apathetic. They were given hot tea while it lasted. But there was nothing else, no glucose, no zwieback. Concentrated meat broths, wine, and so on would have helped them to regain strength, but the worn horses (and there were not many of these left either) yielded a broth without any fat. The first deaths from dysentery, weakness, and starvation began, and they were only the beginning.

Christmas came.

German Christmas, the glistening tree, marzipan, nuts, spice-cake, tinsel, angels with golden wings, fragrance of baked apples, golden-yellow roast goose, presents and green pine needles and the laughter of children. Captain Bäumler and Lieutenant Huth also thought of the special significance of this day. Although the remaining horses were urgently needed, Bäumler had one more slaughtered, so that at least on this day the patients would be able to fill their empty stomachs. He had received chocolate from the supply service, enough to distribute a bar among each five men.

In the afternoon he went on an extra round through the huts. "Well, how are things?" he asked.

All of them found things tolerable.

"I'm satisfied."—"Good to be here where it's warm."—"Much better, doc."—"Be all right soon, doc." Those who complained of pain or that they had no room to stretch out or that they had not yet been flown out, were not the sick but the wounded, who were still physically strong. The sick did not complain. These enfeebled men no longer felt pain or hunger. They sat, dozed, dreamed, answered in weak voices, or merely by a look of their glistening eyes. One, who was on the point of death, breathed, "Getting better, doc."

Huth, too, made his rounds.

It was already dark and every hut had received a Hindenburg light. Huth looked into one of the rooms. In the dim, misty glow of the light not a single face could be distinguished clearly; there was only a gray mass covering the floor and the rattle of mucus-blocked air passages and diseased lungs could be heard. Without saying anything, Huth went on. In the next hut and in the next was the same vapor-laden air, and the presence of human beings could only be guessed. Huth called out to one or two of the invisible phantoms on the floor and listened to their answers. Then he went on. Outside he inhaled deeply of the cold winter air. He strolled over to the other side and entered one of the mud huts. The building might have housed a family of a dozen souls if, in the summertime, the empty sheep stable and the half-open shed were put to use and if in winter everyone crept into one room. Even then the room would have been terribly overcrowded. Now some four dozen sick, bleeding, dying German soldiers lay here. And because it was Christmas Night they had a Hindenburg light—a tiny wick in a paper shell filled with tallow which would burn for an hour, after which the darkness would seem even denser. Huth looked for the Remscheid cutler, Georg Ketteler. Ketteler was not a young man, but in the rapid process of dissolution his childhood countenance had been revealed, a trustful, believing boy's face. Huth had seen him several times after receiving him; now he found him bathed in sweat, just awakened from a spell of delirium and still bemused by it. Ketteler recognized the doctor. "Doc, doc, I was flying the way I never could before. Do you know how you get the gift of flight, doctor?" Yes, how do you? Huth found out; he learned that in a vast city, full of lights and movement and people, there were, of course, magic creatures in the street, and if you touched one in passing you had the gift; at any rate, that was how this patient

53

had acquired it. And Ketteler recalled (he spoke in a thin voice and carefully tried to reconstruct the fine cobweb of his dream) what the fairy was like; she was in the form of a little girl in a worn, poor dress and had been leading a blind man. "But what did I care, I had the gift," he said. Huth listened closely while the dying cutler with his dilated child's eyes recounted the story of Otorvanovka and the history of the shattered army. Ketteler had swum, he had "done the crawl" on the surface of the atmosphere. It was sheer delight, he said. The sea of air below him was a blue expanse; there was a patch of yellow dust where the desert began. . . . Rivers, woods, farmlands, steppes were spread out beneath him; everything belonged to him and he could descend wherever he wished. It was a gigantic game, a reveling in his own strength—you understand, doc? Huth understood. And you understand, doc, that it doesn't end well. . . . Huth already knew that. No, it could not end well because of that poor girl with the blind man and because of his own boundless folly: "But what did I care, I had the gift." And then it happened. By chance the swimmer dipped his head into the gleaming ocean of air and his own eyes were blinded. Numbness seized his limbs as well and he sank precipitately, plunged down like a stone. And then he lay in blackest darkness and around him and within him was a murmurousness and stirring, and close by someone told him what was wrong with his stomach—that it was just a nest full of little mice living inside there.

Huth had heard hundreds of men talking in delirium and under narcosis, uttering incoherent words, groans, shrieks, commands, endearments, obscenities, vanities, and fears. Most of the time he had not listened; this time he marveled at the exactitude with which a brain in dissolution could express both its own personal existence and, simultaneously, a great social process. Could reflect these and find the simplest imaginable formulation for them. For it was all quite true—faith in the extraordinary gift, the reckless reveling in the new powers, the ruthlessness toward another who was, into the bargain, the giver of the gift; it was all true, including the inevitable giving out of the power at the moment of its greatest effort and the inevitable fall. And the darkness and the mice in his stomach were realities—in the present case the hut in Otorvanovka and the diphtheritic tumors in the large intestine caused by the disease. But that was not the essence of it. Huth sat holding Georg Ketteler's perspiring hand and staring at the flickering Hindenburg light which rested on a ledge in the mud wall and illuminated only itself, leaving the nest of misery below in darkness.

He continued to sit holding the man's hand when he heard a Russian "sewing machine" above the hut, one of the old models, a small, slow plane of the kind that drifted over the front every evening dropping explosive bombs no bigger than flower pots, but big enough to worry the men crouching in their snow holes as well as the wounded above ground in Otorvanovka.

But what did I care, I had the gift!

Huth continued to think about it as he made his way back between the huts to the members of the medical company, who were sitting gloomily hunched up in their quarters. He was still thinking about it afterward while he sat in the bunker with Bäumler. Bäumler still had a bottle of cognac left and decided that this was the night for opening it. They talked about Christmases and about last Christmas which Bäumler had spent in Kharkhov and Huth in Berlin on furlough. Later they turned on the radio and listened to music from Berlin. Once they were disturbed, this time not by a Russian "sewing machine" but by the heavy boom of artillery which sounded clearly through the frosty air from the south. It was an artillery attack on Marinovka and Karpovka, and when they stepped out of their shelter they saw the glow of fire on the southern horizon.

"Perhaps they're Hooth's tanks," Bäumler said. "Perhaps they've reached the ring. They were supposed to open the pocket by Christmas."

"I don't believe it," Huth said.

Then firing lasted for ten minutes; then the night silence descended again. Once or twice more a "sewing machine" passed over; except for that there were no other sounds. Bäumler and Huth went back to their cognac. The German radio announced a round-up: Berlin, Hamburg, Frankfurt-am-Main, Königsberg, and other cities called the various sections of the front, called Narvik, called Tunis, called Velikie Luki, called Stalingrad.

"Calling Stalingrad! Come in, Stalingrad."
"Kharkhov . . . here is Stalingrad."

"Ladies and gentlemen of the radio audience, Stalingrad speaking. I am talking to you from the shores of the Volga. Before us lies the snow-covered, silvery-gray ribbon of the great river. Here stand the men of Stalingrad, the German watch on the Volga. The drumming you hear is firing from the Russian trenches opposite us. The Russians are up to something; they want to disturb our Christmas celebration.

"But here is our lieutenant. A splendid figure of a man,

55

a typical soldier of our glorious army. Steel helmet on his head, hand grenades at his belt. But a moment ago, in the cheerful and comfortable atmosphere of this underground shelter, his eyes were resting upon the shining Christmas tree. Now they are boring into the snow-swept, howling, hostile winter night. The lieutenant turns smartly to his men. 'Tighten chin straps,' he orders. Ah, you ought to see this, ladies and gentlemen, this lieutenant and his men, these mettlesome German faces and the change that comes over them in a moment's time. Tightening the chin strap of the helmet has a remarkable effect. For the result of it is that the soldier becomes, so to speak, one with his helmet, that, so to speak, he . . .'"

Captain Bäumler groaned.

"What's the matter, Bäumler?"

"Damned if that's Stalingrad!"

"No, of course it isn't. Maybe it's Kharkhov or even in Berlin. In any case it's a fake."

The broadcast droned on. The man in Kharkhov or Berlin or wherever he was plugged away at the chin strap.

"... It is a psychological preparation, too, an inward tensing—you ought to *see* these men, ladies—crouching for the spring. And if a man's courage should tend to slacken, the chin strap acts as an outward aid, holding the jaw set. . . ."

"Do you want to hear the rest, Bäumler?"

"No, that's enough. Turn it off."

But Huth did not turn it off. He was familiar with the broadcasting times of a number of stations. Twirling the dials, he set the radio to a different wave length and they heard, in German again, a report on huge German tank losses at Kotelnikovo (Hooth's tanks) and of fighting at Morosovskaya, Tatsinkaya, Millerovo (good God, Millerovo; where in the world was the line of the front?), and of the encirclement of German forces at Velikie Luki. . . .

"Shall I leave it on, Bäumler?"

"Yes, let's listen," Bäumler replied bleakly. And from that day on, the two of them, whenever they were alone in their bunker, listened to the Russian communiqués and to broadcasts from London.

Afterward Bäumler stretched out on his cot. Huth made another round in the cold night, past the reception and operating house where half the medical company slept on stretchers or on the floor while the other half stood watch. He walked by the huts, now completely dark. At the company's vehicle park stood a few sleds and a troop of small, shaggy horses, their heads pressed close together, a gray, ice-crusted heap in the snow, only the white mist rising from their nostrils indicating that there was anything alive here.

Huth returned to the shelter and lay down. What did I care, I had the gift, he thought as he fell asleep.

The land had gone back to the shape it had had when it first emerged from nature's hands, to the form that fire and water and ice had given it. In the west lay the Don, in the east the Volga, in the south the Karpovka; running parallel to the Don was the line of the Rossoshka hills which sloped down to the little Rossoshka River; in the south was a low plateau running parallel to the Karpovka and sloping down to the Karpovka valley; in the east, flanking the Volga, the land was also hilly. Between these hills, like a gleaming plate cracked in a few places by ravines and fissures was the steppe, lashed by frequent snowstorms. The edges of this big plate were, in the east, the bend of the Volga and Stalingrad. And here, on this snow-swept plain, the fate of the German Sixth Army was sealed.

The land was waste and void.

The traces of human beings who had lived here and set up their homes had been wiped out. Highways were no longer highways, railroad lines had vanished. The villages, the sheep and cattle farms, had been bombed and shattered by artillery; only abandoned ruins were left. Those who had come in place of the inhabitants, the German soldiers, found no shelter left. The staffs lived in bunkers among the ruins of the villages and the common soldiers lay in holes in the ground up front and often merely in holes scooped in the snow under the open sky. Never before had such huge masses of men occupied the land between Don and Volga, and never before had men died here in such numbers.

In a dugout on a slope of the Rossoshka hills a face gray with frost bent over another face that also showed the traces of the murderous cold.

"Matt, are you dozing?"

"Yes, August."

Matthias Gimpf lay on a cot, staring up at the ceiling of the dugout. Standing over the cot, August Gnotke was laying a handful of old rags down on it. He hesitated for a moment as if he wanted to say something else; then he turned away from Gimpf, who lay motionless in his coat, cap, and boots. Gnotke

57

buttoned his coat, covered his hands, ears, and throat and left the dugout. It was his turn to stand guard for an hour.

Two hours in the dugout, one hour up front in the trench was now the division of watches. Life had regained normality to that extent. Sergeants were also required to do sentinel duty. Gnotke had been given his collar tabs and shoulder straps again and had even been ordered to sew them on. However, that meant little now. He was as ragged as the others; his feet were wrapped in rags like the others. Under these conditions a bit of braid meant little and a non-com had the same duties as a private.

Christmas was long since past, and the date set for the attempt to break out to the west had also passed without anything happening. On Christmas night they had left their holes in the snow and gone up closer to the hillside. There they had found a trench and behind it a dugout, a former Russian dugout that had later been enlarged by services-of-supply soldiers. And since Georg Ketteler had gone off to the clearing station, and since the boy from Ottakring and the men from Ostermiething and Billerbeck and Hohengüstrow and others had been buried in the snow farther west, there was plenty of room for them all in the dugout. It was quite different from the cramped holes in the snow and the hole in the ground that they had later completed. Those had had only room enough for a few men at a time.

January had come and the icy gray mist now drifted in from the east, from the Volga. When the wind left off playing with the gray tatters of cloud and took up its games closer to the ground, it swept the surface of the steppe clear and whipped hard-frozen grains of snow into the men's faces. This was one such day; the ground was free of snow and gray with frost. All the snow was now in the air, sailing past in perfectly straight lines. Through the drifting snow a pale white ball could be discerned, the only fixed point visible in the incessant movement. This ball was the sun.

A face suddenly appeared at Gnotke's side. Bluish lips, a large nose, a pair of glasses above the nose. He was the sentry from the other end of the trench.

"Christ, that soup today—starvation rations again!"

Gnotke peered at the eyes behind the glasses. From the look in those eyes he saw the inevitable outcome; if it did not happen at once it would certainly be soon. The man before him, who stood with shoulders hunched, had once been a drawing teacher; he would never teach again.

"I counted the peas in the soup. Fourteen of them, the rest pure water. Don't they have any horses left?"

Gnotke looked straight into the man's eyes.

"And the damned lice. It's not so bad out here, but you don't dare to get into a warm place." Actually he had wanted to say something different.

"Do you feel so knocked out too?"

"Yes," Gnotke said.

They stood side by side and looked at the moving stream of air. The snow floated close to the ground. Their eyes were level with the surface of the ground and the view was broken by a grating of ice-coated twigs that had been stuffed into the hole in the tiny earth wall.

"Such weather. Nobody, not even a Russian, could keep his eyes open. Today it would have to succeed." This was a proposal and the teacher expected an answer. Gnotke continued to stare out into the drifting snow. The other sentry turned away and went back to his post.

So The Gravedigger (that was what they called Gnotke in the company) didn't want to help. The teacher stared out through his own peephole. His gaze no longer had the steadiness of days past when he had been sufficiently calm to draw the scene on a piece of paper with a long, even stroke, and even to sketch in a foreground—to draw that flat, barrel field with the prominent hump in the middle: the dead horse toward which his every thought was now directed.

After a while Gnotke observed that the teacher had abandoned his post. The man was outside the trench, pressing close to the ground, pushing himself forward an inch at a time. Gnotke knew what was going to happen. The teacher was not the first to go this way.

Two weeks ago a group of engineers in the vicinity had chased a skinny nag. Unluckily, the fleeing animal had run between the German and the Russian lines and a shot from the other side had killed it. The body still lay there, swollen and frosty gray. Beside this gray mound were three dark spots— in clear weather they could be recognized as human bodies. Two of them were engineers who had been reluctant to lose their prey, the third was a man from Gnotke's own company who had ventured out there and been shot by a Russian marksman. Now the teacher was going.

Gnotke had seen in the man's eyes that he was done for—today or tomorrow. In the snow holes down below he had also looked at faces and into eyes and sensed, more than once, the inevitability of a man's fate. If it had been practicable, he

59

would have preferred to return to the coventry of his former occupation. It had seemed to him more bearable to deal with corpses as one's daily work. They showed their gaping wounds, their glazed eyes, their gut; some of them grinned as Sergeant Aslang had done, but they did not talk and they no longer hoped for anything.

The men in the snow holes, on the other hand . . .

There had been that boy from Ottakring, his nose already pinched, obviously as good as done for, who placed all his hopes on a Christmas package from home and talked about cookies and candy and cake and lobster salad. Gnotke had listened to him and tried in vain to banish the definite image that this pinched nose and daily gaunter face evoked in him. And then there was that farmer from Ostermiething who swallowed every pill he was given or could barter from others and still did not get rid of his diarrhea. At the same time he thought of nothing but his fields and his horses. Were the mares going to foal, he wanted to know, or had they failed to get bred? Behind this farmer who worried incessantly about his cattle and crops and who would not cut the hay and carry water to the barn, behind him too Gnotke had seen the open grave. And he had watched them reach the point where the boy from Ottakring stopped wishing for cookies and cake for Christmas and longed only for half a loaf of black bread—and did not receive even that. And Gnotke saw the farmer from Ostemiething who had bargained so hard about the price of every pill grow feebler and feebler, until one day he sat up and wrote, with a hand numbed by cold, a letter that could never be mailed. *"Dear parents, sisters, and brothers,"* he had written, *"pay for two holy Masses for me, so that I'll get out half alive. I don't care at all what they cost. . . ."*

As Gnotke stood there, staring into the snow that whipped over the field, he thought of faces, the faces of men who had been at his side and vanished again, of hopes that had outlived the men and were now cherished by others on their way to death. He looked for the teacher again. The man was merely a gray streak on the ground, a fallen twig in the welling chaos. The teacher was moving so cautiously he seemed motionless; only by steady observation could it be seen that he was slowly approaching his goal. This teacher had a wife, children, a house, and beehives back of the house, and here he was risking wife, children, and life for a hunk of horseflesh. But what could you do? A man in that state could not be talked out of it. The dead horse was more alluring than any number of words and lofty ideas could be.

Gnotke thought of Stüve, whose feet had swollen and who had hardly spoken a word since Ketteler's departure. Now, to cap his misfortunes, his glasses had been broken. He thought of the red-haired sergeant, Urbas, who lay on his cot with some peculiar disease; he also thought of his cracked bell, Gimpf. In Vyazma, it seemed, Gimpf had not been with the troops at the front, but with a detachment of guards, and while with them something had happened to him that had been more devastating than the penal battalion and everything else. This much Gnotke had by now found out about Gimpf.

Dingelstedt had reached the dead horse. He raised his hand and with his knife cut out a piece of meat. Gnotke heard nothing but the tempestuous howl of the wind, saw nothing but the movements of that hand with the knife—movements shrouded by billowing curtains of snow. Perhaps the man would be lucky and come through! Gnotke thought. At that moment a shot rang out.

On January 8th, some nineteen miles from Gnotke's shelter, at the northern end of the German line of resistance, the snow was also sweeping across the steppe and the sun hung like a pallid disk among the gliding layers of mist. Second Lieutenant Lawkow, a small, pock-marked man, held a telephone in his hand and was crying excitedly into it, "Look here, are you off your head? Can't you see those are negotiators with a white flag?"

"No matter, if they're Russians we fire," the neighboring trench replied.

Lieutenant Lawkow was the adjutant of the battalion, but since the battalion C.O. had fallen sick and gone to the rear, he was now acting commander. He hung up, cursed his neighbor, and again stared over the edge of the trench at the drifting snow. He could distinguish a white flag fluttering in the wind; under a volley of rifle fire the flag withdrew.

Lieutenant Lawkow telephoned regimental headquarters and was informed that the lieutenant of the adjacent battalion had behaved correctly, formally speaking, since orders from the army directed that negotiators were to be rejected by fire. Then the regimental commander in person came to the phone and received Lawkow's report. Half an hour later the commander, Colonel Lundt, came up to the front-line trench.

Shortly afterward the Russian negotiators reappeared. Again the large white flag fluttered in the wind. Again a bugle call sounded across the snow-covered field. This time no rifle shots were fired. Colonel Lundt sent Lieutenant Lawkow out to meet the Russian negotiators. Lawkow led them through an unmined path across the no man's land and into the German lines. There were two Russian officers and a bugler. They informed the colonel that, on behalf of the Soviet High Command, they had a document to transmit to the commander of the German Sixth Army.

Colonel Lundt had them blindfolded, led them to his car, and drove to his regimental staff headquarters. Here he called Army HQ and spoke to the chief of the army general staff and then to the commander in chief. He then asked the Russian officers to give him the document for transmission to his superiors, and to consider themselves his guests until his return.

Colonel Lundt got into his car, drove toward Pitomnik airport and then on the road toward Gumrak and stopped at the bunkers near the end of the landing field where, in a former Russian anti-aircraft battery, the Army High Command had taken up quarters.

The document that was handed to the commander in chief read:

"To the commander in chief of the German Sixth Army, Colonel General Paulus, or his representative, and to the entire force of officers and men of the encircled German forces at Stalingrad.

"The German Sixth Army, units of the Fourth Panzer Army, and reinforcements sent to their aid have been completely surrounded since November 23, 1942.

"The troops of the Red Army have forged a solid ring around this German Army group. All hope that your troops might be saved by an offensive of the German Army from the south and southwest has proved vain; the German troops coming to relieve you have been routed by the Red Army and their remnants are retreating toward Rostov.

"The German air transport fleet, which has been supplying you with starvation rations of food, ammunition, and fuel, has been forced by the swift and successful advance of the Red Army to shift its bases frequently and to fly great distances to reach the pocketed troops. In addition, the German air transport fleet is suffering tremendous losses in planes and crews at the hands of the Russian Air Force. Help for the surrounded troops is becoming illusory.

"The situation of your surrounded troops is desperate; they are suffering from starvation, disease, and cold. The fierce Russian winter is only beginning. The hard frosts, cold winds, and blizzards are still to come; but your soldiers are not supplied with winter clothing and are living under extremely unhygenic conditions.

"You, as commander, and all the officers of the surrounded troops, understand perfectly well that you have at your disposal no real means for breaking out of the pocket. Your position is hopeless and further resistance senseless.

"In view of your hopeless situation and in order to avoid needless bloodshed, we propose that you accept the following conditions of surrender: (1) All surrounded German troops, with you and your staff at their head, are to cease resistance. (2) You will turn over to us intact all troops, weapons, combat equipment, and war supplies.

"We guarantee life and safety to all officers and soldiers who cease resistance and, after the end of the war, transportation back to Germany or to any country to which the prisoners of war wish to go.

"All troops who surrender will be permitted to keep their uniforms, insignia of rank and decorations, their personal property and objects of value; the higher officers may also keep their swords.

"All officers, non-commissioned officers, and soldiers who surrender will receive normal rations at once.

"All wounded, sick, and frost-bitten persons will be given medical treatment.

"Your reply in writing is expected at 10 A.M. Moscow time on January 9, 1943, to be delivered by your personal representative, who is to travel in a passenger automobile bearing a white flag along the road from Konny junction to Kotluban station. Your representative will be met by fully authorized Russian officers in Sector 'B', one-half kilometer southeast of Junction 564 on January 9, 1943 at 10 A.M.

"Should you reject our offer of surrender, we must warn you that the forces of the Red Army and Red Air Force will be forced to proceed to the annihilation of the surrounded German troops, and that you will bear the responsibility for their destruction.

> (Signed) VORONOF,
> Colonel General of Artillery, representative of the Supreme Command of the Red Army.
> (Signed) ROKOSSOVSKI,
> Lieutenant General, Commander in Chief of the Don Front."

Neither Sergeant Gnotke nor any of the other men on the Stalingrad west and north fronts knew that on the following day at ten in the morning, another dark page in their book of fate would be turned and their final destruction ordered. That day, in the trench where Gnotke stood guard and in the field in front of him, only a single shot was heard. The bullet struck close to the dead horse and churned up some snow. The arm that had moved so slowly and the hand that had cut a piece of meat out of the dead horse, fell back. Then there was no more motion and everything was the same as before, except for the fourth immobile figure which by morning would be covered with snow and would then appear to be a dark spot like the three others out there in the drifting snow.

After half an hour Gnotke was relieved.

His relief, a hunched figure in crazy-quilt wrappings, with weary eyes blinking from under his cotton hood, was Corporal Liebich, a clerk from Merseburg in Thüringia who had been one of the Vertiachi staff company and therefore felt this plunge into hunger and darkness more acutely than the others. It was Gnotke's duty to state that all was well at the post, or else to inform his relief of whatever was wrong. But Gnotke merely pointed briefly out into the field at the fourth dark spot that now lay beside the familiar three near the dead horse.

Liebich understood at once. "Dingelstedt?" he asked. Gnotke nodded.

Before he returned to his own dugout, Gnotke had to inform the commander of the guard of Corporal Dingelstedt's disappearance and to make a report on what he had observed. The commander of the guard, Staff Sergeant Pöhls, who only a few days ago had been mess sergeant back at the staff company, wrote the name "Dingelstedt" in his notebook. He did not want to hear the details and was glad that this close-mouthed fellow Gnotke and not someone else was reporting. The mere mention of the dead horse beaded his forehead with sweat, and the vehement motion he felt in his intestines was not imaginery, even if the doctor in Otorvanovka had said that his diarrhea was based on an affected central nervous system, on strong emotions, fear or fright, say, so that shifting him up front would change and might possibly relieve his condition.

The company commander, Captain von Hollwitz, had to strike two men off his muster roll that day—a soldier who had died during the night and been buried in the snow that morning, and Corporal Dingelstedt. The company then had thirty-two men left: one officer, five non-commissioned officers, and twenty-six privates.

Von Hollwitz had had some three hundred men when he led his newly-formed company across the Don from Vertiachi. Enemy action, hunger, and disease has taken nine-tenths of his men. The time could not be far off when not a single man would be left to hold a gun.

Von Hollwitz thought of Vertiachi, the last place where life for him had been relatively normal. He thought of the campaign that had taken them to Vertiachi, of the furlough just before, of his home and the fields and woods and his "old man" who was still running the place, and he thought of Ilse of the neighboring estate. His dugout was only a few dozen yards from the foremost positions. They had been lucky here in finding former Russian dugouts; such shelters were a rarity on the Stalingrad west front. But how long would it last, how long could they hold out here? A kerosene lamp was burning on his desk, but kerosene was giving out too. On the table lay Corporal Dingelstedt's personal property. A watch, a wedding ring, a wallet with some money, a few photographs, and a packet of letters. Hollwitz examined the photographs—a cottage, a backyard garden, an old pear tree with high grass underneath it. A bench with a young woman and a boy of about ten sitting on it. A man in a straw hat, the shadows of branches and leaves on his face. This was Corporal Dingelstedt himself. Hollwitz placed the pictures beside the letters. As he did so he noticed a letter written in a child's hand. He read it.

> "Dear Papa,
> We have a new little brother. The doctor and the lady who came, they call her the midwife, say he looks like you. Frau Late wanted to take him home, but we won't give him to anybody, because mama almost died and the doctor is still coming every day. Mama can't even sit up in bed, and we have to be very good because she is so sick. What will we do if our mama dies? Papa, please come, mama keeps calling all the time 'Heinrich come to me.' Then Aunt Liese has to go to the telephone and call the doctor and then she has an injection in her leg and goes back to sleep again. When they ask mama what the baby's name is she just looks at us and does not say anything, so I said his name will be Heinz Viktor.
> Love and Kisses from
> Walter"

"The squad room is the soldier's home and should be kept as homelike as possible," state the army instructions on the care of barracks and squad rooms. West of Stalingrad a hole in the snow, a foxhole, in rare cases a dugout, was the soldier's home. In this sense the dugout of which Gnotke was senior officer had been fitted out. Doors and windows, doorframes and windowframes, had been taken from the huts of near-by villages, as well as tables, benches, and other articles. In the dugout a door might be used for a door or for something entirely different. Windows and windowframes and carved shutters seemed ideally suited for dugout cupboards. The first inhabitants of this dugout must have had certain definite ideas in mind when they painted on the door the words: WINTER REST HOME. But the thoughts of those soldiers had vanished like themselves and no trace of them remained. The steps by which Gnotke descended into the dugout were badly worn at the edges; the onetime wooden framing had been removed and used for heating. The chairs, except for one bench, the built-in cupboards, and the wooden revetment of the walls had also gone into the stove and turned to smoke. The night before the cot (formerly the door of a peasant hut) of the second dead soldier had been burned. When Gnotke came down into the dugout and went up to Dingelstedt's cot to pack the man's possessions, the men in the dugout looked up and watched him by the dim light that trickled in through a crack in the ground. When he returned shortly afterward Dingelstedt's cot too had been dismantled, and Private Altenhuden was busy hacking it into firewood with his bayonet.

Gnotke squatted down beside the still-cold stove. He had seen at a glance that Gimpf was still lying motionless on his cot, as he had been when Gnotke went out to stand sentry duty. Gimpf had not removed his boots, had left untouched the rags that lay ready at his side, and was still staring up at the ceiling prop. He too, like Sergeant Pöhls, was suffering not so much from his slightly frost-bitten feet as from an affliction of the central nervous system. But fear or fright could scarcely have affected Gimpf; such emotions had entirely disappeared since his service in the disciplinary battalion.

Altenhuden brought an armful of firewood to the stove.

"Kindling, and a few minutes ago it was a cot. Well, he don't need it no more."

"No, he doesn't need it," Gnotke said.

That was Corporal Dingelstedt's epitaph.

"'S a good thing we got some stove wood again," a high voice declared—that of Corporal Riess.

"Shut up, Riess," Gnotke said irritably. "You would have done better to bring back some horsemeat."

Altenhuden lit the fire and the iron stove—a converted gasoline can—began to glow and belch smoke at the joints and from the fire door. There were two things that could revive life in a dugout (the third, a square meal, was no longer to be thought of): a Soviet attack or a lit stove. When an attack

66

took place, all of them were up, no matter how wretched they felt, for losing the dugout would mean losing everything; outside the dugout lurked the blizzard-swept, naked steppe. This time the cause of their revival was a hot stove, and Altenhuden was not sparing with the wood; he stuffed into the stove as much as it would hold. Even the acrid smoke was pleasant in this hole in the ground, sunk into a clay and limestone soil, with walls that looked like frozen granite. Although the warmth was not all-enveloping, the smoke that streamed along the walls to the exit created a home-like atmosphere and the men, lying like withered flies on their cots, began to stir, to become animated. First Stüve got off his cot and crouched down beside the stove; a second, third, and fourth followed him, and from outside came Liebich and the other sentries who had been relieved. Gnotke put a pot of water on top of the stove, and when it was hot he carried it over to Gimpf's cot. He nudged Gimpf who, with Gnotke's eyes fixed upon him, reluctantly unwrapped the rags from his shoes and took them off so that he could cover his feet with the hot rags Gnotke handed him. Gnotke had already told him more than once that sound feet were more important than a sound mind. "Your feet are better than Stüve's and better than Kalbach's too," he had said to Gimpf. For Stüve's feet were swollen from starvation and Kalbach's from starvation and a weakening of the heart action. Gimpf continued to lie on the cot with the hot compresses on his feet. Gnotke brought him another pot of water and then, although he did not take over Gimpf's turn at sentry duty, he exchanged with him so that Gimpf would not have to go out until later.

When Gnotke returned to the dugout after being relieved for the second time, it was already night. A few of the men were still sitting around the stove; others had gone back to their cots. The glow of the fire flickered on the faces of the men by the stove, played across the ceiling and walls of the dugout and from time to time illuminated those who were sitting on their cots with knees drawn up or were lying stretched out in the smoke and darkness.

As Gnotke entered he heard someone say, "We just have to be content, because if the Russians had succeeded in doing what they intended . . ." The speaker interrupted himself, then added after a pause, "We're still alive."

"We're still alive!" someone repeated from the darkness.

Another man spoke up: "The Devil himself has surrounded us here. Only praying will help."

That was the end of the conversation. The man who wanted

to practice contentment and who was "still alive" was Kalbach of the weak heart and swollen feet. The one who no longer believed in Russians or a Führer and clung to prayer alone was Corporal August Fell. Gnotke found a place among the men by the stove. They did not move to make room as he sat down. They sat motionless, their unkempt beards looking unreal, as if they had been pasted on, their heads drooping. The men sitting on the cots looked at their knees; the men lying down stared at the red reflections on the ceiling.

The carnival, the orgy that had sprung to life here for an hour, was over. They might have used this gift of warmth differently, as had Private Altenhuden, for example. He had taken off his shirt, picked out two hundred and thirty lice, and dropped them into a tin can filled with water. Or they might have washed the rags on their feet and patched their socks, or else, as Gimpf had done on Gnotke's urging, have tended their feet on which their lives would soon depend. But the warmth and the unexpected quiet of the front had been too precious for utilitarian purposes. They had enjoyed it to the full as in other times they might have enjoyed a large portion of whisky, and the effect had been much the same. They had again mustered up all the conversational material that they had already eked out for weeks and had chewed it all over again. Naturally, they could no longer talk about Hooth's tanks; by this time that theme was a dead horse. On the other hand, all of them had seen with their own eyes a tremendous glow of fire in the west. Corporal Riess, for all his failure to bring back horse meat from the regimental rations office, had at least returned with an explanation of the glow. "You see," he said, "it's true after all. There's fighting beyond the ring. The Russians are still in Kalach, but a whole SS army is slamming into them there." Then Sergeant Urbas had put in a word—Urbas who lay on his cot with some kind of "manic disease," so that they never knew what to expect of him; at one time he lay like a stick, idiotically counting his fingers and hearing nothing at all, even when he was shouted at; at another time he would listen like a beast of prey for every faintest whisper, put in his oar about everything and rave furiously until he again fell back, his face blue, into his former rigidity, so that more than once the others thought he had died. So he had lain all day. But when Riess spoke about the SS army in Kalach, Urbas suddenly threw off his blanket, shelter half, coat, and everything else, swung his legs over the side of the cot, and sitting there with his blue, swollen face, screamed: "Sure, there's no doubt about it. I know it. They're over the bridge already and cutting their way through."

The others did not like to look at Urbas or listen to him, even if for once he should chance to be right. They were therefore relieved when he collapsed again after adding some incomprehensible nonsense to what he had already said. Altenhuden replaced his dangling feet on the cot and covered him again. After that Urbas kept quiet and Riess went on with his report of what he had heard at the rations office. When he had finished, August Fell clasped his hands and said: "I want you all to hear this. I'm making a vow and if it's true I'll keep it; if I get home safely I'll put a hundred marks in the collection plate." The others, Kalbach and Liebich and Riess and Liebsch and Altenhuden and Stüve and even Gimpf all contributed a few words to fan their common hope, so that before long the iron ring was virtually shattered, Stalingrad won, and the Russians at last driven into the Volga.

"You can see it in the way the Russians are fighting—their stubbornness is an indication."—"They don't want to surrender Stalingrad, but sooner or later it will have to fall."—"After all, we have nine-tenths of the place; only small groups are still fighting there. The trouble is they're so well fortified that their positions are almost impregnable." —"Even when they attack in masses, the soldiers are all convicts and the commissars are whipping them on." —"Sooner or later the Russians will feel the pinch; they can't stand their tremendous losses forever."

Somehow, the Russians' "tremendous losses" made their own losses seem smaller, and by talking about "hunger in the Russian lines" they tried to talk away the hollowness in their own bellies, but this they could not do. Still, Liebich suddenly started to his feet and exclaimed, "You can see it already; we've had it quiet here for days."

"Christ, no, I wouldn't say days," Sergeant Maulhard replied. Three days ago, during an assault on the trench, he had been shot in the buttocks and since had been lying prone on his cot, waiting to be transported back to the clearing station. A medical aide had placed an emergency bandage on the wound and he now lay with rising wound fever. There were no morphine injections for him; his one consolation was the medical aide's suggestion that a tetanus injection he had received several months ago, after being lightly wounded, would probably still be effective and would protect him against tetanus. To this one hope he clung. But Maulhard was certainly no more edifying a sight than Sergeant Urbas, and at this time, when all the men were getting warm and trotting out their remaining reasons for hope, they were not eager to hear him talk; they turned again to Corporal Riess to hear what other news he had brought from regimental headquarters.

Riess, like Liebich and the staff sergeant, had formerly belonged to the staff company. While he had waited vainly for hours for the issue of horse meat, he had sat down with his old comrades and played "twenty-one" with them, and by the time he returned without the horse meat he had picked up a deal of information. Now, one after the other, he relieved himself of his latest slogans. Altenhuden refueled the stove until the sparks flew, and although these men in the dugout had been inside the pocket for fifty days and had seen their hopes shattered fifty times, they now gathered up the pieces and put them together again for the fifty-first time. In about a week, then, normal postal communications should be re-established and they would be able to send letters home as usual. And in about five days, say around the 15th or 16th of January, the issue would be decided; that was as sure as that Hitler was the Führer and the Führer would keep his word.

"Loyalty repays loyalty," Riess had said.

"Things are bad here, but after all it was even worse last winter in the Valdai pocket and they got out," Corporal Fell recalled.

"What I want to know is why we didn't break out on the third, as we were supposed to," Altenhuden said.

"No need of that; we just stay where we are and they'll break through to us," Riess said. "According to headquarters, we'll be able to leave the pocket by January 26th at the latest. And of course there'll be furloughs, first for the men with lots of dependents, but later on for all."

"The Führer's said so."

"So we'll not falter and not retreat a step; we can be sure of being liberated."

"Emil, is it true they've got a plan for furloughs all worked out?" someone asked Riess.

"You know, the plan for all of us to be taken home by plane immediately . . . ?"

It was all true, all tangible.

So they sat around the stove; their hair had not been cut for weeks and was caked with dirt, their faces were unshaven, their eyes glistened with hunger, but they felt that the end of their suffering was so near, that all the pain and dying had not been in vain, for they had "defended" the fortress of Stalingrad and had held out till the end, until they were relieved and liberated; and tomorrow they would be transformed; they would be passengers in a transport plane, human beings, lovingly tended by their women and children and the whole nation. It was all true, all true.

All this had taken place before Gnotke returned, and it had ended by the time he joined the men crouching around the cooling stove. There was no longer any wood beside the stove; it had all been burned. The fire was down to embers, the red glow on the ceiling was growing fainter. Fell, who had spoken of prayer as the sole hope, and Kalbach who had asserted triumphantly that they were still alive, had already returned to their cots. Liebich and Riess were still at the stove; they were the two who had not moved to make room for him. They could not stand his cold glance. And Gnotke, for his part, could not get rid of the impression that the sparse whiskers on Liebich's face were hairs stuck on a wax doll's face, nor could he help his exact knowledge of how colorless those blue eyes of Riess's would someday look. The two soon stood up and clambered onto their bunks. Only Altenhuden remained, and he and Gnotke fell asleep beside the stove.

Gnotke awoke once more to hear Stüve saying, "That swine Liebsch, done it again. . . ." "Don't make a fuss," another voice called out in the darkness, but Stüve would not calm down. "Pig-headed as a tank and too goddamn lazy to get up and unbutton his pants and piss outside, and if you're underneath him you get it all on you," he growled, and in the wretched light from the tiny kerosene lamp he lit he could be seen to stand up and shake out his shelter half. Liebsch, however, could not be seen or heard; he did not stir.

That was nothing unusual; it happened every day and Gnotke went back to sleep.

On November 19, 1942, the deputy chief of the general staff of the German Sixth Army had 330,000 men on his tables of organization. By January 10, 1943—in fifty-one days—he had to write off 140,000 men. They were casualties from Russian arms, starvation, cold, and disease. There remained 190,000 men.

On January 10, 1943, these men began their flight over the frozen, empty steppe. It started at ten o'clock in the morning of January 10—the time limit of the Soviet High Command's ultimatum.

In Gnotke's bunker the general dissolution began ten minutes earlier; Private Altenhuden opened the doors of chaos with a touch of his finger. He put his right forefinger on a red

71

spot, a spot this size and shape of a lentil, on the neck of Sergeant Urbas. When he withdrew his finger, the spot, which had vanished under the pressure, immediately returned. Altenhuden did not know that he was still holding his finger in the air while his other hand opened Urbas' shirt. There, too, on the man's bare chest, were the same red spots. Then Altenhuden stared at his forefinger as if something had been imparted to it that he would never be able to erase, that was already coursing through his blood and would assail his heart and brain. He stared at Urbas, at the bloodshot whites of the half-closed eyes, at the swollen face, the large black nostrils, the thick lips also black and parted, revealing the teeth; he smelled the man's stinking, stertorous breath. And then Altenhuden staggered back, thrust his finger under his armpit, and said tonelessly, "Typhus!"

"Typhus," someone repeated.

"The bastard!"

"And he said he had a headache."

"Wouldn't eat anything."

"Headaches and chills, that's what it is."

They talked all at once, a helpless, confused babble. Here it was, the disease of besieged cities, of beaten armies, of shattered countries, and they did not what to do. It was a few minutes before ten o'clock. The light that trickled into the dugout was of an earthen gray and the faces of the soldiers standing around the sergeant's bunk was of the same color.

"What are we going to do?"

"Get him out of here—where's the medic?"

But where was there a medical squad to remove him and where could he be taken? To Otorvanovka? For days there had been no room there for Sergeant Maulhard with his buttock wound. Or to Pitomnik airport to be flown out? Or to the hospital at Gumrak where the patients were lying out in the street and dying under canvas tents?

"This brainless bastard," Corporal Riess repeated. "Nutty as they come and it's his own fault; he shouldn't have drunk unboiled snow water. We were ordered not to."

"Cut the guff. What are we going to do? He's got to get out of here."

Corporal Riess, a former SS man attached at one time to an SS concentration camp in occupied Poland, was familiar with the radical procedure in cases of typhus: a bullet in the back of the neck, burial fourteen feet deep, quicklime on top. "Let's make a report and isolate him for the time being," he said. "Right now we can lay him out in the snow."

But Sergeant Urbas was also familiar with a number of different practices. Formerly a sergeant with the supply train, he had come all the way to the vicinity of Moscow with the army and then from the Dniester through Kiev, Kharkhov, Rostov, and Kalach to the steppes of the Don and Volga, and he had seen a good deal on the way. It had never occurred to him that he himself might be the object of methods for extermination that were practiced upon sick inmates of camps and infected civilians. Moreover, it was not clear how much he understood of what the men were saying about him; but as he suddenly sat up and dangled his legs again over the edge of the cot, as he opened his eyes and saw the group of gray faces all looking at him, he understood a great deal all at once. Shaken by fever though he was, with buzzing head and almost sightless eyes, he nevertheless heard what they were thinking. He saw and heard again——heard the sly tone in what Riess had said, saw the wretchedness in the others' faces and the terror lurking in their eyes.

"Urbas, look here, man," Riess called out to him, and this being addressed by name was all that was needed to recall him to himself, to clear momentarily the haziness of his mind. He was Urbas, a man, a hard-pressed living creature, and this band of starving, helpless, cruel men had surrounded him, were his antagonists. In the confusion of men and objects Urbas' eyes fixed on one point, the gasoline can that had been converted into a stove. In a flash he had flung himself from his cot, seized the stove, crammed it with its contents of flaky gray ashes on Corporal Riess's head and crunched it into a formless mass with a powerful blow of both fists. The stovepipe fell apart, black particles of soot flew about the room. Urbas reeled into the table, and in a moment, under his pounding fists, no table was left. The man Urbas was transformed into a whirl of hands and feet, and whatever he laid hands on became a club or missile. Whenever any of the others approached the raging madman, he was clubbed and kicked simultaneously. Urbas was a short, square-set fellow with bristly gray hair that now, grown long and softer, hung down over his inflamed eyes and fluttered around his puffed face. He had been a packer and later a warehouse manager for a Leipzig export firm; he had a wife at home named Brigitte and a son who was also in the field. This monster who seemed exempt from the laws of gravity and equilibrium, who filled the dugout from end to end, who had become a maelstrom of flesh and muscle, could see and hear now. Erich Urbas heard curses and shouts; he saw Riess, who had managed to remove the stove from his head,

73

kneeling on the floor and wiping ashes from his face and eyes; he saw Liebich and Liebsch tumbled over one another; saw Stüve, Fell, and Altenhuden rushing at him again; saw Sergeant Maulhard hitching up the bandage and his bloodstained trousers and fleeing from his bunk; he saw Gnotke standing by the earth wall of the dugout and staring; he saw Technical Sergeant Pöhls coming down the steps into the dugout even before the door was flung open; he saw through walls, through mist, he saw with supernatural keenness. He was holding a heavy object in his hand and he let fly with it. And this other thing in his hand was certainly not a rubber hose, this thing that came whistling down on a human body. And yet it was also the same stout rubber hose that hung behind the hall door at home. Suddenly he saw it all again: a Sunday afternoon, flowered cups on the coffee table, Brigitte pouring the steaming coffee, he himself sitting in his suspenders, the top buttons of his pants open, sitting on the sofa where he would lie down after coffee; and he had just picked up a thick slice of pound-cake when the woman next door came in and said, "There's a tramp upstairs by the attic steps." And he saw himself, Urbas, with the rubber hose in his hand, and the tramp hunched up beside the attic steps, sleeping the "sleep of the righteous" (but a tramp might break open the attic door and steal things; that happened every day). And the heavy rubber hose slashed down upon the wretched, homeless creature, struck the face and the terrified eyes of the awakening tramp. And warehouse manager Urbas rode high; he was fighting misery and misfortune with a rubber hose; he was a policeman, a landlord, a property owner, a defender of law and order. He beat the reeling fellow down the stairs and returned to his apartment, hung the rubber hose behind the hall door again and sat down on the sofa, while Brigitte put the cold coffee aside and poured him a fresh cup from the steaming coffeepot.

That was Urbas then, that was Urbas now.

But now he was holding not a rubber hose, but a cot torn off its hinges, and he swung it around in a circle. If the edge of this murderous weapon had struck someone, it would have killed or crippled; when the flat of it did strike, it bruised and tore out bits of hair and skin. Urbas was fighting misery and he struck all wretches and unfortunates. But he was no longer Urbas with his rubber hose; he was no longer a landlord and property owner, no longer a defender of order; he was not even a soldier of the New Order any more.

This Urbas in the dugout was no longer the Urbas of Leipzig with a wife and a son and a three-room apartment and an allotment garden and a cottage out in the countryside. He was no longer that Sergeant Urbas who could pass unmoved by gallows from which hanged men and women dangled and who could drive without a second thought past anti-tank ditches that he knew were filled with the bodies of executed civilians and prisoners of war. He was an Urbas who felt each blow he dealt, felt them all painfully. The Urbas in the dugout was a desperate, dying man and he howled and shrieked; sweat dripped from his face and he foamed at the mouth. In the end he could not stay the ebbing of his strength. The cot or stable door fell from his hands, the others pilled on him, threw him to the floor, struck him repeatedly, and held his hands and feet tightly.

He writhed. Half a dozen men lay on top of him. The fragments of the dugout furnishings were scattered all around. Sergeant Pöhls's voice became audible: "Idiots, you pack of crazy idiots. Didn't you hear the alarm? The Russians are attacking." The company commander, Captain von Hollwitz, had come in also. "Are you off your heads, what the devil's the matter with you. Alarm! Get out of here."

"The Russians . . ."

It was 10:00 A.M. The heap of men on top of Urbas suddenly found that not only Urbas was writhing under them, but that the earth itself was vibrating. The Russian artillery fire began; a first heavy salvo, a booming echo, a second reverberation. The men, reeling to their feet, could already hear a new series of discharges; the subsequent echo and then the following second echo merged with the detonations as the shells struck and the mill began to grind.

Altenhuden, Fell, Gnotke, Gimpf, and Liebich, bruised and battered as they were from their struggle with Urbas, and Riess, still blind from ashes, limping Stüve, Kalbach with his weak heart, and the apathetic swine Johannes Liebsch—all of them clumsily buttoned their coats, plumped their steel helmets over their rag-wrapped faces, rushed up the dugout steps, ran into the communicating trench, and hurried up front to their action stations. Even Sergeant Maulhard with his buttock wound limped behind them; after all, he might just as well lie still behind the machine gun as on his cot.

The western sky was flaming. The ravines, the steppe with its little villages sprinkled here and there down to the Karpovka valley—the whole of the snow-covered landscape seemed to be burning. Smoke rose as from a mighty conflagration. From the regiment's observation post the individual muzzle flashes from the Russian artillery could be seen, but it was necessary to assemble the observations of many regiments and

75

of a whole series of divisions, and to mark all these observations and reports on the strategic map at Army Headquarters, to grasp that the entire western half of the heart-shaped pocket was being compressed by a clenching fist.

HILL 126 WAS LOST.

"Right away, colonel!"

"Right away, general!"

"Emergency call."

"Emergency call."

"The chief of staff or the commander in chief personally."

"Hill 126 . . ."

The G-3 stood before the desk of the army chief of staff. The chief gave him a piercing, frozen glance. Both knew that the attempt at relief from outside had failed; Hooth had been defeated at Kotelnikovo and was retreating toward Rostov; the formations of Manstein's armies were also withdrawing toward Rostov. The German army was being defeated, the Stalingrade Sixth Army was lost; its matériel could not be saved and the only remaining task was, or should have been, to preserve the living men of which it was composed.

It was the beginning of the end. The chief of staff was pale; his eyes glistened with ill-concealed rage. "Sons of bitches," was his conclusion from the sum of his strategical and tactical information and reflections. The 44th Infantry Division was not holding. The 376th Infantry Division had brought disaster in its train ever since the battles around Kletskaya and could scarcely be considered reliable. The 3rd Infantry Division (Motorized) had stuck there in that damned salient so long, had held on so desperately to its dugouts and bunkers, that now it was too late and it too was in a devil of a fix.

"The Third has to be pulled out of that sack. In this position fast retreat is the only chance. By liquidating the 'nose' of the pocket we'll free the 29th Motorized and send it to Damme. For the rest: hold! The breaches in the line of the 44th and the 376th must be cleared again and held."

"And in the south?"

"Retake 129 and hold."

The army chief of staff had marked on his maps a rear defense line indicated by the code word "Violet"; farther back was another for which the code word was "Sunflower." But aside from his order for the 3rd Division, which in any case had been attacked from the rear and was in dissolution and flight, he issued no orders for retreat. The adjustments that took place in the fronts would have to be drawn in blood. The orders could no longer affect the army as such, or any conceivably attainable goals of that army; at most they could affect the lives of 190,000 men. But these orders, streaming from Army H.Q. to Bolshaya Rossoshka, Baburkin, Novo-Alexeyevka, Karpovka, Voroponovo, and Pestchanka concerned not the lives, but the deaths of these men.

The divisional commanders sat in their bunkers, bent over their maps laid out on tables, over radio messages, telephone messages, teletype messages which were handed them by their G-3's. One held his head between his clenched fists, another let his hands lie slackly on the table before him, a third ground his teeth, a fourth . . . all of them swore, all functioned, all conferred with their operations officers, issued orders, had their orders radioed, telegraphed, transmitted up front by special-missions officers, messengers, truck drivers, motorcyclists, tank drivers. One of these was General Geest; his headquarters were in a *balka,* as the deep ravines were called here, in the vicinity of Bolshaya Rossoshka. Here he was far from the front and at a greater distance from the endangered positions than any of the other staff headquarters. Nevertheless, he wore his steel helmet in the bunker, with the chin strap buckled tight. If disengagement, retreat, or even flight should prove necessary, he would again be on the inner arc of the movement. For this reason he had received an order to withdraw infantry and anti-tank troops from his division and throw them into a threatened point. Since the emergency company he had set up under Captain von Hollwitz was still fighting outside of his division's area, he again had the supply troops, the clearing stations, and the collecting stations combed through and another emergency company activated. This he placed under the command of a Lieutenant Wedderkop and sent off toward Baburkin.

The second, a commander at the northern switch position, also had to send reinforcements to the west front. He sent Colonel Lundt, and one of the two battalions that Lundt took with him was still temporarily commanded by the adjutant, Lieutenant Lawkow.

The third was General Gönnern. At this time he was in the large village of Karpovka, in the midst of a confusion of crates being nailed shut, of trunks being packed, and of wounded being carried out into the street and loaded on trucks. The news of the breaches in north and south had made it evident that both Russian thrusts were directed toward Karpovka; it was high time to shift headquarters farther to the rear.

The fourth was General Damme in Novo-Alexeyevka. His G-3 sat bent over a map, making pencil marks on it with one hand while his left hand held a telephone to his ear. Damme paced back and forth in the narrow shelter. Once he paused, looked over his G-3's shoulder, and examined the new entries on the map. He drew on his cigar, noticed that it had gone out, lit it again, and resumed his pacing.

His adjutant entered, followed by a mud-coated figure; even on the man's face there were layers of dirt and dried sweat. It was Colonel Vilshofen.

"Well, thank God you're here!" Damme exclaimed, shaking both Vilshofen's hands heartily. "A tank man at last—tanks are what we need here."

"I have no more tanks, sir."

"What . . . no, I see, of course not."

"Four tanks are all I have left."

Vilshofen had other disappointments in store for Damme. He and the assortment of troops who made up his combat group had not been sent to aid Damme, but to fill in the gap on Damme's right wing, between Damme's division and the adjoining division.

Damme went over to the map again. "What am I going to do?" he groaned. "The corps promised me help. An hour ago a Lieutenant Wedderkop with two hundred men passed through here. You ought to have seen that—gleanings from the hospitals. A troop of cripples rather than soldiers, each one with ten cartridges in his pocket. What kind of help is that?"

Damme, Damme's operations officer, and Colonel Vilshofen sat down at the map table. The adjutant took over the telephone and noted down the constant flow of reports from the front. Damme explained the situation to Vilshofen. "The Kasachi Hills have been fought over for weeks. They keep changing hands, and since they only meant casualties, both sides finally left them unoccupied. But now we've also lost Height 126 and we must retake it; there's no choice." The pencil in Damme's hand marked a number of dots rather than a continuous line on the outspread map. Vilshofen's violet-blue eyes followed the indicated line. The pencil touched a few more dots which indicated five Scythian burial mounds and three prominent hills. "You must take over the mounds and this northernmost hill, in addition to your other commitments, Vilshofen."

"Very well, sir. I'll have the hill occupied tonight."

"The hill must be held, at least until the new positions have been taken up. The 3rd Motorized Infantry Division is retreating from the 'nose.' The new line will then run along the road and curve south toward the railroad embankment, approximately in the direction of Atamansk."

Vilshofen rose.

"The hill, Vilshofen," were Damme's parting words. Then he turned back to his G-3 and conferred with him about the evacuation and shifting to the rear of the rations depot and several repair workshops and clearing stations. The G-3 took over the telephone again to receive the current reports from the front. The neighboring division called on the second telephone and informed Damme that the enemy had deepened his penetration.

Meanwhile Colonel Vilshofen went out, took a seat in a motorcycle sidecar, and sped off into the night over the ice-coated road.

The shelter Vilshofen had appropriated on the road to Dmitrevka was a root cellar of a former collective farm, intended for the storage of potatoes and other vegetables. Its walls and roof were of earth and it was situated right on the road. Eight steps led down into it, and the clank of caterpillar tracks, the creak of wagon wheels, the footsteps of marching detachments, and the noises of services-of-supply forces headed toward the rear and of reinforcements headed toward the front could be heard inside. Whenever the heavy door opened, letting in a cloud of white mist, and the figure of a major, a captain, or some other front-line officer emerged from the mist, the shelter was for moments also filled with the acrid stench of sweat, of blood, of unwashed bodies, and much dying.

"Well, gentlemen . . ."

Colonel Vilshofen stood up; the three officers also rose. He had been sitting on a barrel of sauerkraut, the others—a captain, a lieutenant, and a technical sergeant—on a feed trough. Colonel Vilshofen shook hands with the three men.

"May God protect you!"

This phrase was addressed to all three. It had sprung involuntarily to Vilshofen's lips, and the three men seemed to feel it entirely appropriate at this time; not one of them showed any surprise. They donned their woolen caps, turned up their collars, drew on their mittens, and vanished into the white mist. Colonel Vilshofen remained behind, amazed at himself.

"God . . ."

What did it mean? Why had he not said, "Heil Hitler!"? Why had no one noticed the omission?

Captain Steiger also thought about the phrase. It seemed to have far more meaning when spoken by the regimental commander than it would have had from the mouth, say, of the division's chaplain. Captain Steiger was leading a column of forty men and ten anti-tank guns. Each team of four was pulling along one light gun. The sky clouded over, but a gap remained where stars gleamed brightly. The gap of clear sky touched the horizon near the huts of Dmitrevka, which towered up out of the deadly flatness of the terrain.

The huts gradually sank beneath the horizon at the rear of the marching column. They made slow progress. The wheels of the guns turned heavily. After a while they moved still more slowly, advanced by fits and starts. The land, mauled during mud time by the treads of tanks and gouged out here and there by bombs, now lay spread out before them like a frozen storm-wracked sea. Over the billows and hummocks the anti-tank cannon with their human tractors bobbed up and down. They passed infantrymen on the way who were working like damned souls; with spades, picks, and axes they were hacking shelters for themselves in the earth. The clay soil was frozen hard as granite. Steiger's column still had two and a half miles to go to reach the hill that had to be occupied before dawn, occupied and held. But the men were soaking wet under their clothes, sweating from exertion and weakness. A corporal whom Steiger had sent to the nearest infantry company to fetch assistance returned alone. The company itself needed help; the ground was so hard that the men could not dig in. By dawn they would still find themselves without any shelter, and there was not a tree, not a rise in the ground, no sort of cover anywhere. Steiger's column slaved on. The men groaned and cursed, swore at the infantrymen who had refused to help them drag the heavy guns. And these infantrymen, a mile or so behind them, hacking away with their axes at the frozen earth until sparks flew and the blood burst through the skin of their palms—these infantrymen also groaned and cursed. They swore at the battalion commander, at the regimental commander—let them come up front and see what it was like to dig in here. And the battalion commander groaned at all the unobtainable needs that were reported to him; he groaned and cursed and sent messengers rushing off to regimental headquarters; and the regimental commander groaned at the insuperable difficulties and sent one officer after the other to division headquarters to describe how impossible it was to establish the planned line and to stress the necessity of further withdrawal to a place where the terrain would be more suitable for defense, say to the Rossoshka valley. And the divisional commander, General Damme, convinced of the untenability of the projected line, talked over the telephone to the corps. When the corps refused him further aide by way of more anti-aircraft and anti-tank guns, he left off pleading courteously: "But look here, now see here, sir, then it's all up with us." Instead he howled, shrieked, shouted, raged, and cursed like a cab driver and finally slammed the receiver back on the hook so hard that the table shook.

At that moment there was a face, the face of a general in the Stalingrad pocket, of which one half was rigid while the other twitched. The mouth dictated twitching, jerky words; the words were taken down, coded, and radioed, and after a period of waiting the reply was received and decoded. The face remained as it was, one half twitching, the other half rigid.

The reply read:

> "The line in the west to the west of the Rossoshka valley, in the south to the south of the Karpovka valley, must be held at all costs and under all conditions. Moreover, a report is desired explaining how it happened that the army abandoned Tsybenko and Kravtsov without having received the requisite permission from the High Command of the Armed Forces."

There were generals whose faces turned purple with rage when they read this reply. There were staff officers whose faces became rigid masks as they received and transmitted orders. There were fits of fury, hoarsely shouting voices, obstinate silences, injections of morphine and veronal, lapses into deathlike prostration. And there was obedience, criminal, murderous obedience. . . .

Commander Vilshofen left his command post. Up front his combat group was dying; there he might also die, but perhaps he could save whatever was still salvageable. He rode up front in a tank and got out into an icy mist and a snow-covered field. Dotted in a long line over the field were men with picks and shovels, their rifles lying beside them. They had dug in barely up to their waists and could go no deeper.

Vilshofen went up to one of the groups.

"How long have you been digging away?"

"All night, sir."

"Had your breakfast yet?"

"No, sir—hot water isn't any breakfast, I guess."

"No, it certainly isn't."

They also had no smokes. Vilshofen distributed the cigarettes he had with him. He looked at the men's faces as one after the other bent over the burning match in his cupped palm. He knew all of them; his unit was so shrunken that he knew the names of the new men as well as those who had formerly belonged to his tank regiment. One of them was Wilhelm Vogt, who had been with the tank regiment; he was a farm boy from the region of the Weser, near Minden. His father at home was so feeble that he could scarcely manage the farm work, but Vilshofen had recently been forced to refuse the boy a work leave home—at a time when furloughs were still possible. Another was De Wede, also a farmer; his wife at home in Celle was running their place with Russian and Polish prisoners of war. The third was a young clerk from Crefeld; the fourth, Wilsdruff, had formerly been in charge of the now dissolved repair squad; he was a metal worker from Upper Silesia and the father of five children. All four of them had the same look, the same bewhiskered, gaunt faces, the same staring eyes.

Vilshofen also lit a cigarette as he talked to the soldiers. He did not hold out any hope to them; he was unwilling to tell them things he himself no longer believed. When De Wede asked, "Do you think Hooth is still coming, sir?" Vilshofen replied, "It doesn't look like it; I'm afraid we're on our own here."

"Then it will be a long time before our young husband will get a chance to be with his wife, and he hasn't even seen her yet," De Wede said. He was referring to the clerk from Crefeld who had been married by proxy a while back and had also been refused a furlough for the occasion.

Vilshofen glanced at the man and said, "His fate is no worse than that of the men who have known their wives for years and still want to see them again."

He turned his gaze back to De Wede and Wilsdruff. "Let me have it frankly, De Wede. What would you do right now if you could do whatever you pleased?"

"Lie down here and not move another step, sir."

"And you, Wilsdruff?"

"May I say what I think, sir?"

"Yes, of course, Wilsdruff."

"Desert and perhaps save my life, sir," Wilsdruff said, jerking his thumb toward the west.

"So that's what you'd do—and what do you think the Russians would do?"

"I imagine they're human, sir."

Vilshofen looked thoughtfully at the soldier's face. The last time he had seen it was that night at Kletskaya, and much had happened since. "If you think that is a feasible course, Wilsdruff, I won't hold you back or let anyone interfere with you; but to my mind, if surrender is necessary all should do it together in recognition of the general situation."

It was not yet dawn. Vilshofen moved on to a hollow that led into a ravine. In the ravine stood a group of men: Captain Tomas and his adjutant, Lieutenant Latte; also Captains Runz and Hedemann, his acting battalion commanders. The rest were the crews of the four tanks; Vilshofen had invited them to the conference because he wanted them to hear what was at stake, what they had to fight and perhaps to die for.

"The enemy has succeeded in making deep penetrations here on the western front and on the northern front as well," he said. "The 'nose' at Marinovka is being evacuated right now and it's no great loss. The front was too extensive there; it could not be held without a great expenditure of forces and the men should have cleared out long ago. But they hung on because they had good dugouts there and nothing behind them. Well, that is one side of the matter; now, at any rate, they have to get out, and by holding here we will help them withdraw. That, of course, is just one element in our general task."

Vilshofen raised his hand and pointed out into the mist.

"Up there on the hill is Captain Steiger; to the right and left, on each of those knolls, is an anti-tank group. The hill blocks the road to Novo-Alexeyevka. You, men, have to support the men on the hill and fend off the expected attack against it—smash the attackers if that is possible. . . . And now. . . ."

He almost said again, "God protect you." But he interrupted himself this time, glanced over the group once more, and merely said briskly, "All right, that's the job."

He shook hands with Tomas and Latte; the scarred face of the older man and the lieutenant's boyish features seemed to force him to make this gesture. Then he stood there and watched Tomas (who limped slightly since he had been wounded), Latte, and the other men get into their tanks. He saw the hatches close and watched the tanks as they rolled down the ravine, climbed up the opposite slope, moved like four bright-blue bugs around the Scythian burial mounds on the flat plain, and vanished. Four tanks—not long ago it had been a torrent of steel and roaring gasoline that darkened the earth; not very long ago he had been commander of a whole regiment of tanks.

"Well, gentlemen, I'm ready."

This was addressed to his battalion commanders, Captains Runz and Hedemann. They led him to the shelter that had been dug for them during the night. It was a hole, hacked waist-deep in the ground, roofed in by a tent that was covered with snow and earth. The canvas that formed the sides had been flapped back so that they could see, after they were seated, one of the burial mounds that rose out of the plain. It was still before dawn; darkness hung heavily in the ravine and fog drifted over the icy land. Beyond the burial mound a star shone through the mist.

The officers discussed munitions, rations, engineering supplies, replacements. They had scarcely any AA guns, scarcely any AT guns, and a few shells for the guns they had. Instead of two hundred grams of bread daily, they were receiving rations of one hundred grams. There was not a single nail left for building emplacements, not a foot of wire. The companies were thinned out, growing smaller day by day, and there were no men to fill the gaps. Vilshofen was aware of this and he knew that conditions were no different in the neighboring regiment. The division was burned out; so was the division on his right. The division on the left—Damme's—was referred to among the soldiers as the DD which meant "dead division" or, sometimes, in memory of an earlier river-crossing that had cost many casualites, the "drowned division" and sometimes the "damned division." Completely shattered and then reassembled, its gaps had been filled with remnants from the combat troops and non-combatants of other divisions; it was so brittle that it began to break up under the slightest contact with the enemy. Only the tank forces that had been assembled behind it gave it some sort of backbone and held it together provisionally.

"Where will it end?"

"Have we been abandoned?"

"The line cannot be held."

"But the Führer will do everything in his power; we ourselves must break out."

Vilshofen listened attentively to Runz and Hedemann. Then he said, "Breaking out was proposed once when it might still have been possible. The proposal was rejected; today it's too late. There is no longer any way out for the half-starved, poorly-equipped soldiery that we are now."

"Good God, the Führer's word!"

85

"Why is this being done to us? What is our crime? Have we been abandoned?"

It was cold, the air filled with granular snow that stung their faces. The hole in the ground was so narrow that their knees touched. White steam from the speaker's breath wafted into the faces of the men sitting opposite him. The rumble of salvos could be heard. The Scythian mound beyond the fluttering canvas was surrounded by a flickering, greenish light. Vilshofen looked at his two officers. Runz was a former civil service official, forty years old. A few days ago he had celebrated his eleventh wedding anniversary in a shallow hole in the ground. Before the encirclement he had received a letter every day from his wife, or two or three whenever mail was given out. Hedemann was also an official and a reserve officer; he had bought a small farm cheaply in Latvia, near Dünaburg, and longed for the end of the war so that he could sit quietly by the Druja, hunt and fish and pursue his marshland farming operations—a subject he discussed with as much eagerness as his experiences during the French campaign. This was all Vilshofen knew about the two men. This morning they looked bedraggled, unwashed, and unkempt, just like all the enlisted men in the foxholes. Their eyes had the same dull look as they gazed out into the snow and listened to the roar of exploding metal.

"To sum up," Vilshofen said, "we have to be sparing of ammunition and rations will be even scarcer. We no longer have any extra horses for slaughtering. We can no longer count on help from outside. Those are the unpleasant facts. We must endure on our own."

Runz puffed out a dense cloud of white vapor. Hedemann stared down at his mittens. The roaring outside grew louder, the explosions came closer.

Dawn had broken, and with it had come the attack. The hill was under fire; from its brow smoke rose into the gray sky. This was the moment when the dikes gave, the moment of the flood, of total disaster on the Stalingrad west front. Vilshofen heard a tumult near the wall of the tent—footsteps, scraps of conversation, a cool voice reporting. Then he made out a sentence: "The whole division is gone to hell."

He threw back the canvas and clambered out of the hole. A number of his officers and a lieutenant from another unit were standing in a group; non-coms and enlisted men were among them. The lieutenant was gesticulating vigorously as he explained something; he was so lanky that the movements looked strangely disjointed.

"What's happened to whom, lieutenant?" Vilshofen asked.

"The division, sir . . . the division has been routed; they're all on the run. Your left flank is completely exposed, sir."

"What division are you talking about and who are you anyway?"

"Lieutenant Wedderkop, sir."

The lieutenant had been the leader of another salvaged emergency company; his whole company had been scattered to the four winds, he said, beaten to a pulp. Wedderkop was only the first to arrive out of breath. In a moment there were others, panting, racing groups. Cheering Russians in white snow capes were pursuing them on foot.

"Everybody over here . . . Runz, the machine gun . . . Hedemann, the AT . . . Wedderkop, hand grenades. Tie them together." The colonel himself lay on the ground behind a machine gun, Runz behind another, Hedemann at an anti-tank gun. Wedderkop demonstrated that he knew how to handle concentrated charges of grenades. Vilshofen also managed to keep a small group of soldiers from running away. They defended themselves against the infantry assault and succeeded in fending off the first wave. Then they worked their way forward and waited for the next wave in the shelter of the burial mound.

Vilshofen, his face blackened by powder, called Wedderkop over. "Now let me have a coherent report, Wedderkop."

The picture that emerged from Wedderkop's report and from other reports and observations was this: There had been a Russian penetration from the north. Damme's division had not held, even though the 29th Infantry Division (motorized) had been thrown in to aid it; both divisions had been crushed and routed, and parts of these divisions, falling like firebrands among the men of Vilshofen's own combat group, had scattered the men as if they were cattle fleeing from a prairie fire.

Vilshofen had remained behind with his small group. He certainly could not stay long at the burial mound, but he wanted to assemble the tanks and the groups on the hills before he began withdrawing. He was able to communicate with Kindt and Bauer, but Captain Steiger did not report. Vilshofen looked in the direction of his outpost. Nothing could be seen but a cloud of smoke enveloping the brow of the hill.

Captain Steiger lay there on the hill. He too had watched the day break over the ice-coated landscape. He had thought of the past and of last night, and he had mused upon the colonel's parting words.

God. . . . If not for Hitler, then for God's sake? Yesterday, Hill 126 and the retreat down the eastern slopes; then the night with his forty grenadiers hitched to anti-tank guns like half-dead oxen. They had been able to bring only two of the cannon up the steep hill—two teams of twenty men each tugging and sweating to get them into position.

Two guns, thirty-two rifles, and the hill had to be held! The men were lying in hollows in the snow like rabbits, and like rabbits they were sleeping with wide-open eyes. Perhaps they were dreaming; perhaps this very minute they were being tormented by sights and sounds of yesterday, recorded without their knowledge by stunned ears and dulled eyes, so that every horrible detail might later be reviewed.

A star set and the sky turned gray. His eyes were turned away from the dawn, toward the west. Toward the west—God's will—was this God's will?

Not for nothing was he of peasant stock. He was a coppersmith from Bopfingen in Württemberg, and his father and grandfather before him had tilled the soil in that region. It was soil that for centuries had been plowed and harrowed by Waldensians, Swedes, Bohemians, and Swiss; from north and south reformers had swept through the land, and in the name of "God's will" men had been burned, racked, beheaded, flayed, boiled, and roasted. At this moment Steiger was uncommonly sensitive; with good reason he felt closer to death than to life and he penetrated to untouched strata within himself that ordinarily would have remained hidden.

"Without a doubt, as long as the world has been, the burners have always been cleverer than the burned. . . ." This phrase flashed through the mind of a man on the brow of a hill west of Novo-Alexeyevka. It was a strange thought and Steiger himself had no idea where he had heard it before or why it came to mind now. The immediate stimulus was the sight of Lieutenant Kindt's hill going up in smoke, the sound of Sergeant Bauer's machine gun rattling out its last desperate rounds, and a stunning blow on the head.

Steiger heard a long-drawn-out "Hooray!" From the cloud of smoke fur-capped figures in short fur jackets emerged. Delicate pale-blue streamers of smoke floated from the muzzles of rifles. Puffs of smoke rose from exploding hand grenades. An anti-tank gun—Amberger, Schuster, and Nitschke—was firing at a lumbering, roaring, advancing target. Figures popped in and out of the crevasses. The heavy Russian tank advanced like a steer, hooked Schuster and Nitschke and their gun in its horns and threw them over backward. Steiger felt a violent blow and collapsed. It was then that the phrase about the burners and the burned shot into his mind; it went on cynically:

"The proof of this may be seen in every kitchen, for the cook is smarter than the wood he burns." But Steiger's heart was with the victims, not the executioners. Who was now the burner, who the burned? After all, what was happening here was happening on foreign soil, on land that had also been put to the torch a hundred times. He had come here with the cooks, the know-it-alls, the cynics. Now who was the cook, who the wood? Is a man after all nothing but wood?

Steiger was no longer capable of answering such questions. He lost consciousness.

The Russian terms had been rejected. The result was the liquidation of the pocket.

The five German divisions fled eastward. They marched, some in orderly fashion, some in disorder, some still supplied with rations, some cut off from all supplies. They broke up, they reassembled. Dmitrevka was overrun, then Karpovka, Novo-Alexeyevka, Baburkin. The various staffs evacuated in panic the dugout villages along the tiny Rossoshka River.

It snowed. The temperature was eighteen below zero.

The stragglers and dispersed soldiers from the front followed the staffs on foot. Wherever they passed they witnessed the same scenes. Cannon overturned, abandoned tanks, trucks athwart the road, heaps of cartridges, bombs, and shells. When the front-line troops entered the bunkers in these "rear" towns, they found open crates, abandoned, half-packed suitcases filled with soap, canned goods, candles, chocolates, cake, hardtack. On the floor lay service manuals and account books. The weary, filthy men from the front lines stared and stuffed some of the food into their mouths, other things into their pockets. Then, hearing the approaching rumble of the enemy's cannon, they stumbled up the steps and marched again on the snow-swept plain. They followed the road churned up by the wheels of trucks and tractors. The beaten army followed in the tracks of the various staffs—toward Pitomnik, Gumrak, Stalingrad. They retreated toward the line known on the strategic maps as "Violet."

On the way discipline triumphed, order emerged from the confusion. Here a small, pock-marked lieutenant gathered his scattered men around him, settled them behind a rampart of snow, fed them from a bogged-down truck loaded with rations, and sent out couriers until he located his regimental commander and again received orders. In another place a flak commander and his adjutant who had lost half of their anti-aircraft guns when the west front collapsed assembled guns that had been abandoned by the road and in the villages and had them transported in personnel carriers. Thus they restored their company to full strength in weapons at least. There were many such Lieutenant Lawkows and Major Buchners and Lieutenant Looses—though there were also many who lost their heads and ran until they were stopped or reached Stalingrad. However, where groups did reform there was another nucleus besides the resolute leader—the field kitchen. The groups resumed contact with their battalions and regiments; the regiments sought and found their supply troops, which had in the main got as far as Pitomnik airport. The staffs crowded into the ravines between Pitomnik and Stalingrad and between Voroponovo and Stalingrad.

Colonel Vilshofen's front-line regiment had been badly mauled. Sergeant Bauer with a few men and Lieutenant Kindt with a few more men had joined the small detachment that he, Runz, Hedemann, and Wedderkop had managed to hold together around the Scythian burial mound. Of his four tanks one had returned with Tomas and Latte and with the wounded Captain Steiger and two enlisted men who had been picked up on the hill.

Thirty hours passed, thirty hours of fighting, of being unable to disengage, of endless marching from the burial mound through Otorvanovka. Vilshofen had hurried ahead in the tank and overtaken the fleeing soldiers of his regiment. He set up a field kitchen on the edge of Otorvanovka and the smoke from it could be seen for a great distance over the open plain. Around that smoke some of his men had rallied as around a banner. Before long Vilshofen had two AT guns, one tank, some hundred rifles, and one heavy MG platoon. He discarded his baggage train, retained his combat and ration supply trains. The carts, however, were no longer drawn by horses but by Russian prisoners whom he had taken along as a labor force since the retreat from Vertiachi. He had had no luck in establishing contact with the division to his right (Damme's) or to his left. Cut off from the rest of the army, possessing only a decimated little group—many were missing, many had fallen, many were stragglers or had drifted into other units—he arrived at the tiny village of Otorvanovka, where a partially evacuated clearing station had been located.

All the way his group had been under artillery fire, although he had so far managed to fend off the Russian infantry. By now, however, the infantry had come up so close that there was nothing for him to do but to make a stand here. As a result, the battle line was drawn right through the middle of the clearing station, and before long the huts shot up in flames.

The medical lieutenant, a young man with unmilitary, un-disciplined bearing, suddenly approached him. The young doctor bluntly demanded what at least one of his battalion commanders, Captain Runz, had hinted at during the last conference—that the white flag be raised.

"Out of the question. Don't trouble yourself about matters that are none of your business," Vilshofen replied curtly.

The roofs of the huts collapsed, the walls were shattered. Under the falling roofs and the fragments of sun-dried mud lay the wounded. When the line fell back again, all the men who still were alive in the ruins of the former dressing station lay under fire from both sides. The doctor appeared again. This time he had no proposals—it was too late for that. This time he asked questions and demanded answers. A lieutenant challenged a colonel—it was an unheard-of thing.

Otorvanovka was a temporary block in a vacuum. To the left there was no longer a line, to the right no longer a line. Men were dying there for no purpose whatever—and this was what the medical lieutenant asserted. He went further; he extended his remarks to cover the whole Stalingrad enterprise and even the grandiose advance on Stalingrad. The man deserved a summary court-martial and execution on the spot. Nevertheless, he remained with the group and moved east in the ranks of Vilshofen's column. He had only spoken aloud thoughts that Vilshofen himself had perhaps turned over subconsciously. Ought the man to be shot for that—even though a good many men were being shot for just that?

Thirty hours passed. Vilshofen's combat group crossed the frozen Rossoshka River. On the other side it marched through a deep gorge and after many hours debouched into the steppe and approached a village north of Novo-Alexeyevka. It was about three o'clock in the afternoon. Snow began to fall from the low-hanging sky. Even this remote little village was under fire. Many of the huts were burning; smoke was billowing up from others. A barn roof collapsed and sent a shower of sparks and burning wisps of straw raining down upon the passing column.

A soldier's hand moved to a soldier's face—that of De Wede, the farmer. With filthy, bent fingers he rubbed his face and wiped the soot from this eyes. De Wede, the man from Crefeld whose name was Robert Brünner, and Sergeant Matzke were marching in the same row. Two days ago they had thrown away their spades, left their rifles, and run for their lives. They had found their way to the field kitchen and the regiment, huddled under pieces of mud wall in Otorvanovka, and now they were passing through a village with sparks flying into their faces. The men plodded sluggishly, their eyes fixed not on the knapsack and mess kit of the man in front, but on his rag-wrapped legs. But these eyes saw nothing; their senses were unaware of the atmosphere of filth and decay that moved along with the column.

They made a halt at the farther end of the village. The train had stopped there, the sleds and the Russians who had been pulling them. The Russians were already hacking a pit in the frozen ground. De Wede, Brünner, and Matzke sat down at the side of the road and waited for the order to break ranks and seek quarters. There were dugouts here and also the plank walls of the houses, which promised warmth and some protection from flying fragments.

"There's still something left here," Sergeant Matzke said.

"Yes, sure to be," De Wede agreed.

Brünner said, "I wonder where Krämer is?" As they were marching through the village they had sent Hermann Krämer out to scout around the village and the dugouts. "If you find anything, come back quick," Matzke had ordered him.

After a while Krämer returned. Like Brünner, he had been a white-collar worker, a teller in a Magdeburg bank. But this man in tattered uniform and with straggly beard no longer looked anything like a bank teller, nor did his sunken face and dilated pupils indicate that he was only twenty-eight years old.

"Nothing left, it's all been cleaned out," Krämer reported. "But I picked up a little something." He took his hoard out of his coat pocket.

"Potatoes?"

"Yes, potatoes."

The potatoes were frozen. Each man received two.

"Good stuff, been cooked already. I found them in a swine trough."

"In a swine trough!"

"Yes, there was a corps HQ here. They had pigs and fed them on boiled potatoes, no less."

"On my farm they haven't let us feed potatoes to the pigs for the past six years," De Wede said.

A body, frozen stiff, was removed from one of the sleds and carried past them. "Vogt," De Wede said. "Yes, Vogt," Brünner repeated. As they sat chewing on the hard, icy potatoes, they looked at the retreating body of Private Vogt. Two days ago they had dug away at a foxhole with Vogt. He had been wounded at the Scythian burial mound and had died in the sled on the way. A second and third frozen corpse was carried

92

past. The third had been the battalion commander, Captain Hedemann.

"He hasn't any boots on either."

"Yes, they've taken them off. Orders."

Wilsdruff came up to the group. "What are you eating?" he asked.

"French fried," Brünner said, his mouth full.

"Real potatoes?"

"Yes. Hermann found them in a pig trough."

"Where is it?"

"There are none left," Krämer said.

Wilsdruff nodded mournfully. After a while he asked, "Is that new lieutenant going to stay with us—Wedderkop, I mean?"

Matzke shrugged.

"Where can he go?" Brünner said. "His whole company is *kaputt*. One of the men says he punished a fellow with extra sentry duty for chopping wood with his bayonet."

"He looks up to anything."

The order to break ranks was not given, and there was no chance for the hoped-for sleep inside a dugout or a hut. The soldiers saw Captain Tomas and Lieutenant Wedderkop return from a brief reconnaissance and report to the colonel. Then orders came to start moving again at once. The Russians stopped digging the grave. The dead—nine other soldiers besides Captain Hedemann had died on the sled—were laid on the bare ground where the snow had been shoveled away. They waited for the colonel who was standing near a sled where the other battalion commander, Captain Runz, lay dying. Before long Runz was carried over and laid beside the others.

The eleven bodies, stripped of their coats, uniforms and boots, lay in a row. Fat flakes of snow sifted down from the low sky. A shell struck near by, and a fountain of smoke, mud, and snow rose into the mist. Captain Tomas, Lieutenant Wedderkop, Lieutenant Kindt, Second Lieutenant Latte, Sergeant Bauer, the doctor from Otorvanovka, medical aides, and enlisted men stood around. A short distance away stood the sleds which had been run together to form a laager. Near them the Russian prisoners crouched in a bedraggled mass. It was on this spot, in this milieu and at this very hour, that Colonel Vilshofen awoke from a fantastic nightmare, one that had lasted not only for these past thirty hours on the march, but for thirty years, from one war to the next, from a Verdun on the Meuse to the Verdun on the Volga.

Vilshofen looked around and saw a great many things under

the gray sky. There were not only these eleven corpses, not only the Russian column of slaves, not only the beat of automatic guns and the eruptions of exploding shells inside the village and even quite close to where they stood. There was also himself, a man of forty-eight years, a mirror of bloody events and of quite ordinary and harmless happenings, a receptacle in which many layers were piled one upon another, and now they began swelling and bursting out. He could no longer accept and submerge the new scenes before his eyes as simply as he had in the past; he could not take them in and forget them; they called for an explanation, not only the faces before him, but the many memories of the past.

There was Hedemann, a local justice of the peace from Central Germany who had a wife and a grown daughter, though he never mentioned them in his diary, even in the entires made on furlough. But the times of arrival and departure on furloughs were noted by hour and minute, as were all the other times and places where he stopped. Hedemann was a precise person; the only unprecise act and the sole adventure in his regularized life had been the purchase of that small estate in Latvia, for which he had used his wife's inheritance. But Captain Hedemann would never live on his pension in Latvia, would never sit on the banks of the Druja with his fishing rod in hand. And there was Captain Runz who had been an assistant principal in a high school and who only a moment ago had made his last request: "Please, sir, give my love to my wife and tell her, sir . . ." Then he had died. And what could Vilshofen tell Captain Runz's wife? What could he tell Sergeant Vogt's father? Could he say: he died defending a Scythian burial mound? Could he say: "I refused him a furlough while there was still time because it was more important for him to die for three mud hovels in Otorvanovka than to continue his life on his farm in Minden? There were other soldiers here, Stade, Burstedt, Scharrenbroich, and they too were farmers or farmers' sons; they too had fathers or wives and work at home; they too were urgently needed. They had fallen defending a road whose other end was in the Russians' hands, a road that the Russians were steadily reeling in like a fishing line, that led across Pitomnik airport and on into the waste of rubble and ruins that was Stalingrad. They had fallen for a road that led from nothingness to nothingness. This cut-off road was no more a military object than the railroad tracks to the south; there could be no military necessity, no military rationale for holding it. What then was the necessity, what then was the rationale for these sacrifices?

We are engaging enemy forces, we are helping the rest of the front, our sacrifice has meaning outside our own immediate sphere of activity. Such answers might have been suggested yesterday, but facile solutions were no longer applicable today. The question went beyond the immediate problem. The hour had come; the cup of sorrow was filled and overflowing.

Here the victims lay, and there were many more than these eleven. There were endless rows of faces, eyeless and mud-colored, themselves earth. And not only the dead of this war but the victims of another were demanding the meaning of their sacrifice. These men were not firmly-embedded foundation stones upon which a proud structure was to be erected—neither these nor the dead of the First World War. There they lay, cast-off shards. . . .

And there the living stood, Latte and Tomas and Bauer and Kindt. And there was Lieutenant Wedderkop whose education had been Nazi from the beginning; as a stripling in camp he had read the inscription: WE ARE BORN TO DIE. And there was that other young man, the doctor from Otorvanovka who met one's look squarely and did not guard his tongue. When Vilshofen first saw him, he had been wearing a rubber apron, had had his sleeves rolled up and his arms red with blood to the elbows. He had stood operating until the roof fell in on his head and on the soldier who lay on the operating table. Undoubtedly it had been partly in consideration of such devotion to duty that Vilshofen had overlooked the man's insidious questions and had not applied the letter of military law. And after all, was it not this young doctor who had first raised the question that he, Vilshofen, was now facing?

What was it all about? What was it all about?

Lieutenant Wedderkop shifted his weight from one foot to the other. Sergeant Bauer stared dully at the bare feet of his former battalion commander, Runz. Latte gazed fixedly at the colonel's face. Lieutenant Kindt and all the men gaped at their colonel. But Vilshofen stood rigid as a post. There was a phrase for these situations—for Führer and Reich or something of the sort—but the colonel did not say it.

He too stared—over the row of dead bodies, over the ranks of the soldiers and medical aides, over the sled laager, beyond the hollow from which Russian automatic guns were spewing fire—back, back through the snow-filled air to Otorvanovka where specters with dangling, torn bandages reeled to their feet, took a step and then stumbled and collasped again and lay under the burning woodwork. Vilshofen gazed still further back and then his sight slowly returned from the distance. "Amen," he said. And that was all.

Snow was shoveled over the bodies on the ground. Vilshofen gathered the officers around him and issued orders for the resumed march. The last tank was to be blown up. The fuel would be drained out first and used to run two trucks that had been abandoned in the village. Captain Tomas, who could no longer march because of his leg wound, would take one of the trucks into Stalingrad and report to the army for other assignment. He would take with him the doctor, the medical aides, and the ambulatory wounded who had been evacuated from Otorvanovka. Lieutenant Wedderkop would take the wounded from the regiment either to Pitomnik airport or, in case they were not received there, to the Gumrak hospital. Wedderkop would also find out where the divisional headquarters was, report the position and situation of the regiment, and obtain rations, fuel, and ammunition. Lieutenant Kindt was ordered to start off at once with the train for a position seven miles east on the road to Pitomnik. Sergeant Bauer would form the rear guard; he was to take up a position on the eastern edge of the village and cover the retreat against probable infantry or tank attacks. Anti-tank guns and munitions were scattered around the village; he would make use of them.

Vilshofen himself led the main body of his combat group. The temperature had fallen sharply, though it had been cold enough—thirteen below zero—when they set out. Behind them heavy fire showered down upon the village; a bank of yellow smoke hovered over the huts. Darkness fell. Everywhere was snow. A forlorn band of men marched along. One of that band was Private De Wede.

De Wede was neither particularly tall nor particularly stocky, but he had once been sturdily healthy. A powerful heart beat in his breast. Although he generally moved and spoke slowly, his heart could drive his blood swiftly through his veins when swift-moving blood was necessary. In his home mowings he had swung the scythe like a man when only a fourteen-year-old boy, had mowed through the morning mist until the first stars rose. Later on, too, he had held his own at country dances and in the brawls that often followed such amusements. And he had fought more than a few fights on account of his wife, Alwine, whom he had taken from a neighboring village. His heart had always fulfilled its function and met emergencies, and he was thoroughly inured to cold. He had rarely worn gloves; at home in the iciest weather he could sit for an hour and longer in his wagon holding the reins with bare hands. His skin would turn red, then blue, of course, but nothing more; as soon as he stepped into the tavern to warm himself, the blood shot back into his fingertips so fast that they prickled. A year ago, before Moscow, he had worn mittens and had wrapped his head in cloths; but even there he had been through days when by all rights he should have frozen to death and had come through unharmed. He had been out in the open in temperatures of forty and more below zero and had not been frostbitten. He had three daughters, no sons. He was forty-one and under normal circumstances would still have had half his life before him. His father had still pottered around the farm at eighty, and at eighty-two had followed his son's unit through the village as it marched away with the temperature fifteen below zero. Old De Wede had walked all the way to the church and then on to the tavern. But now young De Wede was tramping on a road that had no churches, no taverns, nothing but snow. He was marching along the right end of his row. Beside him marched Brünner and Sergeant Matzke; behind him a man shuffled along with his feet wrapped in an old horse blanket that he had cut in two and fastened with a string. De Wede was weary and hungry; so were the others. After an hour's march his face was blue; so were the faces of the others! But it was the heart that made the difference. De Wede's heart had weakened. At route step, in loose formation, by threes, with the train far ahead, the regiment marched through the snow.

It was a cloudy night, but not utterly dark. The snow shone. Slowly as the regiment moved, the train moved even more slowly, but it had a start. It consisted of a column of sleds laden with rifles, ammunition, tents, instruments, and all sorts of odds and ends. Instead of horses, men were hitched to these sleds. A main rope and fifteen or twenty spokes of rope radiated out from the front of each sled, and on these ropes fifteen or twenty Russian prisoners of war tugged. Curses and blows with rifle butts could not make them change their pace; the same slow speed was maintained on smooth road and through snowdrifts. Sometimes—it happened on every march—a man fell out of the noose of rope. Then the man beside him took up the empty loop and the march continued without pause. Among the men in the sled column the soldier who remained behind had a name that was written in their memories, and one day an accounting would be demanded in his name. But the regiment that brought up at the rear knew nothing of his name, his origins, or his rank. When they saw such a gray blob lying beside the road, they scarcely noticed. At most one or two of them might say, "A pack Russian."

De Wede had seen three such "pack Russians" that night lying along the road. The first and the second he observed sharply as they lay on the white snow. He scarcely saw the third; although it had grown no darker and the figure was only two paces away from him, he noticed only a gray spot in a featureless landscape. De Wede also could no longer hear; he had become deaf. The men's feet behind and ahead of him stamped and scraped and shuffled and slogged through the drifted snow, but De Wede did not hear them. He was marching in a parade of silent phantoms. And yet he knew exactly what was wrong with him and what could save him. He thought of a half bottle of brandy that he had left in a cupboard at home. Or Alwine or Liese, his eldest daughter, might make black coffee or hot tea for him. His hands and feet no longer ached; he no longer felt the weight of his very bones as he had done before. But he was walking through a mass of absorbent cotton. De Wede's face was no longer blue. If a light had been flashed into it, his features would have appeared chalky. Brünner at his side did not notice, and Wilsdruff did not notice, although the man's snow-white, frozen nose might have attracted their attention even on so cloudy a night. All the other men were concerned with themselves alone; all of them plodded and slid along, struggling through a haze that was not outside, but inside themselves. De Wede walked on through cotton, but no man could keep that up for long. He went on a few paces more, then stepped to one side of the row and reeled into the ditch. For a moment he stood there, up to his knees in a snowdrift. "Maybe he just wants to piss," Brünner said. The man in back with the horse blanket around his legs did not notice the gap until some time had passed. De Wede sat down and then he collapsed completely and crumpled into the snowdrift. In a moment he was insensible and neither Alwine nor any of his flaxenhaired daughters was at his side. A gray blob lay beside the road—the fourth. Perhaps one of the men in the rear ranks muttered, "A pack Russian." But probably not, for this was the fifth hour of the night march and all the men of the entire regiment were asleep on their feet as they plodded on, eastward, toward their new positions.

That same night Lieutenant Wedderkop rode toward Pitomnik in the truck. Wedderkop was twenty-two years old, a lanky, blond-haired boy. If the command had been given he would have stuck a cigarette into his mouth and run with fixed bayonet against a whole entrenched regiment or even against a fifty-two-ton tank. He had been trained for such courage, not in the army but in a "special camp of the Hitler Youth." A sense of physical and moral strength had been carefully nurtured in him; he had been trained to reckless courage whose goal was not so much self-preservation as self-destruction. SS cadet Wedderkop had entered life an artificial product, a half-formed thing, a figure sketched only in whites. Life might kill him; he had been raised for that purpose. Or it might melt him in the furnace and begin forging him anew; but then the time and effort that had been expended in breeding such a type would have been wasted. As he was, he could not be incapable of facing life. He could not cope with a reality in which there did not simply exist on one side masters and superman who alone possessed courage and who owned the world, and on the other side slaves, submen, and cowards who owned nothing. Life distributes good and evil, competence and incompetence, courage and weakness in even measure in every human soul, and Wedderkop had not been taught to stand up to that kind of life.

But now Wedderkop was immersed in life, in a boiling crucible of life. A hard lesson was in store for him tonight on this road; like the boy in the fable, he was going to learn what fear was. He had to go through with it; there was no escaping the evil. It did not help him to recall that fear was something "alien to the race" from which he sprang, that it was "a characteristic of Jewish and mixed, Jew-corrupted blood." There was no escape; his own Aryan blood rushed to his tips of his ears; he felt a hand clamping around his heart, and his blood withdrew; he paled and quivered like a terrified animal. He would have collapsed if he had not been sitting in the front seat of the truck with the driver on his left and Captain Steiger on his right—he was supposed to leave Steiger with the other casualties either in Pitomnik or in Gumrak. He trembled and was unable to help Steiger when Steiger asked him. His hands failed him and the driver had to assist. Wedderkop opened his mouth, but he could not utter a sound. The trouble was not Steiger, not Steiger alone or the foot that Steiger had laid in his lap; the trouble was not one foot but a great many, and still it was not that alone. What was happening outside, the terrible scene that the headlights illuminated—faces against the windshield, faces at the side windows, hands clinging to the door, the door handles, the running boards, the ice-crusted wheels; the tangle of arms and bodies gripping the radiator and the hood, the cluster of human bodies falling back into the snow—it was unnatural, it could not happen, it was inconceivable. The driver put Wedderkop's state into words. He did not say, "Sir." He said, "For

Christ's sake, man, stop bawling; there's nothing we can do about it."

Wedderkop remembered. Once upon a time a horse had fallen and been propped up again. He had gazed in terror at the unnatural position of the animal's dangling, broken leg—he had been five years old at the time—and his aunt had taken him home and put him to bed. There he had lain and cried and for days had suffered nervous attacks. That was the child he had been. And now, after being picked for the SS and sent to the special leaders school at Sonthofen, after punitive expeditions in the Brest area, after trench and pillbox warfare, after reaching the age of twenty-two, he was so weak, so weak. And he was—Steiger said he was getting somewhere. "Go on bawling; you're getting somewhere."

One half of Captain Steiger's face had been torn open by a fragment from a tank-gun shell and his right arm had been smashed, but his feet had not been harmed. At least, they had been all right when Tomas rescued him from the hill. But since the sled ride something had been wrong with his feet, with one foot anyway. They had had to lift him into the truck. And it was this foot that had started all the trouble.

The road they were on would have been bad enough even without snow. Although the terrain was for the most part level, the road frequently dipped into hollows, dropped into a ravine or a dried-out stream bed and climbed up the other side. It was far from being the shortest route between the villages of the steppe; it wound along with many twists and loops, following the lay of the land pretty much along the paths that, ages ago, the cattle must have trodden into the open plain. This particular night fine powdery snow had in places drifted into sheer walls. The road was marked out by holes with waving wisps of straw attached. Wedderkop had some twenty-five odd miles to traverse, no small distance. But that night battalions spent twelve hours struggling to make six miles and many never reached their destinations. German soldiers writhing on the ground often could not drag themselves a few yards through the snow to the running board of some truck that stopped for them.

Wedderkop, leaning back in his seat, his coat collar turned up, his fur cap pulled down over his forehead, blinked through the windshield at the flat landscape. It was a wasteland of white, dry powder, of wind-swept billows and lavish filigree work. Again and again the driver reached for the gearshift and went into second and then into first; then he would turn on the headlights for better vision and the motor would roar, the wheels would churn in the air until they found traction again and the truck plowed through a spraying wall of snow. At such times the full horror of this suddenly-illuminated night would penetrate into the cab of the truck.

They had come upon a large truck with its radiator and front wheels in the ditch, the rear wheels still up on the road. There had been a figure standing in the middle of the road, two more crouching beside him. The driver had stopped and got out. The man on the road was unable to speak; he had already shouted himself hoarse and toward the last had simply held up his arm in its bloody bandage as if it were a signal flag. The two men on the ground babbled a few words, but they could not move their legs. The driver, with Wedderkop's assistance, carried the three into the truck and placed them beside the other wounded men. Then they glanced into the canvas-covered body of the other truck. The corpses of twenty or thirty wounded men had slid forward on the sloping floor and, with their blankets, blood-soaked underclothes, and bandages, had frozen into a solid mass.

They rode on, passing a second, a third, and a fourth truck. A truck column of wounded had gone over this road that day and had broken up.

Once more the driver stopped their truck, and then he drove on without halting.

A fifth, a sixth, a seventh wreck.

In the snow they saw drivers, ambulance men, whole columns of wounded who had left the trucks with their frozen loads and were trying to make their way on foot. They reeled into the glare of the headlights, waved, gestured, raised clenched fists, scrambled out of the way of the rushing vehicle at the last moment.

Captain Steiger and his foot—or perhaps the fact that the boot and the rags around it were thawing in the heat of the motor—was the cause of what happened next. Captain Steiger, tormented by pain that mounted to his knee and higher, had asked Wedderkop to stretch out his leg. Since the cab was crowded, Wedderkop had to take Steiger's foot on his lap. After a while Steiger asked him to remove the rags and the boot and wrap the foot in a scarf. Wedderkop began unwrapping the rags and untying the boot lace. The road at this point dipped into a hollow, ran along a gorge for a while and then climbed again. The gorge, with its precipitous sides so white and frozen, could scarcely have looked any different in the Ice Age when the retreating glacial waters first cut it into the plain, drawing a long slash down into the valley of the Volga. The truck began climbing the other side of the gorge. Wedderkop had managed to get the rags off and the lace untied. Steiger clenched his teeth; the gnawing pain was not in the foot, but higher up; he was sure of that. "Please, please, jerk the boot right off," he said. To do that Wedderkop needed more room. The driver turned on the headlights to make certain that there was no human soul in this wasteland, none of the snow-covered phantoms of this night. Then he stopped the car.

But the snow-covered phantoms were there nevertheless.

The road, to reach the level plain again, doubled around and ran westward through a cleft. There, invisible from the side of the curve where they had stopped, two trucks were stuck fast. Their cargo of wounded men had frozen to death like the others. But on the curve and on the rising end of the road, where approaching trucks were forced to drive slowly, all the men who could make it had gathered. They hid behind the banks of snow in the cleft, for they had the desperation of dying men who did not want to die, and the experiences of the night had already made them as cunning as the Ice Age hungers of prehistoric times.

Everything happened at once.

Wedderkop tugged at the boot and with it—leather, rags, skin and flesh were one solid mass—he pulled off the frost-rotted boot and found that he had in his lap the neatly-peeled skeleton of Steiger's foot. Steiger should have been the one to cry out, but it was Wedderkop who shrieked and shrank back. He tried to turn away to escape the sight, but the only place to look was through the windshield. And there he saw in the bright glare of the headlights a figure sliding down the road toward him. He saw it fall forward on its face as its feet snapped off like pieces of glass. And there was not only this one, there was a whole band of similar shapes. They rose out of the cleft with bandaged heads, arms in splints and plaster casts, blankets, rags and canvas wrapped around them; they limped, staggered, fell and shattered bones as they struck the ground. Some of the fallen struggled up again, and all of them, even those who lay on the ground, moved as fast as they could toward the truck. "One, two . . . ten," Wedderkop counted mechanically. Ten gray human worms, crawling and writhing along the ground, were making the same attempt as those who still had feet. A bloody head rose up out of the snow and fell back helplessly. Another propelled himself forward by digging a pointed object into the ground, the handle of a truck jack. The one who had first fallen flailed about with his arms, thighs, and midriff and managed to move closer. They all came closer, and those who still had feet began throwing themselves onto the truck.

Again there were hands reaching for the door handles, clinging to the radiator, the running boards, the edges of the body; hands tearing the canvas top, gripping faces and eyes, pulling other men back. Behind, in the body of the truck, the wounded howled as they were crushed under the weight of those who piled in on top of them. The motor panted, the truck started again, swayed up the slope in first gear. As soon as he reached the top of the rising ground, the driver shifted into second and third, stepped hard on the accelerator. At full speed they raced along, and in the wind the tangle of hands and bones clinging to hood, running boards, and body fell off again.

This thing that raced along in the night was not some beast pursued by primitive man, not some mammoth stung by stone axes and mad with pain; it was a Daimler-Benz truck powered by a ninety horsepower Diesel motor, with three axles, front and rear-wheel drive. Howling, it fled through the night, sagged into holes, bounced over bumps, and left behind it a high, streaming cloud of snow. All this took place not three hundred thousand years before our era, but on the night of January 12, 1943, on the Karpovka-Pitomnik road.

On January 12th the dressing stations in Karpovka, Dmîtrevka, Novo-Alexeyevka and Baburkin were evacuated. From each one, hundreds of seriously wounded men, wrapped only in blankets, were loaded onto open trucks. Some of the trucks had run out of fuel on the way; others had been stuck in snowdrifts. Of thirty trucks, only five reached their destination. Only one of the doctors had refused to obey the order for evacuation. He had silently listened to all the curses, howls, imprecations, and pleas of the wretched victims, used all available narcotics on them and told them that it would be better for them if they remained behind. But the casualties from all other clearing stations had been sent off, not toward Pitomnik airport where they could be flown out of the Stalingrad pocket, but to the field hospital between Gumrak and Stalingrad, which by now was nothing but a receiving station for the largest of the Stalingrad cemeteries.

"Go on bawling. . . ."

The man whose foot had been pulled off like a dirty sock, who now sat in his place with a scarf and a scrap of blanket wrapped around the bare bones and with the pain burning to his knees, had said that.

Is a man made of wood?

All the creatures who had been shaken off this careening vehicle, who had remained behind, crushed into the snow, had mothers, were born of women who gave themselves to love and who, loving, dreamed of strong, free sons. But not all had grown strong and none had been free.

"Go on bawling; you're getting somewhere now."

Where was he getting? Wedderkop did not ask the question. He still saw the faces, still heard the splintering of bones as they broke; he was still paralyzed with horror and could understand nothing at all.

Steiger went on: "Calloused hands are not a sign of strength. And a calloused heart is usually empty. Go on bawling; it's the best thing you can do."

He went on talking about strength and about freedom and even about God. Then, numb with pain, he closed his eyes and slumped in his seat. When he came to again he was looking out into a white void, and the eyes of the man on the seat beside him were utterly vacant. Steiger thought of other men's eyes, of those who had borne witness with their deaths. Some had been cast into the fire like wood and had spoken, even as they were burning, words that men had preserved, words that had guided humanity onward. But those men back there, those men left on the road. . . .

"Those men back there, why have they been cast off like dry sticks? What are they dying for?" he asked Wedderkop.

"For the Führer," the driver said.

Wedderkop rubbed his forehead.

"We are dying for nothing at all . . . it's horrible," Captain Steiger said.

A SMALL ROOM, BARE WALLS, WHITE CURTAINS, A plain desk, two men in the light of the desk lamp. One was Colonel Schuster, adjutant to the chief of the Adjutant General's Office in the Army High Command at Berlin. The other was Lieutenant Colonel Carras, who at this late hour had received a telephone call at his apartment ordering him to report to this office.

Though he was forty-eight, Lieutenant Colonel Carras looked very young for his years. In this he seemed to vie with his wife who still, after nineteen years of marriage, looked about twenty-eight. He was also a man of quick understanding, but he was somewhat haggard now; the orders he had just received had taken him completely by surprise. He stared in perplexity at his fellow officer, whom he knew very well in unofficial capacities and with whom he was quite friendly.

He recovered his composure.

"*Heil* and no thanks," he said. "You know I'll go anywhere. I volunteered for El Alamein. And for all I care I'll go to Tripoli now, or Tunis or Iraq, or parachute into the United States. I'm ready for anything that makes sense. But this . . . lunacy! Stark raving mad, by God. It's absolutely senseless."

His friend Schuster took an official tone. He reread to Carras the order for his transfer to the Sixth Army. Absolutely senseless—Carrass stuck to his opinion. The Sixth Army was in a mousetrap and neither the Devil nor Hitler was going to get it out. He had seen that young captain they were ordering out there; but he had a general for an uncle who had gone pretty far in criticizing the Supreme Command. An uncle like that could do a man a lot of harm. Having one was a death sentence, in fact. But he, Lieutenant Colonel Carras, hadn't any. His loyalty and services were well known, his future assured; God damn it to hell, it was impossible, it was incomprehensible, absurd. . . .

But the thing had been decided.

Schuster sent him in to see the chief. When he came out again and walked down the funereally quiet corridors to the stairway, he was no longer Lieutenant Colonel Carras, but Colonel Carras. He had been informed of his promotion and received a transfer to the Sixth Army simultaneously. Nominally his assignment was for the purpose of familiarizing him with the routine of an artillery commander. In addition, however, a specially delicate and highly flattering mission had been conferred upon him; the orders came virtually direct from the Führer himself. The great thing was, though, that he must take a plane the next day.

Colonel Carras returned home.

He lived on the old West Side of Berlin, near the Spree, in an apartment that had formerly been occupied by a distinguished Jewish physician. The metal furniture in the rooms—tubular steel and glass—had been bought by Carras; the rest, the huge desk in the study, the heavy bookcases, the rows of books, the statuettes of Buddha, the Chinese idols on the shelves, and the engravings on the walls, had been taken over from their old owner. They lent the apartment a somewhat old-fashioned atmosphere, but Carras had introduced a modern note with a "charming" portrait of Hitler, all in golden-brown tones, the bulbous nose and the upper half of the face shaded by the large visor of the military cap, the shadows a sunny gold.

The promotion would have to be celebrated—and he would have to say good-bye. He did not tell his wife about the transfer; he did not want that bitter pill to spoil the last evening together. When she asked, "Don't you think we ought to telephone the Schultes or somebody?" he said, "No, let it go, I'd rather spend the evening alone with you. Just get dressed."

A little later he placed his wife's moleskin cape around her shoulders. Both of them were standing in front of the wardrobe mirror, and early in the evening as it was, he betrayed his secret in the look he gave the reflection of her face, her hair, and her shoulders. But he continued to play his part. He was celebrating his promotion, not a gloomy departure, my God, perhaps forever. The elevator was as usual not running. They groped their way down the dark stairs. They went two stations by tram and then continued on foot.

It was damp and cold in the fourth winter of war. Yesterday wild rumors had been afloat and there was a mood of depression in the air. Margot shivered as they walked through the dark area between the Zoo Station and Wittenbergplatz. "When the blackout's finally lifted we won't be able to find our way around," he joked.

106

At Horcher's in the Lutherstrasse everything was unchanged. Warmth, light, noiselessly efficient waiters, a little older than in peacetime. At a near-by table an Air Force major sat with an actress.

"Have you been in Africa?"

"Yes, and I could tell you stories . . ."

Carras heard a few words—Crete, Sicily. So they were retreating to the "inner line" there too. A little way off sat a panzer general, still a young man, must have been a regular career hound, as they said. There were some officers Carras knew from the Army High Command; the rest were civilians.

Margot showed no sign of concern when he ordered dinner, although she must know that it would cost half his pay. Usually, when they went out together they would go to Kempinski's or Rösch's, where the food was decent and the prices not too outrageous. As far as Margot was concerned, when funds were low she had not been above a sausage or two at "Wurstmax"—before all the sausages disappeared. But tonight it was Horcher's, caviar and vodka and turtle soup, Moselle with the fish and a fine Bordeaux with the pheasant, pastry and fruit and cheese for dessert. How pleasantly one could live if one was allowed to! Their glasses clinked delicately. They glanced into one another's eyes, floated for a moment in infinite depths.

"Margot!"

"Hans!"

That was all; not a word was said about the "colonel." Margot understood that something quite different was being celebrated. Twenty years had passed like a breath. She was looking at him with the same glow in her eyes. Nowhere else had he encountered quite that combination of dreamy abstraction and pagan frankness. Twenty years ago . . . she was still a girl and they had stolen out of the house at daybreak, walked through the morning mist, and stopped at a Friesian farmhouse where they drank milk still warm from the cow and sat on the floor in front of the fireplace. A gnarled, smoldering tree root dried their feet and stockings which were wet from the dew. That day, had it not been their real wedding day? Twenty years, and no one could tell from looking at her that she had an eighteen-year-old son, Hans Otfried, fallen at Velikie Luki for Führer and Reich. Tonight, proud in her sorrow; she wore the pretty Paris necklace her boy had brought her.

After Horcher's, with its atmosphere of elegance and its lordly waiters who treated outsiders so haughtily that they lost all taste for returning, Hans and Margot descended "to the people." They sat in the Frasquita Café near the Zoo; it was open all night, and Carras had always wanted to see what it was like. Soldiers on furlough and bombed-out persons who had the money sat here, chatting and waiting for the next day, for the next move.

Cabaret. "Hans Moser and Paul Hörbiger present. . . ." Although he was in no mood for such nonsense, he had to sit and listen to Moser's patter. Presently they escaped to the bar where they spent another pleasant hour, the two of them like a self-sufficient island amid all the turmoil. When they finally decided to go home, the trains were no longer running and there were no taxis or busses. They had to trudge across the Tiergarten. Margot was wearing black satin shoes; they were ruined, of course. But they were home at last.

Carras had not only played the rôle of a young lover. It was really like the early days of their love, and her hands caressed him with all the tenderness of youth. When he awoke it was day and he was alone in the bed. He stretched luxuriantly in the warmth and was not sure who he was—the eighteen-year-old Otfried or the forty-eight-year-old Hans Carras. Nor was he sure whether he had told her. . . .

But she already knew.

He bathed and dressed, and by the time he sat down to breakfast everything was ready. His suitcase was packed. There was no need for him to look; he could be certain that nothing had been forgotten.

"So it's Stalingrad!"

"Hans!"

"Margot!"

The hall door closed behind him. Carras knew that it was more than an ordinary door closing: it was the door to life, and it might never open again for him. An hour later he sat in the plane.

Under the Junkers' wings lay the gray stone sea of Berlin. He glanced around, looked through the cockpit window at the pilot busy with his instruments and at the radio operator who was letting the trailing antenna sing out. When he gazed down again, the city was already behind and he could see the railroad line to Adlersdorf and the eastern industrial suburbs. Then the bare wintry fields, the Spree, the Oder, and even farther.

Carras was accompanied by a number of men who had been assigned to him for his special mission. Captain Döllwang was also in the plane, the young man who had an uncle who was a general, the one who had received the death sentence. He was twenty-four and an unusually gifted young man. Like Carras he had worked at headquarters and had now been assigned to the Sixth Army "in order to obtain command experience."

Lvov was their first landing point. Planes were arriving and departing incessantly. "What a traffic jam," Captain Döllwang exclaimed. Carras and Döllwang went to look for the flight director of the air base. While they were walking, a whole formation of Junkers landed, rolled across the field and stopped, parked in the snow. A cabin door was opened as they were passing and a whiff of carbolic reached their nostrils. All these planes had come from the east and all of them were loaded with wounded.

They found the flight director surrounded by a group of men from a squadron of fighter planes; they had come from Sicily by way of Munich and Krakow and wanted to spend the night here.

"Out of the question—we've just flown thirteen hundred miles and it will be dark in two hours," Carras heard the air commander saying.

"I can't help you, sir," the flight director replied. "It's an order from Marshal Göring himself: no plane making an intermediate landing may remain longer than is absolutely essential for servicing and refueling. Any delaying of planes fit for service at the front will be punished by immediate court-martial."

The fighter pilots had to start off again before dark. Carras' Junkers was also ordered to continue its flight. They went on to Kalinovka in the Ukraine. Here they refueled and flew to Vinnitsa.

Next day they reached Mariupol, where they spent their second night. Even while he was still in Berlin, Carras had read his own interpretation into communiqué phrases like "defensive battles," "planned withdrawals," and so on. But the stories he heard in Mariupol, the casual way in which fliers mentioned that on their last missions they had bombed railroad stations and trains laden with German, not Russian matériel—twenty trains here, thirty there, forty freight cars at one place, fifty, sixty at others—these things sounded to him like madmen's fancies. At first he was tempted to assume that the whole squadron and all the rest of the personnel at this base belonged in psycho wards.

He heard the names of towns that were supposed to be far in the rear. "For God's sake, where are the real front lines?" Döllwang asked. "You'll see soon enough," an Air Force captain replied.

Another passenger joined them at Mariupol. He was Captain Henkel, a reservist who had commanded a company that ran a military printing plant back in Kharkhov. Since, as he put it, he wanted to be in the thick of the fighting for once, he had volunteered for Stalingrad service.

Next day, on the last lap of their flight, they did see. At first they stayed close to the ground, often at an altitude of less than a hundred feet. Carras sat at the window. Beyond Taganrog they had the Don estuary below them. The frozen blue fingers of the river had been turned into military roads. Marching columns, among them cattle, peasants, peasant women, horse-drawn vehicles, and sleds moved like crawling processions of ants toward Azov and the sea.

They passed over fleeing troops. Incredible—yet unmistakable! The troops were German; they were flying low enough to see that clearly. They stayed close to the ground. On the left was the frozen Don. Farther out on the steppe were columns of light and heavy motor vehicles trying to overtake one another in the snow. Then damaged vehicles and winding infantry columns sank below the horizon. Expanses of white steppe, dead horses, overturned guns. A group of medium artillery pieces stood in the midst of an empty field, the horses hitched up, the reins tangled, and no drivers in sight. There was not a human being to be seen in the entire area. Where was the front? Suddenly anti-aircraft batteries began firing upon them, and still they had seen no front. The plane shot up through the clouds. Above the cloud cover it was bright and sunny. Some two thousands yards to their left was another Junkers, also flying east. Nothing else in sight. After another hour's flight they glided down, penetrated the clouds and found themselves above a vast, oblong city—or was it a quarry? There were roofless houses, hollow concrete skeletons, broken façades, stone pylons like huge toothpicks. It was Stalingrad. Circling, they flew back and made a smooth landing on Pitomnik airfield.

The expanse of white came to life—had begun to while the Junkers was still making its approach. Now hordes of wounded men limped and stumbled across the field. The plane was surrounded at once. The cabin door was blocked by heads, arms in slings and bandages, by ragged figures and faces blue with frostbite. It was almost impossible to get the baggage out. The guard had to clear a lane and then struggle to carry the severer casualties on stretchers into the Junkers. The plane was to start on the return flight in half an hour. But what had happened to the second Junkers which had been loaded with rations from Mariupol? Nothing was to be seen or heard of it.

Carras took his suitcase, the crushed wreck of a suitcase. "I was just able to save it, sir," his orderly reported. "The whole mob trampled on it and it busted open." The orderly lifted the lid, which would no longer lock, to show him. Everything had been thrust back helter-skelter, pyjamas, shaving kit, snow from the ground, a photograph album—all the things that Margot had so carefully packed only forty-eight hours since. But Carras had no time for musing, or for snapping at his orderly or the wild men around them. An officer in furs and fur cap, a second, third, and fourth officer wanted information from him. Had he brought rations, oil, fuel, bread, a suitcase with a submarine radio, an ultra-short-wave receiver? All were furious at his ignorance and rushed off. His own questions remained unanswered.

At last the Junkers with its heavy cargo of wounded lumbered off through the snow and rose into the air. Some few had been carried in on stretchers; the rest had got places for themselves by sheer strength of arm. Carras was left alone with the limping, stumbling rabble (he could think of no better expression for this crowd of hundreds), who now struggled toward the edge of the airfield. He found out who was the control officer and who the airfield commander—the latter a captain totally at his wit's end. He learned that Army H.Q. was no longer in Gumrak, but in a ravine farther to the west. Unless an armored car had been sent for him—which was doubtful—there was no transportation available.

It was 15.10 hours and dark before a truck finally drew up in front of the cave where Carras was waiting. Carras took a seat in the cab beside the driver; Captain Döllwang and Captain Henkel had to get into the body of the truck with the enlisted men. They started off toward Gumrak and Stalingrad. The air was filled with drifting snow. The windshield wiper swished incessantly. Carras could see nothing of the landscape; there were only billows of snow. He had the feeling of having left the ground and that he was flying again, though with incredible slowness—the driver was unable to shift into second, and for the greater part of the way they ground along in low gear.

Finally the truck stopped. They had arrived at Captain Döllwang's destination. Döllwang's face appeared at the cab window. The driver opened the door.

"Where do I go?" Döllwang asked.

"Over there; if you go that way you can't miss it, captain," the driver shouted, pointing across the road into a boundless waste of white billows. "You go about two thousand yards ahead, then the ground slopes and you'll come into the ravine. Division has been located there since yesterday."

"Drive over there," Carras ordered.

"Yes, sir—but we don't have enough fuel for detours, and if we get stuck nobody's going to pull us out."

Captain Döllwang said good-bye. Carras watched him trudge off, a small suitcase in one hand, sinking into the snow over his knees and even up to the bottom of his short fur jacket. Following him, a gray phantom, was Henkel.

Döllwang undoubtedly carried a death sentence in his pocket. But what about himself, Carras—why was *he* here? What was *his* task? The artillery command was sheer camouflage, of course. The highly special and honorable mission entrusted to him by the highest authority, was to stiffen up a crew of spineless officers—whose names he had. He was to set them right, to use every possible means, gentle or drastic, to raise the morale of the officers and men of the whole army. He was to go to extremes, if necessary, to screw up their courage. Stalingrad was the key position!

All very well . . . but it was absurd, utterly senseless, that only forty-eight hours ago he was still in Berlin.

A cavern, a table, a staff map on the table. Bowed over it were a number of heads—the tanned, bald pate of General Gönnern, the heads of his G-3, of General Vennekohl, the corps artillery commander, and of Lieutenant Colonel Unschlicht, chief of staff of the corps. Beside the table stood the new arrivals, Döllwang and Henkel.

On top of the map lay one of Vilshofen's overlays which Lieutenant Wedderkop had just brought in. The officers' attention was fixed upon this sketch. It was certainly an emphatic commentary upon the position.

The sketch showed the area between the Volga and the Don, with the city of Stalingrad at the tip of the Volga salient. The front line, running from the northern end of Stalingrad westward and then curving around back toward the Volga, enclosed a space shaped like a human heart. This was the front line yesterday and the day before.

Three enemy spearheads were aimed at the village and airdrome of Pitomnik. The men looking down at the sketch could see that the heart had already been cut in half. The question was, could this half heart go on living? Would it be possible to seal off the bleeding wound once more? Vilshofen had asked this very question in a note appended to his sketch: "How can 'Violet' be established, and if 'Violet' cannot be, what conclusion must be drawn? Have you gentlemen of the staff decided that?"

112

The defense line dubbed "Violet" had been drawn to include Pitomnik airport. But all the reports were bad; the enemy had made deep penetrations on north, south, and west; the divisions withdrawing from the west had occupied only a part of their assigned positions, and two of these divisions no longer existed. Of a third, only remnants were left (Gönnern, Vennekohl, and Unschlicht, however, were not yet able to swallow this last fact.) It should have been clear to them that the line was nothing but a mark on a sheet of paper, that out in the snow-covered fields the reality consisted of beaten, bloody hordes streaming chaotically eastward under the temporary protection of the few strong points that were still holding.

The others turned to Unschlicht who as chief of staff of the corps was expected to have a more general view of the situation than they themselves. But Unschlicht shrugged and said: "Intelligence and reports have been so scanty up to now and there are still so many to come in that it's hard to form any picture of the whole situation."

"Then why has Vilshofen come to such calamitous conclusions?" Gönnern asked.

"Oh, he thinks he can hear the grass growing," Vennekohl said. "But still and all, I see only your few men, Gönnern, in the whole area—yours, Lundt's regiment, and Vilshofen's combat group, of course."

"It does look as though the 113th, the 76th, and parts of the 44th have withdrawn," Unschlicht admitted.

"The farther south they were, the farther they had to move on to the outer end of the pivot, and I don't think they could've managed it," Vennekohl said. "If you ask me, Vilshofen's sketch there hits the nail on the head. 'Violet' can't be held any more; I'll bet on 'Sunflower.'" "Sunflower" was the projected line of defense still farther to the rear. This line omitted Pitomnik airport and ran from the area of Borodkim in the north, southward along the narrow-gauge railway line to Voroponovo station, then turned and went on to the southern outposts of Stalingrad itself.

"But suppose the divisions can't make it and are unable to take up even their 'Sunflower' positions?"

"It's not our responsibility to answer these broader questions," Gönnern exclaimed. "No, it's not up to us, it's not." And it was not, unless they had disowned their "Leader" and made the fate of their men their principal concern.

A pause ensued. After some minutes of gloomy silence Gönnern said, "Everything depends on Pitomnik, our only usable airport. We stand or fall by Pitomnik. We must block the road to it—that's our mission now." He was well aware that he was talking nonsense, but he was glad of this opportunity to switch the subject. "That applies to you in particular, my dear Döllwang," he said, turning to the young captain. He knew old Döllwang, had known him for many years. "You ought to have a battalion, but I no longer have a regiment, and we don't have any battalions either. We've had to amalgamate; right now we're organizing our remnants into combat groups. I think we'll send you to Vilshofen. Is that all right?"

This last sentence was addressed to the chief of staff of the corps. He nodded his agreement.

"I've kept Wedderkop back," the G-3 said. "He can take Döllwang with him when he goes up front again."

"And Captain Henkel also?"

"Captain Henkel has been detailed to Lundt's regiment."

"Very well then, let it stand. Good luck."

As Döllwang, accompanied by the G-3, left the bunker, Gönnern stared after them. He gazed into space for quite a while after the captain had disappeared. For the third time within an hour he had the same thought. It had occurred to him first in connection with himself and his own position, then with regard to his old comrade, General Döllwang. Now he included the general's nephew, this twenty-four-year-old captain, and this time, before he turned back to his affairs, he voiced the thought: "We are expendable."

Döllwang and Wedderkop, both young men, both educated along military lines, were very different from one another. There were differences in their education, too. Döllwang had been taught to value objective facts and real possibilities, while Wedderkop's training had stressed irrationality and impossibilities, and at the same time a rigid formalism. These differences had brought into relief the environmental and inherited traits of the two men. It was no accident that Döllwang loved music and could surrender himself utterly, to the point of self-forgetfulness, to a melody or to the cascading, harmoniously rushing stream of a composition. If he had to solve an abstract problem, say, the transportation of a thousand-ton load over a distance of a hundred kilometers, the problem depended for him upon the sum of facts about horsepowers, conditions, the difficulties that would be encountered, and the chances of overcoming them. Even as a boy he had observed that wagon wheels on a sandy country road rolled more slowly than they did on the highway. On his uncle's estate he had learned that a cow that has been hitched to a cart all day will yield less milk than when it has rested. Warmth, attachment to others, quiet, were familiar to him in their most elemental forms—a nest of fledglings, the velvety soft muzzle of a horse, the pointed nose of a dog nuzzling into his hands, the massive calm of a ruminating cow.

Wedderkop had his antecedents and his family too, like everyone else, but of his family he knew little more than their pictures in the photograph album. The deacon in the black frock coat, with the seamed face, was his father; the woman with the vertical fold between her eyes his mother; the other woman with the pious, submissive expression, an aunt who lived in his house. This Potsdam deacon and his wife had brought him into the world and had supported him for a number of years; but they had remained alien to him and he rejected them just as he rejected most social considerations. They had served chiefly to provide him with an unimpeachable genealogy and a number of phantom ancestors.

These two, Döllwang and Wedderkop, had to travel the same road that Wedderkop had traversed the night before. In Pitomnik they stopped at the rations depot, but no new planes had come in with food and there was nothing to be had. (The day before Wedderkop had received only half a rations unit, instead of the three or four that the company was counting on.) Then they drove on to the stragglers' collecting station, where they were to obtain replacements for their decimated combat group. Wedderkop got out and soon returned with a sergeant and eight men. He lined them up in front of the truck and asked their names. The sergeant's name was August Gnotke; the others were Corporal Riess and Privates Altenhuden, Gimpf, Fell, Liebsch, Stüve, and Kalbach. The group clambered into the rear of the truck, Wedderkop got into the cab again, and they drove on.

"Funny-looking bunch," Wedderkop said. "Not really stragglers, but the remnants of an emergency company. There was a technical sergeant with them, but he shot himself this morning."

They were all a funny-looking bunch, Döllwang thought, the men waiting in front of the rations depot and those men from the headquarters company in the ravine where the depot was situated, as well as this first lieutenant and the driver here in the cab. Formerly, in Germany, he had sometimes come across trainloads of men on furlough and had noted their weary, exhausted faces. He had also seen trains of wounded. But here all the air was suffused with an unbroken weariness, was a single malodorous wound. Not Wedderkop, the line officer who had participated step by step for fifty days in the process of decay, but Döllwang, the young general staff officer for whom two days earlier Stalingrad had been nothing but an abstraction drawn with red and blue lines on a map, felt most deeply the hopelessness of the situation. He had been inside the ring for only four hours, but it was already clear to him that here was no army, only a battle-weary, exhausted, lice-ridden, bloodless, enervated mass of men. It might become an army again, but only if it had rest and proper care, then more rest and care, than combined-arms drill and new equipment. But he was not here to worry about the needs of the army; he had been sent to work in a small unit and to acquire experience in leading troops.

Their road was covered with snow. At the outset the snow had been flattened out by the wheels of many vehicles, but farther on there were fewer tracks. Trucks lay by the roadside. In the distance they appeared like boulders in the moonlight, but as he passed Döllwang saw that they were nothing but wrecks powdered over with snow. In the middle of the road or close to the edges of it lay gray bundles. At first there were only a few, isolated, scattered along the road; after a while there was a continuous succession of them, coated with snow like the wrecks of vehicles, with now a foot, now a hand protruding. The road led down into a ravine. Here there were two wrecked trucks and it looked as though a battle had taken place. Wedderkop groaned. The driver turned his head and looked at Wedderkop and Döllwang in turn. Wedderkop said, "Yes, lots of things have gone to pot, gone to hell, lots of things. . . ."

His voice was leaden. He was obviously referring to something specific, but Döllwang could not know what it was. He waited for an explanation. But Wedderkop changed the subject.

"At any rate they had to take Steiger off my hands," he said. "Captain Steiger, the defender of the Kasachi hills. Naturally that didn't make any impression in Pitomnik—what he'd done, I mean. The sawbones there haven't the faintest idea what it's all about. They just stand and cut and saw all day and hear nothing and see nothing. They didn't want to take Steiger. But I laid him on the table right in front of their noses. . . . By the way, he's the man you're replacing, captain."

There was a silence. After a while Döllwang said, "Well, driver, I should think we'd be there soon, or else we'll be landing in the Russians' laps." They did not, in fact, have far to go. They drove up to a sentry standing in the road.

116

"Combat Group Vilshofen?"

"Other side of the road."

Vilshofen's combat group had moved into some unoccupied caverns to the north of the Baburkin-Pitomnik road. Together with another group across the highway they were blocking this route to Pitomnik. Those two groups formed part of the line of defense known as "Violet." This line was one that changed every night. By day the men lay and died in their positions; at night they marched and died on the march. Threatened everywhere with annihilation, the troops avoided close contact with the enemy, fought only rear-guard battles, or lay shivering in the icy wind. They had given up trying to dig in. They retreated now in disciplined fashion to their new positions. If they did not find old fortifications or dugouts, they crouched along the railroad embankment, in some crevasse or, if they were in the open field, behind a wall of snow. This ring of infantry, hammered thin and with its temper burned out, still enclosed an area of more than two hundred and fifty square miles of steppe—which left sufficient room in the rear for artillery and tank units, for workshops, headquarters, hospitals, depots; the crumbling army had ample space for despair, paralysis, panic, disease, and death.

This thin ring of infantry troops had to hold. It served the same function as the shell of an egg; if it broke, the contents would instantly spill out and there would be nothing left but pus and blood and stench, for the egg was rotten.

Such was the image in the mind of one man. And like all images it reproduced what had once been seen—but in magnified form, swollen in furious motion. Blue sky and plunging down from the sky a dark ball. But the ball was talons, wings, ruffled plumage. A shower of feathers and it is over. The ball can and does split, becomes two creatures again. And the light will shine on, there will be joy and fertility without end. A vision of creation.

But what was happening here was not creation. No storm giant had infused the breath of life into men. An empty bellows had pumped convulsively and abused a nation, and nothing would result, no light, no happiness, no fruitfulness.

"We are expendable!" General Gönnern had put it. Not all were aware of this, but all were dejected, naked, and it was happening to all.

It was Colonel Vilshofen who thought about the blue sky. The vision of procreation came to him, and horror at the perversion of the act. He lay stretched out on a heap of old clothes. He was wearing his boots and furs and his fur cap with the visor

117

down. In the midst of issuing orders for the disposition of his troops for the night he had been overwhelmed by his weariness. He had told his adjutant to wake him again in two minutes. The adjutant sat on a box. It was cold; there was no door. An hour ago the place had been a deserted cave. A niche in the earthen wall was the fireplace; in it the wreckage of an automobile, including some pieces of rubber from the tires, was burning. Smoke billowed up and floated slowly toward the exit. From the ceiling black flakes trickled down.

Black flakes fell upon Vilshofen's face. Black flakes—he had seen crows sitting like thick black flakes on the carcass of a truck and they had not flown up when he marched past them alone. They fluttered up at last—he heard them screeching—when the head of his column, marching behind him, reached the same spot.

Earlier there had been dead horses on the road, with the crows feeding on the cadavers; now there were trucks filled with frozen human flesh. The crows, wings beating hard, whirled up; there were such numbers of them that they spouted into the air like black smoke.

Colonel Vilshofen groaned. His adjutant, hovering over him with watch in hand, was tempted to wake him up at once, but he waited the remaining half minute. Vilshofen felt a hand upon his shoulder and looked up into the smoking lamp hanging from a nail and then into the youthful features of his Lieutenant Latte. He was still absorbed by his dream. But this was not a dream—the wall of earth, the lamp, Lieutenant Latte was reality. A fluttering monster beating its wings . . . a horrible convulsion and a monstrous abortion expelled . . . a stinking, dripping eggshell . . . streams of suppurating foulness in the snow. . . . And Gönnern and Damme and the commander in chief—what did they have to do with it, what did he have to do with it? Who was the throbbing, sterile giant bellows and who the suffering, necessitous puppets that died a thousand deaths . . . ? And who had lost his honor in this act and forfeited his life?

Colonel Vilshofen reeled to his feet. Then he staggered back. Döllwang stood before him, shaved, washed, neat, eyes bright and intelligent. Another apparition! And yet it was as true as the horror that still vibrated in his nerves.

Walter Döllwang took a step forward.

"Assigned to your combat group, sir. . . ." Vilshofen heard, and he saw the hand the captain held out. No, this was the last straw. Döllwang, for his part, saw before him a haggard, exhausted face and eyes glowing like torches, and he had to pull

118

himself up sharp to conceal his alarm at the changed appearance of this old friend who had been almost a father to him.

Vilshofen's attention, however, was distracted almost at once. Wedderkop reported back from his transport assignment. He had left Captain Steiger at the field hospital in Pitomnik. The other eighteen wounded men, except for two, he had delivered at the Gumrak cemetery rather than the Gumrak field hospital. And he had brought back—this made the strongest impression upon Vilshofen—half a day's rations for the men.

Half a day's rations. Fifty grams of hardtack (one wafer and a sliver of another), eight grams of midday rations (seven peas), twenty-five grams of supper rations (a morsel of meat) and five grams of beverage were the full day's ration at this time, and Wedderkop had brought back half that amount: Döllwang stood beside Vilshofen, who at once had the rations distributed (except for the peas) and stood by to supervise. As each man came up and held out his hand, Vilshofen gave him a word or a look. But he consoled no one; his words of encouragement were distinctly grim. Döllwang had known Vilshofen as a taciturn man who weighed his words carefully and phrased them precisely and he at once recognized the suffering, battered human being who spoke now.

Vilshofen looked at the dirty soldier's hand clutching the sliver of hardtack and the bit of canned meat, which was the size of a thumb, and he said, "Damned scanty, isn't it, Hannes?" And to another, "Stretch it out so you'll have something for breakfast." To a third: "How many pigs does your old man have in his pen back home, Vogt?" "Just one, sir." "There you are; they're on short rations too." To the fourth, a former schoolmaster: "Don't forget to chew it; it makes it last longer." To the fifth: "How many kids have you got, Wilsdruff?" "You know, sir; five." "Lucky you don't have to share this with your family." To the sixth: "Well, Matzke, you poor devil. When you're on your way to the gallows, they might have given you a better last meal."

He left no one out.

"See how nicely the table is set." —"Up front now and you'll have a Strauss waltz for dessert." (The nightly propaganda broadcasts from the Russian positions always began with musical transcriptions.) "What was that they played last night?" he asked the next man. "From *Rigoletto,* sir." "Yesterday we had a symphony on the Stalin organ [A Russian type of mortar]." —"Desert to Ivan—I've told you that once before."— "Go on, run off to Ivan; you'll only croak here. I won't keep anyone back."

So he went on, and whether he was encouraging one man or bidding good-bye to another who was already marked for death, whether his remarks sounded like high treason, Vilshofen was in deadly earnest. The dismal procession passed on, human ruins, men whose age it was impossible to tell. Everyone was addressed personally; not one passed by without at least a glance, a grim smile, and there was not one of these dulled faces that did not show animation for a moment.

The new men from Pitomnik came up.

"What is your name, sergeant?"

"Gnotke, sir."

"Where were you before?"

"At Dmitrevka, sir."

"And before that?"

"Before Moscow, sir."

"And before that, before your military service?"

"In the SA, sir."

"And before that, Sergeant Gnotke?"

"At home in Klein-Stepenitz in Pomerania, sir."

"I guess you liked it best of all there, eh?"

"Yes, sir, it was best there, sir."

"Well, let's hope you'll be back there some time, Gnotke." But Gnotke was not yet dismissed.

"Well, tell me about your men. Who is this fellow?"

"Corporal Riess, sir."

"All right, and what else? What is there to say about Riess?"

"Riess is healthy; in Dmitrevka he always fetched the rations. Before that he was in the SS. He does his duty. In his free time he plays cards."

"That right, Riess?"

"Yes, sir."

"And the next?"

"Private Altenhuden comes from Pomerania too, sir."

"Very well. The next?"

"Private Gimpf, sir."

This time Vilshofen did not say "Very well, the next." He fixed his eyes—a few days ago they had been of a violet-blue color and a few minutes ago they had struck Döllwang as glowing torches—searchingly upon Gnotke's face, which displayed the slow, clumsy workings of incipient thought.

"Well, sir, I really don't know . . . there's not much really wrong with him. During the breakthrough at Kletskaya he lay at the bottom of a hole and he wanted to stay there, and afterwards, when we were marching, he wanted to lie down, and at

Vertiachi he didn't give a damn and at Dmitrevka he still didn't give a damn about anything. . . ."

"Then you've come a long way together?"

"Yes, and he was with me in the penal battalion too."

"I see. Where does Gimpf come from?"

"From Alten-Affeln. He has a mother at home there and I guess she thinks he's a good, dutiful son and will come home some day to run the farm. . . ."

Gnotke paused again. For a whole year he had not made such a long speech.

"Tell me about Kletskaya and the hole there."

"Yes, sir. Sergeant Aslang was sitting on the edge of the hole —he was still sitting and the others were lying and the hole was half full and I didn't look around and then I pulled him [Gnotke looked at Gimpf] out and on the way I kept making him go on, and it was the same in Vertiachi and in Dmitrevka; sometimes I had to push him along . . . and yet there's nothing special about him, so why . . . ?"

"Yes, why, Gnotke? There are many other mother's sons, aren't there?"

"Yes, sir, many . . . this morning Sergeant Pöhls shot himself. He used to work in the kitchen and couldn't stand going hungry. Yesterday we left Sergeant Maulhard in the snow; we couldn't lug him any farther. And at Dmitreyka we left Sergeant Urbas lying in the dugout, though he was as good as done for anyway. . . ."

Yes, why was Gnotke concerned about this one man? The question seriously interested Vilshofen. He had not failed to notice how Gnotke's face, hardened to immobility from having seen too much of dying, had flickered faintly as he considered this question, hinting at a true face beneath the rigid mask. Even the sun cannot awaken a stony wasteland to life, but the light can burst forth at any moment from a human wasteland, Vilshofen concluded. A human being, no matter how crushed and shamelessly abused he was, no matter how blind a puppet he had become, was not hopeless rubbish as long as he still breathed and as long as he could still think of his fellow men, even if it were only one of his comrades. But what was it he, Vilshofen, had really meant? Had he not really given himself up as hopeless . . . ?

Who could understand the labyrinthine ways of his thoughts —Gnotke or Döllwang or Wedderkop or any of the others standing there? None of them knew the reason, but the effect was obvious. Gnotke and Döllwang and Wedderkop and the others standing there at the bottom of the ravine, with the nocturnal winter sky pocketed above them between snow-banks, saw a smile on their colonel's face; they saw it in his eyes and watched it flicker across his haggard features like a flash of red sheet lightning. The gleam remained as Vilshofen spoke, his gaze fixed on Gimpf. "So that's Gimpf. We want to go on keeping an eye on him. But the others, too, Gnotke—at least their feet. Who is that—his hoofs look in sort of bad shape?"

"Private Kalbach, sir. It would be hard on his wife and kids if he went. He has swollen feet and a weak heart."

"And who is this man, and this one and this one?"

"Private Stüve, sir. He feels bad because we used to have three men from his town with us. Private Liebich; he's worried about taxes; he has a small house in Masserberg in Thuringia. Private August Fell; he prays. Private Liebsch; he has a weak bladder and when we have a bunker he has to sleep at the bottom."

"Very well. Riess, Stüve, Liebsch, and Liebich are off duty now and can crawl into an empty cave. If you ever have a bunker and cots again, Liebsch will sleep at the bottom, of course. Sergeant Gnotke, Gimpf, Fell, and Altenhuden will go to posts up front."

Vilshofen watched the men as they departed, and he saw them twice—with full, healthy faces and raised heads as they had been once, and then as they actually looked, their faces sunken, their throats withered like old men, their eyes dull.

Some two hours later the sentry on guard in front of the "headquarters" heard whistling from Vilshofen's cave. The sentry pushed aside his earflaps to hear better; then he shrugged. There was no doubt about it; it was a gay, carefree melody. Lieutenant Latte, who had gone out to check the guard posts, was no less surprised when he returned to the cave. As he stepped in he saw Vilshofen standing in front of the niche where the fire was burning, tall and gaunt in a tattered coat, the ends of his scarf dangling loose, the earflaps on his fur cap protruding. In the flickering glow of the fire he reminded Latte of a picture of Don Quixote.

Vilshofen was whistling a tune from *Carmen.*

Glancing lightly at Latte, he said, "Life is a great thing." Latte was returning from the front line where Sergeant Matzke had just died and been buried in the snow.

"Life, sir . . ." Latte stammered.

"Did you see that fellow—Gnotke is his name. I took his paybook and checked up on where he's been and what he's

been through. A chap like that ought to be so dead here"—
Vilshofen thumbed his fist against his hollow chest—"that cannon or mines or firing squads shouldn't be needed. And that's
what the regulations intend—I know them. But he clears
mines, buries corpses, sweats in the Don Bend, stews at Vertiachi, roasts in the Stalingrad pocket, and could have been
maimed a dozen times, but even then it would only have been
something external. The thing is, he finds a Gimpf, a helpless
baby, and he takes care of him—takes care of a helpless man.
Just imagine it—his hands are good for something besides
hauling off the dead. They can handle life and that's why he's
alive himself and will live like a man to his last hour. That *is* a
triumph. Get yourself a Gimpf, Latte, and you'll live. For us I
suppose it has to be the whole crew out there; more than that,
we must think of our whole nation. But then we must ask ourselves where we're leading our men and where, in the end, our
nation is being led. Where, Latte, where?"

"What do you mean, sir?"

"To death, Latte, and for no purpose at all. There can't be
anything worse than that."

"And yet you whistle the Toreador's song, sir?"

"Yes, Latte. Yesterday I wanted to surrender. Today . . . what
do I want to do today, what is there left for a man who finds
himself humiliated, flat on his back? I wanted to lead a shock
troop assault and be done with it all; but even that was no
longer feasible. It was another matter when Stalingrad was
still a goal, but it has become a death trap and we're sitting
right in it . . . right in it. The strong eat up the weak; the weak
fall; the sick lie and are left behind. It's all logical. If a man is
sick and can no longer crawl to the feed trough, it shows poor
breeding, inferior racial stock. But those who steal from others
and fill their own bellies will live a few minutes longer and are
therefore of superior stock. Latte, have you had a chance to see
those corpses with skulls cracked open and the brains eaten
out?"

"Sir!"

"Yes, Latte, I've seen them—and the men that can do that
are the chosen people in this death trap and may survive."

"Permit me to point out, sir . . ."

"Don't talk to me about the Rumanians; they've been
blamed for too many of the things we've done. The Rumanians, at any rate, didn't invent the slogans about the superior
race. I've seen it, I tell you. I've seen several broken skulls like
that on the road. And that is the logical consequence, that is
the goal we've been heading toward, not only since yesterday

123

and not only since we crossed the Don and the Kalmuck Steppes and penetrated into the factory quarter of Stalingrad. That is the logical consequence of the doctrine of superior races. . . . Do you hear something screeching, Latte?"

"No, I beg your pardon, sir."

"Well, what is that, Latte?" Vilshofen's hand shot out and his finger touched the eagle on Latte's uniform, the national emblem of the new German Reich of Adolf Hitler.

"The crow would be a more appropriate emblem," Vilshofen said. "And it really is that; it sits, fat and swollen and beating its wings, on the edge of our death trap. It is with us all the time, wherever we go." He hooked his nail between the coat and the edge of the emblem and said, "We shall have to part with it, Latte; we shall have to get rid of it."

"I beg your pardon, sir. May I go now?"

"Yes, you may, Latte. Sleep on what I've said and tomorrow we'll talk it over again."

We're in it up to our necks, Vilshofen thought as he watched his adjutant go out. Shock troop assaults and similar evasions won't do . . . just won't do any more. Now we must keep still and realize what we've done to cities, countries, and peoples. We've come a long way and many a village has gone up in smoke and many a man . . . those chaps were fed like prize steers; they kept their bellies stuffed, had razors and shaving cream, and we carried along all sorts of stuff, all sorts of plunder in those tanks that were like homes to us. We were arrogant and the world that rolled along under us was ours for the taking, and there were a good many men who didn't jump aside in time; sometimes whole platoons were ground under our triumphant tracks.

Now it was January. In September he, Manfred Vilshofen, had been the man in the tank, the conqueror of the factory quarter of Stalingrad.

And now . . . fleeing hordes, running for their lives and finding death all the sooner. Cannon cast aside in the deserted villages of the steppe, plunder strewn about the comfortable shelters, boiled potatoes in the pig troughs. A main dressing station turned into a main defense line and the paralyzed wounded creatures in the huts covered for the second time by fire and splinters and lumps of clay. Trucks stuck fast in the snow at night, men lying on the ground, and not a hand stirs to lift them up again. A planned defense line without emplacements organized and built in advance. Döllwang flown into the pocket and old Döllwang at home, cashiered.

What was it all about, what did it all mean?

A shock troop assault—ought that to be the end of thoughts that could not be thought through to the end? But others did think things through—that doctor, for instance, not so young any more, but he looked young and he thought and talked about what he thought, went beyond the limits that had been set for him and poked at fundamental principles that even a colonel did not dare to touch. And that sergeant, a convict soldier whom hell had not been able to burn; he had not been turned into slag, for he still had a sense of comradeship with his fellows (not only for Gimpf; he had a shrewd understanding of the others, knew where the shoe pinched them). Fearless thinking and a sure, instinctive urge for life could exist even here in this death trap, and so life was still a great thing and the fight was still worthwhile.

But a fight against what, against whom?

Vilshofen stood in the cave that had been scratched into the side of this ravine, but he did not see the earthen wall. His gaze—the same gaze that had once swept the steppes, peering through the lookout slot of his tank at the clifflike heaps of ruins and at factory chimneys belching smoke and fire from holes in their sides—was fixed once more in the distance. But the regions he saw lay beyond that city which now clumped like a congealed stream of lava. The goal was no longer Stalingrad.

A few steps away was the cave into which Latte had clambered after his visit with the colonel. These caves had been dug in the summer by Croats attached to the supply train; they lay close together and somewhat resembled a village of Indian pueblos. Latte's, like Vilshofen's, was without a door or a window. The ceiling had fallen in at one place, and this hole, as well as the entrance, had been stuffed with canvas. Here, too, a hole for the fire had been hacked into the earth wall, and in this hole all sorts of junk smoked thickly. Here, too, the smoke billowed up to the ceiling and eddied through the half-collapsed wall into the neighboring cave where the enlisted men lay, closely crowded.

Sharing the cave with Latte was Lieutenant Wedderkop, Lieutenant Kindt, and Captain Döllwang. They lay stretched out on a shelter half, in their uniforms and boots. The coats they had spread over themselves were clammy, and the shelter half on top of the coats was frozen stiff. They had come in here after the distribution of the rations and gone almost directly to sleep, without much talk. Wedderkop, however, had first relieved himself of the news he had brought back from headquarters. "The pocket is a hell of a lot narrower now, on the

125

west and on the south too," he had said. "It's shrunk to half the size by now. The staff has moved again, into a ravine beyond Gumrak. There they kicked out General Hartmann and his whole staff. That was the place they called Hartmann's Village; they had a marvelous setup there, and now they've had to move to Stalingrad. . . ." Kindt was too done in to comment and Döllwang was too busy with his own thoughts. "Stalingrad with its resident staffs is the head; we with our diarrhea are the behind, I suppose; and Pitomnik with its airport is the navel that feeds us. Until the cord is broken it can go on that way." With this rather garish picture Wedderkop completed his "situation report." Then he pulled his cap down over his eyes and went to sleep.

Döllwang had lain for a while staring into the glowing, rust-red smoke; he had listened to the snoring of the men on the other side of the wall and thought of his quiet, clean room in Berlin, of his aunt's unobtrusive, busy hands that kept everything in order. He had also thought of his plane trip here, of the fleeing army, the landing at Pitomnik, then headquarters, the front, the distribution of rations, and Vilshofen. Above all his thoughts had lingered on Vilshofen.

Hours had passed. Now Latte stood over the sleepers. He awakened his relief, Lieutenant Wedderkop, and crawled into his place as soon as Wedderkop had got up. But Latte, too, could not fall asleep at once. Through the wall he heard the sentries who had been relieved come in. One of the men was Wilsdruff, one the Magdeburg bank clerk. There was also one of the new men, Kalbach, the one with the sore feet.

"We were here once before," one of the men said. The others, too, had recognized the area where they had once rested during the hundred-day assault on Stalingrad. "The Croats were here in the ravine," Kärmer recalled. "They had a fine time. The place swarmed with Russian women they'd kidnapped. The women carried water and did the laundry and darned socks, and at night they had to share the bunks."

"Come now, that sort of thing didn't happen in our army," Kalbach exclaimed.

"Think so?" Wilsdruff said. "All I know is that right here in the ravine, back there where the tank men were in rest camp, the ground was littered with used french letters. That's the way things were here while we were advancing."

Latte lay still, listening to the men's talk until it gradually died down into silence. Even then he was unable to sleep. He kept thinking of Vilshofen—of the tank commander Vilshofen at Kharkov, at the Mius, on the Don Steppe, crossing the

126

Tsymla and the Don, driving into Stalingrad; he thought of how Vilshofen, his tank regiment destroyed, had become the commander of a combat group, and he thought of how Vilshofen had talked tonight. And he was not only cold outwardly; he was chilled to the heart.

The commander of the adjacent unit had gone mad; another had shot himself. Every day someone shot himself, someone lost his mind. What about Vilshofen? A shock troop assault to get it over with, he had said. He had said a number of other things, but this last had made the profoundest impression on Latte. Did he intend to organize an assault battalion and take his Latte along? Latte was still young, but it was a time for dying.

At this point Latte at last fell asleep. He was awakened by a peal of laughter that boomed throughout the narrow cavern. Looking up, he saw Wedderkop standing over him and heard him say, "Now our own old man has gone nuts too."

"What's the matter?"

"Who's crazy?"

"They ought to have been shot on the spot. That's what we always did with these sub-humans. They set a sled on fire and gave a signal."

"What's that? Who?"

"The Russians in the train. But instead of making hash of the whole crew of them, he's given orders that the Russians are to be left behind next time we withdraw."

"Who will pull the sleds?" Kindt asked.

" 'Sleds ought to have horses hitched to them,' he said, 'and since we have no horses, the sleds will have to be left behind and everyone will carry his own gear. Ammunition and equipment will be loaded on hand sleds and pulled by the column.' "

"Impossible!" Lieutenant Kindt said.

Lieutenant Latte's eyes grew vacant; his mouth twitched and it looked as if he were on the point of weeping.

"I tell you he's off his nut," Wedderkop insisted. " 'We have no horses and we have no feed for horses,' he said. 'We have no food for prisoners nor any extra men to guard them or to transport them to the rear. Therefore the Russians stay behind.' "

"That isn't craziness; it's the logical conclusion," Döllwang said.

Kindt shook his head and Latte looked perplexedly from one to the other. But Wedderkop said, "Shooting them would be the logical conclusion."

"To shoot men because they can't be fed and can't be guarded would be murder."

"I beg your pardon, captain," Wedderkop said, "it's obvious that you've been only one day on the Eastern Front."

Hunger and cold and groups of soldiers huddling in the snow; no communications to the rear and no communications from one group to the next—such was the defense line known as "Violet." Other troops were fleeing, struggling toward it from the west. Some never reached the line; others, reaching it, did not take up positions there, but marched on. One of the few groups that had taken up positions was Vilshofen's combat unit; another was Keil's combat group; another was Lundt's regiment, and another Buchner's flak battalion.

Across the road from Vilshofen's group was Keil's. Major Keil was the successor to a regimental commander who had shot himself when the west front collapsed. His group consisted mainly of dispersed soldiers from other units; the core of it, however, was the Ninth East Prussian MG Battalion. Keil, a young officer promoted above his seniority rating, was also an East Prussian; he was the son of an automobile mechanic who had later acquired ownership of a garage and gasoline station on the highway between Königsberg and Cranz. Keil had been in position here a half day longer than Vilshofen and had already laid a telephone line up front.

Keil was holding the telephone receiver to his ear.

"Who's there—oh, hello, Vierkant. Listen, Vierkant, on the way here we found some brandy in a headquarters bunker. No, not two cases; unfortunately, just two bottles. What should I do with it? If I distribute it, everyone will get no more than a thimbleful and even then there won't be enough to go round."

"If I were the major I'd drink it myself and not worry about it," Private Vierkant, the machine gunner up front, replied.

"I think so too," Keil said. "Very well—with the idea that I'm drinking for all of you. We'll divide it up here in headquarters, right away. Now one more thing, Vierkant. Listen sharp, this has nothing to do with brandy. On our right we're in touch with Vilshofen's combat group, but we have nothing at all on our left flank. Schwandt's regiment ought to be poking around somewhere near here. Tell the first sergeant to make up a patrol and to scout around until he finds out what's going on over there. O.K.?"

Vierkant repeated the order and Keil hung up.

He turned to his staff. The "staff" which shared the cave with him consisted of the unit's cook, Heinrich Halluweit, who had been Keil's orderly and messenger for years, machine gunner

Karl Wischwill and Technical Sergeant Göritt, a former rural schoolmaster.

"All right, let's have the stuff, Heinrich."

Halluweit opened the first of the two bottles.

"A bit of a snack to go with it would be the thing, but there's no chance of that." There was in fact no chance, for here too the ration was seven peas and twenty-five grams of meat per man, and not a single pea or a single fibre of meat extra was taken by the staff. Such things did not happen in Keil's combat group.

Keil was not yet thirty years old. A long scar on his face ran from his left eye down to his mouth. At Belgorod a shell splinter had torn open his face. The wound had healed since then; the scar had formed fast. But a wound he had received before Moscow in the winter of 1941 had been slower to mend, and on long marches he limped somewhat. If the marches were too long he would sit on one of the hand sleds and his East Prussians would take turns pulling him.

This evening the four of them drank up the two bottles of brandy. Later, however, Keil was still able to visit the foremost positions; he wanted to determine how far his unit could fan out to the left to cover the deserted terrain there.

At another point in the defense line known as "Violet" lay Buchner's anti-aircraft battalion. This battalion had been destroyed once at Verkhnaya Businovka, again at the Kasachi hills, but each time it had come to life again. Its resurrections were due largely to a young, energetic second lieutenant named Stampfer and to Technical Sergeant Minz; these two had always managed to get sufficient supplies of fuel and had seen to it that reserves were stored at a safe distance from the front. As a result, the battalion had twice been able to fill out its complement of guns from equipment abandoned on the roads by other retreating units. Buchner had been able to bring into the new line a full battery of heavy 8.8 cm. flak guns in addition to the 2 cm. guns that had been brought up in personnel carriers.

Major Buchner, Second Lieutenant Stampfer, and Technical Sergeant Minz were sitting in their bunker. Before them stood Sergeant Januscheck. Januscheck had just returned from regimental headquarters and from the rations office at Pitomnik, and the news he had brought from headquarters, confirmed by the flak battalion at Pitomnik, had made such an impression upon the commander and his aides that they sat numb.

Sergeant Januscheck stood there and grinned.

"What are you grinning for, you bastard?" Buchner asked.

"I beg your pardon, sir, but I heard it from Welisch and he heard it from Sepp Reisinger who's in the signal company and saw it, and when he heard the report the regimental commander sat there like a wet cat just the way you're doing, and the staff captain and the adjutant too, and they talked about a sinking ship and rats, even though it wasn't a ship at all, just a Junkers transport plane, and there was no rat, just our general inside of it."

"Shut your trap, Januscheck!" Buchner said.

But Januscheck was not through. "And they said the colonel was indignant, which in plain words means that he kicked his table to pieces."

Sergeant Minz, who had brought Januscheck in on charges of rumor-mongering, stood by with a bleak expression. Major Buchner said impatiently, "Where the devil is Loose?"

Lieutenant Loose, the adjutant, had been sent off to telephone the regimental adjutant to find out whether there was any truth in Januscheck's gossip. The story was that the commander of their flak division, General Pickert, had flown out of the pocket to make a report and had not returned; instead he had pretended that he had made an unsuccessful try. He had sent a radio message stating: "Tried to fly back. Unfortunately not possible account strong enemy attacks." Januscheck had investigated the matter carefully; the flak men at Pitomnik airport had informed him that on the night in question some twenty Junkers transports had landed without difficulties.

At last Lieutenant Loose returned. He confirmed everything Januscheck had said and brought, moreover, a second radio message from General Pickert, which was to be read to the troops in an order of the day. It read: "Richthofen forbids further flights. Am organizing new Ninth Flak Division. Revenge for Stalingrad!"

"Good God . . ."

"Organizing new Ninth—what does that mean?"

"That was just what made the regimental commander raving mad, according to what I heard from the adjutant," Lieutenant Loose said. "He radioed an answer that General Pickert won't pin up on his wall."

"What was the answer?"

" 'The Ninth Flak Division is fighting as hard as ever in the ruins of Stalingrad.' "

"Damn it all, I still don't understand it. That's as good as saying that we've been written off."

"That's right, written off."

"And the rat flies out."

"Januscheck, will you kindly keep your mouth shut."

"Well, you see, sir, if a man's written off, I mean if he's as good as talking from the grave, he might as well say what he thinks."

"No, you've got to keep your trap shut even in the grave. And now get out of here and don't let me hear any more of your rumor-mongering, understand."

"*Jawohl*, Herr Major."

After Januscheck and Minz had gone, Major Buchner said to Loose and Stampfer: "Gentlemen, I don't know what to say. This is absolutely unheard of. It really means that he's deserted us, left us in the lurch. Mentally we're buried already. But the colonel is right: we're still here and there's nothing left for us to do but to go on fighting in the ruins."

"I still don't understand it, sir," Lieutenant Loose said. "How can a man in a position of command, who by the way has helped to get us into this disaster, simply sit himself in a plane and leave us to our fate? What kind of moral stature is that, sir?"

"Good God, moral stature!" was all Buchner replied.

Another group along "Violet" was Lundt's regiment, which consisted merely of a headquarters in a ravine and a few troops scattered around a mile or two ahead; the regiment had shrunk to the size of a battalion. Since the retreat from the west front this unit had been led by the battalion adjutant, Lieutenant Lawkow. Now, however, an acting battalion commander was coming to take over. He was Captain Henkel who had flown in on the plane with Carras and Döllwang.

To save gasoline, Captain Henkel was driven, not to the ravine where Colonel Lundt's staff was located, but directly to the front line, a point in the middle of a snowy desert where Lieutenant Lawkow had established his headquarters.

Captain Henkel clambered down from the truck cab. The driver followed him. The two stood there, the captain and the driver who held Henkel's two suitcases. Before them lay a white expanse, above them motionless stars. Henkel looked around.

"It's along here somewhere, sir," the driver said, and he led the way down a path tramped in the snow. The path sloped downward and continued along the bottom of a crevice that was scarcely higher than a man, then led through snowdrifts and ended in front of a notched cave.

"Here it is, sir."

"What's that? There must be some kind of dugout. . . ."

"Here it is, sir," the driver repeated.

Another step forward and Henkel was still standing under the cold stars, his feet deep in the snow; but he could now see that a hole had been scooped in the wall. A fire was glowing dimly on the floor and smoke that smelled atrocious billowed up into his face. He saw a hand stretch out and fan the fire, so that in the red glare the scene in the cave was visible for a moment. There was nothing but a bed made of coats and rags, a fire, a few mess kits and tin cans around it, and between the fire and the bed was a box with a telephone standing on it. On the bed, with his legs tucked under his body and a coat propped on sticks tentwise over his head, sat a small man with a pock-marked face. He stood up and introduced himself as the acting battalion commander, Lieutenant Lawkow.

"What's the idea of sitting here in the middle of the night; where's your bunker, lieutenant?" Captain Henkel asked as soon as he recovered from his initial amazement.

"This is the battalion combat command post, sir."

"Why, it's impossible. And where are my quarters going to be?"

"I'll just have to move over. There's room enough under the coat here."

"But this is frightful. And look at these conditions—there's nothing here, nothing at all. Where are the quarters for the other officers?"

"I am the only officer in the battalion."

"My God!" Henkel said.

"Won't you sit down, sir?"

"Sit down . . ." There was nothing else for him to do; Henkel crawled under the coat. Lawkow, too, sat down again and tucked his feet under him once more. "That's the best protection," he said.

"What do you mean?"

"It's the best way to protect your legs against freezing—by keeping them close to your body."

My God, what have I done? Henkel thought. There I sat in the army printing plant in Kharkov, a nice quiet post, and I thought it was too quiet because there were no chances for promotion. And so I snatched at the opportunity to be sent to Stalingrad because they told me I'd be handed command of a battalion right off.

And now he had his battalion. But my God, this wasn't true, couldn't be true. A battalion headquarters like this was unthinkable, unheard of; what could have brought things to this

132

pass? He had better familiarize himself with battalion affairs as soon as possible.

"Where is the battalion stationed at present, Lieutenant Lawkow?"

"Out there," Lawkow replied, pointing out over the snow-drifted crevice. Since, however, he meant the steppe beyond, his head actually pointed to the clear, starlit winter sky.

"Out there in the holes—two, three, five men in each. We are flanking a highroad leading from Bolshaya Rossoshka. The men have had nothing to eat, so I have to give them something to chew the rag on at least."

"Chew the rag on—what do you mean by that?"

"Well, sir, since they haven't anything to sink their teeth into, the least you can do is give them something for their brains to work on. That's what I've always done."

Captain Henkel was in civil life a lawyer from Bautzen accustomed to a precise and moderate way of life and to precision and objectivity in language. Now he was beginning to grow suspicious of this little lieutenant with his legs tucked under him and his face disfigured by pockmarks and by quite ordinary dirt. He could not tolerate such vague phraseology, Henkel said—phraseology which conveyed no exact or definite idea whatsoever; moreover, it was highly improper in an official report and in transferring a battalion—he stressed this latter point. Lieutenant Lawkow at once adopted an official tone and informed Captain Henkle quite precisely that the troops up front had had no warm food for three days and today had received nothing at all.

Captain Henkel started to his feet. "Then the field kitchen must be set up there at once."

"We don't have any field kitchen, sir. And anyway, there isn't a scrap of anything to put in a pot. Today the regiment has again failed to deliver any rations to us."

"But these are dreadful, intolerable conditions. I must telephone the regimental commander at once."

"*Jawohl*, I'll connect you immediately, sir."

Lawkow reached out for the telephone, pulled the box closer to the bed, and connected Captain Henkel with Colonel Lundt, the commander of the regiment. The conversation lasted several minutes. Lieutenant Lawkow sat by, looking quite swollen from the coat, scarves, and other rags he had managed to wrap around himself. He watched the captain's face and saw the blood drain out of it.

Weakly, Henkel replaced the telephone. For a while he said nothing, but he gazed at Lawkow's face in the dim glow of the fire as though he were seeing him for the first time. After a while he said, "He's an extremely nervous sort, our colonel, isn't he?"

Colonel Lundt had told him in reply to his questions about rations: "Do whatever you think best; I can't help you out. In general rely on your lieutenant; he knows his way around in these matters. Above all, fortify your position with all available means and don't waste any time about it."

In line with this order Captain Henkel decided to inspect the most advanced outposts at once. Before he got up to have Lawkow show him around, he returned to the question of rations once more. "The colonel says you know your way around and know what to do in such emergencies. Provisions must be assured; I mean, provisioning must be put on a solid basis."

"Sir, we don't have a solid basis for anything at all. There are no regular supplies of rations or munitons or anything."

"Well, what have you done about food?"

"It's all a matter of chance, sir. En route we've picked up things that the supply services threw away when they skipped out. And when all the headquarters moved off to the east, sometimes horses were driven by or a herd of cattle, and then of course we lay in wait and caught a horse or a cow. Then we'd throw a rope around its neck, drag it along behind a car, and slaughter it. Of course that sort of thing is living from hand to mouth."

"But this is simply frightful, frightful."

"It wasn't so frightful as long as there was anything to pick up, sir. But now, when there's simply nothing left at all, not a thing to eat. . . ."

"Nothing at all to eat—no human being can stand that."

The lieutenant grinned. His grin was so incomprehensible and so repulsive in this grave situation that Captain Henkel quickly changed the subject. "Well, let's go to inspect the positions."

After they had left the niche in the wall and the captain's voice could be heard once more, loudly lamenting the darkness and asserting that he could not see his hand before his face, the driver who had crouched down by the fire shook his head pensively. The driver was thinking: we won't have him around long; we might as well bury him on the spot.

Hours passed. The driver woke up at the sound of Henkel's plaintive voice again. Henkel and Lawkow had returned from their tour of inspection and the driver heard the same refrain:

"But it simply isn't possible. No dugouts, no trenches, no barbed wire; there isn't any line at all. It isn't possible."

Then Henkel said:

"I can tell you this, Lieutenant Lawkow, I'm not really an ambitious man and I didn't care at all about commanding a battalion."

And after a while:

"They told me in Kharkov that the army here would be relieved without the shadow of a doubt."

"I no longer believe there'll be any relief," Lawkow said.

Every day someone shot himself; every day someone went mad. But this was least true of the front, that thin ring which daily grew thinner. Along the ring men might relapse into utter torpor, but death took place in normal fashion, from failing lungs, exhaustion, freezing, or wounds. Inside the ring, however, in staff bunkers, in garrison headquarters, in the rations and administrative offices, among the repair companies and the other rear services, the incidence of suicide and madness increased daily. Here conferences went on, plans were forged, plans for escape and for breaking out of the encirclement were toyed with; here men played cards, did not sleep or barely slept, bargained and exchanged, lost and won, raged and swore and prayed, sang hymns and discussed all the varieties of suicide, aimed pistols at their own temples. A single word could bring all this ferment to the boiling point and transform human beings into horned, tailed, cloven-hoofed monsters—into a blind, maddened herd that would trample down all other life and violate all the limits imposed by reason and law.

"Tanks!" was one such word.

The area was the sector in front of Pitomnik, on the southern rim of the broad airfield. Here, according to the plans of Army Headquarters, the 376th Infantry Division and the 29th I.D. (motorized) were to take up positions. But both divisions had been routed in the area between Dmitrevka and Novo-Alexeyevka, and no troops at all took up their assigned positions. Gray hordes emerged from the snow and moved across the land. Trucks, too, churned their way through the snowy wasteland, but neither trucks nor men on foot stopped; all continued on across the airfield and through Pitomnik.

Perhaps it was a cry from someone among these hordes, perhaps it was the sight of those worn-out, wearily shuffling men who for days had been fleeing from tanks, that drew the outcry from someone else. Who can say who was the first to utter that shout? When a pack of mad dogs races out of the hot dust of the plains and streams through village upon village, who can say which of the dogs is first?

135

"Tanks!" the word echoed through sprawling Pitomnik.

"Tanks!" someone shouted at the airfield. The word flew into the traffic control room, into the airdrome commander's bunker; it screamed through the tents of the dressing station, through the collecting station for stragglers; it reached the jam of horse-drawn and motorized vehicles on the highroad, shrieked through the horseshoe-shaped ravine that branched out from the road and along which ran a line of caves and bunkers filled with stores of hardtack, meat, peas, beans, coffee, and cocoa. Here the rations supply office was located. It coursed like a spark through tinder to Pitomnik village, more than two miles away.

In the surgeon's hand the saw trembled. The radioman in the traffic control tower threw away his earphones. The gravedigger at the cemetery dropped his spade; the airdrome commandant shouted for his chauffeur. The already scattered troops scattered again. The wounded at the dressing station writhed on their pallets. The paymaster at the rations depot left his bread, his meat, and his beverages. Those who could reach some kind of vehicle rode; those who were able ran. The mob that raced out of Pitomnik onto the highway—it numbered thousands—was nothing but a pack of shaggy, two-legged creatures. The direction was prescribed beforehand; it had been the one possible direction in this area since the days of the triumphant advance, and therein lay the curse, the perversion that turned victory into death. The direction, always the same, was toward Stalingrad.

During the day a leaden sky had discharged its burden of snow; now, toward twilight, the mists rose up from the Volga. The landing field was still clear of ground fog and two approaching Junkers had just reported to the traffic control officer. The transports appeared over the airdrome without fighter protection, circled several times, then penetrated the scraps of mist and landed.

The ambulance orderlies had begun their work of carrying some forty critically-wounded men out to the landing field. As it had been for days at every arrival of a plane, that was the signal for the others. By the hundreds they limped and hobbled as fast as they could from their tents to the field.

One of the Junkers had come to the end of its landing run. The propeller was still turning, but the plane stood still. The cabin door opened and unloading began. The second Junkers touched the white field and the landing gear churned up the snow. Its approach was observed with feverish interest by eyes half hidden under white dressings, by all the severely wounded men who were still able to see. Thirty-eight of them lay there, the strip of cardboard bearing their names on their chests. One of these thirty-eight on the stretchers who were to be flown out was Captain Steiger.

Captain Steiger's left leg had been amputated up to the knee. The doctors had been unable as yet to remove the shell fragment from his arm; his head wound had apparently turned out to be not dangerous. He had reason to hope that he would reach a hospital at home and later be sent to Bopfingen, and although one leg would have a prosthesis instead of a foot at the end of it, he would again be able to take possession of his little kingdom, the smoke-blackened forge, the bellows, the anvil, the vise, the hammers and drills. The stretcher on which he was lying, the cardboard identification on his chest, the road back—Bopfingen, his smithy, his small, humble house in the Untere Kochengasse, his wife in the kitchen of his home, after work his pint at the pub, a chat with a drayman or a farmer from Härdtfeld—after all he had been through these things implied so much happiness that he could not grasp it, and this snow-covered field with its great, broad-winged birds that were to carry him back to such a wonderful, simple, natural life seemed to be sheer fantasy to him. He could not believe it; it would go against the stern law that now—he had known this for many days—governed his life.

And it was all fantasy.

Steiger was probably the only one of all these men who understood from beginning to end what he now witnessed, whose eyes took in all that one man could of the many-footed, rioting monster. He saw, he understood, and he assented. For when his chest was trampled, his ribs driven into his lungs, and a bloody foam appeared on his lips, he breathed the words, "Yea and Amen!"

For days the flak regiment had had standing orders to fire upon the mob if necessary. Now the guns had been cranked down to fire at ground level, but the gunners did not fire. The snow was being trodden by hundreds of feet, feet shuffling along wrapped in rags, blankets, scraps of canvas. There were others who moved faster, who burst through the ranks of those with leg and foot injuries and, with dilated eyes, gaping mouths, and distended nostrils, panted up to the plane. The shrieks that filled the air did not come from the men who had been knocked down and trampled—they lay still with their faces in the snow—but from those who were too slow and remained behind.

Sacks of beans, chocolate, bread, round jugs of whisky were

trampled to bits, and among these things, looking scarcely different from the sacks, were the bodies of soldiers, the faces of men who had fallen. They did not rise again; kicked down repeatedly by felt-wrapped, swollen feet, they became a solid mass and served as the ramp to the cabin door and the interior of the plane. The ramp grew, it rose so high that "the strong, the victors, the winners," had to stoop to get into the cabin. The men of the guard were stunned by the piercing screams and the air impregnated with death. They used their rifle butts to clear a path to the entrance, but when they reached the top of the heap they threw away their weapons and themselves pressed into the plane. Stragglers, wounded men, stretcher bearers, soldiers, and officers thrust and pushed and forced their way in. There was room in the cabin for only twenty men and as yet no more than half the plane's cargo of rations had been unloaded. But the pilot had no choice; there was no time, no help in sight, and the mist was rising. He scrambled into his seat. The motor and propeller roared, snow was churned up, the mob screeched and fell back. The cabin door was still open. Arms, legs, and bodies hung out. The plane bounced back to the ground twice, then rose clumsily into the air.

It happened when the second Junkers started.

As the plane—also encrusted with human beings—began to move forward with a roar, the mob reeled back out of the way and stumbled into the row of stretchers on which lay the critically wounded men. Some of these wounded were killed, and one of them was Steiger. He did not die immediately; he raised his head once more. He saw the huge bird skimming through the snow, saw it shake off dark clusters of human creatures. He saw the horde of the condemned who were left behind on the field.

Dying, Steiger asked himself a question and answered it. Have I set fire to a house? No. Have I taken away a peasant's cow? No. Did I have any need of the Volga? No, no, no. But others needed it and others set fire to houses, stole cattle, filched bread from widows' cupboards. And I have seen women and children carried off. Captain Steiger, Coppersmith Steiger, you went along with it. . . . There is no returning to your forge, your bellows, your house on the Untere Kochengasse. You are dying . . . not for Bopfingen, not for Germany, but for the land of the Kalmucks. There is the guilt.

He looked once more with dying eyes. The wide, white field had narrowed. With its mass of howling, despairing figures who feebly toiled eastward, it had become a white-hot pot with gray bubbles of foam rising to the top. It was a melting-pot—and the scum was being skimmed off and thrown upon the refuse heap.

"And the crooked shall be made straight. Yea and Amen!" So died Captain Steiger.

It grew dark over Pitomnik. In the middle was the broad airfield, surrounded by a line of pillboxes. In rows stood dead tanks, trucks, canvas-covered wagons, hundreds of them pointing in all directions, capped with thick masses of snow, without fuel, without life. Between the rows of vehicles ran lanes that resembled the streets of a deserted city. And a few miles to the south Pitomnik village (it had been bombed to bits; only a few huts were still standing and life had long since moved underground and into concrete shelters) was deserted, abandoned. Doors stood open and banged back and forth in the wind. Scraps of canvas hung from the tents that had housed the wounded. On the doors and walls of bunkers were inscriptions: "Garrison Command Post—Army Post Office—Armory—Ammunition Depot—Delousing Station—Rations—Airport Command—Stragglers Collecting Station. . . ." But there was no one in sight, no men at all. In trucks, horse carts, wagons, and sleds, or clinging to these vehicles and falling off and limping forward on foot, scattered again, run over or kicked by the horses of the columns that followed, the frantic mob had swept on eastward. Some got as far as Gumrak, some as far as Stalingradski, and some even reached Stalingrad.

The trumpets of Jericho. Not a shot from a tank, not the sight of a tank, but a cry of fear from a human voice, taken up and passed on by a thousand terrified men, had unleashed this fantastic flight. And now Pitomnik was depopulated, deserted, abandoned, and only the icy breath of the Volga passed over the vast graveyard of vehicles and the ruins of houses and shelters. The only sounds that emerged from the mist were the whimpers of dying men, and somewhere in the mist monotonous questions and sobbing answers could be heard. Somewhere in the mist a kneeling figure was bent over an outstretched soldier, and from the uniform depended a gleaming silver chain with a crucifix at the end of it.

"No, I don't want to . . . just for once I want . . ."

"What do you want just for once, my boy?"

"Eight years in the Hitler Youth, then labor service, then farm service, then a soldier . . . for once, chaplain, I want to live without dress inspection, without falling in; for once I want to be alone for a while, and I don't want to . . . I don't want to . . ."

"An infant does not want to go to sleep, my son. But when its mother lays her hand upon its eyes, the eyes close of themselves. . . ."

The dying man's throat rattled, his body writhed.

"Our Father Which art in Heaven . . ."

The chaplain's fingers reached out and closed the soldier's eyelids. He took the man's paybook from his breast pocket, broke off the lower part of the identification tag (perforated for the purpose) and put it away. His fingers performed mechanically an action practiced hundreds of times. His lips murmured: ". . . Father, grant him eternal rest. And may he behold the Eternal Light."

The chaplain walked on slowly. Army Chaplain Kalser was on his way from Pitomnik to Stalingrad. Once he had been vicar in Höxter on the Weser. He came from the Westphalian coal region, was the son of a miner. When one day he had been faced with the alternatives of concentration camp or becoming an army chaplain, he had chosen the army.

"I am the chaplain of the 376th Infantry Division," he introduced himself whenever he knelt beside one of the figures lying on the road. The 376th Infantry Division had been virtually destroyed fifty-six days earlier on the other side of the Don. Its commander had reorganized it on this side of the Don and it had again been beaten and routed at the Kasachi Hills. Leaderless groups were all that was left of it, and these eddied westward through the snow. The chaplain had not fled with division headquarters. He had remained where the men were dying and had followed along behind one of the groups, accompanied by his Protestant colleague, Martin Koog, and by his sexton, Hans Schellenberg. They had carried their baggage on a toboggan which they pulled by turns. Now, for no visible reason, these groups of stragglers had also scattered to the winds; Koog, Schellenberg, and the toboggan had vanished and Kalser had continued on his way alone.

He closed the eyes of Protestants, Catholics, Germans, Russians. That night the dying proved not to be men who had been shattered by shell splinters and rocket fragments; these men had been crushed, had fallen from vehicles, had been spitted by the shafts of wagons, trampled on by horses, run over by cars, mashed by heavy eight-ton trucks; or else they were freezing to death—wounded men who had fled from the dressing station and been unable to go on through the snow.

The weather had changed. During the day dry snow had

fallen and in the evening it had been foggy, but now the temperature dropped sharply, the sky cleared, and a murderous cold descended.

Chaplain Kalser bent over the next man.

From the look with which the man greeted the priest, Kalser recognized a Catholic. He took out a small purse with the letters OI—*oleum infirmorum*—embroidered on it. Inside was a wad of cotton that had already touched the foreheads of hundreds of men, and a golden vial no bigger than a thumb which contained the holy oil. The oil was viscous from cold.

"Do you wish to have the Saviour?"

"Yes!" the eyes glowing in the mist replied. The hand that reached out for the little purse could not complete its motion. Under the beneficent touch upon his brow, under the soothing hand, the dying man's death rattle grew feebler. Perhaps he saw once more the Eternal Light in his village church, perhaps breathed once more the air of his native soil, saw once more his mother or his wife at home. Then the eyes dilated, the body twisted in the last agonies, and it was over.

"Chaplain, stay with me!" the next man pleaded.

Please take this letter with you, please write to my wife, others requested. Almost all of them asked for transportation. Many wanted a cigarette, many wanted bread.

Dying men who wanted to smoke a cigarette! Dying men who asked not for holy bread, but for a piece of ordinary black bread. The chaplain had no cigarettes and no bread. Five wafers were all he had left and he did not know to how many dying men he would have to offer the viaticum. And he had to keep the holy oil deep in his trousers pocket to keep it from freezing, and he had to keep at least one hand warm to bless and to administer the last sacraments.

A face in the snow. The snow white, the face yellow.

"What is your name, my boy?"

"Hollwitz."

"How can I help—I am the chaplain of the 376th."

"A cigarette—then I won't need anything more."

Von Hollwitz recognized the chaplain, and Kalser also recognized Staff Captain von Hollwitz who had taken over an emergency company in Vertiachi. The chaplain listened to his story —the words emerged stertorously from the man's failing lungs. Von Hollwitz had been wounded and taken to Pitomnik airport to be flown out. One frightful night (the snow had blown into the tent and the wounded men had been dying silently, one after the other, with no doctors or medical aides present) he had got up from his cot, gone to the doctors' shelters, and demanded that as many of the wounded as possible be shifted from the tents to the shelters, so that they could be kept alive until they were flown out. But nothing was done; instead the commander of the medical company had said to him: "Let me see your flight certification, captain; it has to be checked once more." And the certificate had never been returned to him, so that he could not be flown out and was condemned to death.

And now: a snowy night, a fearsome sky, a chaplain.

A rude peasant of a chaplain. . . . Von Hollwitz recalled very well the last time he had seen this chaplain, that day he was burning his letters. Good God, no . . . all the wretchedness of it gripped young Hollwitz. He lost his self-control; he sobbed and red, bloody foam rose to his lips. His arm and one side of his chest were bandaged, his coat draped over his shoulders. Like all the wounded men who could still walk, he had fled from the tent. On the road he had waved at the cars, but in vain. None of them had stopped. He had tried to force one to stop by placing himself in the road; the car had hit him and knocked him down, and there he had lain. Twenty years old. In his pocket he had the last letter from his father, the only one he had not burned. ". . . Yesterday, right from our shooting box, a fourteen-pointer. I had my sights on him—but no, I'm saving him until you come back. He's for you." A fourteen-pointer . . . and Ilse, my God . . . and a scoundrel of a medical company commander and a scoundrel of a driver and snow and night and in the night a chaplain . . . My God, it couldn't, couldn't be so.

But the rude peasant's hand was human warmth, a reassuring contact in the last agonies. Hollwitz stopped struggling so violently against death; his groans died away to a low whimpering. After a while Chaplain Kalser closed the young officer's eyes, folded his hands over his breast and broke off and pocketed the half of the dog tag.

The road stretched out before him, the earth white, the sky above it gray. In the snow lay dead, dying, and living men. In the snow were bogged-down automobiles, cursing drivers. Men were making use of their steel helmets and bare hands to shovel the wheels free and to clear patches of road. Sweating brows, arms lame from cranking, frozen motors that would not start. Sleds pitched on their sides, overturned wagons, stray horses plodding wearily away and vanishing into the night beside the road.

Groups of limping figures staggering slowly on.

"Where to, boys?"

"To Stalingrad."

"But what's the good of going to Stalingrad?"

Uncomprehending looks, idiotic bursts of laughter. The snow crunched under their feet. Beside the road a dark triangle bobbed up; a dying horse thrust itself upon its forelegs, collapsed again.

Stalingrad! Where else was there to go, what else was real in this cold white chaos? Snow crunched, knees shook, weary feet dragged the burden of exhausted bodies. Noses white with cold. Ears falling off. Freezing tears. Thick, meaningless babbling.

"Where to?"

"Stalingrad!"

"What's the matter, my boy?" —"I must sit down—my heart." —"Sit still, I'll stay with you." —"My heart and my feet too . . . and that skunk, Wedderkop."

"Who is Wedderkop?"

"In Pitomnik, he . . ."

In Pitomnik Lieutenant Wedderkop had driven off to Stalingrad with the truck, leaving the driver and his companion behind.

"And what is your name?"

"Kalbach, chaplain."

"Feel better now?"

"Worse—I must lie down."

"Go ahead. Here's your pack for a pillow and your blanket over you. I'll stay here. Where are you from?"

"Urbach in Thüringia . . ."

The face dissolved; the man spoke in a changed, distant voice: "Martha, you must not lift such heavy weights now. . . . Now, sir, you'll have to help thresh, because Martha can't work now, and in this cold I can't do it either. . . . No, all that's keeping me going is will; otherwise I'd break down . . . have to deliver a ton of rye and three hundred pounds of oats and a ton of hay and five tons of potatoes . . . it's too much. . . ."

The delirious man's voice faded to a murmur.

"Tomorrow I'll thresh the last of the grain, then deliver the hay . . . why to Stalingrad . . . all right if only they'd let me alone. . . . They're loading straw at the station again . . . but we won't give them any, do you hear, Martha . . . Martha, do you remember. . . ."

A snowflake fell upon Kalbach's nose, another on his lips, and did not melt. Again half the identification tag was broken off and placed with the others in the chaplain's coat pocket.

Protestants, Catholics, atheists . . .

He blessed them all. He gave the sacraments to those who

wanted them; he did not admonish those who preferred to die without them. Words had become cheap and without force. He held the hands of the men who were afraid, laid his fingertips upon the dying, and when they had died he breathed a mother's kiss upon their brows. With each dying man he died, and with each sufferer he felt his own guilt swelling.

The Chaplain of the 376th, who was the son of a miner from Oberhausen, was not learned in the Scriptures; but the symbol of grace was within him and he saw it rise out of the snow and tower up to the sky. That it was only a symbol, and that in other geographical and spiritual zones of humanity other symbols, such as Tao, Justice, Reason, are set in its place, was no concern of his, for he was a simple son of his Church.

Many symbols—what matter if they express the same thing? Many signs, but only one truth. But truth had no abode, truth was dethroned, the bonds of humanity broken. There was no longer any obligation to speak the truth, to do right. Words were cheap. Might had become Right. Killers in the army of Hitler had succumbed to the madness, priests in the army of Hitler had succumbed to it, some in apostasy, others overcome by their guilt and drawn into the vortex.

Sin . . . atonement. If cause could remain without effect, sin without atonement, the equilibrium of the world would be upset. There could be no order; all men would only turn away from God.

But that was impossible!

Bones jutting through clothing, intestines oozing from bellies, eyes lit with madness, men trampled in gullies like broken crockery. The kneeling priest demanded of none what his sin might be. He asked of none, he wanted to hear nothing, no confession. What confession could Kalbach, or young Captain von Hollwitz, the blanched boy who wanted to be alone just for once—what confession could they make? Their tiny contribution could never have raised the scale of wrath so high; those who did penance all the way from the Rossoshka ravine to Pitomnik, and on from Pitomnik through Gumrak and to Stalingrad—none of these atoned for their own guilt alone.

They were the sacrifice. And sacrifice atones for all.

† This symbol the priest saw rising from the snow and towering into the sky. There it was, come again, challenging and pointing the way, making order out of chaos, mending all that was broken, making the crooked straight. The priest walked through the snow towards the sign. He blessed the dying no longer. His fingers were frozen and his hand, clutching

144

the capsule of holy oil, was like hard wood. And it was not only to the icy wind blowing from the east that he bowed his head.

He wandered over an apocalyptic land.

General Vennekohl had been right.

" 'Violet' can't be held any more; I'd lay my bets on 'Sunflower,' " he had said. And "Violet" could no longer be held. A huge hole had been revealed in this defense line. The remnants of the 376th Infantry Division and the 29th Motorized Division which had been routed on the west front had poured through Pitomnik without stopping, a horde of weaponless and dying men. The 3rd Infantry Division (motorized), coming out of the Marinovka salient, had been destroyed by the snowstorm and panic; many had died under the wheels and caterpillar treads of their own vehicles. The sector of the defense line assigned to this division was never occupied. It was impossible to stuff the gap with fleeing troops stopped en route and led back to the front. The troops in other parts of the line had to fall back, and these included Keil's and Vilshofen's combat groups and Lundt's regiment.

Although the line was falling back in defiance of orders, the generals were determined that Pitomnik must be held, at least for three days or two or one—until the ration depots there could be evacuated. Vilshofen's, Lundt's, and Keil's groups were among the units in the flood of retreating troops which were ordered to form a wide arc around Pitomnik airfield and village. There was also a unit known as Schwandt's regiment.

At the same time that Pitomnik was being evacuated in panic, Brigadier General Gönnern sat in a shelter in a *balka* that branched off from the Tulevoy ravine; opposite him, his coat still on, suitcases, sleeping bags, and other paraphernalia all around him and more being carried in by the drivers, stood Major General Damme, who had just arrived. His division which was popularly called by the soldiers and Three D Division, had now ceased to exist. It was in sober truth dead, drowned, damned. And the men that were still left applied the same words to their commander. Damme, as he stood there with his jaw slack, and his blue eyes like those of a dead fish, looked dead, drowned, and damned.

"There's something left," he replied in answer to Gönnern's question about his division. "Steinle, Colonel Steinle, is outside rounding up all the men he can. We'll probably get a combat group out of it yet."

He turned to his orderly and snapped, "Come on, now, unpack those things. No, not that one. The cigars must be in the brown suitcase." He glanced around the bunker for the first time. "Not bad here. Revetted all around, built-in bunks, curtained too, and pictures on the walls—nudes and all. First rate!"

"A unit of field police was stationed here," Gönnern said. As a married man and the father of three grown daughters he did not relish being suspected of having papered the walls of his bunker with naked girls and pages from picture magazines.

"No doubt, no doubt, Gönnern," Damme replied.

The orderly had found the cigars. He handed the box to Damme, who offered them to Gönnern and then took one himself. After the first few puffs he began to grow more animated.

"Yes, Gönnern, it's one hell of a mess. Everything, absolutely everything has gone to pot. Kletskaya was bad enough." He spoke as if Kletskaya was a place out of another life. "But now —on the Kasachi hills two hours of barrage wrecked everything. Wasn't a chance to hold there."

Another puff at the cigar.

"You should have heard Hube. . . ." At Dmitrevka General Hube, the commander of the tank army, had been Damme's nearest neighbor. "Yes, you should have heard him shooting his mouth off. And all the time he could see the way we were melting away. He flew out to report to the Führer. You'd think he would have said that it was crazy to go on here and plain suicide. But when he came back: We have to hold out. And that's all he brought back. Not a tank, not a man, nothing but words. At Dubininsky he had a foxhole dug for himself. 'For defense at close quarters. We'll stop them here,' he boasted. You know what came of that? He flew out again, and this time he hasn't come back. But we're left holding the bag."

"What, Hube too?"

"Don't tell me there's someone else?"

"Pickert flew out a few days ago." Gönnern recounted how he had returned, circled the airdrome, radioed down that he was sorry he couldn't land, and flown off again. "It raised the devil of a stir in the flak division," Gönnern said. "Bewilderment, discouragement, sheer fury."

"No doubt, no doubt."

"And now Bär has come back."

"Was he out too?"

"Yes, to report to the Führer."

"What did he bring back?"

"Definite promises with regard to supplies, I hear. Reich Marshal Göering himself is going to take the matter in hand now."

146

"Let him come out here himself and take a look at the way things are bitched up in Pitomnik."

"At least he ought to inspect the base airdromes at Shachty and Mariupol."

"What! Shachty and Mariupol? I thought Morosovsky and Salsk were the base airdromes."

"Once upon a time, Damme. Nobody knows just where the front is today."

"Pickert cut loose at the right time. But we're still right here in the trap, and everything's falling to pieces. It's sheerest idiocy to go on holding out here. I've got to admit it, Gönnern. In our present situation there's nothing left to do but to capitulate."

"No such thing. That was another message Bär brought back. The Führer is said to have called for Draconian measures. 'There is no such thing as capitulation,' he said. We are to take him as our example."

"What is that supposed to mean, Gönnern?"

Gönnern shrugged. "Am I supposed to turn teetotaler, like him—that's what I've come to now, anyway. The cigars are running low, too. Good God, he can't want to see all of us stretched out in the snow."

"Speaking of teetotaling, I still have a bottle of brandy left," Gönnern said. He had, as a matter of fact, several bottles left. Conditions being what they were, he was going easy with the brandy; most of the time he used it only as a nightcap, to help him sleep. Now, however, he had the open bottles and two glasses brought in. He had not yet filled the glasses when his G-3 burst in, followed by his adjutant. They had with them the mess officer and a civilian official of the supply administration.

"Pitomnik has fallen, sir!"

"What? How? How is that possible?"

The G-3 pushed the mess officer forward. The man seemed more dead than alive; he looked as if he had just been picked up out of the snow. His coat was open, the buttons missing, the pockets ripped out, His face was bruised.

"A tank attack."

The man stammered incoherent phrases—tanks—at the airfield, at the ration office, at Pitomnik village—vehicles jammed up everywhere—forty-four trucks at the loading area—inconceivable, sir—fleeing troops—indescribable scenes. . . .

But no precise information as to the strength of the attack, the direction from which it had come, or the troops that were opposing it, could be extracted from the captain.

The telephone rang. The G-3 picked up the receiver and talked with the G-3 of the army corps. Troops were to be withdrawn from the west front and transferred to the south. Head-quarters was considering pulling Vilshofen's group out of the division's line.

Gönnern flared up. "Out of the question," he snapped. "The front isn't holding anyway. Pulling Vilshofen out would . . ." A thought suddenly occurred to him. "But where is Vilshofen if Pitomnik . . ." Vilshofen's combat group had been stationed far to the west of Pitomnik.

Gönnern pounded his fist on the table. He glared at the mess officer.

"Did you see any tanks, Captain Wenzel?"

"No, sir."

"Has there been any attempt to get in touch with Vilshofen?" he asked his G-3.

"Not yet, sir."

"Do so, do so."

Vilshofen's group responded as usual. Vilshofen was still fronting west as he had been doing for the past ten days, fighting defensive battles and rear-guard actions. At the moment the group was heavily engaged against tanks and infantry, but Vilshofen knew nothing of any penetration to his rear.

Moreover—the telephone connection with Vilshofen passed through Pitomnik.

"What the devil is wrong here? This is the worst devil of a mess in this whole stinking war. What's going on, Captain Wenzel? Did you evacuate the rations?"

"No, sir."

"Why not? I'd like to know why not, if you please!"

"The rations office has . . . has . . ."

"Has what?"

"Has been liquidated, sir."

The corps telephoned again "The Commanding General wishes to inquire what deviltry has been going on in the territory of your division and requests an immediate report."

"Am launching inquiry, will report when clarified," Gönnern shouted to his G-3, who passed on the message.

Meanwhile Major General Damme had applied himself to the bottle of brandy. He merely shook his head and looked at each of the excited men in turn.

"Just the way it began in Novo-Alexeyevka," he remarked. "The whole army is ripe for the madhouse."

*At that same momen*t acting battalion commander Lieutenant Lawkow tramped through the night. Snow was sifting down steadily. He was weary; his every bone ached and his shoulders felt bowed by an intolerable burden. He walked with bowed head; the bottom of his coat trailed on the ground and was heavy with frozen snow. He scarcely knew he was moving, but step by step he marched across the white terrain toward a ravine where Colonel Lundt and the regimental staff had their headquarters.

Captain Henkel had lasted only one night with the battalion. When the attack began and a mortar shell hit the crevice where the "combat command post" was located, Henkel had crawled into the farthermost corner of the hole. That would not have been so bad; Lawkow had done the same. But Henkel had lain as if dead, unable to utter a word, to think or to issue an order. Then, when the attacking Russians' "Oooray," rang out, he had sprung to his feet and run off. He had not been seen again and Lawkow had resumed command of the battalion.

Lawkow tramped on through the night. Snow eddied around him, automatic guns flashed, and mortar shells threw up geysers. Lawkow tried not to think of how many men were walking behind him. The battalion had numbered nearly a thousand men when it was pulled out of the northern switch position; there had been four hundred left when Captain Henkel came to take over. . . . He tried not to think, but in spite of his leaden weariness scenes, faces appeared to him, voices sounded in his ears. They were the faces of yesterday, they were voices that would never speak again.

Lieutenant Lawkow reached the ravine. He passed the sentry, strode through the tiny anteroom of the bunker, and entered the main part of the plank-revetted dugout. There the regimental commander sat at a table in the glow of a lamp.

The commander looked up and gripped the edge of the table with both hands as he stared at the little lieutenant who ought at this moment to have been in the front line.

The images of the past rose again in Lawkow, and he said, "Here I stand, God help me."

He stood, indeed, straight as a rod. Colonel Lundt sprang to his feet, his face white, his voice trembling. "What's the matter, Lawkow? Where is your battalion?"

"The battalion is waiting outside," Lieutenant Lawkow replied. "I must inform you, sir, that the battalion now consists of four men."

At that same moment Colonel Carras was sitting in his "furnished toothpick," where he had just established himself. He had visited Army Headquarters in a ravine near Stalingradski; they had sent him to Stalingrad, where he had been assigned quarters in the ruins of a large department store, the seat of a regimental command post. The constant coming and going had disturbed him and the damp cellar air depressed him, and so he had moved to a temporary billet at the top of the ruin, adjacent to an artillery observation post. All day long he had a fine view of the wreckage of Stalingrad, of the broad flat land on the other shore of the frozen Volga. He had found an armchair in the rubble, and a bookshelf held an ashtray and a few utensils. The window opening was stuffed with wood and rags. So he sat in his coat and sheepskin shoes, a writing pad on his knees, summing up in catchword notes his first impressions of the Stalingrad pocket.

"Most obvious: complete breakdown of supplies. Shortage of everything. Rapid decline in troops' fighting power. Loose behavior, lack of discipline, wild rumor-mongering. Confusion in all the staffs, a dangerous prevailing atmosphere of nervousness. Hope of help from outside coexists with loss of faith in own strength. . . ."

These notes were an outline for a written (or preferably an oral) report to the Army High Command in Berlin. Naturally, Carras could not permit himself to stray too far from the official view of the situation, but he had already drawn his own conclusions and personally he went much further than his report would go. He had been in Pitomnik, in Gumrak, at the northern switch position, and on the southern front. Although he had been inside the pocket for only a few days, he had talked with dozens of officers, with chiefs of staffs, with commanders, and even with two corps commanders. For all his mental toughness he had been shocked. Everybody outside the pocket, every captain on home duty, such as the man he had met a week ago in the sleeping car between Munich and Berlin, to say nothing of the officers at the Army High Command, knew more about the situation than the encircled men themselves. At GHQ there were no longer any illusions about the fate of the Sixth Army; those officers who called attention to the number of men, the almost 300,000 soldiers inside the pocket, and based a show of optimism on that, were doing so only because that was the official tack to take. Everyone knew that the figure was by now meaningless, that military sins would not go unpunished, and that in this case the disaster would be all the more shattering.

The commanders of troops were presumably men of judgment and decision, given to sober examination of the facts. Yet they, who were most concerned, whose personal affair it was, knew nothing. In the existing situation Carras would have considered nervousness, panic, and despair only natural. But to see the pendulum swing the other way and to find the commanders of regiments, divisions, and even whole army corps, men forty and fifty years old with twenty or thirty years of service behind them—to see such men obsessed by an innocent, childish, almost mystical belief in "the Führer's promise" was shocking to Carras. After all, these were generals and colonels whose business it was to guide thousands and tens of thousands of men. They talked about attempts to break out of the ring and went so far (as they had done in planning "Operation Thunderclap") to issue orders for blowing up ammunition and equipment that the army would not be able to take with it on its "trip." Then, on the following day, they would cancel the plan, only to find themselves poorer than before, lacking even more of the barest necessities. Nevertheless, they immediately began planning new operations, and when these too could not be carried out or were forbidden by the Führer's headquarters, they said, "Very well, we'll stay where we are and they'll break through to us." Who was going to break through to them—the Japanese? For Manstein and the defeated Don army group had not yet recovered from the destruction of Hooth's tanks and the collapse of the Don front. They were all saying kind words about the sad situation of the Sixth Army (which belonged to Manstein's army group), but not one of them would have given a red cent for its chances.

Carras had met one man, a general from an old Prussian military family, who had his hand on the patient's pulse and was clear-sighted enough to observe the progressive paralysis of the organism. No wonder the man's nerves were quivering, no wonder he was disturbed. For he himself, his army corps, and all his man were a part of that organism; he was a cell in it and could not help recognizing that all the symptoms indicated the impending death of the patient.

He had met one such man; perhaps there were two or three others. But most of them exhibited nothing but flickering hopes, clouded judgment, numbed wills. The pocket would really provide a field day for a psychiatrist, Carras reflected. Here was a specimen stretched out on a board for observation, an exhibit of mass psychosis unique in history. What notes could be taken here for a paper on the slackening of physical activity, on the dulling of intellectual, moral, and physical resistance, on the pathology of the new "pocket disease," an epidemic resulting in mass deaths. But he had not been sent here to act the psychiatrist; the Army High Command and the Führer's headquarters were not interested in this side of the matter. There was no need for him to observe the symptoms. And, God help him, not only the commanding general, not only the wounded men at Pitomnik airport, but he himself was already caught up in the decay; he was already part and parcel of it; he too was a cell in the organism which was writhing in its death throes.

At that same moment Lieutenant Stetten of the signal corps was sending and receiving messages in the snow-covered radio station at Gumrak. One message to the Chief of the General Staff at GHQ in Berlin, General Zeitzler, read: *"We are nearing a disaster here. Almost no rations, little ammunition, little fuel.* Question: *What does the Führer say to this?"*

Some incoming messages read: *"Congratulations to command and troops for great defensive success. Am awaiting proposals for decorations.* Signed: *von Manstein." "Express my gratitude and admiration to 2nd Grenadiers Regiment 134.* Signed: *von Manstein."* (To whom could the gratitude and admiration be expressed? The regiment no longer existed.) *"My gratitude and congratulations to Vilshofen combat group. Colonel Vilshofen is promoted to brigadier general, effective 1 / 1 / 43.* Signed: *von Manstein."*

At that same moment, just before the first houses of Stalingrad, a large truck skidded on a steep, icy patch of road. The driver was inexperienced with trucks and applied the brakes. The truck whirled around, slid across the road, went over the bank and overturned. Beside the battered wreckage, amid truck parts and quantities of provisions that had been loaded on in Pitomnik, Lieutenant Wedderkop sat up. He might have remained sitting there until the next day and until he froze to death, or he might have been picked up by a patrol and delivered to the city military government headquarters. But he was picked up by another kind of patrol, by a sergeant named Lachman who was hunting for loot. As soon as he caught sight of the lieutenant sitting bolt upright and had exchanged a few words with him, he realized what had happened.

"The umbilical cord has obviously been cut," Wedderkop said, speaking distinctly and without expression. "Yes," Lachman replied, "it's quite obvious to me too, lieutenant." —"But the main thing is our fighting spirit; that remains."—"Of course, that remains even without an umbilical cord."—"Fighting spirit, alliance with nature, becoming part of nature itself, that is the basis of our profession. What, by the way, do you think of our general situation?" —"Somewhat cloudy," Lachman replied, "but still I think I see the silver lining." He enumerated what he saw: "Peas, chocolate, bread, beef. And there's schnaps in there too, isn't there?" —"Yes, a full day's

152

ration for the group." —"Splendid. But how about standing up now? It must be getting cold around the seat of your pants." —"Yes, rather cold."

The situation was quite clear to Lachman. The lieutenant had obviously skipped out with the whole load of rations, skidded into the ditch, and was now suffering some sort of concussion of the brain. But what should he do with him? It wouldn't do to let the man sit here—might attract others to this rich hoard. He pulled Wedderkop to his feet. The fellows's limbs were sound; only his head had been injured. Still and all, he was a disciplined fellow. Lachman loaded him like a pack mule and himself took everything he could carry. Then they set out, by bypaths that avoided sentry posts, toward Stalingrad. They passed over fields of rubble, through barbed-wire entanglements, through holes in buildings, and finally descended steps into a cellar. So Wedderkop entered one of the dens of the "Stalingrad underworld," one of the hiding places of the marauders whose numbers were constantly increasing.

THE DEATH BLOW CAME FROM THE SOUTH.

Seven days had passed since the Soviet High Command had made its offer of surrender terms. For seven days the pressure from the west and southwest had persisted. Breaches had been made in the ring of defenders; they had withdrawn and again closed these gaps. But there were new penetrations, the lines were rolled back, from the west toward Pitomnik and the railroad line and from the southwest toward the railroad line, which represented the last line of defense.

Pitomnik had been abandoned in panic. Army Headquarters ordered the supply services to visit Pitomnik again and evacuate its supplies. It was quite late, toward eleven in the morning (darkness fell shortly after three) before the finance officers with their retinue of supply sergeants and corporals and their long columns of trucks arrived at the airport. Several trucks also carried the flight control officers and the ground crews—those who had been stopped in their flight, that is. It was high time they returned: two Junkers and a huge four-motored Condor were circling like bewildered birds over the abandoned nest. They did not dare to land without signals or instructions from the ground and without knowing what they would find on this vast cemetery of machines.

They were given landing signals and settled to the ground. The pilots left their seats, clambered out, and stretched their legs. They left motors and propellers running, for unloading and loading had to be finished in ten or twenty minutes and they must be ready to start immediately. They looked around; one of the two Junkers pilots who had been here frequently wrinkled his nose and sniffed suspiciously. Something had happened here, something was different about the place. The perpetually excited flight director was not excited; his face was gray and he said nothing. The pilot looked at a near-by Stork. A bus had run into it and smashed the cabin. There had been other collisions on the field. He noticed a jeep that was running

154

around from one group of parked planes to the next, stopping briefly near each. Then he turned and looked in another direction over the field. Dead men lay in the snow. The pilot glanced at the other pilot and they sauntered toward the dead. A row of stretchers upon which lay men with bandaged heads, arms or legs in splints, set faces. They had frozen to death here.

"Twenty-eight," one of the pilots counted.

"I've never seen anything like this."

Where were the ambulance men, where were the wounded who were to be flown out? Not that there was any lack of passengers; all of them were wounded or had eyes glittering with madness; but this time all of them came forward on their own feet.

"That fellow over there," one of the pilots said, pointing to a figure in a high fur cap who was tramping across the expanse of snow, "that fellow had eight pieces of blue cloth in his hand and he offered them to me if I'd take him along."

The man in the fur cap was on his way to the Condor.

The pilots walked over to the Condor. The plane stood there with its tremendous wings and its four propellers straight lines against the winter sky. They were standing still. The Condor pilot had turned off the motors. He was standing beside his plane, hunched up and shivering with cold. His eyebrows were white with frost, his face gray; plainly, he was dressed too lightly.

"Say there, what the devil are you doing, turning off your motor? It'll freeze up on you."

"Freeze up?"

The pilot did not know or had not thought of it. He was an Atlantic flyer, had flown from Bordeaux to Mariupol only the day before. He leaped to his seat and tried to start the motors. They turned over, stopped again, started a second and a third time, and then it was over. The starter had burned out.

Where would he get a starter? There was none for a Condor.

For a few minutes the Condor pilot gave no thought to his situation. But when he came up to the flight director he received a shock. "The Russians are advancing on Pitomnik; rocket guns are firing four miles from here," he heard someone saying.

"What about my Condor?"

"Hell, your Condor!" The flight director glanced at the huge plane and then his eyes drifted out over the field where some hundred and fifty planes stood, with starters but without fuel. There's room for a Condor on a pile like that, his glance seemed to say.

The jeep, which was still circling around, stopped in front of the flight director. A captain with a scarred face stepped out.

"I'm sorry, Captain Tomas," the flight director greeted him. "I've been telegraphing around the whole area, but no one knows anything. There's not a trace of him."

Captain Tomas sped off. Army Headquarters had ordered him to find a certain Colonel Schwandt whose unit was supposed to hold Pitomnik village until nine o'clock the following morning, by which time the rations depot would be evacuated.

The two Junkers started off. The Condor pilot watched them rise, then glanced sadly over the airfield. Troops of soldiers were marching past. Like smoke they rose up out of the snow and drifted diagonally across the field. The Atlantic pilot forgot that he was shivering with cold. How could rifles and even machine guns ever fall into the hands of such bands of men, of trash, rather? They had no feet; they moved along on rag bags. Their coats might once have been coats; now they were nothing but stuffed sacks. On the backs of these creatures were blankets, mess kits, sometimes a gay colored quilt and bits of wooden wreckage they had picked up to serve as firewood in their next shelter. Rags, rags everywhere on them. Faces, eyes, cheekbones, and nose showed out of a tangle of mud and beard and scraps of cloth.

One of these men went up to the pilot, put out his hand, and indicated the cigarette the flier had in his mouth. The hand the man had taken from his pocket was wrapped in bandages to the knuckles; the nails protruded like polished black claws. Nearsighted brown eyes were set in a seamed face. The man must once have worn glasses; there were circular rings of scab where the rims had touched the skin and a scabby swelling on the bridge of the nose. The pilot stopped puffing his cigarette; he stared at the man.

"An ally?" he asked.

The man did not understand.

"You're a Croat or something, aren't you?" the flier wondered.

"Think you're funny, hey? Give me the butt," the soldier said. He was handed the half cigarette and greedily took a puff. The man was Private Evald Stüve. He took another puff and passed the rest on to August Fell. Liebsch also had one puff. Then the men tramped on. Mess kits rattled, the bundle of blankets and odds and ends on their backs swayed. Front-line German soldiers! the pilot suddenly realized. That was the moment he forgot how cold he was.

At the rim of the airfield the jeep stopped. Captain Tomas

jumped out, went up to a man and examined his face closely before he gripped his shoulders. "Latte, old boy!"

"Hannes . . . Captain Tomas!"

"Call me Hannes. What are you doing here?"

"We're withdrawing—to Voroponovo."

"How is the old man?"

"Vilshofen . . ."

"What's the matter, what's happened?" Tomas asked quickly as he saw the change come over Latte's young face.

"Nothing, nothing has happened. Everything's all right, he's all right."

Something was not quite all right, Tomas realized. The last time he had seen Vilshofen had been when they laid Runz and Hedemann in the snow. What was the matter with Vilshofen, what was wrong? He had no time now to draw Latte out. On the steppe machine guns were chattering; the wind carried the sound of them as well as the howls of rocket guns. Along the German line smoke and mud and snow mushroomed up and white lights flickered.

Both men looked toward the front.

"They've mounted those damned rocket guns on their tanks and are bringing them up close," Latte said.

"Do you know whether Schwandt's combat group is over there?" Tomas asked.

"No, that's Keil's group—old acquaintances. You know those East Prussians, don't you, sir? MG Battalion 9. The commander is over there in the ravine, sir."

"Come now, call me Hannes."

"Very well, Hannes!"

They shook hands. Latte moved off behind his men. Tomas went back to his car. He decided to drive over to the ravine and talk to Commander Keil. This ravine was the horseshoe-shaped gorge which contained the storage bunkers of the rations office. As in the past, vehicles were jammed up at the entrance to the ravine; this time they were the vehicles mobilized by the supply services to carry out the provisions. Truck after truck rolled down into the ravine, drove up to the bunkers and returned loaded to the road at the other end of the horseshoe. Tomas was about to get into his car when a chattering began up ahead. A machine gun was firing, and farther away an antitank gun. There was a loud, high-pitched explosion, and for seconds a cloud of fine powder hovered above the ravine, then trickled off into the dun sky.

After a pause several more tank shells burst. These detonations acted like a signal. The noise was too much for the nerves

157

of the paymasters and their assistants, and Pitomnik recapitulated its experience of the previous day. The trucks, loaded and unloaded, manned and unmanned (the men who could not reach the trucks shouted, cursed, and tried to run after them), began to move. Tomas was glad that he was still on the airfield, off the road. He saw trucks roaring up toward him, first one, then two, then three abreast, then a group spread across the full width of the road, then the whole lot of them, each trying to pass the other. Fenders were ripped off, sides scraped, and the wreckage remained behind—vehicles that had been forced to the side of the road and had tipped into the ditch or stuck fast in deep snow. Madmen sat at the wheels of these trucks, madmen stepped on the accelerators and shifted the gears; and the others, sitting or clinging behind them, had also lost their heads completely and trembled whenever the wheels slowed for a moment.

For a second time it was not Russian tanks that had scattered this column. Shots fired by a single tank that had broken through had exploded over the ravine. This was enough to produce a flight as wild as that of the night before. Keil's group still lay under rocket-gun fire and under the fire of Russian tanks, but it held its line. Major Keil was a daredevil and had always been lucky, in his assignments, in the execution of his assignments, in winning swift promotions, and in making things comfortable for himself. He had been assigned to defend this ravine and the condition in which he found it (open doors revealing stores of bread, meat, chocolate, and beverages), the fact that he was sole master of this utopia, was only one more point in his long career of lucky chances. It might turn out to be the last time—therefore make the best of it. One never knew. Not that Keil had failed to do everything in his power to bring the paymasters and their men to their senses. "But there was no doing anything with them; they refused to pay attention," he said to Tomas, who had found him sitting at the telephone in a cleared storage bunker.

Keil was giving instructions to his lieutenants, describing the line to which his men were to withdraw as soon as darkness fell. Then he added: "Beef stew tonight . . . and what else, Heinrich?" he asked the mess sergeant who had just come in. "With noodles, do you hear? . . . No, I'm not kidding, the kitchen's going strong. Just take a look around; you're sure to see the smoke rising over the ravine."

He certainly was not kidding. All the cook had to do in order to fill his pots was to reach out into the snow. There lay heaps of supplies that had fallen off trucks—cabbage, meat, sacks of flour. There were mounds of crates all around—clothing, camouflage suits, engineering equipment, cola drinks, cigarettes, tooth powder, canteen supplies.

"When the tank shell exploded over the ravine," Keil continued his account, "they stood there like someone had hit them over the head. Then, when one of our sergeants came sliding down the side of the ravine with his face bloody, nothing could stop them. . . ."

Keil had studied at the Technical High School and had intended to be an engineer; when conscription was introduced he had interrupted his studies and entered the army. At the time the war broke out his father had been running a filling station and garage on the Königsberg-Cranz highway. In the winter of '41, when Keil returned home on convalescent leave after being wounded, he found two new sheds—grandiloquently called "production units"—where his father was engaged in manufacturing parts. Germany was expanding and the private person—if he were efficient and loyal to Führer and Reich—could also expand. A filling station could grow into a factory —such was Keil's simple view of the war. Naturally, difficulties cropped up, shortages of raw materials, scarcity of labor and so on, and some factories were being merged. But Keil's father was a good Party member and had obtained priorities for materials and labor; moreover, he had orders for the first half of 1943. For the time being it was tough going; you had to fight your way through. Stalingrad, too, was tough going and you had to fight your way through.

"This ravine is going to be held," he said to Tomas, "until these bunkers have been eaten bare or until Judgment Day, whichever comes first." He went on to give Tomas his views on the general political and military situation. Things were looking pretty bad in Africa, he admitted. And on the Eastern Front there had been enough of these everlasting withdrawals. It was high time the Führer asserted his authority. Our U-boats would take care of the English and the Americans and chop them down to size. The Russians . . . yes, the Russians were a hard nut to crack, but they were bleeding themselves to death; the very fanaticism of their attacks was a sure sign that they were on the downgrade.

"The main thing is—Stalingrad must fall! If we have Stalingrad, the Japanese too will gradually take the offensive. And meanwhile Tiflis will be taken. Then we'll have the Turks behind us; they'll enter the war too. Then we'll be over the hump. If only we didn't have so many stinkers among us, the situation would be a lot better at the front and in general. One of these days a lot of heads will have to roll."

Keil informed Tomas that Colonel Schwandt had been located south of Keil himself, on his left flank, and had been pressed back so that he was now probably near Pitomnik village. Tomas said good-bye and started off at once for the village. Tiflis and the Turks, the Japanese and the U-boats—there was optimism for you, he thought. But of course that was the way you had to look at the situation; at least you had to make an effort to look at it that way. Still, if Schwandt was in Pitomnik village Keil's left flank was exposed and perhaps Judgment Day would dawn for him and his East Prussians very soon indeed.

Tomas found Colonel Schwandt in a bunker near Pitomnik. The colonel was sitting in front of a kerosene lamp, his head propped in both his hands; on the table lay a pistol. He stared at Tomas as if the visitor were a ghost.

"Captain Tomas," Tomas introduced himself. "I have an army order to transmit to you, sir. Pitomnik village is to be held under all circumstances until tomorrow morning at nine o'clock to permit the evacuation of the airport."

Colonel Schwandt neither moved nor invited the captain to sit down. Tomas was not sure the man had heard his message. His thoughts were obviously far away.

After a while he replied, speaking as if the matter were something that lay in the remote past, which he could recall only with difficulty. "Pitomnik village is an open door. There isn't anyone left there."

Captain Tomas repeated his message. Schwandt repeated what he had said about the open door. That was all. Tomas could get nothing more out of him. Obviously, the situation he had stumbled into was one that no longer related to the world of the living. The colonel again began staring into the smoking kerosene lamp; he stopped listening to Tomas. Tomas glanced once more at the haggard, numbed face with its gray whiskers and light, vacant eyes; he glanced again at the dull-brown weapon on the table, and then he climbed the stairs into the night.

In another bunker he found two soldiers, who started to their feet when he entered. They were eating; they had bread and canned meat which they were extracting from a can with their fingers and eating frozen. They continued to chew as they answered his questions.

"Why no, there's no fighting; that's ammunition being blown up," one of them said. It was ammunition that had already been loaded on trucks. They told Tomas something of what had happened to them, and he realized that Colonel Schwandt no longer had any troops at all. For seven days he had been in flight through the snow from the Karpovka valley. With the remnants of his regiment he had reached Pitomnik village, and there he had lost control of his troops when they encountered the fleeing vehicles from Pitomnik airport and from the west. The rest of the regiment had scattered with the groups that were racing madly eastward.

Tomas thought of Keil's threatened position. He returned to the colonel's bunker. The man was still sitting in the same posture and did not stir when the captain picked up his telephone. But Tomas was unable to reach the airport, the rations depot, or Keil, and so he left again.

Since he had carried out his mission, he started back toward Stalingrad. The road ran into the village, where it met the broad highway from the west that passed through Gumrak and Stalingrad. The surface of the highway lay glistening in the moonlight, marked by countless tracks and deeply rutted. Rifles, machine guns, knapsacks, crates of ammunition, and dead men lay in the snow. In the middle of the road a wrecked bus rose up like a black cliff. Then came a pair and later a group of vehicles that had crashed and had to be skirted. A few men on foot were still coming from the west. They appeared suddenly out of the snow, groups of two and three or five and six. These men struggled on to the farther end of the village, where the road narrowed like a funnel and where, wheel to wheel, radiator to radiator, fender to fender, a tremendous conglomeration of abandoned vehicles blocked all traffic.

There were four thousand, perhaps five thousand vehicles, Tomas estimated. AA and AT guns, trucks and personnel carriers, motorcyles and self-propelled gun mounts, command busses, ambulances, rocket projectors, radio cars, howitzers, tractors. And there was a similar scene only a few miles away at the airport! And had it been any different earlier at Marinovka, Dmitrevka, Novo-Alexeyevka? How many such junk yards had the dying army left behind on the roads over which it had fled?

These graveyards of vehicles were abandoned, but not entirely deserted. Once more, before the wave came and passed over them, life writhed and twitched in them, a wretched, desperate, ugly, tenacious life. Fires flared up in these graveyards, tanks of gasoline and crates of ammunition exploded; there were wounded and dying men there, and sleeping, eating, and swilling men also; there were looters.

Tomas got no farther. He might stay here and the Russians would arrive by dawn at the latest. He might set out on foot as hundreds before him had done. But his little car could do what others could not; he might try to work his way around the rim of this vast parking lot. The jeep with its four-wheel drive began bucking into the snow, backing and smashing forward again. Tomas got out, and while the driver forced a road yard by yard, Tomas fetched boards, coats, and canvas from the abandoned vehicles and laid the things on the surface of the snow to form a road.

In this way Tomas worked his way into the mass. Although he kept to the outer rim of the huge assemblage of wheels and truck bodies and snow-covered cabs, and although he could not know all the secrets, all the suffering that went on in this strange burrow, he saw a good deal.

Some of the things he saw were familiar to him from the past week. On his way from Vilshofen's group to Stalingrad he had seen Karpovka and Dmitrevka abandoned in panic. He was aware that for weeks there had been a standing army order requiring every gallon of fuel to be drained and used exclusively for combat vehicles. But when the grand evacuation and flight began in Dmitrevka and the other rear-area villages on the Stalingrad west front, ample quantities of gasoline had suddenly appeared and the most incredible vehicles, convertibles, coupes, limousines, heavy trucks, and huge busses had rolled out of the farmyards. A whole army of officials, surveyors, economic warfare squads, repair companies, and supply services had started moving. And the most fantastic stuff had been loaded on these vehicles and taken along—only to tumble off or spill out of the cars on the way. Tomas had seen radio sets, surveying tools, and precision instruments smashed with axes, but beds, furniture, suitcases, pictures, plunder, barrels of beer, and sack upon sack of food were loaded on to these vehicles. In Dmitrevka, where the battle line had run right through the rows of tents at the clearing station for wounded, a senior paymaster had not had room for a single casualty, but he had had two fattened pigs loaded into his car. And these were not for his men; Tomas had inquired and found out that they were his "private property." Another vehicle, a small bus, had also had no room for wounded men, but space for three Russian women—cook, laundress, and cleaning woman. And while the wounded wanted to leave, these women wanted to stay behind, but they were made to sit among the sacks of provisions.

At first, as he made his way among the jumble of vehicles,

Tomas saw nothing that he had not already seen in abandoned railroad cars or at Stalingrad during raids upon the hiding places of the Stalingrad marauders. In one truck he saw a man crouching over a torn bag and stuffing dried fruit into his mouth with both hands. In another three men, their hands and faces smeared a sticky red, were scooping jam out of a pail and slobbering it into their mouths. Inside another truck, among the soft upholstery of blankets and assembled rags, he saw a group of five men sitting over a complete banquet. They had quantities of bread, ham, and preserved sausage as well as chocolate and whisky.

"Looters are to be shot within twenty-four hours after capture," the army order read, but Tomas did nothing. What was the sense; the man who was gorging himself on prunes would be writhing like a horse with colic by morning; the others with their pail of jam would also almost kill themselves with eating.

Less out of conviction than out of habit and disgust with the picture they presented, he growled at the five men over their meal. What, after all, could they do under the circumstances but eat their fill for once and follow up the meal with a drink or two?

"Get out of here and rejoin your unit," he snapped.

The five men merely gaped at him and went on eating. He persisted for a moment and found out that three of them belonged to Colonel Schwandt's regiment which was supposed to be defending Pitomnik village. The other two were members of the routed 29th Motorized Division and had been on the road for a whole week.

Tomas went on. He heard a rustling sound inside a truck. When he switched on his flashlight he saw a man bending over an officer's suitcase he had broken open. He had a silver cigarette case in his hand.

"Swine!" Tomas said, and let darkness blot out the scene.

He found a solitary drinker who did not notice Tomas at all and continued talking to himself. More rustling; Tomas heard wounded men groaning inside a truck. One said in a weak voice, "Where are you, comrade? What are you doing? Is help coming? Are we going to start again?" No one answered the man. The only sounds were those of a suitcase's being broken open and the heavy breath of a looter as he rummaged through it.

Tomas walked away quietly.

More rustling and more groaning, more imploring voices. A dying man babbled deliriously. Others pleaded for aid, for a drink of water. The looters ransacked the baggage of furloughed men, dying men, dead men, and paid no attention to anything else.

A shot sounded, then a second and a third. A shell exploded somewhere. Many voices cried out in response. A bleeding soldier ran past, shouting, "We're surrounded. Russians in white snow capes."

Tomas reached his car and took his seat beside the driver. The jeep fought its way through the worst of the snow. By occasionally backing up and plunging ahead again, it made slow progress. The firing continued; tanks shells hit. Trucks filled with ammunition exploded, fountaining up and strewing fire and fragments all around. The huge vehicle park sweated human beings; like black droplets individuals and small groups stumbled through the snow and fled eastward.

The sky was already graying.

Tomas reached the open road at last, passing groups of fleeing men on the way. His car dipped deep down into a gulch and when it regained the level road, Tomas saw before him a whole column of soldiers—without arms, in torn coats, limping along with the aid of sticks on rag-wrapped feet, swaying unsteadily as they moved. Many of them raised their hands and shouted; they all wanted rides, they all wanted to get to Stalingrad. Tomas took along a bareheaded, grayhaired sergeant with a gaping wound in his face.

That night the Russians entered Pitomnik airport and village. A new defense line formed, consisting partly of retreating troops, partly of dispersed and hungry soldiers who for the sake of a crust of bread suffered themselves to be thrown into the front lines again. The new line formed a few miles in front of the tram line, ran south, crossed the Stalingrad-Marinovka railroad line and turned at an acute angle at Pestchanka, from where it led down to the Volga. Voroponovo was the center of the sector of the front facing southwest and south which now became the center of the fighting. Army Headquarters found it necessary to send hastily-assembled troops marching toward Voroponovo. Among these troops were Vilshofen's combat group, Steinle's combat group—which was all that was left of Damme's division—and Keil's combat group, which had also been subordinated to Damme.

Vilshofen arrived at Voroponovo at noon and moved into an unoccupied bunker that had belonged to the rations office. There were other bunkers and a farmstead. Vilshofen ordered the buildings evacuated for his men. His distraught host, a paymaster with the rosy face of a devotee of port wine, came shuffling up in house slippers (although it was already after noon).

Paymaster Zabel had reason to be distraught. At home in Braunschweig he was known as "Bernhard Zabel, Fine Foods, Wholesale and Retail." When, during the German advance, he had been posted on this farm, he had spread himself quite a bit and arranged for a long stay. He kept two horses, a wagon, and a sled for the winter, had a cow, pigs, and a variety of fowl in the barn. He slept on the stove (he had learned to appreciate this Russian comfort; it was like lying on a heating pad all night) in the big "master house." He kept one peasant for tending the stove and another for the barn. Women took care of the housekeeping and all the other inhabitants had been driven away. A master sergeant kept his account books; his chief aide, Sergeant Kulicke, with eight enlisted men, managed everything else. This carefully organized autarchic economy (or semi-autarchic, since it did depend on subsidies) had recently been assailed by the demon of disorder. Zabel had been forced to give up his horses and his cow as well. Now even the poultry feed was running low and his whole beautifully arranged system was going to pieces, or had already done so. Only ruins were left: a few hams, the lard in the crocks, and a pair of ducks. And the stories he heard from the mess officers about the front were far from pretty—were, in fact, horrible. He felt that his informants were trustworthy; many of them had formerly been his overnight guests and he and the veterinary lieutenant who lived next door had spent many pleasant hours with them. It was best, apparently, to take no notice of what was going on at the near-by railroad station of Voroponovo; since ordinary traffic had ceased, all sorts of scum seemed to be assembling there. For his part, he had no direct contact with them; he never went to the station and was satisfied with what the master sergeant, the veterinary, or his right-hand man, Kulicke, told him about it. That was certainly enough. Zabel had done his best to protect the household against the incursion of negligence and anarchy. After all, this turmoil would subside sooner or later; eventually the pocket would have to be opened up again. Meanwhile he must do what he could. However, for the past few days he had been unable to close his eyes to the facts, and he had a foreboding that hard times were coming.

Then, this morning, during the gray noon hour, a dirty, grimy figure, thin as a fence rail, had suddenly appeared in his yard and revealed himself as a colonel and the commander of an alien regiment. And Zabel had to go out as he was, in slippers, and show this apparition around the place. For the paymaster it was the first step of the descent into the abyss. The unit that turned in at the farmyard gate two hours later was the beginning of the end. From then on, whenever he stepped inside the house or in the sheds or in the yard, he ran into these creatures; it made him feel as if he was wading through muck. Still, most of them did move off after a few hours of rest. They might call it "rest"; to him it was anything but restful when they sprawled over the premises and slept with their mouths open. He could not refrain from letting the captain know what he thought of the men he commanded. This captain gave him the impression of being the most civilized of the lot; he never would have mentioned the matter to the colonel, that gloomy fence rail with his vulture's face and burning eyes. But he had ventured to address the captain; he had buckled his belt and put on his cap, gone up to the fellow and said: "Captain, sir, I must inform you that my two ducks which I've had on this farm right along have been stolen by your men." And lest the captain think that a pair of ducks were a trivial matter in times like these, he had added: "I've fattened them for a long time and used to allow myself a duck for Sunday dinner."

At this moment Sergeant Kulicke came up and whispered more bad news in his ear. Zabel added this latest report to his complaint: "I have just learned that the special provisions I keep for the mess officers so they can have a bite when they come back after a strenuous journey have been broken into. A ten-pound pail of jam has been stolen."

The captain appeared to be impressed at first. Then he went over to his men, who had just fallen in, and said: "Look here, men, if any of you have eaten two fat ducks, I wish to inform you that you've eaten the paymaster's Sunday dinner." Then he turned to a man whose face bore the traces of raspberry jam and said, "Private Stüve, ask your sergeant and he'll tell you that under special circumstances a soldier should wash his face not only before, but after a meal."

In short, it was scandalous, it was sheer mockery; the paymaster could not see any other way to interpret it.

"Left face, route step, march!" he heard the captain command. And there Zabel stood, his belt buckled, his best cap on his head, utterly dazed. He saw grinning faces and the tramping of feet of the soldiers. This thing was more serious than just two ducks and a pail of jam. Principles were being trampled underfoot—and by such feet, feet wrapped in rags and scraps of leather. The paymaster turned, confusion in his soul, and went back into his "master house."

Paymaster Zabel's instinct had guided him rightly when he thought that the appearance of Vilshofen's combat group represented the incursion of the underworld and the beginning of an eclipse. No more than forty-eight hours later the main line of defense ran diagonally across his farm. Vilshofen's combat group was now being divided into two sections, one being Döllwang's and the other Latte's. When Döllwang left the farm with his section it was already growing dark; it was night by the time Latte's section departed (at this same hour Captain Tomas was approaching Colonel Schwandt's bunker). Both Latte's and Döllwang's groups crossed the railroad track, left the huge collection of motionless freight cars behind them—a feeble light gleamed in some—and turned southwestward over the frozen snow of the steppe.

Vilshofen remained behind with a few men. He maintained communications with his two groups up front through couriers. A telephone line led back to the headquarters in the Tsaritsa ravine, and he also had a telephone line running cross-country to the adjoining regiment whose commander, a Colonel Enders, had been flown into the pocket three weeks earlier. Enders' headquarters was in a brick factory and he himself was living in a chimney! From Vilshofen's conversation with him over the telephone, he seemed a peculiar sort. The fact that reinforcements were being brought up seemed to indicate that the box around Voroponovo was going to blow sky-high very soon. But Enders seemed to have spent half the night reading Lao-tse. And he asked Vilshofen whether there was a chaplain with his combat group; Protestant or Catholic, it didn't matter. If there was one he wanted to talk to him and would Vilshofen please send him over.

At three o'clock in the morning Vilshofen reported back to headquarters that both his groups had occupied their new positions. Then he lay down for a while. He was tired, but found it hard to fall asleep. Major Hedemann, Major Runz, Captain Steiger, Tomas (Latte had mentioned meeting him earlier in the day), Private de Wede, Gnüssel, Wahler, Dusch, and all the rest of them who had remained behind in the snow. An endless procession of fleeting faces, a succession of fleeting thoughts. The philosophy of Lao-tse . . . and Lieutenant Colonel Unschlicht, a precise, sober officer undeviating in the performance of his duties, gathering a barber-shop quartet around himself and making them sing, "A Mighty Fortress is Our God," and other hymns, with Unschlicht himself accompanying on the flute. . . . and Voroponovo, a vast assemblage of railroad cars and the whole town full of exhausted or pillaging soldiers. . . . And he himself, holding together a group of hungry but still disciplined, still fighting soldiers, and with them a loyal, trustworthy officer he had known as a child. He recalled the first time Döllwang's uncle had lifted the boy to the back of his plow horse. Now, grown up, Döllwang had justified all the hopes that had been placed in him, and Vilshofen felt toward him as a son. But what was he doing? Instead of preserving this group, instead of trying to keep them alive for whatever lay beyond this his death pocket—and surely something would, something would have to, come out of it—instead of saving his men for that something beyond, that better goal, he was letting them march up front again, in order to preserve this suppurating boil and let it ripen for a few more days, although in the rear the stench of it was already rising to the heavens. . . . Why were men like Colonel Enders and Captain Döllwang being sent into the pocket? And they were not the only ones. Was Stalingrad already marked out as an ideal execution ground?

"Beyond Stalingrad"—he remembered that the doctor at Otorvanovka had used such a phrase. Beyond Stalingrad—what did it mean, where must one stand in order to judge it, what could one do when one already lay, a bound and disgraced sacrificial victim, upon the execution block? What was the commander in chief doing? Why did not the generals speak out? Where was the place to stand on from which one could move this world of false calculations, vain arrogance, and vicious contempt of human lives?

Beyond Stalingrad must mean: struggle against military madness, against military (and, no doubt, not only military) criminality.

But, God, what would that lead to . . . ?

Thirty years from the First World War to the Second World War. Didn't we prepare for both, didn't we stake everything on one card, didn't we march triumphantly to the Volga, didn't we think we could derive a one-sided right from the success of our arms?

One-sided view! Fatal faith!

Who could have made us do what we have done voluntarily —serve short-sighted, avaricious interests and sacrifice the lives, the welfare, and the future of our people? Stalingrad was necessary, not for us to triumph, but for us to learn a lesson. Beyond Stalingrad must mean to fight against military— and not only military—criminality. It must mean to turn away from the long wrong road we have traveled, to turn away from our own wrongdoing and above all from the wrongs we have committed against our true selves.

To fight . . . why not start . . . ?

But then his weariness overcame him. Vilshofen lay, for once without his coat, his jacket, or his boots, and for the first time in many days he slept soundly under a real roof.

Before dawn he stood on the platform of the prominent water tower of Voroponovo, amid telephone lines and men wearing head-sets, and stared out into the graying sky. During the night reports had come in of the abandonment of Pitomnik airport and Pitomnik village and the withdrawal of the line to the railroad. Latte, Döllwang, and Colonel Enders had observed movement in the Russian positions. It was clear that a major Soviet attack was impending. Vilshofen looked southwest over the snow-covered steppe. The attack would have to start from there; out there the Russian tanks must be standing. He felt as if he could see them through the snow and mist, spread out in a wide semicircle.

Beside him stood Buchner, the flak commander. Vilshofen remembered him from Kletskaya; he had slept in the same bunker with Buchner one night.

Buchner was talking about fuel.

"If we have to clear out of here too, we'll have a tough time of it, sir," a lieutenant was saying to him. "If we do, we might just as well throw away the heavy flak."

"Out of the question, Stampfer. Drive over to Verkhnaya Yelshanka, to Minina. Go through all the ravines and shake up all the staff headquarters. Take Januscheck with you; he's got a nose for that kind of thing. He'll smell out the gas wherever it is. We've got to have gas, or we're done for."

"I wish I knew why they've sent us here," Buchner said to Vilshofen after Lieutenant Stampfer had left. "There's a gap left on the west front where they took us out and I don't think we'll fill any holes here. We used up almost all of our fuel on the way here—and that's about all the good that will ever come out of it. . . . What's the matter, Loose?"

Buchner's adjutant, Lieutenant Loose, had come up. "I beg your pardon, colonel. . . . Orders from the corps, Herr Major. A change in disposition; the batteries are to be pushed forward."

Major Buchner reached for the telephone.

"Yes . . . what's that? . . . connect me with the chief . . . with his G-3 then. Flak at close quarters—have you gone mad? The

169

guns fire best at two thousand yards. . . . But, sir, they'll pop off my guns like clay pigeons. . . ."

Vilshofen guessed what it was about. There was no doubt that the thin line of his own men stood in need of help. But there was also no doubt that the flak guns would scarcely get a chance to fire in the front lines and would therefore not help very much.

"Very well, sir," he heard Buchner conclude the conversation. In tone it was as if he had said, "Kiss my ass."

Struggle against military madness. But that was not the kind of struggle he had been thinking of during the night. Good God, where was the commander in chief, where was the general, where the officer who would put a stop to this shameful spectacle, who would give the signal for disobedience? It would no longer be disobedience; it was the command of the hour, obedience to a higher duty. And, if the signal did not come, where were the people, where were the men who could cast aside their false leaders and act for themselves? Where were there signs of revolt, of independence, of wrath? What was the matter with the people?

Have we, Vilshofen asked himself, have we so crushed them, so burned out their souls, that there is no spark left in them? He mentally reviewed the faces of his men. And all were empty, no light in their eyes, no hope, no despair. Nothing. Nothing.

Gray day. From the steppe to the southeast and from the Volga Bend a light breeze blew. A flare, shimmering a reddish-yellow, rose up above the steppe, then a second and a third. These signals relieved Major Buchner of the necessity of moving guns up front. They would have to stay where they were now.

For Vilshofen the bursting flares and the flashes of artillery fire that instantly followed were a liberation from his tormenting dilemma. The apparatus that began to function at once took charge of him, required his experience and his decisions, claimed his full attention. There was no room left for questions; there was nothing but fighting.

A motor runs even when it is idling and the power is being put to no use. The range finder reads off distances, the commander entered artillery positions on his map even though he did not have and never would have ammunition with which to combat the enemy batteries. There was just sufficient ammunition to fire against massed tank or infantry attacks.

Minutes passed. The boom of the Russian artillery merged into one long roll of thunder. The smoke, too, the trailing streamers of rockets rising out of hollows in the snow and the muzzle flashes of the batteries coalesced into a single cloud that rolled heavily over the white landscape toward the German positions.

Through the battery commander's telescope Vilshofen observed a movement in the snow. White on white, a whirling and churning of snow. Tanks moving in to jumping-off positons.

"Major, don't you see . . . ?"

"Already spotted."

"Can't you break them up?"

"Can't . . . no ammunition."

A few minutes later. Russian fighter planes. As the formation dived it looked like a dark planet splitting into fragments. The howl of motors, crash of bombs, spurting fountains of earth, debris, flying wreckage of freight cars. A wave of intensely heated air splashed up, passed across the faces of the men on the water tower.

The flak did not fire. The guns were not turned up; they were set for ground fire, for fending off tanks. There was not enough ammunition for any other work. Weak from helpless rage, the flak commander clutched the railing of the observation post and stared out into the cauldron of smoke and fire.

Observation post—but the only thing that men there could observe was their own defeat. The smoke thickened and the billows of smoke from the steppe washed up against the tower, surged high and flooded everywhere. The platform of the water tower floated like a vessel on a dark, heaving sea. The rending metal screeched and the thunderous detonations of the cannon crashed in Voroponovo. The water tower shook like the mast of a ship in a hurricane. It cast off its concrete dress and suddenly stood naked on its long iron legs.

"Yelshanka is under fire."

"Stalingrad is under fire too."

"Heavy artillery is firing across the Volga."

The rear, too, was aflame. Over Yelshanka with its division headquarters and its corps headquarters, and over the ruined city on the Volga as well, the billows of smoke seethed. The explosions could be heard dozens of miles away. The whole surrounded area was one bubbling, boiling crucible. Throughout the pocket, from countless fires and explosions, black seas of smoke rose into the sky. And within this dense black blanket of smoke a thousand objects were blasted—earth, barricades, cobblestone walls, lathes, boilers, instrument panels. . . . Whole garages, munitions dumps, and batteries hurtled into the air, and among them were human beings without limbs, without heads. The fragments flew forty yards into the air, fell to earth again, and were again whirled up, pulverized, disintegrated.

In a shelter in Verkhnaya Yelshanka sat General Jänicke, the corps commander of the southern front, which was at this moment falling to pieces. The shelter shook as bombs and shells struck incessantly outside. Then a bomb hit near by. The doors flew open, dust, snow, and boards whirled through the air. The general felt his cheek, then saw that his hand was bloody. He acted with a wonderful promptness. He sent for the doctor, sent for the commander of an infantry division, sent for his orderly and got a telephone connection with Army Headquarters. The doctor bandaged his head. The orderly packed his bags. Two hours later he was ready.

By radio Jänicke's report that he had been wounded reached the Personnel Office of the Army High Command in Berlin. The chief of the Personnel Office, an old friend of Jänicke's, acted instantly and Jänicke was sent orders to fly out of the pocket. The infantry division commander entered Jänicke's bunker and listened impassively to what his commanding general had to say. He took over the affairs of the corps—that is to say, he took over two beaten infantry divisions, several artillery battalions without guns, a Rumanian division that not only lacked AA and AT guns, but was also for the most part without rifles or bayonets. General Jänicke left for Gumrak, whence he would be flown out. The officers of his staff shook their heads and exchanged significant glances.

"Dangerously wounded—just what did happen?"

"A board grazed his head."

"Slick work, wasn't it? Jänicke and the chief of the Personnel Office used to be in the same regiment."

Colonel Carras had just entered his room in the ruined Stalingrad department store. He was freshly washed and shaved (the water for the purpose had had to be brought from a water hole down the near-by street that lay under the fire of Russian sharpshooters). He had time for another look around this place (a last look, he thought; and at the frozen Volga before he set out for Gumrak airdrome. An hour ago orders had come for him to fly to GHQ to report. As he looked across the river, he saw the flares rising and noted the red muzzle flashes from the long-range cannon on the other side. You had to count ten from the flash—it took that long —before a 24 cm. shell struck, exploded, and turned what had been a building into an eruption of concrete, falling beams, and metal. And during the explosion it all vanished—the ride to Gumrak, flight to Berlin, headquarters and report. When Carras was able to close his gaping mouth again, when he regained control of his shaking knees and saw opposite, in place of another tall building, a "toothpick" similar to the one he was in, then he also regained his vision of what was to come—the ride, the flight, the report, Margot, the eyes he would look into. Not eyes of "dreamy abstraction and pagan frankness," but large staring eyes above a bulbous nose (reporting to GHQ meant, after all, reporting to HIM). At that moment, as new hits registered near by and the floor swayed underfoot, as smoke rose and there emerged out of the dust nothing but a great block of stone with protruding beams, remnants of floors, and articles of furniture dangling in the open air, as the trunk of a man spitted on an iron post rose to third-story height and rosy spots were mashed against the gables—remains of an infantryman who had just been walking past the building—at that moment Colonel Carras looked into his Führer's eyes more intently than ever before.

Not far from the department store ruin were Lieutenant Wedderkop and Sergeant Lachman. With a band of ruffians they huddled in the narrow ovoid of a Stalingrad sewer main. The gang had just returned from one of its nocturnal looting expeditions. They had eaten and drunk and had the remains of their meal still spread before them. When the bombardment began, they tried to outshout the rumble of guns. A cup of whisky passed from hand to hand. One man played a harmonica, another accompanied him on a comb, the rest bawled in a semblance of tune. Wedderkop had recovered from his concussion of the brain, but he had become wholly irresponsible and neither wished to nor knew how to get away from the group of which he had become a member. He drank with them and bawled, if anything, louder than the others. As they were carrying on this way, a tremendous detonation shook the earth. Dirt, smoke, and dust filled the air. When it was over, Wedderkop and Lachman alone crawled out to the light.

In an area guarded by a detachment of men picked for their stature there was an unusually sturdy bunker. In the bunker, surrounded by generals and colonels, sat a gaunt officer of high rank, decorations of the First and Second World Wars splashed across his chest. One half of this high officer's face twitched.

Dirt trickled down from the ceiling. The water glass on the

table jumped. The general who had been talking paused, listened to the sand trickling behind the revetment, and then continued: "To my mind the collapse can no longer be staved off. During the night only a single Heinkel III flew in; the whole attempt to hold out is ridiculous. What we need principally is heavy ammunition and fuel—and there isn't even enough fuel to send the corps and the divisions the limited supplies we have." Another near miss, more rumbling. Again the water glass on the table jumped and earth trickled down behind the walls. With a despairing gesture, the gaunt officer with the facial twitch turned to his chief of staff and dictated a radio message:

"The fortress can no longer be held. Starving, wounded, and frozen German soldiers are strewn the length of the roads. (1) I have therefore arranged for an orderly attempt to break out to the southwest. (2) Request planes be sent in time to fly out specialists (officers will be recommended by name). Myself not to be included."

Signed:
Von Paulus.

Under that same smoky sky the commanding general of the army corps whose front faced north and toward the Volga tramped restlessly through the snow. His chin was stubbled, his white hair unbrushed, his elegant riding clothes hidden under a fluttering camouflage cape. He was a general of artillery—but his cannon were silent. He tramped down a path trodden in the snow from his bunker to the road and back again. Once he, one of the five commanding generals in the army besieging Stalingrad, had protested against the command to dig in and had urged the army commander to break through to the west even against orders from the High Command. Nearly sixty days had passed since then and on his walk, in the fields and in front of the bunkers to the right and left of the ravine, lay the corpses of frozen soldiers whom no one now bothered to bury. As he turned into the tributary ravine where his own bunker was located, he came upon two infantrymen. Both were kneeling, one was clasping the other about the waist and holding his head. "Don't lie down, August, or you won't ever get up again; you'll be done for." The other man lay down nevertheless. The man who had spoken stayed with him; he continued to kneel, supporting himself with his hands in the snow.

The general gritted his teeth. And he too suddenly thought of the face with the large staring eyes and the bulbous nose.

The general, a man of sixty, suddenly thought of the time his father, a young company commander, had responded to an insult by attacking his colonel with his sword in the presence of the assembled company.

Gönnern and Damme sat in their bunker in the Tulevoy ravine, while near by a 15 cm. battery fired from all four barrels. Colonel Lundt was with them; he had been driven back all this way and the generals had had to find a place in their bunker for him to sleep. The three sat around the table, a piece of canvas stretched like a canopy over their heads, for here the earth did not merely trickle down; whole clods of it broke from the ceiling and thudded upon the floor of the canvas.

"I've just come from corps headquarters; Unschlicht is sitting there and playing the flute," Damme said. "Saw it with my own eyes. He says he's practicing a particularly difficult passage that requires concentration and calms the nerves. As long as the barrage is going on there's nothing else to do anyway, he says."

"If I knew how I'd play the flute, too," Gönnern said.

"Yes, all of us are gradually going crazy," Lundt said, but quickly added, "from the rank of colonel down, of course. By the way, that new man, Captain Henkel, has been found."

"Well. Where was he?"

"At the 'Tartar Wall.' A lieutenant of mine pulled him out of the mob there."

"I hear that there's quite a crew over there."

"I looked it over, the place where they found Henkel. It's just a crude hole in the ground with more than thirty men in it, officers and civilian officials. And all of them older men, scarcely one under forty. Filthy, done in, morale zero. Their uniforms in shreds, wearing soldiers' blouses, chauffeur's coats. They seem to have drifted there from every quarter of the pocket. When I entered the hole someone had just brought in a piece of sheet iron with a roasted horse liver on it. 'Gentlemen, can't you keep it a bit cleaner here?' I said. 'No use any more, sir,' one of them answered. What can you say to that?"

"Yes, frightful conditions," Gönnern agreed.

"Well, what happened to Henkel?"

"I had him brought back up front. He never arrived, disappeared again. I don't care if it's the last time I see him. What I want to know is why they send such a man into the pocket? The man never saw any fighting; he spent the whole war in his printing plant, printing up forms."

Gönnern, Damme, and Lundt sat in silence for a while and waited for Vilshofen, who had now been made a general.

"He's taking his time."

"Well, he'll probably have to crawl into a hole somewhere on the way here."

Outside the guns of the battery shook.

"We'll never put out the fire with water pistols like that. They might just as well save the ammunition for the infantry attack." When neither of the others answered Damme, he went on, "Well, there's nothing to do but stay put and stick our necks out until our heads get lopped off. But at least we ought to know what it's for. What do you say, Gönnern, what for?"

"To fight. I don't know any other answer either."

"Tell me, Gönnern, what did old Blücher do at Radkau?— the corps commander mentioned that recently."

"He had no bread and no ammunition left, so he surrendered."

"Exactly, that's just what I mean."

The detonations of the Russian artillery came nearer.

"Those damned toy cannon out there are drawing the Russian barrage down on our heads. Where the devil is Vilshofen? If he were here we could start a rubber of bridge to relax our nerves."

When the door finally opened it was not Vilshofen who entered, but Koog, the Protestant chaplain of Damme's division.

"Well, has Kalser turned up again? . . . Kalser is our Catholic chaplain," Damme said in explanation to Gönnern and Lundt.

"He's been seen at Voroponovo. But I've come about something else, about the matter of Private Krämer."

Private Krämer had left his post, crawled inside the ruined farmhouse where he was supposed to stand guard, and had slept for thirty-six hours uninterruptedly. For this he had been sentenced to death.

"It's absolutely impossible; I've talked with the man and that sentence must not be carried out, sir," Koog shouted into his commander's ear, while outside the battery thundered and the roar of the front did not pause for a second. The floor of the bunker shook and pieces of ceiling broke off and fell.

"The man is not accountable for his actions; he talks nonsense, babbles like a child. . . . No, he was like that days earlier, at the time he abandoned his post. The man comes under Paragraph 51; he's crazy—it's impossible to shoot him."

Damme shrugged. There was nothing he could do about it, he said.

"Krämer used to be an anti-tank gunner. Most of his unit was driven westward at Kletskaya; he and a few other men made their way to the east, to our side and into the pocket. He came all the way with nothing but a pistol in his hand and a pair of rubbers on his feet. Because of the rubbers his feet froze. Then he was in a combat group."

"Yes, and there too he deserted."

"I could bring up formal grounds. The man does not even belong to our division. . . ."

"He was picked up and assigned to us."

"Sir, the decisive factor is that this man is not in his right mind and cannot justly or legally be executed. Finally, he's the head of a family; he has a wife and two children. He's still young and will recover. The fate of a whole family depends upon his life. . . ."

"I can't do anything about it. There are hundreds of cases like his, desertions while on guard duty. None of the men are good for anything and nobody around here is sane any more. The army corps has picked out this particular case and insists that the sentence be carried out as an example."

Koog had no time to do anything. The execution squad was already on the way to the place where the sentence was to be carried out. He hurried to the other end of the ravine and spoke to the chief of staff of the army corps, Lieutenant Colonel Unschlicht, who lowered his flute without putting it aside and kept his lips pursed and his eyes fixed on the page of music, a seventeenth-century hymn. He listened abstractedly to Koog's arguments. There was no one in the whole army, he said, who did not want to sleep for thirty-six hours or longer, and for that very reason the execution of the sentence was a military necessity. That was all he would say about the matter to Koog.

During the past weeks Koog had held the hands of hundreds of dying men and had offered them consolation. But this was something different and as he left Unschlicht's bunker his knees shook. He saw three men with rifles, led by a sergeant, marching through the snow. He hurried to arrive before the squad at the dugout where Hermann Krämer, once a twenty-eight-year-old bank clerk, was waiting to be taken out for his last steps.

The squad arrived. Koog walked along beside Krämer. The sergeant, his three men, and the provost marshal followed. There were only a dozen paces to go. Between the entrances to two bunkers Krämer was placed against a wall of drifted snow. Nothing about the man with his tattered coat, his feet and head wrapped in rags, his hollow face framed in a straggly beard, his shining, dilated eyes—nothing recalled his civil life, his desk, his teller's window; nothing bespoke a home with lamp on the table, a sofa, pictures on the walls.

"I would so much have liked to wait for the next distribution of rations. . . . But tell me, chaplain, do you go right to Heaven or is there a kind of in-between state where you still don't get anything to eat?" Chaplain Koog was helpless; he could think of nothing to say, no consolation to give—fortunately, none was expected. He stammered something about a message. Could he give one to Krämer's wife and children?

"My wife's name is Ilse and the children's are Ilse and, yes, and Gustav," Krämer said, unbuttoning his coat and taking out a packet of letters that had been read to shreds. "There, send these back and please write to her. Write that I would have been done for soon anyway. I'm nothing but skin and bones, don't weigh more than ninety pounds. . . ."

The provost marshal was growing impatient; he took a step forward and raised to his eyes the sheet of paper he held so that he could read the sentence. A black billow of smoke rolled over the ravine. The whole scene was phantasmal; the men moved like marionettes. The provost marshal refolded his sheet of paper. Three soldiers—their coats too were tattered, their faces were also gray, their eyes dilated and shining with hunger—raised their rifles. There was a puff of fine blue smoke from the rifle barrels, but no sound of shots; the roar of the front and the rumble of cannon in the ravine drowned out everything else. The soldiers shouldered their rifles again, and led by the sergeant, tramped off. Chaplain Koog closed the eyes of the corpse in the snow. No one was interested in it any more; no one looked back at it.

Koog went back to his divisional commander with his rucksack packed and his sleeping bag draped over it. "I should like to be detailed to Steinle's combat group, sir."

"If you insist on getting into the thickest of the mess, I won't hold you back, Koog," Damme replied.

All this took place while the Russian artillery was hurling thousands of tons of searing metal into the pocket and while the whole front broke into flames. Men were crushed, roasted, suffocated, torn to pieces, buried or tossed forty yards into the air. Buildings collapsed; the earth seethed. Radio messages were dictated and sent out. New battalions were recruited from dugouts filled with dying men. A flute was played. A man was shot. Combat groups were wiped out and others— the men squeezed into crevices, their faces pressed against the ground—others survived and waited for the end of the barrage.

The gunfire lasted for thirty minutes. Then came three and a half hours of concentrated fire from mortars and rockets. There then remained three hours to darkness—three hours of infantry and tank attacks. The men of Döllwang's and Latte's groups had had experience with previous terrible barrages in the Don Bend, at the Kasachi Hills, and near the Rossoshka valley. They knew what dugouts and fortified lines meant at such times. And so, when the signal flares mounted into the sky and the artillery began its work of annihilation, they left the positions they had occupied during the night and sought refuge in crevices and holes to the rear. From there they watched the roofs of the dugouts, the fortifications, and the barbed-wire entanglements go flying into the air. They themselves suffered few losses from artillery fire. But the mortar and rocket fire proved all the more costly; they lost almost half their personnel. Even so, almost all the men who fell were new to the fighting, soldiers picked up out of repair crews and supply units during the march from Pitomnik to Voroponovo.

Three and a half hours of mortar fire!

Theoretically, Döllwang knew what that meant. He knew that the man who could not endure the incessant screeching, whistling, and hissing and the cloudburst of pattering splinters and who ran out into the sea of smoke that was being fed constantly by more falling shells—in nine cases out of ten he would be killed or wounded and lost to his unit. Battalions that lost their nerve under mortar fire had as many as ninety per cent casualties; others who stuck it out during the same bombardment in crevices and shell holes had escaped with losses of only three per cent. Döllwang was familiar with the theory and he knew that to overcome the urge to jump up during a long shelling it was necessary to cling to the ground, to grip it with all your might. Now, for the first time, he had an opportunity to observe the demoralizing effect of such attacks on his own nerves, from the way his little finger twitched to the complete breakdown of his whole nervous system and a panicky longing to jump to his feet. From his hole he could not see the hollow in the snow some five hundred yards away, but he could see whole schools of shells rising up out of the hollow like dolphins with plump heads and shimmering fishy tails, and he saw them rise, then slow down and crash among his own men to the right and left.

It was an endless, roaring, shattering torrent pouring down upon the frozen ground. Döllwang crouched in a hole so narrow that his shoulders touched the earth on both sides. He was knee to knee, face to face with another human being, Sergeant Gnotke. Time stood still and his little finger stopped obeying the commands of his brain. And where were the others?—five, ten, fifteen, a hundred yards away in other holes. No corridor led to them; there was no way to see them. The rim of this hole formed the horizon, the border of the inhabitable and transversable world. The little finger quivered. Someone who had overstepped the permitted limits screamed near by. "Lung torn open," Gnotke breathed; he made a practice of distinguishing types of wounds by the kind of scream. When the howling of the wounded man died away in a death rattle, Gnotke's momentary tension relaxed. He kept his hands concealed in the wide sleeves of his coat and did not move a muscle. His breathing was quiet and regular. Red-hot splinters flew into the hole. In the summertime such splinters had traveled so close to the ground and were so sharp that they had mowed the grass. One of them dropped down and burned a hole in Döllwang's coat. Gnotke instantly opened his eyes, picked up the splinter in his bare fingers, and flipped it out into the snow. It was at this moment that Gnotke noticed his captain's state. Now it was not only Döllwang's finger but his whole hand that was shaking. Gnotke glanced from the hand to the captain's face and eyes. Döllwang's lips were parted, showing teeth set firmly together. That was not necessarily bad, though it was a sign of extreme tension. But the officer's hands and his eyes, wide and staring into nothingness—these were danger signs. Half an hour of the heaviest kind of barrage, followed by hours of mortar fire, no end in sight, the impossibility of believing that it could ever end—this left, it seemed, only the alternatives of dying or going mad. But this is not true; it is a rhetorical falsification of the truth. In reality there are many gradations of reactions, trembling, numbness, screaming fits, praying, involuntary evacuation. And all these reactions occurred in the holes and crevices surrounding Döllwang and Gnotke, among the battle-hardened soldiers as well as among the surveyors, mechanics, and others who up to yesterday had worked in the rear. But such reactions were not the worst of it. Gnotke had seen men jerk their heads around toward a spitting, exploding shell and then, paralyzed by terror, be unable to move their neck muscles; he had seen men in this state helplessly submit to being bayoneted. The captain in front of him had, he knew, been sitting in some office in Berlin only a week ago. And Gnotke was no longer the indifferent observer he had been when he had read Dingelstedt's intentions in his eyes and yet had not lifted a finger to save the teacher. Now he was the man who had pulled Gimpf out of the pit of the dead—but even then his motives were different. Then he had been moved by the terrible fear of being alone; here it was something else, a real human sympathy.

Döllwang did not know that he was deaf, almost out of his senses, and completely unconscious of his immediate surroundings. He began slowly to realize it when he felt the pressure of a hand upon his own and a face began to take shape in front of him. Strangely, he saw at one and the same time both the dirt-smudged face of this soldier and the face of his aunt. Both Gnotke's gray eyes and his aunt's were suddenly fixed upon him at the breakfast table, so that he felt compelled to say: "I beg your pardon, aunt, I was thinking of something else and wasn't listening." But here the something else that occupied his mind was not a problem in mathematics or physics; here he was completely absorbed by the murderous roaring and his limbs were fluttering with terror. All of a sudden he noticed this, and in the noticing, a part of his self-control returned. Gnotke was talking to him, had evidently been talking for some time, although he heard only the last few sentences.

"Yes, I suppose they're all 'new' men, the ones who are jumping up," Döllwang replied at last.

"Yos, they're all new men. Never went through anything like this in the rear."

"Well, it really is hard on the nerves," Döllwang said, and Gnotke gently withdrew his hand.

"Anyone who jumps up is done for," he said.

The conversation was fragmentary enough in the unceasing roar. But nevertheless it was a human relationship, a hand reaching out to hold him when he was on the point of being swept away.

A few yards away Stüve sat in a hole so narrow that he had to keep his knees bent and his head bowed. The trouble with him was not his nervous system; he could stand the unending rumble and the bursting of a thousand shells. But his muscles could scarcely endure it. Since he was unable to stretch his legs, he kept wagging his head back and forth, back and forth. Then he began wiggling his toes and twisting his hands at the wrists, for it was frightfully cold. The end of the affair would be, he knew, that he would have to face an infantry assault with his feet swollen and his limbs asleep, and then he would have to counter-attack!

Another few yards away August Fell crouched. He no longer prayed, no longer thought of putting money into the collection plate; he was numb and deaf, physically and mentally. In another foxhole was Liebsch, the soldier with the weak bladder. He was too numb and deaf, dulled to everything, unconcerned with questions or answers about God and fate, with only a single thought that had been hammered into his head once and had stayed there. He kept thinking this one thought: We must hold the position, we must hold the position. In a fourth hole crouched one of the new men who was not really a soldier. He was Robert Rebstock, a mechanic from Berlin-Oberschön-weider who up to now had been working in a garage at Dubin-insky. He had gone along with a fleeing column to Yeshovka where he had been picked up by a reception commando and assigned to Vilshofen's combat group. Now he sat here with a rifle between his knees, cartridges in his pocket, not daring to move while the world howled and roared and went to pieces. Thoughts raced through his mind like rats on the deck of a sinking ship. He thought of a Hans, a Lisbeth, a Hitler, of "Russkis," and a Lotte. Hans had been right after all; he had stayed at home in Obserschönweider and was now foreman in a factory, lording it over a group of Russkis. Lisbeth was his sister, a Jehovah's Witness, and he had laughed at her phrases; but here it was, the "glassy sea" and the howling and gnashing of teeth; here it was in reality, not merely on paper. And Hitler —it was maddening, nothing to eat and snow and a rifle between your knees and Hitler saying: "I'll get you out." Doing nothing and saying, "Take me as your example." Dead men everywhere; this was the kind of thing he himself had been hurrahing for when he was in the SA, and if anyone had carped or criticized he'd been shoved off into a camp. And Lotte (his wife), Good God, Lotte; if he got killed now like everybody else, Lotte would probably marry Hans. Maybe she was right and maybe Lisbeth had been right too; perhaps he should have given the Russkis a slice of bread or a cigarette once in a while. It was his own fault; he was being hacked to pieces here because he had been so dumb and had really wanted things this way.

Farther on, in other holes, others of the group were huddled, Altenhuden, Gimpf, Liebich, Wilsdruff, Riess, another new man, more new men. Altenhuden, twenty-six years old, was as crushed as if he had already lived a thousand years. Gimpf made up his mind not to take another step; he was going to stay in this hole and be buried there. Liebich had reached the limit of endurance; he pressed his head between both hands, ran his fingers under his hood, and then looked at the hairs that remained in his hands. Wilsdruff had forgotten who he was and where he was; he no longer knew that he had a wife and children; he felt no more than a lump of clay might feel. Riess wept and cursed alternately and swore that this was his last barrage, his last mortar assault, that he was quits with it now. He'd had enough of this goddamned mess; he was going over the hill; he'd strike out for himself the way so many of the others were doing. There was enough stuff lying around on the roads for a man to live on.

Altenhuden was sharing a hole with Gimpf. "Where'd you get those boots with the thick fur lining?" he asked. "They're swell stuff."

"Gnotke gave 'em to me on account of my frozen foot," Gimpf replied.

"Where did he 'organize' them?"

"Didn't organize them at all. The colonel gave them to him. The colonel is wearing felt boots instead now."

"This is going on here forever," Altenhuden said after a while.

"For all I care a shell can bury us both here. Then I won't have to keep going on and on."

"Well, I care. I want to get home to Nemitz some time and help get in the hay once more. Don't you ever think about home?"

"Home . . ." Gimpf said. It was a feeble, lost sigh under the bleak sky and amid the ferment and roar all around.

A clod of frozen clay dropped into the hole. Altenhuden reached for it. A scrap of paper was attached to it, and printed in huge letters on the paper was the message: "When firing over lie still. When the tanks come, let them roll over. Don't shoot. Save ammunition for infantry. Let them come close. Hold fire until order is given."

Altenhuden tossed the clod of clay to Liebsch in the next hole, and so it passed on down the line, reaching Fell, Wilsdruff, and the others. The order came from Döllwang who had it from Vilshofen at the water tower in Voroponovo. A messenger had carried it through a ravine and down a communication trench, then started it toward the foremost line by throwing it in this manner.

Altenhuden, Gnotke, and Fell and some hundred men, "old" and "new" men under Döllwang, and another hundred led by Latte, lay for three and a half hours under the mortar fire. Bit by bit their bodies lost all capacity for feeling. Their stomachs, which at first had swelled out like balloons, had by now shrunk to empty sacks. Their bladders no longer bothered them; they had involuntarily relieved themselves. They lay on their sides or, if there were no room, crouched. Their brains had stopped functioning. There were those who had continued to think of their former lives or of Adolf Hitler's responsibility for it all, or of their wives. They had, (like Rebstock,) long since leaped up and been punched full of holes by a thousand tiny splinters, as a piece of meat dropped into tropical waters is instantly gobbled up by a thousand little fishes.

For three and a half hours the torrent of iron and smoke continued to fall from the sky. The silence that settled when it was over did not mark the end; it was rather the climax in the scale of horror. Earth and sky became numb; the men did not dare to breathe; they had to make themselves as small as possible. They crouched, knelt, lay on their bellies and pressed their faces into the earth.

Then it came, the clank of steel, the rattle of treads, the creaking of the frozen earth, the heat of exhausts, sudden darkness as though a shadow were moving over and past, and loose lumps of snow falling into the holes. The tanks rolled right over these crouching foxholes. Only in the larger holes did the tanks linger for a moment, turn on their axes, and crush hole and men and snow into an ugly pulp beneath them.

Artillery, mortars, tanks, all the machinery of hell developed by German technique, produced by German labor in immeasurable quantities, misused by German generals to crush other peoples—here these things emerged in the quantities that action and reaction had engendered, and they rolled over German soldiers who lay, turned to stone and shrunken like mummies, hugging the ground.

Then the tanks were past.

A new wave of silence. The cannon fire was now directed farther toward the rear. The silence lasted until the small noises made by human beings became audible: creaking, rattling of mess kits, spades, grinding of teeth, snorting, howls, bestial outcries. A wave of assault troops. Up now! The stiff limbs moved, the men stood on numb feet, ran on prickling feet. . . . Hand grenades, submachine guns, frozen urine in trouser legs, but shout, shout for all you're worth!

"Hurrah!"

"Oooray!"

Gnotke, Gimpf, Döllwang, Ukrainians, Cossacks . . . Fell

184

and an Usbek . . . Altenhuden, Liebsch, Riess, Kalmucks, Siberians, Russians, White Russians. . . .

"Oooray!"

Fire sprayed into eyes, skulls cracked like eggshells, Russians propped their tommy guns against stomach and belt and fired until the chambers were empty; then they threw the guns aside and attacked with knives. Lieutenant Latte, critically wounded, lay in the snow. He heard from the direction of Voroponovo an 8.8 cm. battery begin to fire. That must be Vilshofen, giving a reception to the tanks that had broken through.

Latte turned his head to one side and died.

It was not Vilshofen; it was Major Buchner's heavy flak. Aiding him were the cannon of a 15 cm. battery that once, from this very spot, had squandered ammunition, had arrogantly fired at solitary targets; once the men had mockingly taken aim at single men who were approaching their positions. Now the battery fired its last shells and fell silent forever.

Vilshofen stood on the platform of the water tower. He was still standing there when night crept over the steppe. The line had held, only to be abandoned under cover of darkness so that on the following day it would no longer exist. Latte dead, half the combat group fallen, the other half captured or dispersed. A small, bloody group of men returned over the steppe. That was the way the line had held.

Captain Döllwang, Master Sergeant Hanke, Sergeant Gnotke forty-two unwounded men and a few who were able to walk by leaning on their comrades. This detachment limped through the darkness toward Voroponovo. Enders' regiment looked no better than Vilshofen's combat group; Steinle's combat group and Keil's combat group had also been bled white. During the night all of them fell back to the railroad tracks to occupy new positions there. The new line that formed was, this time, not a slender ring of steel; it was nothing but tin hammered so hopelessly soft that at the next blow it would give, be smashed to bits.

With dulled senses, weary and heavily laden, Döllwang's unit marched through the night and the snow. The road had been tramped smooth, had drifted over again, been tramped down and had again drifted. It dipped into hollows, cut across walls of snow. Nothing could be seen in this blue night, not even the prominent water tower in Voroponovo. There were still markers along the road, but these consisted no longer of posts driven into the ground. The posts had all been used for firewood. Now, every twenty, thirty, or forty paces, some bolt

185

upright, some leaning aslant in a snowpile, stood the new road markers—horses' legs with the flesh gnawed clean off. Some stood with hock and hoof pointing up, others with the thigh and broad pelvic bones upward. Döllwang's group marched on, and behind it, in a serpentine line, wound the remnants of Enders' regiment. Ahead lay Voroponovo; behind was no-man's-land (that is, for this night it was still no-man's-land) and the abandoned battlefield which here and there was still under the fire of automatic guns.

Many well-trodden paths ran from the front and from dug-outs into the marked main highway, and men who had been scattered during the fighting at close quarters, or those whom for a time terror had so benumbed that they were unable to move, were warmed with hope when they saw a protruding horse's leg. Then they held the thread in their hands; they could hope to find their way back to their units. One of these "fortunate" men was Private Evald Stüve; another, from Enders' regiment, was Corporal Hans Daussig. When Stüve caught sight of Daussig, who was crouching down and listening on the other side of the road (one could not know how far the Russians had already infiltrated), he remained quite still and observed the other man's movements. What followed was little different from a nocturnal meeting between two wolves. They sniffed at one another for a long time, and when they finally set out together and, after a while, sat down to rest, their shadows on the blue snow were remarkably like those of two hunted, mangy wolves.

"What've you got?" Daussig asked.

"My arm—bayonet wound. You?"

"In the side—tommy gun, I think."

"All your fellows gone?" Stüve asked.

"Dunno. I opens my eyes and there I am in the snow. Just before there was bayonet fighting, but then everybody disappeared."

Both men fell silent. Suddenly Daussig broke out into peals of laughter. Stüve looked at him suspiciously. "Guess you got one in the head too, didn't you?"

"No, I was just thinking about something."

"Must've been funny."

"I was thinking about home. . . ." The recollection had not been funny, had been fearful, in fact. But nothing could bother him now; it was a joke, the way you could suddenly think of a thing like this.

"Where're you from?" Stüve asked.

"Berlin."

"Me, I'm from Cologne. But we'd better get going toward Voroponovo."

They had to get to Voroponovo; they did not think of what lay beyond that goal, and before long they did not think of anything at all. The snow veiled their eyes; Stüve forgot about Cologne, forget the worries of a woman named Tilla, concerns that for eight years had been his own. And Daussig—Daussig had once been a musician, had had a job and an apartment with a rented piano and a wife of whom he was fiercely jealous. But all that was far away; it did not matter to him now whether his "sweetie" was still a "race horse with a jockey" or whether things had changed with her since. Stüve and Daussig leaned against one another; each held the other one upright and so they tramped on, both desiring nothing more than a hole into which they could crawl.

They had only a few thousand yards to go, but it took them hours to make it. On the way they met a third, a fourth, a fifth straggler. After a while it was a large group reeling along. Then they reached the station and groped their way past a row of dark freight cars. They were looking for an emergency hospital train, and they found it. On the way one of the men had talked about this train and had asserted that there would be room enough in it for all of them. But where had they ever found enough room, except on the naked steppe and in the snow? None of them wanted to admit this to himself. The idea of cars marked with the Red Cross and equipped with beds, blankets, and stoves, had taken firm hold of their agonized brains. Beds, blankets, and stoves with wheels underneath them, wheels that stood on rails, wheels that might eventually roll—perhaps only to Stalingrad, perhaps to. . . . Dying was so easy; why should not life too be possible? And now they were here, stumbling along the row of cars. They could see clearly the red crosses in spite of the snow that half covered them. The cars were freight cars with sliding doors; tiny windows had been set into them. Behind one windowpane a dim light showed. Smoke rose from the iron stove pipes that protruded out of the roofs of other cars. These cars were inhabited, but whenever they knocked or pounded on the wooden walls, there was no answer, no doors opened, and nothing stirred. The men staggered on. They stumbled over frozen stumps that lay along the path, dropped here and there the whole length of the train. They did not look closer at these six-foot objects; they did not want to see them. A cot, a space in which to lie down in one of those heated cars, was all they desired.

At last they found a car whose door yielded. It was empty,

or at any rate no longer defended by its occupants. There were cots in it too, and a stove; so far, everything was well. The men on the cots no longer moved; they were stiff. The new arrivals picked them up, dragged them to the sliding door, and threw them out. There was room for all; in fact there were cots enough for all. But since it was difficult to clamber in and the one step was far too low, they looked around and finally brought over some of the frozen logs. The first step was widened and a second built on top of it. Now even the men with leg wounds could get into the freight car. But the men who brought the frozen stumps over the steps (similar steps led up to the other freight cars) could no longer help noticing that one end was a pair of stiff human legs and the other a frozen human head. . . .

Stüve stood outside. He saw Daussig crawl into the car on all fours. A face appeared in front of him, a large nose, pale blue eyes. It was the face of August Fell, who had also lagged behind. Stüve reached out for Fell with his sound arm and drew him close.

"Let's get out of here," he said. "The others are probably at the rations office."

"Yes, I guess they are," Fell replied.

The two left the hospital trains and the railroad station.

Next day the main defense line, which was nothing but a concept on a map, included Voroponovo railroad station, ran diagonally across the farmstead where the rations office was situated, and continued on northward to Siding 44, where Keil's group lay, then on around Gumrak and eastward from Gumrak.

Dully, like gray smoke, the new day dawned. The men who rose to their feet that morning in the yard of the rations office themselves looked like little more than shapes formed of gray smoke. Sergeant Hanke, Sergeant Gnotke, spoke a few words and one group or another marched off, settled down in a shed or on the roof of a shed, or in a dugout. So the new "line" was occupied. It was a highly formless and unmilitary procedure. The only group that had a military look—in fact, a trim, martial appearance—was the paymaster's combat group, composed of his master sergeant, his Sergeant Kulicke, and the soldiers attached to the rations office. These men had steel helmets on their heads; their straps and belts were shining; pistols dangled at their waists. A sentry stood at the gate, another in front of the rations depot, a third in front of another room. And these sentries each had a can of kerosene ready,

188

just as the orders required, so that if the Russians came they could set fire to the rooms and dumps. The master sergeant scurried around checking the sentries. Every few minutes he went up to the paymaster's hut, asked the sentry, "Where is the chief?" and then reported: "Report: all quiet."

Since the night before when the thunder of the front had paused and he had come out of his bunker, the paymaster had been—not quite "on his feet," but in constant, restless movement. He was waiting; there was nothing else for him to do. The division had ordered the rations office evacuated and had sent several trucks for the purpose. These trucks had been overdue for several hours and there was still no sign of them. The paymaster could not stay in one place for long. Again and again he ran out into the yard and looked down the road, then up at the sky. He kept listening to the crack of rifles that came from the railroad station.

At one point he entered the room that Captain Döllwang had taken for himself. "Captain . . ."

Döllwang waved his hand reassuringly. "Everything in order, paymaster."

"But, sir, don't you think . . . wouldn't it be advisable . . ." The paymaster stopped talking abruptly. His face, under the steel helmet, turned white. Outside there was a humming as though a flock of little birds were swooping through the air.

"A few stray rifle bullets, paymaster."

The paymaster left, intending to go back to his room and telephone his neighbor, the veterinary lieutenant who, he knew, had located an automobile and was now on the hunt for a can of gasoline. On his way he saw a figure lying in the yard. A sergeant—his own Sergeant Kulicke.

He stared at the man on the ground. "Sergeant . . . Kulicke!"

The sergeant did not stir. His face was blue; a fine red thread showed on his temple.

"Good God, is he dead?"

Paymaster Zabel must have seen dead men many times. Moreover, he would have only had to go as far as the railroad station to see corpses being used as steps. But these dead men as well as the ones he had occasionally seen lying on the road had been frozen stiff as as posts, had been covered with grime, unrecognizable, with frozen masks for faces. But Sergeant Kulicke—a man could fall at his side and no longer move! The idea would not penetrate to his mind; it was a possibility he had never considered. He forgot his steel helmet, his natty straps, the pistol at his side; he forgot all about his martial getup. He raised Kulicke's arm, then dropped it again. Bewildered, he clasped his hands; his eyes widened.

"Good God, is he dead . . . is he dead?"

"Dead—shot in the head—dead and gone—dead as a doornail!" he heard a whole chorus of voices, saw curious eyes, grinning faces. Fell covered his mouth with his hand to keep from bursting into laughter. The others did not restrain themselves. Fell, Altenhuden, Liebsch, Gimpf, and Gnotke stood around the paymaster.

An hour later Paymaster Zabel, the master sergeant, and the veterinary sat in a personnel carrier. The car rolled out of the gate not an hour too soon. By now not merely stray rifle bullets but well-aimed mortar fire was raining down on the farm, and even before the car turned into the road leading toward Tsaritsa ravine flames burst up out of the buildings. Not only this farmyard, but the neighboring huts and ruins and the railroad station of Voroponovo were objects of the Soviet attack. The offensive embraced the entire front, and no single point where the fire was concentrated held out for long.

The hour of collapse had come.

Freight cars filled with frozen human flesh stood at the station in Voroponovo. In one of these cars lay Hans Daussig, the thirty-two-year-old musician. He had heard all the sounds of death audible inside his own and other cars—the rattling of mucus-filled air passages, the whistling of shattered lungs, the wailing for a slice of bread, a drink of water, the howls of delirium, and the thrashing of the dying. Then the hoarfrost had coated the walls more and more thickly. Lumps of it had come loose and fallen on blankets and faces. After that there had been a long silence. The stove remained dark and cold; there were no hands to feed it with wood, no lungs to blow up the fire or to cough; there was no more chattering of teeth, no more groaning, no more whispering. Daussig had a bullet in the abdomen and the inflammation heated his body and kept him from freezing to death quickly. The silence lasted for a long time; then a different kind of sound came, the explosions of 12.7 cm. shells. To Daussig's ears the detonations were only a faint crackling. A shell fragment tore a hole in the wall of the car and admitted the daylight into this grotto of recumbent snow men. The door was pushed open and a creature, no longer Corporal Daussig, no longer Daussig the musician, a creature barely alive reeled to its feet and fell into the arms of a Red Army soldier. He was placed on a sled and taken to the rear. In a bunker where a red-hot stove poured forth warmth, the frozen blood on Daussig's coat thawed. He held

190

a slice of bread in his hand and sipped hot tea. A probe dug into his body and removed a submachine gun bullet. A drain was placed in the incision and pus flowed out in a thick stream. When Daussig recovered consciousness some time later, he caught sight of light in the darkness, a tiny chink admitting light. The chink might widen; if he had enough strength left he might live again to see the full daylight.

This was happening not only to Daussig, not only to the few survivors in the eight freight cars at Voroponovo station, but to other men in other cars at Basargino and near the field hospital at Gumrak, where such trains stood row upon row on the tracks.

There were wrecked houses filled with abandoned wounded men in Kravtsov and Pestchanka and Voroponovo, at Yeshovka, Gumrak, Stalingradski—all along the highways down which the German army fled toward Stalingrad. Private Stüve sought admittance to the dressing station on the road from Voroponovo to Yeshovka. He was turned away; the dressing station had capacity for sixty men and already sheltered four hundred and fifty. To obtain a bandage he had to surrender part of the lining of his coat. A medical aide let him glance into the ward. Wounded men lay on the bare floor, covered only with their blankets, their faces the color of clay. They lay so close together that when one stirred the movement and the groan passed down the entire row. Their shirt collars were coated with what looked like hoarfrost, which was in fact lice moving up and down the seams. Stüve asked about the rations. "Half portions of horse meat," the medical aide replied. Stüve was given a sliver of hardtack and sent on to the next dressing station. He tramped on, one of thousands of wounded men who could still walk and whose pilgrimage seemed endless. At each successive dressing station, Stüve was turned away. He gnawed the horse bones that had been set up as road markers, rested in caves or in bunkers that had been abandoned by the staffs and rear services. When he came upon a bunker, he often had to move out a dead man in order to make himself a place for the night. Then he would spread out his rags and lie down on them. He would put down a tin can, borrow a spark from a neighbor, and start a tiny fire in the can, using pages from some account book, splinters of wood, or pieces of automobile tire that he had picked up on the way. Such a fire sufficed to warm his stiff fingers and his nose. The others all had similar fires; they lay close to the ground and the smoke rose up over their heads. Sometimes, too, Stüve and the others would spring to their feet at night and race out into the darkness, to scatter in all directions over the snow-covered land. This happened when the sound of an airplane flying low reached their ears and a plane, laden with bread, chocolate, and canned meat, circled above their heads, unable in the mist and drifting snow to find the drop point. It would jettison its cargo somewhere, and the men would rush around in the darkness, sinking up to their necks in snowdrifts. Finally they would stumble back exhausted to their shelters. Occasionally one of the men would actually find one of these rations packages with its seventy pounds of food and would stuff his pockets. Afterward there was sure to be someone who would lie in a corner munching all night long; he would over-eat and disturb everyone else in the bunker with his curses and groans.

Cellars along all the streets in Stalingrad, right into the very heart of the city, were filled with wounded men who had never had any medical treatment. Daily these cellars were combed for men fit enough to be thrown into the front lines again.

An entire army writhed in agony. The army was breaking up; the center of the huge organism was numbed, its com-munications no longer functioned, its peripheral parts were paralyzed. Men died and the dead were no longer buried. In the streets of Stalingrad, in the ravines and on the steppe, corpses lay like logs of wood and snow piled up on them until they resembled fallen birch logs.

A young man—a short time ago he had been in school at Breslau—came through Tsybenko, Kravtsov, and Pestchanka. A hundred times he should have been stuck by bullets or shell fragments, like the others whose corpses he had seen on his way; in the tumult that raged over the Kalmuck Steppe it would have been the most natural event. But somehow he reached Voroponovo as he had earlier reached Pestchanka. Here, too, black smoke billowed up out of the railroad sta-tion and the houses; here, too, snow fountained into the air and human beings howled in agony (though their voices sounded to him like those of animals). Here too were hordes of fleeing men who had thrown away their rifles, their ruck-sacks, their blankets—some had even discarded their boots! He ran along with these hordes of Germans and Rumanians until he reached and recognized the path leading to the rations office.

The group of buildings was burning. Flames were leaping up out of the doors and roof of the paymaster's house. The adjoining house, where the young man himself had been quartered, was a pile of ruins topped by the collapsed roof. He recognized the threshold and doorframe of his own former room, but of the room itself only a mangled hole in the ground was left, and in this hole a captain sat hunched over a field telephone.

"Yes, general. The Russians are in Voroponovo. For an hour I have had no communication with the brick factory on my left. The replacements have arrived. Some of the men are sick; they were sent off without rations. I could not give them anything; we ourselves have been without rations for two days. The supplies in the buildings here were soaked with kerosene and burned by direction of the paymaster, in obedience to his orders. . . . He received the order from his division or from the corps—The chain of command is in such a state of confusion here too that no one can make anything of it." This was certainly the case, and at the last moment, while the southern front was collapsing, Vilshofen's (now Döllwang's) combat group had again been placed under the command of Gönnern, while Enders' regiment and Keil's combat group were given to Damme and Buchner's flak battalion which held the portion of the line between Döllwang and Keil remained under the command of the tank corps. These changes and this failure to make a change did not help to clarify matters.

"Yes, sir. With the replacements and the paymaster's personnel I have one hundred and eighteen men. But I beg you to consider that this farmyard is extremely ill-suited to defense. General Vilshofen, too, pointed out the railroad embankment two hundred yards to our rear as far more suitable. —Yes, sir, the Russians are attacking with mortars, automatic guns, and single tanks. . . . Yes, general. Yes, sir. . . ."

This conversation went on to the accompaniment of exploding shells from automatic guns. Captain Döllwang put down the receiver and looked at the young man who had come in during the conversation and was standing by with an expression of bewilderment. He looked strange—hatless, coat unbuttoned, no belt, no pistol, hair hanging in a tangle over his face.

"Come now, fellow, pull yourself together. What's the matter, where are you from, anyway?"

The young man swallowed. "All over—the Russians broke through—Tsybenko, Kravtsov, gone."

"Of course they're gone. Pestchanka is gone too and so is Voroponvo."

Captain Döllwang noticed the silver epaulet that still hung by a thread to the man's coat. "You're a paymaster's assistant, aren't you—belong to this rations office here, I suppose?"

"Yes, sir . . . belonged . . . I went up front with my regiment, a regiment of grenadiers."

"And where is your regiment now?"

"Gone, everything is gone. Torn to pieces, just torn to pieces by tanks. God, I can still hear them behind me."

"Sit down and take it easy. How did you yourself get through? Tsybenko is ten miles from here."

"I don't know—I can still hear the screams. And then the Russians came, sir. . . ."

"Sit down, man."

Schweidnitz sat down on one of the fallen beams. He could scarcely bear to look around. Good God, this was the house he had thought of as an island of peace. This was his room, filled now with the reek of burning. Through gaping holes came the flashings of exploding shells. The air was filled with howls and hisses. A messenger entered. He was August Fell. "Six tanks from the direction of the station, sir."

Döllwang rushed out.

An hour passed before he returned, and with him a wave of ashes, snow, sulfurous fumes. Altenhuden and Gimpf followed, carrying a wounded man—Lieutenant Kindt. Before they laid him down they had to push Schweidnitz to one side; they could not awaken him from his leaden sleep.

Döllwang picked up the telephone. "Urgent, urgent!" he cried in a hoarse voice. "The G-3 personally."

In a bunker in Tulevoy ravine the telephone clanged. Gönnern's adjutant, Dr. Weichbrot, a young captain with the face of an angelic baby, picked up the receiver. The G-3 was not there at the moment, he said, and the commander was busy with another emergency call. "Yes, I will give the message to the commander: the buildings are rubble, insufficient ammunition, one belt left for each machine gun, twenty shots for each rifle, five shells for each mortar. The farm cannot be held. The captain suggests withdrawal to position on the railroad line two hundred yards to the rear."

The door to the adjoining bunker stood open. There, over a map table illuminated by two unshaded electric bulbs, sat General Gönnern. Near him, with his back to the wall, in coat and field cap, stood General Vilshofen. Gönnern had overheard the conversation outside. He waved the adjutant away. He had the telephone at his ear and was at the moment discussing Döllwang's position with the corps.

". . . but the farm simply doesn't exist any more. Tell that to the command. No, it doesn't exist, it's nothing but rubble,

194

rubble, rubble, do you understand, Unschlicht? Two hundred yards. . . . High Command insists—but that means the end of everything. . . ."

Gönnern laid down the receiver and looked at Vilshofen who stood in silence close to the wall. The light of the bulbs fell upon the map; all around was the darkness of night. Outside were the blizzard, the automatic guns, the tanks that had broken through. But here was the map and here the line determined by the High Command. Voroponovo, a brick factory ahead of the railroad embankment, and a farm lay within this pre-established line. Only yesterday Pestchanka, Tsybenko, and Kravtsov had lain inside that line. No orders from the High Command or the Führer's headquarters, but blood alone had erased that line. And the day before yesterday and the day before that there had been other lines, other points, other farms, and they too had been wiped out in blood and not on orders from the High Command or the Führer's headquarters. Sixty or seventy days earlier the High Command had fixed the line in the northeast at Latashanka on the Volga, in the west on the Rossoshka heights, and in the south beyond the little Karpovka River, and when the troops fell back from those points there had been startled inquiries from the High Command, angry inquiries from the Führer's headquarters, and lamentations and epistles about the "needs of the hour" from the Führer himself.

"Why, when the trouble began in the west at the Kasachi hills and in the Rossoshka valley . . ."

Vilshofen snapped: "The trouble . . . I know we don't like to say the word. But let us say it now: when Height 126 was nothing but a hill of corpses and the Rossoshka valley nothing but a valley of death. . . ."

"All right, put it that way if you like. When the army continued to fall back there were more inquiries, orders, lamentations, threats, and not only threats of court-martial, but actual courts-martial."

"At this moment and in this concrete case the fate of Döllwang's group is at stake, and no one but the commander can judge this situation and decide what the requirements of the situation are."

"But you've heard what the corps and the army, too, has replied. The High Command has fixed the line and not one unit may be withdrawn without permission from the High Command."

"So the High Command is now issuing local orders! What is left of the army's independence, what is left of the field commander's right to issue battle orders in accordance with his estimate of the situation?" Vilshofen asked.—"That's a question that has been asked more than once, my dear Vilshofen."

"This isn't a question of my dear Vilshofen. It is a matter of life and death for the men. And the question is whether their dying helps anyone, or whether it is senseless!"

Gönnern stared at the map, at the broken line that represented the railroad, at a black circle that was Voroponovo, and at a cross that indicated a farmstead. Then the line, the cross, and the circle swam before his eyes.

Unceasingly, the grinding of the Russian artillery could be heard, even though muffled by the thick walls of earth. The canopy over Gönnern's map table sagged in the middle from the weight of lumps of earth that had fallen from the ceiling. Dirt lay on the map and clods of earth on the floor around the table.

"Why have they made us stay here so long?" Gönnern groaned. "There are so many disturbances that efficient work and calm judgment are impossible."

"Efficient work and calm judgment indeed! The best I can wish for you, Gönnern, is more and healthier disturbances. The problem must be solved right here and now; the question is one that confronts not only us, but all of Germany, and it must be answered right here amid the thunder of artillery salvos."

Gönnern gave him a tormented look.

Vilshofen went on. "They told us that Hooth, Manstein, the army group would break the ring and help us—they haven't broken the ring and they haven't helped. Then we were told that our sacrifices were of assistance to the army group and would make it easier to establish a new front. But the front fell farther back, and so we didn't help the army group either. Now there isn't much left of us, and our remnants are falling back to lines that cannot possibly be held. Whom are we helping now, who is profiting by our sacrifices? Won't you explain to me just what it all means, Gönnern?"

Gönnern rubbed his hand over his bald pate. It was possible to talk with Damme and the others. But this hothead who always went the limit in everything (oh, he had been magnificent while the army was still advancing)—you just couldn't get anywhere with him.

"At the moment the question is the fate of Döllwang's group and of Enders, Steimer's, and Keil's groups. But it is more than that—the lives and deaths of an army, of a whole army of men are at stake. And the question is whether there is any sense to their dying or whether it is utterly senseless."

"Well, I must say 'my dear Vilshofen' once more. It seems to me that the question of sense or senselessness is not quite in our province; it would be extending our authority to attempt to answer it. After all, we have our orders, Vilshofen, and we have to stick to them."

Vilshofen laughed grimly; he was, in fact, half out of his mind.

"And finally: we must provide an example," Gönnern made himself say.

"Hooth doesn't break the ring and get us out, but he piles the bodies of his men up at Kotelnikovo; that's one example. Our commander in chief makes gloomy predictions and sends off one radio message after the other to the High Command and the Führer; he demands freedom of action and piles up corpses at Stalingrad. That's another example. I tell you, we've had enough of such examples. Examples of dying are not what Germany needs, but examples of living, of doing what is needful when it is needed and, if circumstances demand it, against orders. . . . No, let me finish, Gönnern. False calculations, underestimating the other side, overestimating ourselves—it's a whole fabric of faulty thinking and acting and it is beginning to rip. And we, all of us here at Stalingrad, are the first to tear. It will go on; such rents cannot be patched with corpses. There is greatness in dying if it is done in the service of a great cause, when it serves the welfare of the whole. But when the dying is only to cover up past mistakes; when the dying is done in an attempt to patch a terrible tear—don't leave, Gönnern—when the purpose of the slaughter is only to sink the cart deeper in the mud, then there is no longer any greatness about it. Then it is petty, wretched, shameful. . . ."

Gönnern was about to break off the conversation when the telephone buzzed again in the adjoining room. Vilshofen and Gönnern listened as the adjutant repeated the message: "Captain Döllwang wounded . . . Lieutenant Kindt dead . . . only one sergeant and thirty-eight men . . . two hundred yards . . ."

Gönnern groaned. Vilshofen was a general without troops, without the power to issue orders. Gönnern reached for the telephone. "Emergency, emergency . . ." He called the army, not the commander in chief, but the chief of staff who was known as "the commander in chief's evil genius." Gönnern preferred to beard the lion rather than to continue the conversation with Vilshofen.

The chief of staff of the army had two telephones before him. Over one wire he was talking with Damme who wanted to pull back Enders' group; Gönnern was calling on the other wire and presumably wanted to do something similar; on his adjutant's wire the commander of the tank corps was objecting to the order placing his flak on the railroad embankment at Voroponovo. At the same time the chief of staff, with his free hand, thrust a heap of papers toward a provost marshal. They were death sentences that he had looked through and confirmed—sentences for cowardice, desertion, theft, looting. In addition he greeted with a nod of his head someone who had just entered—Colonel Carras who had flown out of the pocket days ago and had just returned in the last plane to land at Gumrak. What had he brought back, the chief of staff wondered. He looked ill, wasn't wearing the "All Glory to our Flag" expression he had had as he was about to leave. No, not a bit of it, the chief of staff thought as he replied to Damme: "I can't help it. Order from the High Command. Not a step back. And listen here, Damme, what the devil has been going on with your Keil group? That bird has let himself be driven back over the railroad embankment. The bulge has to be ironed out again at once. . . ." Then he spoke to Gönnern. "Two hundred yards . . . no, not even ten yards. I can't help it. More is at stake than a few yards or a few men. The situation is grave. Tell your captain, tell the men that the fate of the Sixth Army depends on them, on them alone. The order is: Not a step back."

His adjutant handed him his telephone so that he could talk to the commander of the tank corps. The chief of staff did not give the commander a chance to talk. "The flak must stay where it is," he snapped out. "The flak is the moral backbone of the infantry. Explain that to your battalion commander—what's his name?—all right, Buchner, explain that to Buchner. Not a step back!"

Not a step back—this was the order. Damme passed it on to Enders and to Keil. To Enders Damme added an apology; to Major Keil he added vigorous curses against the High Command, "the top brass," and fate. Enders replied by cutting the telephone line and tossing the telephone into the wastebasket. Keil immediately attempted a counterattack and was thrown still farther back. Then he telephoned again from a hole in the snow on the road to Yeshovka. General Damme did not respond with informal imprecations against orders; he spoke in cold, official tones and administered a reprimand, using phrases that made Major Keil flush hot. Since the fighting on the Mius front

Major Keil had worn the Knight's Cross. What Damme said to him made him forget his home town of Cranz, forget his father, his young wife, a factory he had once thought of taking over; made him even forget himself. He bobbed up out of the hole into the howling night and called his men together. "Hans, Heinrich, Georg—who's coming? A shock troop assault!"

After cutting the wire to his brick factory, Colonel Enders did something more. He was not actually living in the big chimney, as he had informed Vilshofen some days ago, but his quarters were inside one of the furnaces. There was room in the furnace for a table, a few chairs, suitcases, books, and various utensils, and Enders had kept it hot as a greenhouse.

Enders wrote out a regimental order, his last. Then he took off his uniform and donned his pajamas. He hung his jacket and trousers neatly on a hanger, had his orderly bring in several white napkins with which to set the table (he had flown into the pocket only two weeks ago and still possessed such amenities), then presented the orderly with a silver cigarette case and dismissed him.

That was the way Chaplain Koog found him a few hours later. After the disruption of telephone communication Colonel Steimer, to the north of Enders, had sent Koog to find out what had happened. On the table stood two glasses, the second full but untouched, a half-empty bottle, and an open book. Colonel Enders lay on his cot in his silk pajamas. Beside the bed, on a suitcase, stood a water glass and an empty cardboard box labeled *veronal*.

In his last regimental order Colonel Enders had written: *"In consideration of the situation every man has full liberty of action. I permit anyone who whistles to save his life to surrender or to do whatever he considers right in the situation and whatever is his indicated duty, especially with regard to his family."*

In the brick factory Koog once more found his colleague, the Catholic chaplain Kalser, whom he had lost during the panic at Pitomnik.

Flak Commander Buchner held the position between the brick factory and the rations office. On his right the factory had been hit by shellfire and was burning. On his left the rations office was a pyre that was already collapsing. Ahead was the railroad embankment and there, according to orders, the men were struggling to place the heavy anti-aircraft guns, all the remaining 8.8 cm. guns the battalion possessed.

Buchner stood in the snow, his adjutant, Lieutenant Loose, and his column commander, Lieutenant Stampfer, at his side. In the glow of the Russian salvos they saw the flak moving into position; it was clear to them that in the sulfurous light the Russians must have an equally clear view of those cannon.

"The flak is the moral backbone of the infantry," the operations officer, the chief of staff, and the commander of the tank corps had replied to all of Buchner's urging and pleading. "But this is madness, sheer madness," he exclaimed suddenly, and still he did not give the order that would have contravened the orders from above. The batteries had not yet reported completion of their task when hell broke loose—fire from automatic guns and mortars simultaneously. The railroad embankment glittered white, then turned yellow and green; fragments, gun carriages, wheels, barrels, rods hurtled up into the black sky and rained down again. That was his heavy flak; that was his battalion.

"Good God . . . Loose, Loose, Loose!"

Buchner wept; he gripped his adjutant's arm. Loose and Stampfer were livid from the reflection of exploding shells. Sergeant Januscheck wiped blood from his face and said, "Now you've wrecked everything, sir."

Four miles away from Buchner and separated from him only by a hill, Major Keil moved toward the railroad embankment, followed by a detachment of his East Prussians. When a salvo rained down near by, the East Prussians threw themselves flat. Heinrich Halluweit, the cook, raised his head and saw Keil, limping somewhat on his bad leg, stalking steadily on, apparently without the slightest intention of taking cover. Halluweit called out, "Sergeant, what's the matter with him?" Sergeant Göritt shrugged and muttered something inaudible.

Other men called, "Major, major . . ." Keil paid no attention. He plodded on through the deep snow.

Halluweit turned to Vierkant. "What do you think is wrong with him?"

"Crazy, he's gone off the beam. Karl ought to try to talk to him."

Karl Wischwill who had been Keil's orderly for years and who also knew Keil's father and wife and the workshop at Cranz, ran after Keil, throwing himself down in the snow once on the way, but overtaking the major. "Herr Major, Herr Major . . ." No effect. "Herr Keil!"

Keil turned his head briefly. He saw that no one was following him.

"Goddamn bastards," was all he said.

The men behind heard him, but they remained prone. "He's
gone clean off his nut."—"No, we're not that crazy yet."—
"We're not ready for suicide yet."

"Major, major . . ."

Major Keil no longer heard, no longer looked around. He
climbed up a section of the railroad embankment that was
covered by heavy machine guns. A cone of fire instantly cut
him in two.

No exceptions, not a step back! The Leader leads—leads
every single regiment; he also leads Enders' regiment and Keil's
battalion and Döllwang's combat group.

In Gönnern's bunker the telephone buzzed again. The adjutant picked up the receiver and put it to his ear. His face was no
longer that of an angelic baby; now it suddenly looked like an
old woman's. He could not force his lips to say the words he
should have spoken ("Not a step back; the position must be
held!"). His nerves gave way; he dropped the telephone on the
table. It buzzed again; the receiver remained where it was and
distant words crackled in it. They sounded very faint and yet
they filled the room and the adjoining room where Gönnern
and Vilshofen were. "I am fatally wounded," the voice in the
telephone said. "I cannot hold on here any longer; only twenty
men are still alive; I urgently request . . .'"

Again there was a ringing and the crackling of words in the
receiver. This time they were: "Order carried out; the combat
group has ceased to exist."

Gönnern was sitting with his head in hands, his palms pressing against his temples. Between compressed teeth came words
that were a groan: "Tragic indecision . . ."

A shadow fell across his table. It was the shadow of Vilshofen, who had no right to issue orders here or to do anything. Nevertheless, he switched the call from the adjutant's
to Gönnern. But Gönnern would not take it, and so Vilshofen
put it to his own ear and called, "Döllwang . . . Hans, Hans! . . .
Who are you, where is the captain?"

He heard the reply: "Schweidnitz, paymaster's assistant. The
captain . . . My God, Oh God . . ."

The receiver dropped to the table with a thump. Vilshofen's
face was ice, his heart, his blood were snow. Behind him he
heard groans and then he grasped that Gönnern was saying
something. He whirled around. "Now you say it! So you too

201

felt it, you knew it, Gönnern, you haven't been carrying out a battle order, you've executed a death sentence. Döllwang, Hans Döllwang, my own Captain . . . and he is only one, but there were many of them, a whole army. And you, Gönnern, are not the only one either, if that is any sop to your conscience. You're not the only one! Good God, generals the executioners of their own army, executioners of their own men!"

Vilshofen staggered toward the door.

"Madman!" Gönnern called after him.

Vilshofen turned once more. "Germany," he said. "That is not a word written in water, nor in blood. Captain Döllwang, Lieutenant Latte, Private Fell, Private Altenhuden, Sergeant Gnotke . . . whenever a man dies senselessly here, Germany dies with him!"

Gönnern was unable to utter a sound. His jaw dropped, his mouth remained wide open, his face was like putty.

Kalser and Koog left the brick factory. Their way led along the inner arc of the railroad embankment. They reached the spot where the ruins of Buchner's flak battalion lay scattered around and where the snow was crushed down by vehicles. Walking on, they came to the place where the remnants of Döllwang's group, wounded, fleeing, and dying, had crossed the embankment and either remained in the snow or hastened on.

Captain Kalser bent over a figure in the snow.

It was Private Altenhuden who had been lying stunned until he suddenly felt a hand fumbling for his dog tag. "I am the chaplain of the 376th; where are you hurt, my boy?" Altenhuden flipped himself over faster than he had moved during the entire campaign. "Oh God, hell no, was I scared. Like the devil himself had me by the throat. No, no thanks, chaplain, very nice of you all the same. Nothing wrong with me at all, I don't need a thing. Oh yes, it would be nice to get transportation; there's something the matter with my leg, a flesh wound."

"I'm afraid there is no transportation. Keep on in this direction and you'll reach the road to Yeshovka."

"Here's something to help you on your way," Koog said.

"Thank you very much, Chaplain." Altenhuden took the slice of bread and sardine that Chaplain Koog held out to him. These provisions had come from Colonel Enders' room; Koog had filled his pockets with food that Enders had brought along from Germany.

Russian Salvos continued to weave gleaming spiderwebs in the sky. The ruins of the rations office towered over the railroad embankment; they stood marked against the glistening horizon like dark shark fins. The face of the dying man over whom Chaplain Koog knelt flickered green in the flashes of explosions.

"Chaplain, now I really can't attack any more," the dying man's voice whispered.

"There's no need for you to attack any more. For you the war is over."

"Legs, legs, legs, kick 'em up high . . ." Another man bawled the words of a popular song, gazed into the green spurts of light with insane eyes, and snatched with both hands at the chaplain who was bending over him. The chaplain stayed until the man grew still; then he closed the eyes and folded the hands over the man's chest.

The next man was August Fell. Fell was badly wounded but fully conscious. His intestines were bulging out between his jacket and trousers. Chaplain Kalser covered the gaping abdominal wound with the tail of his coat, so that the dying man would not see it. But Fell knew his condition. His last anxiety was that he would be unable to swallow the holy wafer. He could not longer swallow and the stench of feces was already coming from his mouth. The chaplain broke a tiny piece from the wafer and washed it down Fell's throat with water from his canteen. Before very long August Fell also was dead.

Koog and Kalser separated at Fell's body.

Koog went on along the railroad embankment and later descended into the Tsaritsa valley. Kalser turned north toward the road that led to Yeshovka. He gathered around him a number of limping, weary stragglers. In this group around Kalser were Gnotke, Gimpf, Altenhuden, and Assistant Paymaster Schweidnitz.

Toward midnight this group was met by a figure in a white camouflage cloak. Others, with submachine guns held at *ready,* were standing around in the drifting snow. Commands rang out: "Stand still. Not a step farther. Come over here, all of you." Schweidnitz was so weary, anguished, and stunned that he did not recognize his superior, Paymaster Zabel, or the sergeant and veterinary lieutenant who had been his neighbors. The others too were so worn out that without a word of protest they let the reception commando lead them to a new line, where they had to take positions beside other men who had been picked up in similar fashion, and beside supply troops who were being thrown in to defend the front.

When Gnotke opened his eyes next day he found that he was lying on snow. Above him was a shelter half, and it too was covered with snow. He was lying in a shallow hollow; all around him were blankets, coats, and rags. Something stirred under the rags. The black head with its dense mass of hair was Altenhuden's. Gimpf, too, was beside him and one of the new men. Gnotke got up, raised the canvas, and looked out. Before him lay an open field out of which an icy mist.was rising; everywhere he looked it was clear, open field. Here, on the edge of the field, were tents and a smoking field kitchen. Altenhuden also rose, looked around, then met Gnotke's eyes.

"On an open field!" Gnotke said.

"So this is the line!" Altenhuden contributed. After a while he raised his hand and tapped his finger against his forehead. The meaning was: they're crazy. And "they" meant the men in the Tsaritsa ravine, in Stalingrad or in Berlin or wherever they were who were still waging war in a place like this.

Altenhuden voiced his thought. "They're crazy."

"I think so too," said Sergeant Gnotke.

Gnotke was in command of his group, which consisted of Altenhuden, Gimpf, and the new man whose name was Franz Schiele. He led them over to the field kitchen. Each of them received a sliver of hardtack and a mess kit full of horse broth —hot water in which horse bones had been boiled. Later the commander of the combat group, a maintenance master sergeant, went up to Gnotke and ordered him: "Take a few men and reconnoiter the terrain."

The master sergeant pointed vaguely toward where the Russians were presumed to be. "Yes, sir," Gnotke replied. He chose Altenhuden, Gimpf, and the new man to go along. Before leaving he went back to the field kitchen and got another slice of hardtack and enough broth to give each man a serving. Then the four set out. They headed toward the skeletons of some houses that towered up out of high snowdrifts. Here they found a long piece of corrugated iron roofing. They bent one end up, fastened their belts to it as a tug rope. This was their sled. In the same place they found a number of charred fragments of boards which they loaded on. Then they placed their packs on the sled and took turns pulling it. So they tramped through the snow, one group among the hundreds like them who were drifting around during these last days and waiting for the end. The direction they had to take was clear—away from the ring of fire that was drawing closer and closer, toward Tsaritsa ravine and Stalingrad.

The Red Army troops crossed the railroad embankment in the south. From the west they also crossed it (it ran in a wide loop out from Stalingrad and back to the city), and rolled on over Yeshovka and Tulevoy ravine; from the north they flooded across Gumrak airport and reached the group of bunkers known, after their former commander, as Hartmann's Village. The commander in chief, who had his headquarters there, had to flee in haste. He and his entourage moved to Tsaritsa ravine; here they found themselves among the hordes from the routed southern front and stayed only one day. Then the commander in chief moved on and set up his headquarters in the center of Stalingrad in the large ruined department store on the "Place of the Fallen."

The Red Army drew the ring tighter. Russian tanks continued on to the fortifications that surrounded the Stalingrad airport. Here the attacks were directed against the regiments and divisions that had fallen back or were still falling back from the west. At the rim of the airport and on Heights 102 and 107 German artillery, rocket guns, and mortars were already in position. Here too was Major Holmers' artillery battalion.

The order was Hold! Not a step back! The main defense line established for this sector was the "Tartar Wall." Major Holmers was at his emplacement, eight hundred yards from the Tartar Wall. The guns, which had once been pointed toward Stalingrad and the Volga, had fortunately been placed for all-around defense, so that he was able to point them toward the south and southwest. In addition, he had ammunition, thanks to his own caution. In the early days of the encirclement, when the plan for breaking out had developed so far that he received orders to blow up his stocks of ammunition, Holmers had destroyed only half of it. What he had left now stood him in good stead; the barrels of his 15 cm. howitzers, which he had taken from Belgorod across the Donetz, the Oskol, and the Don all the way to Stalingrad and the Volga, would once more have a chance to get hot.

The day was a gloomy one. Thick vapors rose up from the Volga and drifted over the stone gulches and shattered ruins of Stalingrad, passed over the airport and then, blocked by the winds from the west, built up behind the Tartar Wall like a dirty-blue, impenetrable cliff face.

Holmers looked out into the mist. There ahead was the "Concrete Wall," the "Old Woman," the "Tin Soldier," and the "Tennis Racket"; such were the names they had given to a factory, a railroad switch tower, an air lookout tower and a loop in the railroad tracks, in accordance with their characteristic shapes. There was also the "Flower Pot," a small group of trees rising out of the level terrain.

Behind him Holmers had the factory quarter of Stalingrad—remnants of walls, rubble heaps, steel skeletons of buildings, bombed-out houses of the Workers Settlements, a factory chimney riddled with holes at the bottom and in the middle, its top torn off, but miraculously still standing. On his left the broad expanse of snow was the old Russian airfield which had been constantly under fire and therefore never used. At the rim of this airfield stood the "Tin Soldier," the bombed, burned-out fragment of a lookout tower. The ruins beside it were what was left of the former Aviation Academy. Between these two sets of ruins a pair of generals with their staffs and the survivors of their staff companies had settled down. In the middle of the level field was the "Flower Pot." This tiny wood was dotted with artillery, rocket guns, and mortars; it represented the core of the defensive system. All of this terrain with its rubble, twisted iron structures, and factory ruins was surrounded by an extensive ridge of earth that ran in a shallow arc for a considerable distance. This was the "Tartar Wall."

The Tartar Wall was the wonder at which Holmers was staring in amazement, and the sergeant at his side was no less surprised. The strangeness lay not in the ridge itself; they had been familiar with it for days, ever since they had moved their tractors and howitzers over it and had taken possession of several miles of it in order to construct dugouts for their men in its side. They knew, too, how it had changed in the course of time when their cannoneers withdrew and new inhabitants arrived. Then the wall had become for the neglected, starving, dying men of the army what it was today—a place where men passed silently out of the world, for starving and freezing men no longer screamed and complained as they had formerly.

Since yesterday this wall had been the new main defense line. Because its occupants, who at best could only crawl on all fours, could not possibly defend it, troops were ordered to occupy it. The 76th Infantry Division, the 113th Infantry Division, and the 60th Motorized Division had been assigned to this sector; but the troops that came up from the west during the night were no longer divisions, not even parts of divisions.

It was for this reason that Holmers and the sergeant were staring at the wall and at the heavy fog bank beyond it. Beyond the wall was the highway that led from Gumrak and Gorodishche to Stalingrad. The wall itself blocked the view of the road from Holmers' emplacement. Only yesterday that road had been full of the din of motors, the creak of wagon wheels, the clank of caterpillar treads, and the assorted noises of marching columns. Those had been the supply trains, still mobile because they still had fuel; there had also been headquarters staffs from towns to the west, the commander in chief's staff, corps staffs from the ravines near Gumrak, medical, rations, and administrative staffs who had evacuated their quarters and were moving to Stalingrad. But now there was silence beyond the Tartar Wall, although now and then motors would roar and snow fly up, indications that Russian tanks were moving in on the other side of the wall. At such times the major would look at his sergeant who would shrug.

There was nothing to do about it. The ammunition had to be husbanded; they could afford to fire only at definite, visible targets.

A soldier whom Holmers had sent up front returned. "Directly in front of us there's nothing, nobody at all," he reported.

"What shall we do, send some of our own men up there?"

"The few men we have. . . ." the sergeant replied.

"Who will work the guns?"

An observer whose position was far forward toward the west reported by radio: "The unit that is supposed to be here isn't here."

"Why, that's the sector of the 60th Motorized."

The sergeant again shrugged.

The observer up front reported again: "Men on my right. They're going on toward the city. What am I to do?"

"Go back with them," Holmers answered his observer.

What else could he do? With the wall only partly manned, long stretches of it completely uncovered, and with the shattered remnants of divisions not finding their assigned positions and wandering around in the vicinity, or finding, if they did occupy their positions, that they had no support on either flank; with the chain of command in complete disruption and "imaginary troops" all around—under such circumstances Holmers felt that he could not expose his observer any longer.

Suddenly a furious burst of shooting broke out; heavy machine guns and tank cannon began firing on the other side of the wall, under the dense cover of the mist. The artillery battalions could not make out what was going on. Height 102 did not fire, the "Flower Pot" did not fire, Holmers did not fire his own guns.

The shooting was directed at Keil's combat group, which for the past forty-eight hours had been wholly leaderless—since Sergeant Göritt fell at Yeshovka. The East Prussians in MG Battalion 9 had marched a long way through deep snow up to this wall, behind which they hoped to find help. When the few remaining men heard the rumble of tank treads behind them

207

and caught sight of Russian tanks charging in V formation over the level field, Heinrich Halluweit, who had taken command, ordered the heavy machine guns placed in position. But there was nothing around them but a level field, and they and their guns sank deep into the snow. The bursts that spurted from the guns had no more effect on the thick steel walls of the tanks than snowballs would have had. They ricocheted, that was all. The machine gunners had expected this, but they thought their fire would signal the defenders of the wall. The wall, however, remained silent; nothing stirred there except the exhausted men who had lain down to die in the abandoned dugouts and who now staggered to their feet and fled toward the city.

The tanks came up closer. The machine-gun group with Halluweit was crushed into the snow. The others sprang to their feet and ran, trying to reach the wall. On their left was one row of tanks, on their right another. The men reasoned that the tanks would not fire on one another and attempted to reach cover along the walls of one row of tanks. They raced along beside the moving treads in the geysers of snow that accompanied the monsters. But the tanks did turn their machine guns upon one another, and the East Prussians who were not killed by the direct fire fell when they were struck by ricochets from the armor plate.

The men at the guns behind the wall heard the chatter of machine guns and waited to see what would happen, but nothing at all happened within their range of vision. They saw a group of those ghosts from the abandoned dugouts staggering through the snow; that was all.

A man with one sleeve of his coat dangling empty crossed the broad expanse of snow. He heard the howl of tank guns and saw balls of flame spurt up into the mist. But the mist cloaked him, and in any case the tanks were not interested in a single man. The solitary man crossed a ravine, the same Balka-Krutaya over which Holmers had, some days before, seen the troops from the broken west front stream into Stalingrad. This ravine was not very deep, but it was split up into a crazy quilt of tributary ravines. Once a bridge had led across it. This bridge still existed, at least sections of it did. Other parts, including the plank flooring, had been carried away and the holes stuffed with frozen snow and the bones of horses, but it would still carry men on foot. The solitary man felt his way carefully across the bridge, continued on through the snow, climbed over the wall, and came to Major Holmers' emplacement. There he stopped. He was a lieutenant, a small man, still young, but with a face seamed and cracked like the bark of an ancient tree.

He introduced himself: "Lawkow!"

He was the adjutant and at the last the acting commander of Lundt's regiment. . . . No, he did not know where the regiment was. He was supposed to take up positions in the Tulevoy ravine; on the way there he had been wounded.

"My arm, yes, it's gone. It was shot up a bit, sir." Lieutenant Lawkow looked around and his eyes widened. He almost fainted from concentrated attention and from the smell that rose to his nostrils. There was the sergeant, stooping over a blazing fire and holding in his hand, as though it were the most natural act in the world, a long-handled frying pan. And in the pan—it was a big one and quite full—sizzled slices of sausage. Lawkow was amazed and quite beside himself. But he pulled himself together and answered the questions addressed to him. "Our division, no, I don't know where it is. . . . Yes, it's true, in Gorodishche I saw our general standing in the street. He doesn't know what's going to happen next and I don't know either." Then he added, "All I do know is that I seem to have worked up quite an appetite."

"Well, then, sit down with us, Lawkow."

Lawkow, Holmers, and the sergeant sat down to a first-class breakfast. And they did not eat with their hands; they had knives and forks; there were three glasses and each of them had a shot of whisky.

"Arabian nights!" Lawkow said. "If you ever come to Pellningken in East Prussia, sir, we'll slaughter a pig and then we'll sit down to it until there's nothing left. Agreed, sir?"

"Agreed," Holmers said.

"Now if only I could sleep for a while."

"Well, lie down right here."

Holmers and the sergeant went back to their posts.

Others passed by. One of them was a Major Buchner who had sent his men to Stalingrad. He was looking for one of his men, Lieutenant Stampfer, who had vanished along with his entire train and supply column.

Several more times the noises of battle could be heard, momentary encounters between Russian and German troops. The attacks were crushing retreating units and parts of units in the area in front of the Tartar Wall. A wave of enemy infantry and a few tanks also mounted the ridge and the guns from Heights 102 and 107 went into action. But for the most part the positions were unchanged that day.

The change came next day, with a simultaneous change in weather. During the night a strong wind had sprung up, a howling northeaster. The clouds were swept away; the sun shone out of a clear sky and it was so cold that crystals shimmered in the air. A number of the artillerymen whom Holmers had after all sent up to the wall froze to death from lying unprotected in the wind.

The Russian attack concentrated upon the artillery nest in the "Flower Pot." The cannoneers in the "Flower Pot" were without infantry protection. An emergency company which should have been there was not. From his emplacement Holmers observed details of the battle. He did not need his telescope; he could see clearly with the naked eye. Trees swayed and bent over like stalks in a bamboo grove. Tanks broke through into covered dugouts and crushed beneath them snow, men, and earth. The tanks moved on, turned to other objects. Fleeing men who rushed out of the grove were felled by machine-gun fire. The "Flower Pot" was crushed, rolled flat, annihilated.

The loss of the "Flower Pot" split the defenders in two. Central Stalingrad was separated from North Stalingrad. From then on the German Stalingrad army was locked within two pockets. Commander Holmers realized that he was not only facing two fronts, but that a third front was rolling closer and closer to him.

Load—fire!

Load—fire!

Until the batteries reported: Ammuniton gone.

Blow up the guns, blow up the tractors! And then there was nothing to do but to flee, to flee as fast as possible into Stalingrad.

Next day, when Holmers awoke in a Stalingrad cellar, he was still bemused, still in the midst of it; he still smelled the cordite and stood between walls of glowing, russet smoke; he still saw the "Flower Pot" being torn to pieces before his eyes, still participated in the general dissolution that had taken place afterwards.

Height 107—he was through with that now, through for good. The guns were blown up, the labor detachment of Russian prisoners of war had been left behind. Just as well; what good would they be now? The rations were gone too.—"Sergeant, the rations were distributed, weren't they?"—"Yes, sir, everything distributed among the men." So there was nothing left.

"What's the outlook for coffee, sergeant?"

"I'll see to it right away, sir."

The retreat—a general flight into the city. Trucks, command cars, tractors, soldiers, generals, specters. Splashing in among them the bursts of light from shells. Metal, iron girders, towering walls—the edge of Stalingrad gleaming bright as day in the light of rockets, and above it the inky sky. A detachment from the south fled northward, a detachment from the north went south. The greater part of Height 107, Height 102, and the Workers Settlements (each one of these places had cost rivers of German blood) and the airfield were in the hands of the Russians. At the moment the attack was surging against the western rim of the city and past the Aviation Academy toward Central Stalingrad.

The sergeant returned. Holmers' breakfast was not too bad. There was no water for washing, however, nor any wood for thawing snow. Moreover, as an artillery commander without artillery Holmers was unemployed, just as were many other officers and the greater part of the staffs that had flooded into Stalingrad.

However, Holmers was given an assignment, though not a battle assignment. The division entrusted him with a special mission: to comb the ruins and cellars of this quarter of town for men still fit for fighting. Today he had to go through the so-called "white houses." Accompanied by his sergeant and his battalion clerk, he set out. His way led down a path trampled in the snow, across the courtyards of buildings, and straight through other buildings. All the structures were burned out stone frameworks, windowless, doorless, floorless; looking up from below one saw the sky through four or five stories, and snow drifted down from above.

"All rubble!"

"Unbelievable, the amount of steel that's been shot into this place."

"But what is going to happen now, sir?" the clerk asked.

"My dear boy, how should I know? There, you see, there's the line we can't possibly cross."

Through a great gap in a wall, down a precipitate slope, they had a sudden glimpse of the frozen gray Volga.

They walked on over fields of rubble. Whole streets resembled vast quarries, and among the shattered boulders lay corpses. When the three emerged from a labyrinthine street into the open air, they saw before them a row of tall ruins. These once handsome tall buildings, now gutted by demolition bombs, were the "white houses."

The courtyards and cellars were inhabited. In the basements, behind window-openings stuffed with sandbags, sat the staffs. Other cellars in this group of buildings were populated by dispersed soldiers, by the drivers of vehicles that had got bogged down somewhere, by sick men, blacksmith personnel, the remnants of dissolved veterinary companies. The entrances to the cellars were barricaded. Paving stones, store signs, iron bedsteads, lantern posts, and all sorts of odds and ends blocked the way—not only to Russian attackers, but to new arrivals and troublesome patrols of officers. Holmers had to hunt around for the more or less secret exits and entrances. He and his men had to stoop and crawl into a cellar and down a long corridor. The corridor was a yard and a half wide, and even here, along both sides of the wall, was one gray face after the other. From the glowing tin cans with their tiny fires an acrid smoke rose up. Between each man, or in a gap between every second man, one of these tin cans was set up, with some kind of stuff burning in it. The corridor was high enough for a man to stand erect, but because of the smoke Holmers, the sergeant, and the clerk had to stoop as they walked, and even so they almost choked. They could not even reach the farther corners and recesses of these cellars. They stumbled over outstretched feet. And as soon as they entered, as soon as they blocked the feeble light from the street, they were met with shouts. "Stay out. This place is filled up." And as they went the greeting was the same. "Scram. What are you doing here? Watch out, keep off my feet." Holmers, after a poor breakfast, unwashed, suddenly wrenched out of his normal orderliness and pitched down into this abyss, was just in the proper mood to flare up and put a stop to such impudence and laxness. But here, in these caves, he could summon up no rage. He nudged his sergeant—there was no sense in bawling out these lemures. The thing was to get this affair over with as quickly as possible and clear out of this plague spot.

"Listen all of you," Holmers shouted. "For the men who are still fit for combat there's a field kitchen outside in the courtyard. Coffee and bread is being handed out, and each man will receive marching rations."

No one stood up or showed any intention of doing so.

Holmers glanced down the row of those faces that were not hidden by the smoke. He met a man's blue eyes. "Is there any chance of help coming, sir?" "Yes, if Hooth were coming it would be different," another man said. The mention of Hooth, the tank general, evoked laughter, and this reaction seemed to Holmers better and more human than the dull, empty staring of the others.

Holmers turned on his heel. "Show me your paybook," he

212

said to one man. He read: *"Private Evald Stüve, born Dec. 28, 1911 in Cologne; occupation: mechanic. Maiden name of wife: Mathilde Rautenberg. Residence: Cologne, Geronswall 5 c."* "Why are you rotting away here, Stüve; why don't you see to it that you get back to your unit and regular rations?" Stüve threw back his coat and the upper part of his jacket; then he raised the rags that covered his shoulder. Holmers saw a mass of pus with the bone showing through. He reeled back from the stench of the wound. "Have you had medical treatment?" he asked, solely in order to say something. "None," Stüve replied.

Holmers asked no more questions in this cellar. He did not bother the man whom he saw sitting dully on half a sack of flour. Nor did he feel any inclination to enter an adjoining cellar where a few men were squatting around a fire and cooking pancakes of flour and water. Climbing out through the window-opening again, he regained the street. Four men followed him nevertheless, four men so driven by hunger that they were ready to let themselves be sent into combat again for the sake of a march ration consisting of four hundred grams of horse meat and two hundred grams of bread.

From another cellar Holmers fetched a few more men. The adjutant at divisional headquarters laughed at him when he ushered in his recruits. What the devil was the matter with him?—the division needed men and this was no time to set the requirements high. No, by God, as long as his belt still held him together, a man was fit for combat.

That was a reprimand, and Holmers was furious at the adjutant and at the lieutenant colonel who sat in the room and who glanced up briefly, looking at Holmers as if he could not be differentiated from the wall. There they sat in their fat, hadn't the slightest idea what those cellars looked like. Easy for them to talk.

But Holmers said, "Yes, sir," and set out again.

He went from cellar to cellar, and this time he did not permit the men to shut their eyes or ears; he did not overlook impudence or laxness. He recruited everyone without exception—exhausted skeletons, stinking dysentery sufferers, starvelings who were nothing but skin and bones. By damn, did they think he was a policeman? "Under these special circumstances persons of authority must take over this function." That was what that son of a bitch had said . . . and that other fellow sitting there and making you feel like a pane of glass that he could look straight through. . . . Throughout the fighting he had scarcely ever seen those staff officers. Up to now they'd sat comfortably in Yeshovka; while the front faced to the east that had been twelve miles in the rear. What had they known then about what was happening up front, and what did they know now? Let them go down into the cellars themselves and fetch out those living corpses.

But it was Holmers who collected a band of pale and feeble men behind him. Some could scarcely move their legs, some were on the point of death; in others the madness of starvation flickered in their eyes. He cursed, set his teeth, and descended into the next cellar. Four hundred grams of meat and two hundred grams of bread was a great deal; it was really sufficient for a marching ration, for the destination was only the edge of the city; in most cases that was the end point of their lives. The spearhead that was driving into the outskirts of the city consumed men, and it would feed as well on skeletons, men with rotted gut and putrescent wounds; it crumbled and crushed whatever softened human flesh still had the vitality to put itself in reach.

Major Holmers was now a recruiting officer. A civilized human being, only yesterday he had eaten with a knife and fork. Once upon a time he had drunk a demitasse after his meals and smoked a cigar. Each time he came out of one cellar and went into the next, he wondered why this curse had to strike him of all people. He no longer looked up at the sky, he no longer heard the rumble of cannon on the rim of the city, no longer heard the crash of bombs in the same street.

Weary, spiritually drained, poisoned by the air of the cellars and by all the wretchedness he had rummaged through during the day, he slumped down in his own cellar at evening. He sat over the rough table, his head pillowed in his hands, and stared into the flickering candle—and three other Holmers sat there with him—his father, his grandfather, and his great-grandfather.

His father said: I also recruited men; in my service they received salt pork, baked potatoes and beans, warm meals three times a day, the stipulated amount of sugar and lemon juice after six weeks at sea, although it was hard for me to manage it all because shipping was no longer so profitable as it had been.

The grandfather said: I too recruited men, and women and children too, from East Galicia, Latvia, Poland, Serbia, and Bukovina. I filled whole ships with them. What became of them across the ocean I don't know. But my recruiting had sense to it; it satisfied a need and was profitable business. And the societies that dealt in immigrants have grown to greatness.

214

The great-grandfather of the Stalingrad artillery officer said: In our families there have been honorable men who continued to deal in Negro slaves after the abolition of slavery. But I placed the trade on a legal and sound basis; I recruited men, contracted for them to labor in Hawaii, and shipped them out there. After I had depopulated the Island of Flores in the Azores group I began with the Island of Pico, and after a long, hard-working life, with coined gold, weighed and counted and carefully packed away in my sea chest, I sailed home and became the founder of our firm and our family.

The great-grandson who stared into the flickering candle had certainly not depopulated the cellars of Stalingrad, for beaten troops were still pouring in from the west and the flayed bodies in the cellars increased and multiplied just as the inhabitants of Flores and Pico had once multiplied to repopulate the islands. But on this one day he had probably fetched as many men out of the cellars as his great-grandfather might have taken on a voyage in his two-masted schooner from the Azores to the Hawaiian Islands.

What was the sense of it?—that was the question!

I had to pay for salt pork and potatoes and lemon juice for them, a voice answered, but they sailed my cargoes.

Every emigrant, man, woman, or child, brought me five dollars profit after all expenses, a second voice answered.

Even though I accomplished no more in a long life than a single earthquake might do in an hour, still I came home with a chest full of gold, a third voice answered.

But here there is no question of cargoes or of five dollars; here there is no thought of personal profit in it.

We too were not concerned only for ourselves. When we earned money and built ships with our money, we were building up Germany. Our shipping space was living space, real, actual *Lebensraum*.

You recruit men and throw them into battle. Very well, I too recruited men, and if my ship sprung a leak, they drowned and I pocketed the insurance; in any case I made whatever I could out of the ship and the men.

And I too recruited men and shipped them to America. There they vanished; perhaps they worked in the stockyards, perhaps they amounted to something—that was their affair. But I pocketed the passage money and made what I could out of the transaction.

And I too recruited men and sailed them to Hawaii; there they worked on the sugar plantations and distilled strong rum, and I kept the agent's fee. That is the essence of trade: I earn money and others earn money. That is good business, which is to say, in every case it is the satisfaction of a many-sided demand.

But can the principles of peace also be applied to war? Obviously, axioms of common sense are wanted here, and those apply as well to the business of individuals as to the business of nations, to peace and to war.

Greater Germany—was there any demand for that as there was a demand for transatlantic trade, for workers in Swift's packing plants or for laborers in the cotton and cane fields? You recruit men—what becomes of your men in the end? What are they changed into?

First of all and quite plainly, into corpses—and to make it worse, they are not men to begin with, nothing but cripples with shrunken stomachs and rotting guts, many of them wounded, all of them with frozen feet.

What for? For Greater Germany. Greater Germany on the Volga—is that good business, is there a need for that, does it satisfy a many-sided demand? A Greater Germany extending to the Volga—no one demands that and no one needs it; it is not a many-sided demand, not even a one-sided demand; not even Germany needs it.

Then was it done without any compelling necessity, for no real reason? Was it nothing but illusion, madness, crime. Not an idea, a nightmare. ...

A nightmare, and here it is falling to pieces and the men who dreamed it falling to pieces with it. And Holmers is falling to pieces with it, Holmers is falling to pieces with it, Holmers is falling to pieces with it!

The artillery officer, Major Holmers, shouted this sentence at the top of his voice.

The sergeant came rushing in. "Major, sir . . ."

"Did I need it, did I need it, I ask you?" Holmers jumped to his feet. Ordinarily he was a calm person, preferring to say a word too few rather than one too many. But now he let himself go; he roared like an elephant. "Colonial country. Colossus with feet of clay. All we have to do is blow the trumpets and it all collapses. They certainly put it over on us. . . ."

Boom.

Whistling. Quivering earth. Crash of ruins. A bomb had struck close by. Obviously, the adjoining building was collapsing. Holmers' room seemed to whirl around its axis several times. Holmers stood in the middle of a pillar of white plaster dust and shouted: "Madness, megalomania, presumption—our own filth is falling on our heads."

The sergeant came back with some officers, including the lieutenant colonel.

"Holmers, look here, man, have you lost your mind?"

"Greater Germany is falling to pieces."

"Good God, it's been hard enough for all of us. Don't you think we're all on the point of going off our heads?"

"We did long ago. Or did you look at Russia and think it was an island in the Azores, sir?"

"Good God, he's really gone crazy."

"Now listen to me, Holmers. All hell is loose in the southern pocket, and when the southern pocket falls it will be our turn here in the northern pocket. Here too the Russians have made deeper penetrations. Report to your division at once. You must immediately comb out those cellars once more."

"I cannot carry out such an order, sir. . . ."

"Sir?"

"The cellars, no sir, wild horses couldn't drag me into them again. Beg to request, sir, that I be sent to the front."

"Not one man, but hundreds and thousands are needed there," the lieutenant colonel said. "And no one else is as good at it as you, Holmers; you proved that today."

"Hundreds, thousands . . . two hundred thousand, twenty-two divisions are gone already sir, except for the remnants in the cellars. Christ, sir, here you are freshly shaved; go down there yourself, sir, and stick your nose up against one of those stinking sores . . ."

"Sir . . ."

The lieutenant colonel snapped the word like a whip, but Holmers paid no attention; it made no impression upon him.

"Stinking sores, the men full of ulcerated wounds, with stiff legs, utterly miserable—those are the creatures you want, and if you want them, fetch your cannon fodder yourself."

Holmers would not stop. "Stalingrad—we've already used up nine-tenths of the men and now we're taking the rest. The rest of wretched, feeble, dying men—that is today's order. What is the meaning of it? Those men can't fight any more; they'll only be flattened out on the ground. I won't take part in it any more. I'm not a policeman and not a gravedigger either. To continue the battle with men who are half corpses, that is, that is . . ."

Holmers crashed his fist down on the table. He lost the last shreds of his self-control. The smooth-shaven face of the lieutenant colonel swam before his eyes and he did not hear what the other officers were saying. He looked around wildly. Something had to be done.

But he was an officer, and he concluded: "That is irresponsible behavior, gentlemen."

Then he went out, slamming the door behind him.

The officers shook their heads. One of them said, "Really, it's enough to drive one crazy." The lieutenant colonel said, "He wants to go to the front, so we'll send him to the edge of the city."

Holmers sat outside amid the rubble of the ruined street. Above him the starry sky was crystal clear. In the south, above Central Stalingrad, conflagrations raged and dense masses of smoke billowed up. Here he was; this was what he had come to. His father had been right; it had been a breach with his whole tradition, a rude smashing of inherited sobriety, solidity, and well-founded self-respect. Four and five generations of merchants who had calculated carefully, sought only the attainable and always attained it—in order that he might commit all at once the thousand stupid blunders they had avoided, in order that he might dash across whole countries with trucks and howitzers, might point twelve cannon at the moon—the unattainable—and might fire them. With trinitrocellulose, steel, and the acrid smell of cordite he had drawn a line under his whole tradition, under all the standards of value and reason that had been handed down to him. It added up to a crushing sum, enough to make a calm man lose his grip on himself.

The sky over Stalingrad was clouded with masses of snow. In its center was a wedge-shaped space that flashed red from exploding shells. Fires flared up and showers of red sparks sprayed down the twisted streets and fell on the snow-covered heaps of rubble. The wedge that divided the two pockets gained ground, but on the flanks troops—combed out of the cellars and constantly replaced—continued to offer resistance. The fiery wedge inside Stalingrad and its reflection in the sky was a sign visible from a great distance, and the soldiers, the officers, and the commander in chief knew what this sign meant.

It was the sign of the approaching end.

At the commander in chief's conference table stood the commanding general from the Gumrak ravine, the one who had once come upon Gnotke and Gimpf on the path. White-haired, slender, elegant, dark shadows under his eyes, his face had thinned so much during the past few days that all his nerves seemed to be showing through the skin.

His face, his voice quivered. "On the way here," he said, "I have witnessed scenes that beggar description. Do you people know what it means to demand, to order that the battle be continued—and a pointless, senseless battle at that?" The general turned to meet an objection from one of the officers at the table. "No, we are no longer accomplishing any mission here. We are not helping the establishment of a new front, neither at Rostov nor anywhere else. That has been true at least from the moment the pocket was narrowed to minimal dimensions and the Russians were able to withdraw part of their forces from here. Today, when the pocket has been split into segments, it is even truer. All we are doing now is prolonging a horrible process of slaughter."

Another general stood up and said: "Sixteen thousand wounded not cared for. Rations, fuel, ammunition exhausted. No emplacements, no shelters, no firewood. Symptoms of disintegration throughout the army. This description of the situation was radioed to the Führer four days ago. You gentlemen know the answer."

The chief of staff repeated the answer once more: "Capitulation out of the question."

The white-haired general looked at the faces of the men around the table. The commander in chief was there, the left half of his face twitching nervously, his eyebrows also twitching. Two commanding generals were there (he himself was the third; the fourth was in the northern pocket; the fifth had been grazed by a board and had flown out). Several colonels were also present, including Colonel Carras who had just arrived with the latest directives from Berlin. The general's eyes lingered on the long horse-face of the chief of staff. The commander in chief's "evil genius" had insisted indefatigably on holding out, yet he himself had wanted to escape the pocket, had wanted to take the last plane out to "report to the Führer." There had been an ugly scene about that; he had kept the last plane waiting for a whole night at Gumrak airport and had spent the night trying to persuade the commander in chief to sanction his plan. It had required virtually a palace revolution to prevent the chief of staff from flying out—the G-3 had protested indignantly and the commander in chief's adjutant had declared that he would shoot himself on the spot.

"Capitulation out of the question," this same chief of staff now said.

The words hung in the air of the cellar above the round conference table. And these officers whose faces were gray, who were irritable and worn out from lack of sleep, at odds with themselves and with the others, their nerves quivering from the incessant bombardments, numbed by the prospect

219

of the grim fate they saw confronting them, sentenced by their Führer to hold out to the last and compelled to execute this sentence upon their own men—these men inwardly performed a ghostly, inaudible clicking of heels that was, nevertheless, very real, and each of them inwardly voiced the obedient phrase: The order will be carried out.

The order would be carried out—even against their better judgment, even against the promptings of conscience and honor. The white-haired general from Gumrak—thirty years a soldier, two hundred years of military tradition behind him —staggered. Was it possible that orders and honor were incompatible? Yes, it was possible; the proof of it was being demonstrated before his eyes. The commander in chief's cultivated face, the chief of staff's horse-face, the green-eyed cat's face of Colonel Carras, the whole roomful of faces, epaulets, decorations, whirled around him.

"Three culminating points—let us sum up once more, gentlemen. On November 22, 1942, we received the order to dig in. It was an order unheard of in the entire history of warfare, especially for so large an army, twenty-two divisions, three hundred thousand men. How could they be supplied? We expressed our doubts. Today we know that Field Marshal von Manstein, Field Marshal von Weichs, the generals of the Air Force, and even General Zeitzler whom the Führer himself picked for chief of the general staff—all these officers doubted that we could be sent sufficient supplies. The difficult weather, the distance the planes had to cover—and this increased daily as the front rapidly receded—the broad, barren plains without a tree or a bush, where the slow transport planes were gravely exposed to ground defenses—those were some of the considerations. But, after all, it had 'worked' on the Valdai heights with six divisions; why shouldn't it work here with twenty-two divisions? That was the argument; the very size of the enterprise was alluring. Today we know that one man, Reich Marshal Göring, stood up and said: 'My Führer, I will take the responsibility for supplying the Sixth Army.' One voice—and against it the doubts of two army commanders, two Air Force generals, and the chief of the general staff carried little weight; against it our own judgment of the situation carried no weight. We received the order and we obeyed it against our dissenting judgment of the situation. That was on November 22, 1942.

"The other key day is January 10th, when the Russians offered us surrender terms. Well, gentlemen, that was the day we literally closed the last escape hatch. We already had dysentery running through the army; our troops were dying of exhaustion. The utter inadequacy of air supply had been proved by the corpses of a hundred thousand of our men. That should have been enough. We advised the commander in chief and requested freedom of action, if not for surrender, then for a desperate attempt to break out to the west. Once again we were denied. You must stand where you are, we were told. Hube stood before us and gave us the orders; he had just come back from Berlin. Well, he's flown out for good now to organize the supply services. Forgive me, but that is the damnedest nonsense; what is there left to organize? I looked around in Gumrak during the last few days we were there. Sheer chaos—and we are not organizing chaos, we're plunging into it with open eyes. And there stood Hube before us and said: 'At the end we must create a kind of Alcazar, so that we can hold out for months.' That was the order he brought, and we who knew better—not the staff officers in Berlin, but we who could see our men dying before our eyes—we obeyed!"

There was a pause. The speaker wiped the sweat from his brow and then said, "Gentlemen, I protest!"

The commander in chief sat, tormented, having already made up his mind to file away this protest and not to pass it on. The commanding generals stood by sympathetically. The chief of staff listened with malicious curiosity. Colonel Carras was receptive and understanding, admiring the word he himself would never dare to pronounce.

"The third key day was January 22nd. We again requested freedom of action. We wanted to avoid complete disintegration. The reply: Capitulation out of the question. That means, where you stand you must die. How has the situation changed since then? The number of wounded without care and even without the most elementary rations has multiplied. The men are falling senselessly, or are starving or freezing to death. The infantry reserves scraped together from artillery, communications, and supply troops have been used up to the last man. The battle is now being fought with men who are half dead and dying. And to what end? Only so that total chaos will result. Our orders are counter to conscience, counter to honor, counter to a soldier's honor. It is this that I am protesting against, and I request that my protest be recorded and passed on."

The company of officers in the cellar were phantoms.

"Gentlemen, what *do* you imagine the end will be?"

The commander in chief, who was burdened more than the

221

others by imagination, did not want to imagine anything at all, nor did he want to hear what others were imagining.

"I shall obey," the commander in chief said.

That was the end of the conference. The advisers were dismissed. They got up and separated hastily, almost fled from one another. Colonel Carras remained standing in the cellar corridor with a lost look. The commander in chief passed him —tall, slender in build. He had already been a general staff officer in the First World War; afterward he had taught at the Military Academy, had distinguished himself as chief of the Army High Command and in planning operations. All very well, but here . . . here something else beside planning and thinking was needed; here the great need was for the rude hand of a commander who not only thought but could act on his own account and who in difficult times could ruthlessly take responsibilities upon himself. But Paulus could not do that, no, not at all, Carras thought.

"He suffers like Christ on the cross and yet he will carry out the order," Carras said to the chief of the corps staff, Lieutenant Colonel Unschlicht, who was also watching the commander in chief stride down the corridor. Unschlicht merely looked at Carras, then turned up his coat collar and slipped out. Never again would these officers assemble around the same table. They were a group of phantoms departing from one another.

And the protest itself had been nothing but a phantom protest. The white-haired general knew that himself. Everything that was happening, here and farther way, and everything that could happen in Stalingrad from now on, was already beyond determination by the will of men; those who were still moving and seeing were already ghosts. This is what the commanding general said to himself as he walked past the gate of the ruined building, past the saluting sentry and the 10.5 cm. howitzer emplaced there, and stepped out into the broad square which at this hour was bathed in the chalk-white glare of floodlights so that the planes circling overhead could drop their loads of hardtack, meat, and canned rations.

The general walked past barricades, sandbags, barbed-wire fences. He saw the sentries of the guard standing around and heard the crack of shots from a carbine whip over the square. He paid no attention and set out toward the Volga and the ruin where he had his quarters. Then he changed his mind. "I shall go to the edge of the city after all," he said to the officer accompanying him. "Kindly have our few things sent there." He turned and went back across the "Square of the Fallen."

Howls, curses. A general's protest. A major's refusal to carry out an order. Lieutenants failing to execute orders. But these gestures could not halt the course of death. Men continued to fall at the edge of the city and along the streets that led to the city center. Reception commandos continued to pick up dispersed soldiers. Officer patrols continued to comb the cellars and mobilize wounded men, sick men, frostbitten men. German soldiers continued to die of starvation and exhaustion in the Stalingrad plantations of death. The detachments detailed to pick up rations dropped from planes had to shoot to defend the provisions from soldiers turned bandit; execution squads continued to fire their volleys.

A hundred paces from the "Square of the Fallen" and the army headquarters was the tall ruin of the former city theater. The side of it that faced the square was dark, the other side was bathed in red foam from the reflection of fires. The tall structure was roofless and burned out; the walls enclosed an area of rubble. But the cellars underneath the rubble were inhabited and from them corridors led to adjoining ruins and adjoining cellars. There, a day and a half ago, Captain Tomas, with a splinter wound in his head, had sought refuge. He had entered a vault filled with screams of pain, of delirium, and of death. In this maelstrom of dying he had almost forgotten the roaring world outside. Everything had become veiled —whether guns outside were firing, whether it was day or night, whether it was snowing or a storm was raging through the streets—such things could scarcely touch him or the others any longer, or could touch them again only if a bomb or a shell should tear open their cavern.

A few steps farther down into the ground was the operating room. Here three doctors were taking turns at caring for some eight hundred wounded men. The assembly line of bleeding bodies that passed across the operating table never stopped, day and night. For Medical Lieutenant Huth it had not stopped since Otorvanovka; it had been going on for sixty days. The only differences between then and now were that he no longer had any bandages, any antiseptics, any anti-tetanus vaccine, any ether, any morphine. The only equipment he had left were his instruments, the scalpel, the saw, the shears, a kettle of boiling water for sterilizing, and the powerful operating lamp dangling over his head. Pain, unendurable pain, was his sole remaining anesthetic, and the doctor could

223

only feel that they were fortunate who lost consciousness under his saw. The difference between then and now was also that the medical assistants were worn out and thin, and that, more and more frequently, they collapsed from the toil and from the vapors they had been inhaling for so many weeks now.

"Next ..."

The next was Captain Tomas.

It was a morass, a tropical morass that he entered. The skeletal figure that showed him his place on the plank and the other phantom who lifted a set of operating instruments from the kettle of boiling water were medical aides. The man with sweat-soaked body under his full-length oilcloth apron was the doctor. The assistants, the doctor, even the earthern walls were sweating. The doctor stood with his feet in a pool of blood. Steam wafted up out of the pot. The big lamp cast a fierce heat. There were no windows, no ventilation openings. As Tomas was laying his head down on the plank that served for an operating table, he noticed a large bucket. It was filled with fragments of flesh, on top an amputated arm. What a delicate hand, the hand of an intellectual, he thought. From the pail dense vapors of putrescence spiraled upward. It was the hot breath of decay, and the dangling lamp over the doctor's head was a blazing tropical sun.

"Hold your head still, captain."

The skeleton who was assisting the doctor gripped the captain's head between his skull and jaw and held him as if in a vise. Captain Tomas was a simple case. The doctor smoothed out the edges of the wound, cut the dirt-smeared loose skin from cheek and throat, then placed the used, blood-crusted bandage back on the wound.

"Next."

A medical aide picked up Tomas' coat and rucksack, led him through a large vault and then down a long corridor, and gave him a place in a small room.

There he spent twenty-four hours. After twenty-four hours Tomas could no longer stand it; he could no longer endure the silence in the room, the silence among the two dozen men who sat or lay there. It was worse than the morass, worse than the large vault beyond, where the death rattles of the dying went on incessantly day and night. What was the matter? This room, like the big vault itself, had a host—the 14th Tank Division—and the occupants had been assigned to a field kitchen. Therefore, unlike the great mass of the Stalingrad wounded, they received coffee brew in the morning, horse broth at noon, and a slice of bread at night. They were not among the uncared-for wounded; their thread of life had not been cut off; and still it was thinner here and the candle flickered more faintly than in other places. Two dozen human beings sitting hunched up opposite one another, and not a single loud word was spoken. It was like a reading room; there, too, faces are pillowed on hands; there, too, there is a sound of rustling and occasionally someone coughs. But this was no reading room, it was a cellar, and its occupants were sergeants, civilian officials, captains, majors, and even a lieutenant colonel. One man had a frozen foot, another pneumonia and damp hands, another headaches from endless brooding, another sciatica, another second and third degree frostbite. They sat in silence and heard nothing but the trickling of plaster from the walls. Now and then a man stood up, walked out stiff-legged, and did not return. During the time Captain Tomas spent in this room two men had done this, an AA artillery captain and a pharmacist. When the third, a captain and commander of a column, also stood up and went out with the same stiff movements and the same rigid expression, Tomas gathered his things together. His coat on his arm and his rucksack and other possessions in his other hand, he groped his way down the long corridor. He met a tank lieutenant he knew whose two hands had been frozen; his arms were wrapped to the elbows in thick dressings.

"Where are you going, sir?"

"I can't stand it there any more. Do you have any room left?"

"We'll make room."

Captain Tomas moved into the large vault. The other captain climbed the worn steps and reached the open air. The sky above the center of the city was red from fires, but he did not look up. Above the "Square of the Fallen" the howl of propellers sounded, but he did not hear it, he no longer cared. He held his head rigidly in the snowy air, looked neither to the right nor the left, and reached for his pistol. A shot rang through the night and the column commander collapsed. Not far from the spot where he fell lay the bodies of a captain of anti-aircraft artillery and of a pharmacist. Snow settled upon the rubble and upon the figures lying in it.

The "Square of the Fallen," which was not far from the cellar of the theater, was surrounded by the ruins of Stalingrad's tallest buildings. Here too lay wounded men and also soldiers from artillery and tank regiments, regimental headquarters, field kitchens. Here too was the ruin of the large Stalingrad department store which was now both the combat command post of the 71st Infantry Division and the head-quarters of the commander in chief.

The entrances to the square were blocked by barricades—sandbags, lampposts, railings torn from balconies, parts of machines, T-girders, smashed tanks, iron banisters, all wound around with barbed wire. Frozen corpses hung in the barbed wire, arms outspread and hands hooked into the barbs. At the lower end of the square lay a German plane that had crashed. This square, surrounded by the fantastic caesuras of the shattered buildings, was at this time illuminated by the floodlights. It was the hour when the propellers roared up above and the hour when the commander of the sector sent his men, armed with tommy guns or carbines, to patrol the square or to hide behind fragmentary walls.

A propeller roared. From the black heights a plane descended, dropped its load, and zoomed up again. Another roar; the sound could be heard at a great distance. A plane circled the square and again dropped supplies. The drops were not attached to parachutes; like stones the cans of meat, the chocolate, the sausage, hams and breads thudded to the ground. And not everything fell directly into the square; some of the loads dropped in the vicinity, in the streets and passageways between wrecked buildings.

There was a soldier there—and who would ever break off the half of his identification tag? Who would care to take his paybook from his pocket and who would care to read in the paybook: *Franz Liebich, shoe size 11, occupation; clerk, born at Merseburg in Thüringia, married, two children;* and who would some day fill out the form in the rolls: *fallen on————buried in ——— or who would ever read: Battle service: Sept. 1, 1939 to Sept. 5, 1939, battle in West Prussia; Sept. 15, 1939, pursuit in East Poland; and later: May 11, 1940, crossing of the Meuse; May 17, 1940 to May 28, 1940 pursuit battles to the Channel, Battle of Dunkerque; and finally: June 22, 1941: assignment in East* . . . Who would ever care about that and who would inquire on that misty, snowy evening at the "square of the Fallen"? The white-haired commanding general heard the carbine shots as he came out of the ruined department store, but he did not look around. The sentry who had poked the barrel of his carbine through a hole in one of the barricades was the last person who had seen that soldier alive, and he had seen nothing but a tattered figure framed in his sight, the coat-tails fluttering over the chalky-white square; he had not seen the madness in those unsteady human eyes; he had scarcely seen more than the coat button over the breastbone, which was what he aimed at. The order was: shoot without warning. And so he pressed the trigger and the soldier fell on his face a few yards from the loaf of bread he was striving to reach. After a while another shot rang out somewhere else on the square.

It was the same in North Stalingrad. There too was a broad floodlighted square not far from the "white houses." There too a detachment received the drops and a company guarded the area; there too a soldier with a tommy gun did not ask whether the man's name was Evald Stüve, whether his wife, Mathilde Stüve, spent her nights in the air raid shelter in Cologne and her days in the armament factory under the light of a glaring lamp. The guard did not know this and did not wish to know that only a few days earlier the soldier had lain in a shower of splinters at Voroponovo, that he had fought in hand-to-hand combat and been wounded in the arm, that he had since been wandering from dressing station to dressing station and had spent days and nights in cellars without a morsel of bread. The guard raised his submachine gun and fired a burst. The bullets tore out a man's liver and kidneys, and Evald Stüve collapsed in the square in the northern pocket, just as Franz Liebich had collapsed on the "Square of the Fallen."

The rations dropped by the transport planes also fell into battle areas, into Russian positions, and into the scarred places between positions; they fell into the rear yards of buildings and among labyrinthine paths between buildings. And here, instead of guards with white armbands, military police lay in wait. Where breads or sausages fell in the passageways among the buildings and where nocturnal shadows appeared for a moment and vanished the next into one of the many holes—there was the hunting ground for the field police. By twos or in patrols of four they combed this cellar world every hour. Their work kept them well fed; in comparison with the front-line soldiers whose faces were gray from a hundred battles, the MP's looked burly and well-filled. Their bearing was not the least bit lax, their eyes were not dulled, and their words were sharp and to the point. They would say: "There's one of 'em. Come on, get up. What've you got in that box? Flour and bread, nicely wrapped in cellophane, eh? Let's see, what's under your jacket? A sausage, a salami. Isn't that nice. Come along. —And you, my friend. Expecting a baby, are you? Don't try and look dumb, I mean your belly. What's that stuffed under your belt? Come on, unbutton it a little faster. Well, well, no baby after all, just a ham. What's this—anti-tank troops, Corporal Riess,

227

former SS corporal, service in Poland—who gives a damn about that? No, we don't care about your blood type, life saving certificate, or race certificate. Come on, get out. Outside, all of you." And out in the snow they did not go far. From another cellar another detachment of MP's came up, they too leading several arrested men. One of the men from the other detachment said, "Quite a party we've got here. You should of seen it. They built a fake wall out of ammunition crates and behind it they had a whole warehouse full, even coffee. All right, this is as good as any place."

Snow fell from the dark sky. On one side a fence, on the other the glassless window of a house. This was the field of execution. "Looters are to be shot within twenty-four hours," the army order read; here not twenty-four minutes had passed. A burst from submachine guns followed by a few additional shots from revolvers, and the eight men lay on the ground. The snow covered the bodies of the suicides and the bodies of the executed. It fell almost vertically at first, in fat, heavy flakes. Then a wind sprang up and scattered the falling crystals, driving them diagonally across the landscape of tumbled stone and girders. The wind grew stronger. It came out of endless space and it swelled and swelled into a howling storm.

It was one of those gales of the steppe such as the human frame can scarcely endure. A Kalmuck on horseback, overtaken by it, would close his eyes, retreat into his sheepskin, and let his pony find the way, and the shaggy little horse would plod unerringly through the snow.

The paymaster's assistant, Schweidnitz, who was wandering over the steppe, did not know the terrain and had never in his life experienced the sort of gale that raged all around him. How he ever at last reached a hut on the road to Verkhnaya Yelshanka, he did not know. It was only because the ground sloped and he had virtually rolled down the slope into the valley like a snowball; a hundred times he had fallen and bobbed up again out of the sea of whiteness. So he reached the middle of the Tsaritsa ravine, where the wind caught him and whirled him along like an uprooted mandrake, pushing him on and on until, like a piece of brush, he came up against a post and clung fast to it. He no longer knew whether it was the wind or cannon that roared so fearfully, and the flash of a bursting shell seemed to him like a lighted window in the snow-filled air.

A soldier found this wretched, stunned creature holding on with both arms to a wooden post. The soldier found out his name and rank and led him to a hut where, he knew, a paymaster, a veterinary, and several civilian officials were staying.

There Schweidnitz sat, exhausted, hunched up, his head sunk on his chest. Finally he looked around, recognized his chief, the paymaster, recognized a veterinary lieutenant colonel and his neighbor, the veterinary lieutenant (he did not know Chaplain Koog), and he smiled. He was home again. Schweidnitz was nineteen years old.

A conversation was going on.

"What have you found out?"

"Nothing."

"Where are your arms?"

"The Russians have them."

Assistant Paymaster Schweidnitz heard this conversation dimly, as though it were being conducted behind walls. He also heard the paymaster, the veterinary lieutenant colonel, the veterinary lieutenant, the provost officer, and the chaplain put on their fur coats and their leather belts, take tommy guns, and tramp out.

Hours passed before the men returned. They had been busy outside stopping fugitives. (The staff officers of the division had meanwhile barred other roads leading into Tsaritsa ravine from the south.) Schweidnitz, when they returned, was lying on one of the cots, sleeping like a log.

This reception commando of officials was not actually the rear guard, but it was more or less the rear guard of the divisional headquarters, or rather of two divisional headquarters and a corps headquarters which had formerly been located in these huts and had now moved on to the southern suburb of Stalingrad. The staff officers departed after their last efforts to stop fugitives, and now the officials were waiting for a personnel carrier which was to take them away. They brushed the snow from their boots and fur coats, took off their coats, and sat down again. On the table stood a Hindenburg light, a wick in a tiny cardboard container filled with wax. Their faces looked gloomy; they gave the impression that their lives were about to flicker out every time the candle flickered. One after the other they moved away from the table and sat down on the edges of their cots. They waited for the personnel carrier and they also waited for Chaplain Koog, who had not come back with them.

"Koog is a long time about it," the veterinary lieutenant said. "He's gone to see the colonel," the provost officer said.— "Hm, he hasn't got an easy job of it, having to talk everybody out of that sort of thing," Paymaster Zabel said.

"Please don't start that again, Zabel," the lieutenant colonel snapped.

"I'm not saying anything, but the men discuss the matter for hours at a time, whether one ought to do it and how one ought to do it. And even if you don't want to do it, you can't help thinking about it and imagining the whole thing. . . ."

The lieutenant colonel groaned. He did not want to hear any more and so he stretched out on the cot and drew his fur collar over his ears. The veterinary lieutenant also lay down. His cot was above the chaplain's.

"That car is certainly taking its time."

"We ought to call South Tsaritsa."

They telephoned, but were merely told to hold themselves in readiness. Fuel still had to be obtained for the personnel carrier and first it had to make another trip.

After a while Chaplain Koog came in, sat down at the table, and stared into the Hindenburg light. He did not seem aware that out of the darkness of the room four pairs of eyes were fixed upon him, trying to read his expression.

He was weary and spoke slowly, as if in his sleep:

"Now the colonel too . . . and I understand it, I can understand how a man can fold up at a time like this and take his own life."

One of the cots creaked. The veterinary lieutenant colonel sat up, a tall, broad-shouldered man who had had a healthy peasant face. But now the skin over his cheekbones was gray and his eyes were sunken. He went up to the table, leaned forward, and brought his face so close to the chaplain's that his nose almost touched the flickering candle. In a hoarse voice he said, "Can you say that, chaplain? To my mind that is outrageous."

"My dear sir . . ." the chaplain replied, and his voice sounded plaintive and imploring, as though he wished to say: please leave me alone for a little and don't you too start. The lieutenant colonel whirled on his heel and slumped down on his cot again. After a while the chaplain also lay down. The light on the table went out, and in the darkness sleep overcame them all.

A heavy explosion awoke them, and this time Assistant Paymaster Schweidnitz also awoke. Zabel cried out, "Tanks!" Immediately afterward a shot cracked and a body rolled from the lieutenant colonel's cot and thudded to the floor.

"Good God. The lieutenant colonel!" the chaplain shouted. No sooner had he spoken than another shot sounded and the chaplain felt something like a wet hand smack into his face.

The fingers he raised to his forehead and eyes sank into a soft, warm mass; it was the lieutenant colonel's brain. Schweidnitz had lit a match and by its flare he saw what had happened.

"The lieutenant colonel has shot himself through the mouth," he said in his boy's voice.

"He might have had the decency to do that outside, just like everybody else. We have a right to expect that much consideration for others." It was Paymaster Zabel who said this and it sounded like a defiant expression of good upbringing and of disappointment with an old comrade of whom he would not have expected such an indiscretion. But Chaplain Koog's hearing was keen; he grasped the significant nuance. And as he looked at Zabel in the dim glow of the expiring match he saw Zabel's hand thrust back in his fur coat and feel for his hip pocket, and then he saw Zabel making for the door. Koog lost no time; he reached for his fur cap, and not finding it, ran out without it. He stumbled down the corridor, reached the open air, and got his bearings in the heavy snowfall just in time to catch sight of the paymaster again. Koog gripped the man's coat, clamped his fingers around Zabel's wrist, and wrenched the pistol from him. He tossed it out into the snow. "Zabel, Zabel," he scolded. "A grown man, forty years old, who has two daughters and a wife at home. The wife runs the store, worries about rationing, taxes, a hundred different expenses . . . and if something happens to Zabel here, if this cowardly wretch kills himself, she'll have a fine time of it. She'll have to close the store and might just as well commit suicide, taking the two little girls with her—what are their names, Irmgard and Hanne, I think. . . . She can turn on the gas or end the girls' lives with a rope or an axe. But of course that's her affair, that won't matter to Paymaster Zabel any more. After all, he showed her the way. No, Zabel, it won't do, a man can't crawl out of it that way. Paymaster! Man! Zabel. . . ."

Chaplain Koog dragged Zabel along behind him to the gate. By the time he got him inside again, the chaplain himself was done in. He couldn't go on; all day long he had been in a house full of suicides. But it was not today alone; for days past, from morning to night, he had had to revive flagging spirits, persuade men to live. Now his own nerves gave out; he sat down on the threshold and no one was there to offer him consolation. He sat and wept like a child.

No Russian tanks had actually reached the hut. There was another reason for the explosion. A detachment of engineers had blown up a near-by bridge that spanned the ravine. Later a sergeant from the demolition party came into the hut. Zabel, the provost officer, the chaplain, and Schweidnitz (they no longer had to worry about the two veterinaries) decided not to wait for the division personnel carrier any longer. They joined

231

the sergeant and his demolition party and marched toward South Tsaritsa.

The road led down the ravine. The violent gusts against the walls of the ravine ceased for a time, but the steady current of air roared on close to the ground, carrying the snow in a straight course along with it. It was a vale of snow; if you could keep your eyes open for a few minutes at a time you saw only snow, walls of it, great spirals of it rolling slowly above the road. The snow glistened on the walls of the gully and over-hung precipitous surfaces like the eaves of a house, and in the wind-sheltered corners it spanned jagged peaks of rock with hanging garlands. But then the power of the storm reasserted itself and shattered the white wreaths, and the men were un-able to see anything at all. They clung together and moved through the drifts like an ice-crusted boat, floating on this white stream toward South Tsaritsa and Stalingrad.

They would reach their port, although they did not yet know the kind of port that awaited them. In a snowpit on the main road between Voroponovo and Stalingrad they found a group of soldiers, a heap of coats, blankets, rags, hands in mittens, faces, noses, a pair of snow-crusted eyebrows. One man had taken off his glove and was blowing on his fingertips to warm them.

"Where is the new defense line?" Chaplain Koog asked.

The man went on blowing on his fingers. "There isn't any defense line any more," he said.

"Where are the staffs?"

"The corps staff has cleared out, as far as I know. The staff of the 297th Infantry Division is still here."

"Where is it?"

"A hundred yards farther back, left side of the road."

The party of engineers remained behind. The chaplain, the provost officer, the paymaster and the assistant paymaster tramped on. A hundred yards back they found a dugout. And they found themselves in a sudden, weird silence. The howling of the storm had died away some time ago. A low ground mist was lightening the night. Beside the dugout stood a sentry with a rifle.

"Is this the headquarters of the 297th?"

"*Nye Ponimayu,*" the sentry replied without expression.

"*Nye ponimayu*—I don't understand." The chaplain and his three companions did not understand either. The sentry raised his hand and pointed into the mist. Then they understood a little more, and they stood still, as stock-still as four snowmen.

A column was marching up in rows of three, dressed in rags

232

but in precise marching order—a sight they had not seen for a long time. The officers headed the column, and ahead of all was the general.

"Company, halt! Order arms! Attention. Dress right, dress!" A major reported. The general thanked him.

Something was not quite in order; there was a missing formula, a phrase not provided for in the drill regulations. The major turned about. "At ease!" And then he added that unmilitary, unforeseen phrase in casual tones: "Put your small arms down in the snow."

This was done. Again he called: "Attention!"

There were some three hundred men; those were all the officers had been able to round up in the vicinity. The major beckoned to the chaplain, the provost officer, Zabel, and Schweidnitz. The chaplain stood still; then he turned and walked away. Paymaster's Assistant Schweidnitz followed him. No one molested the two of them. The provost officer and the paymaster took their places with the officers at the front of the column.

The general crossed the white field alone.

He came to a stop and saluted. Opposite him stood a Russian officer, a silvery-gray lambskin cap on his head. He was the commander of the 38th Russian Guards Division. The Russian officer returned the salute. For a moment he stood silently looking at the general and at the company of men drawn up in line. He looked at ears wrapped in rags, gray faces, frostbitten noses, at starving, sick bodies. The air was suddenly filled with the stench of plague.

"Where are your regiments, general?" the Russian asked.

"Need *you* ask?"

The Russian did not need to ask. This division had confronted him at Tsybenko, Kravtsov, Pestchanka, and Voroponovo. He knew only too well where the German general's regiments were.

The formalities were completed. Food, shelter, and medical treatment for the wounded were available, the German general was informed. He himself would be permitted to keep his pistol and the other officers their swords. The staff officers took their seats in a car. Paymaster Zabel remained with the company that followed on foot. They passed a number of wrecked trucks, then a small triangular grove of trees as they marched back toward Voroponovo.

"Three hundred men," said a soldier who was walking beside Zabel. "When our division set out, we were seventeen thousand."

THE 297TH INFANTRY DIVISION, WITH ITS GEN-eral and officers at the head, had surrendered. This took place at the southernmost extreme of the pocket. Stragglers from Tsaritsa spread the rumor. It was only one more rumor among so many and scarcely made any greater impression upon the other divisions and their staffs than did the host of other ru-mors. In the streets of Stalingrad, around the ruins of buildings and in cellars, the fighting went on. But day and night the sign stood in the sky above Stalingrad. By night it was a fiery wedge, by day it was smoke that billowed up from the burning buildings and was caught by the wind and swept like a black bog over the land.

Not all the men in Stalingrad saw the sign. Those in the plantations of death saw only the wall of the cellar and the thread of smoke from the warming can, or they saw the dying face of the man at their side. Not all saw the sign, but it stood above them, all. And it was written far away from the scene of fires and smoke and rubble and crumbling houses, far away from the collapsing front, far from the night and the drifting snow, far from the days and nights of endless retreat. The sign was there for all to see in Germany.

The newspapers published banner headlines:

A MAGNIFICENT EXAMPLE. INTENSIFIED FIGHTING AROUND STALINGRAD IN CON-CENTRATED AREA. IMMORTAL HONOR OF THE STALINGRAD FIGHTERS. BRAVE AND LOYAL UNTO DEATH. FOR FÜHRER, FOLK, AND, FATHERLAND. SO THEY FIGHT AND SO THEY DIE, GENERALS AND PRIVATES SIDE BY SIDE. GERMAN COMRADESHIP IN ARMS SURMOUNTS HORROR AND MISERY COMRADES IN DEATH TO THE LAST CAR-

TRIDGE. THAT GERMANY MAY LIVE. THEIR SACRIFICE IS NOT IN VAIN.

A whole nation knew what these headlines meant and saw the horrible, grinning mask behind the empty bathos.

A shrunken old woman sat with the newspaper open on the table in front of her. Her glasses had slipped down to the end of her nose and she gazed out through the window of the peasant house, over the pots of geraniums and through the clean net curtains at the deserted village street. The village was Pelleningken in East Prussia and the old woman sat there with an absent look, her rough, hard-working hands idle in her lap. She was Lawkow's mother. She thought of her son Hans and she saw him as he was when he came down the street and would come in the door a moment later. He was a capable, tough boy, her Hans. He had been in France and in Poland, had been made an officer at the Battle of Moscow, and at Stalingrad, according to his last letter, he had become the battalion adjutant of the 261st. She saw her boy, a powerful physique in a small frame, like a beetle, his face scarred and seamed as the bark of a tree, but his eyes bright and young. That was her Hans, and a tear rolled down her lean cheek and fell on the newspaper page with its loud, hollow words.

Not far from Pelleningken, in the village of Kraupischken, Heinrich Halluweit had his farm. Frau Wischwill and Frau Göritt had come on a visit to Frau Halluweit, carrying the paper with its bad news in their hands. Frau Halluweit and Frau Wischwill were under thirty; Frau Göritt had only a few streaks of gray in her yellow hair. Their three husbands were in the same unit; Heinrich was the cook and Karl and Johann were machine gunners in the 9th East Prussian Machine-Gun Battalion. The three women sat and scarcely touched the coffee that Frau Halluweit had prepared. Their mood was like the atmosphere after a funeral; everything was incomprehensible and all the questions the three women asked remained unanswered. Did it have to happen that way? Did they have to go all the way to the Volga? What was going to happen now? Am I never to see Heinrich again? No, no, it can't be. And am I never to see Karl? How can I go on alone at the farm, with Poles and Russians all the rest of my life? No, if he doesn't come back I'll take my own life.

In the Himmelpfortgasse in Vienna lived a Frau Charlotte

Buchner. On her apartment door was a brass plate with the words: FRITZ BUCHNER, CHEMIST. Now her husband was in the army, a major and the commander of a flak battalion at Stalingrad. Frau Buchner had already prepared her meals for the following day and had picked up the kitchen. Afterward she had looked at old snapshots, and this had made her sad. Fritz at his desk, Fritz in a room filled with looms and women workers—that was in Hungary where he had been manager of a factory and where they had met. Fritz among the looms again and surrounded by more working women—dark-eyed and dark-haired ones this time. Fritz at a table under a bamboo-roofed veranda; Fritz in a white suit and panama hat on a white seashore. That was in Viña del Mar, Chile, where he had also managed a textile factory and where they had lived for five full years. They had returned from there with a four-year-old baby daughter.

This wretched war, and her Fritz of all men had to be trapped in Stalingrad! Frau Buchner kept opening drawers, but what was the point? Everything was in perfect order and she was not looking for anything in particular. But she took out a shawl, a hat, and a few other things and replaced them again. Each thing reminded her of irrecoverable times they had spent together. Finally she held up a long white dress. It was of silk, unweighted, unadulterated raw silk such as never entered the ordinary channels of commerce. Not even the wife of the Hungarian Foreign Minister had ever obtained such a dress. It was her wedding gift from Fritz's employer, her wedding dress. As she held up this dress, all the flood gates suddenly gave way. Everything she had heard from neighboring women these past few days, remarks she had caught from utter strangers in the street, the whole horror of it fell upon Frau Charlotte Buchner all at once. She dropped the silk wedding dress recklessly over the back of a chair. Frau Buchner could no longer endure staying within her four walls. She scarcely knew how she reached the street. She walked down Seilerstätte, down Kärntnerstrasse, turned into the Kärntner Ring and ended up at the Ferdinand Bridge. And whenever she saw two women talking together, she heard: "Her man is at Stalingrad too."

In a one-family house in Berlin-Dahlem, in a quiet room shielded still further against noise by an insulated door, a woman sat. She sat on a chair by the wall, her slender hands resting on the arms of the chair. Her gaze was fixed upon the too-clear empty expanse of a desk. On the desk stood nothing but writing materials and blotters, a calendar and a framed photograph under glass. Of herself. There was another photograph of her grown daughter and another of Ulm, Ulm with its Cathedral. That was where her husband had been born. How many times had she sat here, often late into the night, something or other in her hands, and whenever she had looked up she had seen the back of her husband's neck, his head bent over papers and enveloped in a cloud of cigar smoke. Now the place was empty and, it seemed to her, had been empty for a lifetime. But certainly she had spent at least half her life in solitude, waiting for him who had taken such strange and fantastic paths. What was he really? Soldier? Diplomat? Conspirator on two continents?

Certainly he was still a dear, foolish boy and besides that a reckless gambler for high stakes and the greatest possible gains (though not for himself personally; that was not in question). Certainly he had recklessly staked his own and her own personal happiness. But if the "game" did not turn out well now—and there were dark hints that it was not going to —then not only his and her personal destinies would be settled. Then it would certainly be frightful, good God, then the happiness and lives of so many, so unimaginably many human beings....

Frau Vilshofen sat staring into space. It was unreal, this house with its cork-paneled walls. The silence was unreal; beneath it a thousand cannon roared; beneath it surged the ruin so eloquently described by the ministerial councillor who had called upon her just a little while ago. And yet everything was real once and when Manfred came home—at long intervals, intervals of years sometimes—then she lived; then sunlight was spread over the whole house; people came day and night; there was not a meal without guests; then she felt that the house did not stand aside from the road of life. Yes, brief weeks like that had balanced out long months of loneliness.

And then the war had come. France, then Russia. Manfred had insisted on being shifted from the High Command to the combat troops. Occasionally she received letters from him. Nothing about the war in them; he spoke of the landscape, the steppe, sandstorms, villages, people. A leave, then the Eastern Front again and a long, burdensome silence, scarcely a sign of life from him. And then a letter about the great "mythic stream and the fantastic city"—the Volga and Stalingrad. And then the last letter from him, a letter of the wildest confusion. An earthquake must have taken place inside Manfred.

After that three weeks had passed; then there had been a brief word of greeting, and then not another word. And today had come that telephone call from the ministerial councillor, and then his visit. Here in this very room she had stood and talked with the official from the Propaganda Ministry. She did not know what had prompted her to say what she did; it had suddenly come upon her. When the councillor described to her the magnificent funeral ceremonies that were being arranged, she could not help answering, No! "Good God, he's still alive," she had exclaimed. "No, I can't do it; I can't promise in advance to participate." Perhaps she had acted wrongly; after all, it was not only a question of Manfred. "It is a question of the symbolic funeral ceremony for the entire Sixth Army, madame," the councillor had replied. "No, no, no," she had exclaimed. She was beside herself; she would not hear of mourning for an army or mourning for Manfred. He was still alive, the army was still a living thing; that was the case, plainly enough. And besides he had just been promoted to a general; what was the sense of that if she was supposed to mourn for him now?

"Perhaps I acted wrongly," she said to the white-haired old lady who entered the room, Vilshofen's mother. "No, you were perfectly right, Irene," the old woman said, sinking into a chair and covering her face with her hands. Then she looked up again and said, "Good God, it had to come to this; under this Führer of ours they dig graves for the living...."

The ministerial councillor had gone on his way. After his visit to Vilshofen's wife he went to see the wife of a party official who was now a lieutenant with the Third Motorized Division at Stalingrad. She too had refused to co-operate. But he had finally persuaded a Frau Lilly Daussig in East Berlin to participate. Thus he had a "genuine soldier's wife" for the great funeral ceremony. When he returned from his mission he learned that the Herr Minister himself was in the Mosaic Hall of the new Reich Chancellery. There he found him in the midst of a swarm of paperhangers, giving orders for the draping of the black satin and black flags of mourning, for the placing of the candelabra and the arrangement of a symbolic bier for the Sixth Army.

The Propaganda Minister listened with only half an ear to his assistant's report. He was busy; he was going full blast like a rotary press. Meetings, conferences with reporters, columnists, correspondents, photographers, artists. Biographies of commanders, officers, and soldiers of the Sixth Army, episodes in the battles, examples of heroic deaths, last words and testaments to the nation at large, had to be thought up, outlined, inspired, and written in huge quantities. The Minister had to multiply himself, to exceed himself. This time it was not a matter of blackening the reputations of a few murdered SA men, as it had been during the crisis of the Blood Purge. This time, with a crisis descending upon the whole Nazi Empire, he had to deal with the corpse of an entire army. Twenty-four generals, ten thousand officers, and three hundred thousand men had to be symbolized by the huge black womb of this bier. And it would be a "handsome corpse"; they had seen to that by promoting the commander in chief to field marshal, the colonels to generals, and by distributing Knight's Crosses, Oak Leaves, and first and second class Iron Crosses en masse.

But the army had to die, from the Field Marshal down to the last man. (And perhaps they had not seen to that with equal thoroughness. It was hard to accomplish such a feat from afar and the few assistants who had been flown in were not too helpful.) A corpse had to be a real corpse. You couldn't capitalize politically on a corpse that was half dead. Everyone who found a rat hole through which to creep and who stayed alive (the higher his rank the worse) handicapped the attempt to work up the entire nation to a gigantic final effort. They had to die, all of them! With an expression betraying his many worries, the Propaganda Minister limped through the Mosaic Hall.

A whole people—mothers, wives, children—groaned under the bombardment of propaganda that robbed them of all hope and made them see their husbands, sons, and fathers dying slowly for days on end. But the men were still alive, and it violated all propriety to call the tailor into the house and have oneself measured for mourning dresses while the patient was still writhing on his bed of pain. That was exactly what the propaganda was doing to the Stalingrad soldiers and the members of their families. Their men were still alive! The flak commander, Major Buchner, was still looking for his Lieutenant Stampfer who had disappeared with the train. The battalion adjutant of the 261st Grenadiers Regiment, Lieutenant Lawkow, the stump of his arm tied close to his body with a rag, had reached the Aviation Academy and was feeling his way slowly on into the city of Stalingrad.

Doctor Simmering, major in the medical corps, had returned from a furlough to the Stalingrad front in November. He had arrived in Vertiachi four days late. The observations he had made during those four days of delay, while he waited for hours at every tiny railroad siding, had given him a fairly clear picture of the situation of his own medical unit and of the entire northern sector of Stalingrad.

At the front there had never been sufficient supplies of ammunition. The transportation of other supplies came only after the shipment of ammunition, and transportation of the wounded had a still lower priority. All the way to Chir the track was never cleared at all for hospital trains. Therefore the slightly and severely wounded (no distinction was made between them) were transported in empty freight cars as far as Chir and even all the way to the Donetz area. Simmering had realized something of what this meant when he saw the tracks in every little station jammed with troop transports and with flat cars loaded with tanks, cannon, vehicles, and repair parts. In this jam were a few freight cars loaded with wounded that stood in one place for hours, sometimes for an entire day, before they could move again, only to be stopped at the next station. That had been in November and those freight cars had been without stoves; they had been utilized for the transportation of the wounded only as supplementary hospital cars. Without stoves—and at that time the land had already been frozen hard as granite and the thermometer had dropped to fifteen and twenty degrees below freezing. How many dead, how many cripples, how many men with frozen hands and frozen feet must have resulted from this kind of removal of the wounded! Even then Major Simmering had thought of what a terrible and thoughtless waste of human lives was being practiced here. And that was before the encirclement, in the course of normal military activities. That had been only a feeble preparation for the frightful fate that awaited the wounded after the ring was closed.

Major Simmering was leading a long procession of wounded. He marched slowly, so that the sick and wounded men could follow. He was wearing felt boots. Many of the men who followed him had nothing but rags wrapped around their feet. He did not look around to see men drop out and the column diminish. With the sleds that followed along behind, carrying the men's slender rations, it was a long enough column in any case. Men who sat down in the snow had to be left there. There was nothing that could be done for them. Simmering left it to a sergeant and the lower non-coms in his medical company to address a last word to these men who were left behind, or to record a last greeting from them. All he, the major, could do was to stick with the group, march ahead of them and inspire hope in those who still had a spark of life left.

But what sort of hope was it really, and where was he leading them? He had come from Gumrak, and these men behind him were former patients at the Gumrak hospitals. At the "Tartar Wall" he had run into tank fire and had been forced to turn southward. After a night spent in caves he was on the march once more. The masses of stone, the shattered gables and chimneys, the façades with empty sockets for windows —that was Stalingrad.

Where was he leading them? To the garrison headquarters —that was the order from the army which had somehow reached him. The remnants of medical companies and the masses of wounded pouring into Stalingrad were to be collected in the building formerly occupied by the garrison command for Central Stalingrad. There they would be cared for.

Collected and cared for—that was how the order read on paper. But, good God, for seventy days, at Vertiachi, Baburkin, Bolshaya Rossoshka, and Gumrak he had seen what happened to men who were "collected and cared for." Wouldn't it be more humane to stop right here, before this shattered city, and scatter all these collected men to the four winds?

But a major in the medical corps does not scatter; he collects and organizes, if there is nothing else to do; he organizes a column and leads it.

Where to? To garrison headquarters was the army's answer. That was the major's answer too. But the human being underneath the uniform went on asking questions. Where to—that was a question of conscience.

The sky was clear, the air so cold that bubbles of crystal formed in the nose and the water from running eyes turned instantly to ice. The sky was clear and high and the sun was shining. The edge of Stalingrad came closer and closer; soon he would be at the stone gorge down which he had to guide his column. Where to? . . . Was this not a phantom procession in broad daylight, and had he not seen it before? He had been thirty years old—to think that he was only thirty-six now!— and on his honeymoon. Just as it shone now on the stone rubble of Stalingrad, so the sun had flickered then on the old walls of the Frauenkloster, and in the cloisters, faded and streaked with plaster and saltpeter, was the mural. That had been in Basle and his bride had pressed closer to him as they gazed upon the figure of Death leading the procession and upon the numerous pallid figures in their shrouds who followed him in the icy air of the vault. Charlotte had shuddered and he had felt her quivering warmth, but he himself had not shuddered, but how could he guess that this was more than a picture, that he was being given a look into the mirror of the future.

The figure of Death leading the procession; the figures following him and the shrouds in which they were wrapped—what was missing in this scene? In the painting the figure of Death was blowing a flute. And here, he himself, the doctor who walked ahead so sturdily, who was the embodiment of hope for those who followed him and expected to arrive at some place where they could once again hold up their heads without giddiness and take steps without pain—he himself was also a flute player.

I am the flute player. God, I ought to stop, turn around, pick up a long driver's whip and set upon them all, thrash the wounded, the tubercular, the typhus and the kidney cases, horrify all these hopeful and trusting souls so that they'll run off, fall on their faces and get up again and run on as long as their breath lasts. Then, perhaps, a hundred or twenty or ten of them would reach the Russians and save their lives. But no, a major in the medical corps did not behave that way, and even though an insane act should suddenly appear to him as an ethical necessity, he was still unable to make such a total psychological turnabout.

Little Lieutenant Lawkow, who was also on his way to garrison headquarters, had reached the edge of the city in a direct line from the west—unlike Simmering's column of wounded who approached it in an arc from the south. Only two thousand yards—torsos of buildings, squares filled with rubble, chimneys towering up like the masts of ships, spurting fire from Russian mortars and German flak cannon—separated him from the large gray building and the medical treatment and horse broth he hoped to receive there.

By the looks of it the going would be damnably rotten. But there was nothing to do but to get through. "Not every bullet meets its mark," as the song went. And a man was such a tiny grain of dust that there simply wasn't enough powder and steel for every single one. Some were hit and some went on. Lawkow had had this lesson impressed upon him anew

on his way from the Tulevoy ravine. He had lain in the
snow to get his bearings; he wanted to determine his route
in advance, and before he could do that he must discover
at what and at whom the firing was directed. And he had
found out again that man is nothing but dirt, that he cannot
determine anything in advance and can depend only on luck.
By the time he reached Gumrak, at the latest, he would secure medical treatment, he had thought. After all, Gumrak
was nothing but one big hospital. But his only chance to observe it had been over the shoulders of the other men who
thronged around the railroad station. He had got far enough
to press his nose flat against a windowpane and look inside,
where the poor devils lay piled in seven and eight tiers above
one another. There was a stove in there at least and they
weren't freezing their limbs off. But what could he do? His
crushed arm gave him pain right up to his neck. His neck
and head were already swollen, it seemed to him, by the fiery
pain that was traveling up his arm. What could he do, what
trick could he try to get into this wonderful hospital while
there was still time and the doctor could do something for
him? The Russian attack and the general flight to the east
that had suddenly begun saved him the trouble of worrying
further about it. He had run also, or rather stumbled, toward
Gorodishche, and he ceased to feel his arm at all, but his
neck and head had become a tremendous weight, almost too
much for him to bear. In Gorodishche everything had
turned out so simply. There was the road with flak cannon
and trucks rolling along it, and even trucks loaded with officers' suitcases (why, I threw my suitcase away as far back
as the Kasachi hills!), and there was no room for him on a
single one of those damned trucks. And along the road the
men marched, with and without their arms. Then, suddenly,
he had come upon the general standing by the side of the
road, his lower lip protruding, wagging his head back and
forth every so often as he gloomily watched this passing circus parade. With amazement Lawkow recognized his own
general, the commander of the 113th Infantry Division.
"Well, now, what's the matter with you, Lawkow." he had
asked. "Smashed me up a bit here, sir."—"Have you had it
treated yet?"—"No, sir, I've been trying to get into a dressing station since I left Tulevoy."—"Well, go right in there,
into this dugout here, and report to our divisional surgeon."
—"Very well, sir. May I ask one question, sir: can you tell
me what's going to happen now?" But at this the general
waved his hand wearily and again began watching with a

dulled expression as a panting, heavily-laden "bathtub" rolled by, followed by limping men and the whole hurly-burly of this Napoleonic retreat.

At Gorodishche Lawkow's arm had been amputated, and afterwards it was easier for him. He had a decent bandage wound around the stump and his head felt better, no longer like a huge balloon that had settled on his shoulders. The next stage had been the "Tartar Wall" and the Russian tanks. He had seen the tanks crushing a group of men, the remnants of Major Keil's battalion. But Lawkow, the grain of dust, had been close to the wall and he had climbed over it in time. Then he had walked across the airport as though it were a peaceful plain at the bottom of a ski slope, had had a first-class breakfast as the guest of Buchner, and then had had his first good sleep in days.

On the following day the peaceful skiing terrain had become a very unpleasant deployment area for Russian tanks; firing blazed on the heights and in the little grove of trees and Lawkow realized again that he was nothing but a grain of dust. But luck was with this grain of dust; he had crossed the Tartar Wall a second time and come again into the familiar chaos—guns, hordes of limping men, and more Russian heavy tanks rolling over trucks and suitcases, over a group of screaming men, cutting off another group. There were five, six tanks on the broad expanse of snow. The hatches flew open and on tanks one, two, and three a Russian officer popped up, a submachine gun in his hand. The tanks on the snow, under the high, clear sky, looked like nothing so much as fishing boats that had spread their dragnet. One officer gesticulated with his submachine gun and pointed to the rear, shouting again and again, "Davai, davai!" This seemed to mean: "Now the time has come, kindly move a little faster." And the men who still possessed feet used them and ran for all they were worth. The grain of dust named Lawkow, however, was on the edge of this huge fishing net and he remained outside the narrowing area of panting, running creatures. He too ran, of course, he too panted, but he ran in the opposite direction. To his right and left exploding tank shells tossed up snow, and more than one man stumbled and remained where he had fallen. But the grain of dust reached first a tower that looked like a tin soldier and then the shelter of a ruined building. Afterward he came to the doors of a number of bunkers. The occupants were busy moving out, and moving no less with cook and barber and a rubber bathtub! It looked for all the world as though the field marshal himself had been here, but it was only a regimental commander and a regimental staff, the staff of the 100th Anti-Tank Regiment. These officers certainly had their nerve with them, you had to give them credit for that. They had a whole truck park at their disposal, and again there were suitcases, radio apparatus, army records, and even gasoline for the trucks. Outside on the Tartar Wall were the flak guns that should have been offering defense against the tanks. They had been discarded for lack of fuel. But here there was plenty of fuel for the moving. If Lawkow had not taken the wrong seat—that is, on a truck loaded with packages of records which was finally left behind, he would have moved with them and ridden into Stalingrad in high style.

However, experience was worth something. He had by now learned that you could always set up house for a time in one of these evacuated headquarters. He stayed there comfortably until the next day, then crept on, right up to where he was now. And now he lay in a hollow in the snow and was "taking his bearings." Now he had only to reach garrison headquarters, and that would probably do as a destination for the moment, for only two thousand yards farther on lay the Volga. Even though the river was ice-covered and could be crossed on foot, neither he nor any other German was interested in doing that under present conditions.

Lawkow had carefully examined the terrain; he had observed where the mortar fire was falling and what places were under zone fire from rifles. He could not make out what was actually going on here, what the fighting was for. Finally he set out. After some five hundred yards he rounded a ruined building and entered a narrow street. For a few minutes hell let loose in this short passageway. The Russians were firing and the Germans were firing, but it seemed quite certain that both sides were aiming at him personally. Mortar hits stood up in the mist like big red cabbages. Throwing himself to the ground seemed the natural thing to do—but no, this time it would have been a mistake; here the wrong course of action was the right one. He ran, took long jumps right inside the ruin. It consisted of nothing but walls with a milky sky above and the first faint star. Then he heard groans and saw someone lying in the rubble.

Lawkow went up to the men, hoping perhaps to find out what was being fought for here and which way he ought to go. But when he saw the man's face he realized that he would learn nothing from him. The dirty soldier's hand was as bloodless as the face. The hand beckoned, and Lawkow knelt, gripped the soldier's coat, and lifted him up, but he let him drop to the ground again at once. Both the man's legs were crushed; one of them lay across the other, the foot and boot turned up. It was only after he had seen this that he met the man's eyes; the soldier had realized his situation, that was obvious. Lawkow heard him whispering in a feeble voice, "Comrade, if you make it . . ." "Yes, if I make it. Of course, if there's anything I can do . . ." The soldier had a piece of paper in his hand and was scribbling a few words on it. The hand fell back helplessly and Lawkow picked up the paper. He stuck it into his pocket and then, since everything had quieted down outside, he went on. Halfway to garrison head-quarters there was an open square to cross. Lawkow wanted to reconnoiter carefully first. So he crouched behind a heap of stone and took the paper out of his pocket. He read "Dear Luise, I am done for, my last thought is of you, remember me. . . ." But who in the world was Luise and where did she live. Stupid of him; he should have removed the man's dog tag. Well, after all, what difference did it make? But perhaps it did make a difference. And if he did make it—he had promised. Ahead of him the square was quiet; behind him the guns were flashing again. Lawkow fought with himself. "What a fool you are! If you end up flat on your face, it will serve you right. After all, you've found a way that goes right through the buildings." So he weighed the pros and cons of turning back. Finally he got up and returned the way he had come to the ruin. It was almost dark by now and a second dead man lay in the rubble. Lawkow found the right one and it seemed to him, as he removed the dog tag, that the corpse blinked with appreciation. Lawkow also closed his half-shut eyelids; after all, they were old acquaintances by now. There, that was done. But now there were so many flashes and explosions along the way he had come that it seemed advisable to wait a while behind these thick walls. He drew farther back into the ruin, noticed a hole and a few worn-steps, and went down. There he found three men huddling together.

"Well now, found yourselves a hideout here, have you?" Lawkow inquired.

"Damn right we have. They're off their nut."

"No more of that stuff for us."

Lawkow was unwilling to chime in with this tone. "What's going on?" he asked. "Are the Russians here or are we here?"

246

"Nobody knows. Right now we're making a counterattack."

"A counterattack, eh? Who is 'we'?"

"Our division. That means that the mess sarge and the company clerk have got themselves shootin' irons. The general's somewhere over there in a snowpit."

"It's on his account we're going through this crazy business."

"How do you mean, on his account?"

"He can't stand it in his cellar any longer; the whole pack of 'em are going batty there."

"No, it isn't that. He went to see the corps commander this afternoon and when he came back the business started. They gave him an order to do it."

Lawkow found out that in a ravine near-by was the commanding general of the Eighth Army Corps. A short distance away, under the ruins of a barracks, the ruins of an infantry division had holed up, and a few hundred yards farther away, in some other ruins, were the remnants of another division. After a visit to the commanding general the generals of both divisions had ordered a so-called counterattack. The division to which these three men belonged consisted of the mess sergeant, the chief maintenance sergeant, the divisional veterinary, the clerks, and some eighty men. Where could they counterattack, what line could they occupy if their attack actually achieved anything? There would be nothing left for them to do afterward but to crawl back into their cellars. The action being carried out here with much racket by the ghostly remnants of a division could not be taken seriously from a military point of view. But for the man out there with the crushed legs and for the Luise who was waiting for him, as well as for many of the others, it was a very serious matter indeed.

This counterattack managed to gain the street Lawkow had to pass through, and so for about an hour it was traversable. Consequently, he was able to reach garrison headquarters without trouble, except for a few rifle bullets that splashed plaster from walls around him.

There, however, Lawkow was to see something he had seen neither at the Kasachi hills nor at Tulevoy ravine nor at Gumrak, something no human mind could possibly imagine. And there he found himself in the midst of a very serious affair.

Another officer had covered the same ground as Lieutenant

Lawkow, except that this man had gone over it three times. The other officer was Major Buchner.

Buchner's pilgrimage during the last days of Stalingrad had begun at Voroponovo. There, after Pitomnik had fallen and the Russians had advanced to the railroad embankment, he had been forced by orders to place his last battery of heavy flak up on the embankment. There it had offered neither moral nor physical support to the infantry (in this case Döllwang's combat group) and had been shot to bits. Part of Buchner's shattered battalion had fought again at Yeshovka and at Gumrak, using flak guns they had picked up on the way, and at these places the battalion had been finally destroyed. Finally Buchner gathered the survivors together in a small clump of woods near Stalingradski. There were a hundred and twenty men left and two vehicles from the train. He himself still possessed a personnel carrier, an "old jalopy," but the wheels still turned.

What was he to do? His batteries were gone, his general had flown out, and while they were still bitching it out here the general had croaked the swan song for them: "Am organizing new flak division." At the southern end of the pocket units were already surrendering. Stalingrad was nothing but a mill for grinding bones and guns, it did not matter what. There was no sense, no purpose to its grinding, just so long as it continued to grind something to fine dust. What should Buchner do now? Use the men he had left as infantry? No, damn it all. After all, Stampfer was a college man; Minz had once been a sewage engineer; he himself had once been a chemist and knew a bit about textiles, and was in any case a brainless idiot for having left South America and got himself involved in this uncertain Hitler business. All of these men wearing the uniform of anti-aircraft gunners were, Buchner thought, something more than ordinary soldiers, and all of them had past lives to resume. And therefore he issued his orders: "Lieutenant Stampfer, take over both trucks with the rations and make for Stalingrad. We'll meet at the 'white houses.' And then we'll rest up and try to make up our minds about this situation."

This was the beginning of their total dispersion and aimless wandering. He himself had traveled in the jalopy, then, when the fuel gave out, on foot, first through fogs and blizzards and then through clear air and bitter, glassy cold. The hundred and twenty men had arrived safely at the "white houses" and had taken up quarters there. But Lieutenant Stampfer with the train vehicles and the rations had disappeared. Buchner began searching for him up and down Stalingrad.

The flak troops remained in their cellar and went hungry. Buchner talked over the telephone with the commander of an infantry regiment. "No, I can't hand out any food. Give me your men and they'll get something to eat." And so the infantry commander secured the flak troops, one hundred and twenty men for one hundred and twenty half loaves of bread. Buchner went on looking for Stampfer. With his adjutant, Loose, he went outside the city again. The trail stopped at the grove of trees called the "Flower Pot." They went back to Stalingrad and then back to the "Flower Pot" again. The first time they returned the "Flower Pot" had been swathed in mist and perfectly peaceful. The second time it was bright and sunny and the "Flower Pot" no longer existed; nothing was left but some smoking piles of wood, corpses, and a detachment tramping through the snow with raised hands, in their midst a man with a fluttering white rag. At the "Tartar Wall" they had come across a dugout full of wounded men. "Take us along, take us along!" the men had cried. How could they take a whole dugout full of men when they had no truck and could scarcely lift their own feet any longer? When they turned and left, the wounded men wept.

Major Buchner could not get this scene out of his mind as he tramped along over the deserted airfield under a starry sky. Grown men crying! Loose at his side could no longer talk; he was so exhausted that he kept trotting along a few steps behind the major. They were trying to reach their regimental command post. The truck drivers' coats they wore were heavy; moreover, they were so long that the two men kept tripping over them. They were both dog-tired and could scarcely keep moving. They came to another dugout, and since Buchner felt he could not endure any more weeping, he asked Loose to go in first. Loose returned swiftly, gripped Buchner's sleeve, and drew him away from the dugout. "There are Russians inside there, the whole bunch of them snoozing." They went on. Half an hour later they saw eighty men moving across the field in single file. Germans? Russians? A man was hobbling along at some distance behind them. They caught up to him and asked, "Who are you?" The man replied in French; he for his part had taken them for Russians. It was an engineering detachment on its way toward Central Stalingrad.

Finally they reached the regimental combat headquarters where, only the day before, they had found the entire staff and a commander unable to grasp that Gumrak was already in the Russians' hands. Now the place was deserted, the bunkers empty. Crates, all sorts of junk, documents, and tin cans lay around.

Suddenly three men bobbed up out of one of the bunkers. They were men from Buchner's own battalion and they reported that in a cellar in Central Stalingrad twenty-four more men from the battalion were quartered. They also had news of Stampfer. Stampfer had fallen; the vehicles from the train had been shot up.

That meant the end of the battalion. He could no longer help the hundred and twenty men he had turned over to the infantry regiment; since he had no rations he would be unable to take them back. Buchner now had three men left of his former eight hundred and he thought he ought to gather the twenty-four men in Stalingrad around himself again. On the way they had to feel their way from wall to wall because all hell had suddenly let loose along the street. Lieutenant Loose suddenly fell. For a moment he seemed merely to have tripped. "What's the matter, Loose?"—"My leg, sir." Loose was lifted to his feet and collapsed again. He could no longer walk. It was a bad wound; a fragment had pretty well cut up his leg. They found two rolls of bandage and wrapped them around. But the wound was so big that these scarcely helped and they had to commandeer a shirt also. A litter was constructed and then they carried Lieutenant Loose to garrison headquarters where wounded men were being collected and treated. On the way they located the twenty-four men of the battalion in the cellar and took them along also. With twenty-seven men and Lieutenant Loose on the stretcher they reached the former garrison headquarters. Buchner, Loose, and the two men who were carrying the stretcher went inside. After a while Buchner returned without Loose and silently took his place at the head of his "column."

There was firing again. Buchner did not change his pace; he did not care about anything now. All for this, all for this . . . the words ran like a refrain through his head. For this the long road from Kharkov over the Mius and the Don, for this the massacre at Verkhnaya Businovka; for this Height 112; for this the Kasachi hills; for this the slaughter on the railroad embankment at Voroponovo—for such an end as this, for that utterly inconceivable horror. And he should not have left Loose there. The man might just as well die out here where at least he, Buchner, could have stayed by him and held his hand.

Finally Buchner stopped in front of a building. They might as well go in here; nothing mattered one way or another. The first thing was to sleep and perhaps to get something to eat. The men had had nothing at all for three days. They were done in. All that was keeping them upright was the mud on their uniforms and their stiff, frozen coats. Well, they'd report to the army in the morning: Major Buchner and twenty-seven men. The remnant of a flak battalion, perhaps the remains of the entire flak division. Request an assignment, sir, and above all request attachment to a feed trough again, no matter what kind of swine fodder it serves. I can't have men of mine going without bread and without anything else; I can't just let them starve to death. That can't be their reward for all their fighting. Poor Loose, I shouldn't have left him there. I had no right to leave a comrade who has gone through all kinds of hell with me in a place like that. . . . We'll go to Army Headquarters in the morning. First we need a good sleep.

All right, let's go in here. What's this? A steam-driven flour mill, the 71st Infantry Division's mill. The 71st Infantry Division had had its own poultry farm and creamery (in the ravine at Hartmann's Village; that was gone now, of course) and its own flour mill too.

They went in. A sergeant blocked their way. "Come on now, fellers, scram. They'll blow the roof out from over us before long anyway." There was something to that; they could see the flashes of mortars and automatic guns. Buchner noticed them at once as he stood in the dark tunnel with the sergeant before him and his twenty-seven hungry mouths around him. But the insolence of this sergeant!

"What are you thinking of, sergeant? We need shelter and rations."

"Very good, sir. There's nothing here, neither shelter nor rations."

The sergeant was well upholstered for times like these; under his jacket he had a regular paunch. His cheeks were plump and rosy; Buchner could see him distinctly in the glow from the automatic guns. All around them there was a hissing like a thousand burst boilers. Buchner shouted above it: "About face, sergeant! We'll see what isn't here." That shout— a sudden fit of rage had overcome him—almost exhausted his strength. He was weary, his shoulders ached, he could scarcely drag his bones along. And obsessive thoughts about Loose and the garrison headquarters filled his mind. They would have to go there and take Loose out again. A man with whom he had shared his last crust of bread. . . .

The flour mill stood in the courtyard; beside it was a large room and another smaller room. The large room was fully occupied, the sergeant said. He himself lived in the small room, with two millers and a corporal.

Buchner ordered him to awaken one of the millers who looked like a mouse in a flour barrel.

"Come now, give us some flour, miller. Rations for twenty-seven men, get me."

"But, sir, I would have to have permission from the division."

"Rot. What have you got here?"

"Unground wheat."

"You're lying."

"Well, some sweepings, too, just a little stuff that's been swept up."

The sergeant intervened "But, sir, the supply officer . . ."

"The devil with him. He'll never show up here again. Where do you think the Russians are? They're right on our heels. They'll be knocking on your door any moment."

"No, without orders from the supply officer . . ."

God, if only he weren't so tired; if only his limbs, his head were not leaden; if only he were capable of a single clear thought. He suddenly remembered a pack of cigarettes he still had left. He took it out of his pocket.

"Here are cigarettes for you. Now give us flour."

"I can't, sir. It's against the regulations. But I do have a little I've saved up, some of my own."

"Let's have your own then."

The miller took the cigarettes, got up, and vanished into a corner. He came back with two pounds of flour. Two pounds of flour for twenty-seven men.

"My last, sir," he stammered. "There have been so many here before."

Buchner should have hit him, should have knocked him down. But he was exhausted, done in. And what difference did it make? They would croak anyway, with or without the flour. Tomorrow the Russians would be here. He took the two pounds of flour and handed it over to Sergeant Januscheck. Januscheck would have to figure out how to make something for twenty-seven men out of it. Buchner himself went to look at the larger room.

No doubt about it, it was really overcrowded.

That was scarcely the expression for the condition of the room. It was a large storeroom and in the faint glow from the stove it looked exactly as though a large net full of fish had been turned over, so that the fish were lying on the ground and thrashing. Wounded men, refugees, stragglers, Germans,

Croats, Italians, officers, enlisted men, sat, stood, pressed close to the stove, coughed, prayed, whimpered, and shook the whole building with their groans. At the sight of it Buchner gave way; he leaned against one of his men. The group stood close around him; there were twenty-six of them now. They were waiting for the twenty-seventh, Januscheck. At last Januscheck came. When Buchner received his biscuit the same as the others, he started out of a trancelike state that was not yet sleep. The biscuit was little more than a thin wafer. One swallow and it was gone. Buchner closed his eyes. Then he opened them again—whether or not any time had passed, he did not know. He saw a man with his bloody trouser leg wrapped around the stump of his leg.

Loose might as well be here; it would have been better. It wasn't right, putting a comrade in hell while he was still alive. They must get him out of there again. At once!

With this thought, Buchner fell asleep.

GENERAL GÖNNERN AND HIS NEIGHBOR, GENERal Vennekohl, had launched a counterattack. It was not like the counterattacks of former days, when a height and a few neighboring villages were taken and held as bridgeheads for future operations. Nor was it the kind of counterattack they had attempted on the former Stalingrad west front, when they drove the enemy out of a few wrecked tanks that had been turned into pillboxes and occupied these tanks themselves, so that the thorn in their own flesh was removed. Nor were they now employing a division with regiments and battalions and divisional artillery. Now they had only the remnants of their divisions. There was a particularly bitter mockery about the affair since Gönnern now had such illustrious guests in his cellar—two commanding generals with their staffs and, in addition, that fellow Vilshofen, who was rather hard to get along with nowadays. And it had been a bitter, mocking phrase that Vilshofen had spoken when Gönnern slung the carbine on his shoulder and got ready. All the more bitter because there was a good deal of truth in it. "Last spasm," Vilshofen had said.

But after all, a defense line wasn't only a line on paper, and when it had bulges in it they had to be ironed out again; you didn't need an order to make up your mind about that. And really, you had to do it, you had to get yourself some breathing space. Those Russians were really too damn close on your tail; they were practically shooting into your coffee pot and it had got so that you felt yourself being watched when, forgive the phrase, you sat down on the toilet. That wasn't a joke; there had been more than one unfortunate example of the truth of it. And even though this counterblow didn't accomplish very much, still it at least cleared the path to the corps commander's ravine and the path to the Aviation Academy and the officers in the cellar there. And that was something, because there just wasn't any room to retreat any farther back; this sort of streetcleaning had to be carried out every day now.

The trouble was you couldn't do it; it was too costly and you were too poor, in men and in rifle and mortar ammunition.

General Gönnern, carrying his carbine ready, marched under the starry sky over rubble and snow. The heap of ruins at the edge of the field was the wreckage of a barracks, and under the pile was the cellar Gönnern occupied, with a master sergeant, the field kitchen, a generator for electric current, and the officers of his staff. He also had room for a number of guests. The general entered a corridor propped up by beams like a mining tunnel. He handed his carbine to his orderly, who was following at his heels. He himself hung his camouflage coat on a nail. Yes, the counterattack had been necessary, and not only for the sake of clearing a path—since by morning that would undoubtedly again be plague-ridden by machine-gun and mortar nests. It had been necessary for other reasons, for psychological reasons. For, as Goethe had put it: "This is wisdom's last decree: freedom and life are deserved only by conquering them anew every day."

In the cellar stood a table, another table, and cots along the walls. The officers who sat around there saw Gönnern go up to his cot and take off his fur coat.

"Damned cold tonight," one of them said.

"Cold and starlit," Gönnern replied.

The air of the cellar was stale and filled with the smells of drying clothes and leather and wicker suitcases. Over the table hung a bright electric light fed by the generator. This was the generals' shelter. Vilshofen sat in front of the stove, in his hand a sock he was drying. He looked pensively at Gönnern as the general slipped out of his coat and stood there in his tunic and trousers with their red general's stripe. But Vilshofen was not even sure that he was seeing Gönnern or looking straight through him. None of the others asked Gönnern how the counterattack had turned out. He was back, well and good. He could scarcely have brought any news from his excursion. They all returned to their previous occupations—sitting with head in hands and brooding, or pacing up and down, back and forth. Whichever they did they always arrived at the same inconclusive results.

They had to wait, and whatever happened had to come from outside. The door would have to be opened from outside, that was all there was to it. There was no hand to open it from within. They had renounced all possibility of making a decision of their own. That, Vilshofen thought, was the tragedy of these men in the cellar, of the whole army and the whole nation. The only decision that remained was: suicide or not.

The orderlies set the table. They had waited so long only for Gönnern. The officers sat down. For supper the food was the same as lunch. Each man had one plate filled with a cloudy soup. In the soup floated six or seven cubes of horse meat the size of small dice. In addition there was a sliver of bread.

Gönnern, as the host, sat at the head of the table. The two commanding generals sat at his right and left. One of them, the commanding general from the ravine at Gumrak, had been separated from the remnants of his troops, who were in the northern pocket. The other, a man of sixty with blue eyes and snow-white hair, was the successor to General Jänicke, who had flown out leaving him nothing but wreckage. This commanding general from the southern front no longer had any troops at all. The splinters of some of his headquarters were on the southern rim of the city; his last division, the 297th Infantry Division, was the one that had laid down its arms south of Tsaritsa.

Vilshofen, who sat beside the commanding general of the southern front, still did not have the insignia appropriate to his new rank, and he was still wearing the black tank man's uniform he had worn from the Mius to the Volga and through all the ravines and dugouts of the collapsing west front. Now, however, it was no longer black, but a battered gray.

In addition there were Lieutenant Colonel Unschlicht, a colonel from the Army Economic Office, a captain, another captain, a rosy-cheeked boy who had just been promoted. Of Gönnern's staff there were his operations officer, the divisional veterinary, and several younger officers. As they were sitting down to their meal another general entered—Vennekohl, who lived in a near-by cellar and commanded a motley detachment. During the counterattack just completed he had been the real prime mover. The officers sat grave-faced over their horse soup. "A little insipid," General Vennekohl remarked. The officer beside him nodded assent. The others overlooked this remark. After all, it was bad manners to carp over a meal to which you were an invited guest, even if the stuff wasn't fit for pigs. But more than one of them thought of the cans, the sausage, and the iron rations in their own suitcases and wondered whether now were not the time to drop formalities and put some of their own food on the table.

It was a gloomy meal.

The dishes were cleared and each of the officers was given a cup of coffeeish brew. Then they had their cigarettes—

256

they still had some of these left. The meal over, they returned to their thinking and pacing, to their staring into space, reading or leafing through books.

The Gumrak general had always been a walker, and his slender, upright frame had been preserved by long morning walks, rather than by the usual morning ride of the German general. He had kept up the habit of walking throughout the war. During the French campaign there had been walks through the dewy woods or along the seacoast in the north; in the eastern campaign the frequent shifts of his headquarters during the advance had afforded him a wide variety of scenery for his walks. Sometimes he had gone along the bank of a river, sometimes through woods with many different sorts of trees, sometimes across open grainland until he found himself in the midst of a great sea of wheat, sometimes across the bare steppe up to a group of wild pear trees and back again. In Gumrak he had first walked across the hot steppe, cracked open by the merciless sun, later over the snow-covered plain, and at the last down the ravine from one end to the other, down and back. He needed movement in order to think, to make decisions; he had to keep moving to preserve his mental equilibrium. But for days now his pacing had not expressed mental balance; it had been prompted by restiveness and bewilderment. Since Gumrak he had changed his quarters several times. One night he had slept under the ruins of a grain elevator, the next under the wreckage of a hotel, a third night in the cellar of the city jail, and now he had moved into this ruined barracks. Here he walked back and forth from cot to wall, from wall to cot.

The other commanding general, the one from the south, sat stiffly in his chair. Although he remained where he was, quite motionless, he was no less restive than the other, no less tormented by raging thought. Only a few days ago he had felt like a boy; now he was fully aware of his sixty years.

General Vennekohl sat with his legs crossed, completely absorbed in swinging one of his legs back and forth without pausing for a moment.

Captain Weichbrot, the veterinary, and several of the younger officers, sat together in a corner and conversed in low voices. Gönnern had taken a volume of Goethe out of his suitcase and had come over to the table with it. Lieutenant Colonel Unschlicht was reading an old hymnal, moving his lips as he read. Sometimes, when he came to a passage that struck him as particularly fine and appropriate to the hour, he would read it aloud. Gönnern had remarked upon the atmosphere in his quarters. "You can sense the approach of something important. Nobody tells any smutty jokes. Everybody is in a solemn mood, like in August, 1914."

The hymnal and the Second Part of Goethe's *Faust*. But why not Rosenberg or Spengler? Vilshofen thought; they really have more to do with the mess we're in and with the general softening of the brain around here. Undoubtedly Gönnern has one or two volumes of the Nazi writers here, but yet he picks up a volume of Goethe. Oh well: "The damned who, seeking rescue, swim with it, straightway are ground within the grinning jaws. . . . In crannies much remains to be discovered, so much of horror in the smallest space . . ." That's a bit more suitable. But I ought to blame myself most of all, as far as Spengler is concerned. Hardly anyone I know was as keen on making sense of that nonsense as I was, and even when I recognized it for what it was I believed the nonsense was useful. A damn fool at fifty, that's what I am, and I had to wander around in the cellars of a wrecked city to learn that nonsense can never be useful and must lead to ruin.

So they whiled away their time in the cellar. The colonel from the Army Economic Office recounted stories of corruption on the part of the German Ambassador to Paris. "Oh yes, that fine gentleman saw the new times simply as an opportunity to line his pocket and discredit the name of Germany."

General Vennekohl at last stopped swinging his foot and said, "Ah, Paris, those were the days." After a pause he added, "Too damn bad we couldn't have carried the counterattack past the Aviation Academy and out to the 'Tartar Wall.' We still have to make that up."

"You won't be making up much more, Vennekohl," Vilshofen said.

"What does that mean, Vilshofen?"

"I mean that after today's attempt you won't have much more at your disposal."

"Hardly."

Vilshofen was perhaps the only one in the group who had understood the curious mental leap that carried Vennekohl from Paris to the "Tartar Wall." So it was true after all, he thought, that Vennekohl was staying out there in a dugout because a few of the last incoming planes had landed in the shelter of the "Tartar Wall." Evidently Vennekohl was still hoping for the miracle of a landing plane and a seat in it when it flew back.

The telephone rang. The corps commander in the near-by

ravine, who had meanwhile been informed about the result of the "counterattack," was calling. Everyone listened to the conversation, or rather to Gönnern's replies. What the corps commander was saying could easily be guessed.

"But what next? We can't do it again, sir."

"You still have ammunition, don't you?"

"*Jawohl*, Herr General. A little rifle and mortar ammunition."

"And you still have food, don't you?"

"Oh yes, today we had horse meat soup and tomorrow morning we'll have horse meat soup again."

"Then continue as you were. You'll defend your post. Give me your word on that."

"*Jawohl*, Herr General. I give you my word."

Down to the last horse meat soup, Vilshofen thought. It was a little insipid for heroes' fare, but then this whole heroic drama with the hymnal and *Faust* was a little insipid. Oh yes, the soup will be doled out to the last spoonful. *Jawohl*, Herr General.

But it wasn't true; they were lying to themselves, lying right and left. . . . They had no intention of dying heroically; they were scared stiff; they would not swallow the bitter pill they had already handed out, each of them, to fifteen thousand men.

Those men had to swallow it; they had no choice. But these men still had a choice. We'll see, Vilshofen thought, we'll see what their choice is. He looked at their faces for the fiftieth time in an hour. What was Lieutenant Colonel Unschlicht seeking in his old hymn book, if not an armor stronger than shattered steel? What did these stories of blackmail, extortion, and organized highway robbery by Nazi diplomats mean? What else could it mean but: You see, that's the way they are; do you expect me to die for . . . Consciously or unconsciously —and what useful work the unconscious was doing here— they were preparing an alibi for their own sad abdication from the heroic role. The lieutenant colonel had obviously reasoned himself into a conviction that religion forbade certain actions, among them suicide; Gönnern, with his Goethe, was obviously also remembering that he was a minister's son who had been brought up to believe in the strict principles of his religion. And Vennekohl, lying on his cot in the dugout all day with his bottle of brandy, a portrait of his wife, and his pistol on a crate at his side, was still dreaming of a plane that would float down and waft him away. He was even launching counterattacks in order fo clear a landing

259

field, a place where at least a slow-flying Stork could come down.

No, no, they will not do it, they will not!

And what about me? I had a wife, a daughter—I still have them. I'd almost forgotten that. The mythic stream and the fantastic city—I myself am a myth, and if not a stream, certainly I'm a fool, a charlatan, a fortune hunter, an idol-worshipper. A fool in a tank, crazy and intoxicated besides. It could hardly be out of order for the road to come to an end now. Sunk without a trace. But how did it happen, how did the last act turn out this way? How? How?

More self-torment, more restless thinking, more nervous tramping, more staring at the wall, more crackling of paper and turning of pages, more stories about Ambassador Otto Abetz and his stealing a collection of paintings that belonged to the French nation, more discussion about the possibility of moving to the jail cellar or somewhere else.

One man out of his mind, restive, making plans and rejecting them again, wanting to move and staying, behaving like a fugitive—that at least was honest, was human and understandable for one within the grinning jaws of hell. The other motionless, sitting as though he were frozen. Vilshofen remembered him as a captain in the First World War—even then not so young—and he knew the man was not afraid of the devil himself. His rigidity, too, was honest and quite understandable, for you could literally see him growing older with every breath as he saw more and more deeply into this frightful finish of a life.

How, how, how...?

"Hartmann!" The name suddenly ran from one end of the cellar to the other. At this time it was more than the name of a Stalingrad general. It was an alarm, and it made everyone stand still, draw breath. The colonel interrupted his anecdote; even the divisional veterinary, who had been asleep, raised his head and looked around in confusion. To Vilshofen, too, the name and the voice that cried it out had sounded strange, and only when he saw that everyone was looking at him did he realize that he himself had shouted.

General von Hartmann had been the commander of the 71st Infantry Division, that "lucky division," two of whose regiments had been the first to drive into Stalingrad in September. His soldiers had got there first and they had filled their bunkers with loot from whole sections of Stalingrad. Their commander's ravine was furnished with rugs and chandeliers and all sorts of booty. Hartmann himself had been master of a whole underground village, of stores of grain, an agricultural experiment station, a vegetable and poultry farm, herds of cows, his own dairy, his own steam-powered flour mill. Brief glory, vanished riches, lost war. At Tsaritsa he had climbed up on the railroad embankment. He had stood there silhouetted against the winter sky, his tall fur cap on his head, had raised his rifle and fired at random. A Russian bullet had struck him in the middle of his forehead. Like a felled tree he had crashed to the ground and rolled down the embankment.

"Yet he had swift and fine death. A bullet in the head and gone like that."

"Oh yes, Hartmann. . . ."

"The way he stood there! That was an example for you, that was the true Prussian."

"He was the last Prussian," Vilshofen said.

"The last? I don't quite get it."

"I still don't see the next man to climb up on the embankment."

"Yes, a fine example!" General Vennekohl said. "But you've got to admit it's just another form of suicide."

"Have you anything against suicide, Vennekohl?"

"How d'you mean that?"

"Oh well, against the principle of it."

"Seems to me our chief has condemned it in sharp enough terms."

"And yet this is all there is to it—that Hartmann went the way he had sent other men," Vilshofen said.

He went the way; he gave them an example!

They were obliged to take a position. It was agonizing. An oppressive silence settled over the room. However, the general embarrassment was overcome for a while when the intelligence officer entered, followed by a captain. The man was a small, dirt-stained front-line captain with the expression of a man who was still trying to see the funny side of things. He had been taken prisoner and the Russians had sent him back. He recounted his experiences. "The Russians aren't so tough. I was at their headquarters. You ought to see the way they scurry around. Click their heels and salute, hip-hep." He imitated the snappy salutes. "That's right, just like that, sir. You would have liked it yourself, general, seeing real military discipline again. I was also fed well. Bread with plenty of jam on it."

Vennekohl began swinging his leg again. "Hm, jam's all very well, but do we have to sit here and listen to that?"

261

Gönnern took his intelligence officer aside and instructed him to isolate the captain circumspectly from other officers and send him off to army intelligence. At this point Vilshofen intervened. "You don't have to be so careful about these things any more, Gönnern. Over there in the jail I talked to a cavalry captain they'd sent back. Nobody thought of sending for the army's G-2."

"I beg your pardon, Vilshofen!"

"Very well, Herr General."

Really, it was none of Vilshofen's business and Gönnern felt justified in putting him in his place. The intelligence officer went out with the captain. The officers regretfully watched them go. After all, Vilshofen was right; they should have kept the captain here. How did things look inside the Russian lines? The captain could have told them a good deal about that. But the door had already closed behind him and now they were left to themselves again. And again they paced, thought, read. The general from Gumrak finally decided to move into the cellar of the jail. Vilshofen too wanted to go somewhere else. He was sick of these conversations about God and the world and suicide. He decided he would rather move off into some soldier's shelter where men were really dying. Things were stirring there, the stir of death, at least, if not of life. He picked up his rucksack and packed his few possessions. But then he lingered for a while. The others had again found an occasion for diverting their thoughts, for postponing the answer to the tormenting question. This time Lieutenant Colonel Unschlicht provided the opportunity. Unschlicht had found an appropriate passage in his hymnal and now he read it aloud. The others listened attentively:

"Lord, how are mine adversaries increased!
Many are they that rise up against me.
Many are they which say of my soul,
There is no help for him in God.
But thou, O Lord, art a shield about me;
My glory, and the lifter up of mine head.
I cry unto the Lord with my voice,
And he answereth me out of his holy hill.
I laid me down and slept;
I awakened; for the Lord sustaineth me.
I will not be afraid of ten thousands of the people
That have set themselves against me round about.
Arise, O Lord; save me, O my God;
For thou hast smitten all mine enemies upon the cheek bone;

Thou hast broken the teeth of the wicked.
Salvation belongeth unto the Lord:
Thy blessing be upon thy people."

"Oh sure, all very fine, I slept and awakened," Vennekohl said. "But suppose I wake up tomorrow and He hasn't broken their cheekbones and teeth—and by God it doesn't look like He's going to—what then?"

There was that question again, that unavoidable question.

Vilshofen had started them going with his tactless mention of Hartmann's name, and now they had to answer one way or another. This time the question grinned horribly at them from General Vennekohl's long, sallow face. His face was all the more sallow because Vennekohl had been drinking too much and his supplies had run out. Ordinarily he was a precise and sober general staff officer, but during the past fourteen days he had finished off an entire case of brandy. For the past twenty-four hours he had had scarcely a drop. Really, he had already outlived his time. When he was on his last bottle he should have drained the last glass, flung it against the wall, and finis—that was how these things ought to be done. The last bottle had been emptied last night and he had not done it. Now he was sober, as he had always been in the days he spent in careful calculation—how long ago that seemed now. But it was a different kind of sobriety; it was emptiness. He felt like a hollow tree, and something was trickling away inside him. He was so hollow that he did not feel in himself the strength for the movement of the hand and the needful pressure of the finger on the trigger, and yet this action seemed inescapable. Now he stood there, hollow, dulled, and sallow, the question gnawing at him inside, his whole presence a frightful question mark to the others.

What should one do, when should it be done, how was it to be done?

"Jänicke, Pickert," one of the officers said as though starting up out of a nightmare. General Jänicke had not received the well-known "ticket home," the superficial wound that incapacitated a man for action; but the board that had hit him on the head had been good enough to get him flown out.

Jänicke had flown out. Wounded, of course, but still flown out. Pickert had flown out—on orders, of course, but still flown out. Hube had flown out, on orders, of course, but still flown out. The quartermaster of the VIIIth Corps had flown out—without orders, and for that reason had been shot without a hearing at the Tarnopol airfield.

They were out of their dilemma. . . . Hartmann on the railroad embankment. . . . Stempel had taken poison. They were out of their dilemma.

What should be done, when should it be done, how was it to be done?

"The commander in chief has issued an oral order forbidding suicide," the general from Gumrak said.

"It's not so simple to shoot oneself," Gönnern said.

"No, it certainly isn't," Vennekohl agreed.

Vilshofen put in a word. "And a counterattack isn't a very sure way to do it either, Vennekohl. Especially when one hasn't decided in advance to stand up and present oneself as a target."

"You've got the right idea there."

The atmosphere in the cellar was charged. Vennekohl had replied more or less thoughtlessly, but immediately afterwards he snatched up his monocle, stuck it into his eye, and stared icily at Vilshofen. The break in the tension came from another corner of the room. The white-haired commanding general from the south, who had already manifested more than one sign of impatience with the conversation, got up, walked to the middle of the cellar, and stood there with a slight stoop. "I? Commit suicide for the sake of that cheap opportunist?" he said. "I won't."

Here was a statement, a clear-cut declaration. They had to repeat under their breath what he had said, and they had to see the tall, somewhat stooped figure and the eyes bleak with anger under the bushy white brows, before they realized fully that this had been said by a commanding general, and not in private. Everyone reacted differently—with astonishment, incomprehension, bewilderment, and even fear, panicky fear. Was it possible?—an idol was being overturned and no thunderbolts shot down from heaven to annihilate the blasphemer? Perhaps some such phrase had been said before in Stalingrad, in those cellars of death, but there it must have been a feeble whisper. Here it had been blurted out with the intention of being heard by all.

The young, rosy-cheeked captain did not know that his face had turned gray. The others looked at each of the generals in turn. The word, the incisive, condemning, annihilating word that should have been spoken was not spoken. A lieutenant, commander of a motorcycle platoon and a former Hitler Youth leader, thought he could read agreement in the eyes of the other commanding general and at least approval in the faces of the others. He jumped to his feet, opened his mouth, then shut it abruptly as he felt the eyes of all the occupants of the cellar upon him. Then, without having said a word, as though it were the obvious thing to do, he took a cigar case out of his breast pocket, bit off the tip of the cigar and lit it nonchalantly. And then, without looking around, he left the room. Gönnern's adjutant, Captain Weichbrot—he was thirty-five years old and before he entered the historical division of the army he had been a Nazi Party official in Berlin—stood up and with pale face and out-thrust chin also left the room. The embarrassment grew; this, if anything, was a final, an ultimate silence. Vilshofen had not even noticed the departure of the captain and the lieutenant. He released his grip on the rucksack that he had been about to sling over his shoulders.

The phrase the general from the south had used meant a complete upheaval. For that . . . that opportunist! he had said. And, good God, Vilshofen thought, I didn't see it either; I too imagined I had to comply with the decree from above by taking my stand on the railroad embankment.

Not for *him*. . . .

How wretched it is. Our lives are still forfeit, now that our battalions and regiments lie frozen to death in the ravines. But the filthy work has to be completed; after the endless rows of soldiers senselessly, mercilessly condemned to death, the corpses of generals are required. To get one more of them they make me, Vilshofen a general; they promote the commander in chief so that they can have a field marshal's corpse to top the heap. Counterattack, railroad embankment, or simple suicide—it's all the same to them, so long as the result is a corpse. A dead man tells no tales. They can do what they want with a dead man. A dead man has died for the cause, for the stinking rotten cause, and they'll use his bones to beat the drums so that the death march can go on.

No, they must not have their way. It must not be. Crushed, penitent, accursed, and condemned by their own hearts, these generals must not permit the last act to take place. Vilshofen felt as though he were strapped to a wheel of fire and the wheel was rolling across fields of rubble, burned-out cities, steppes littered with dead bodies, whirling, whirling, cursed and still living, not yet dead and already reborn. "Gentlemen, do you see it . . . the green flickering of the world's end and the light of Eastern morning both in the sky at once?"

They did not understand; they had failed to understand their commanding general and they understood still less this Vilshofen, this dry stick suddenly sprouting in the midnight waste. How could they understand a general who spoke in parables?

This Vilshofen was really a madman, and worst of all he seemed to multiply himself like Krishna. Suddenly he had become the burning hub of the vibrating world; he had something to say to each of them.

"Look here, Gönnern, the door is giving way. The road is clear. You can, you must get out now, out of this entanglement. . . . And you, sir, you can shut that hymn book without a worry; you don't need it as a shield anymore. . . . Colonel Ringhardt, the corruption in the Nazi Embassy counts for a good deal more than mere material for anecdotes; it's serious evidence for a court of law. . . . And you, Vennekohl, I beg your pardon if I got in your hair; forgive me for it, because since the Kasachi hills I've been stumbling over the same problem you've already left behind you." Vilshofen held out his hand to Vennekohl. But his hand remained in the air; Vennekohl refused to take notice of it. In fact he actually did not notice it, nor did he hear what Vilshofen was saying. His face was a ghastly white; even without the monocle his eye looked like a sightless piece of glass. He did not realize that the general's outburst had provided a way out for him too. All he saw was that a grave breach had been made, and that everyone here had felt it. Vilshofen looked around. Gönnern too looked as if he had not understood, perhaps not even heard. He was staring at the door that Lieutenant Hesse and Captain Weichbrot had closed behind them only a short time ago. Lieutenant Colonel Unschlicht was leaning forward so that the others could not see his long face; he had clasped his bony hands around the closed book. The divisional veterinary was surprised at the commanding general's expression, but he had been utterly nonplussed at seeing a whole package of cigars again; he looked as though he were prepared for all kinds of miracles. Behind the veterinary, his hand on the back of the latter's chair, stood the captain whose face was ordinarily of a cherubic, rosy hue; it now looked utterly deflowered and overwhelmed.

Gönnern was still staring dispiritedly at the door. "There we have it," he said at almost the same moment that a pistol shot sounded.

The door was thrown open and a captain entered. "Captain Weichbrot, sir . . ."

"What's that, Weichbrot, which Weichbrot?" Gönnern asked distractedly. He continued to stare at the door, or rather

266

through the doorway into the dark maw of the corridor beyond.

The captain said: "Dr. Weichbrot took the picture of his wife and their three-year-old son and put a match to it. . . ."

Gönnern did not seem to grasp a word of this. His whole being seemed to be concentrated in listening, listening to something outside in the corridor, somewhere. Others in the room were also looking out into the darkness. But the general from the south stood stock-still and it would have been impossible to say whether he was aware of what Vilshofen was saying to him.

The captain hesitated a moment, then resumed:

"He held the picture in his hand until it was burned to ashes. Someone said to him, 'Look here, don't do anything foolish.' But he ran out . . . and in the corridor . . . he's lying there. Bullet in his right temple. Yesterday he asked the divisional surgeon where was the best place to shoot."

What all of them had been expecting came. This time it sounded like an attack by a column of infantry; simultaneous roar of multiple explosions. The table where Gönnern stood and at which a general, a colonel, a lieutenant colonel, and two captains still sat, shook with the violence of the detonation. General Vennekohl took out a handkerchief—it was really a large, vivid ladies' silk kerchief that he had bought in Paris—and wiped his pate. The lieutenant colonel's expression was humbly submissive. The young captain's lips twitched.

"Now the calamity is complete," Gönnern said. Within an hour's time in his own cellar a senior party official and a Hitler Youth leader had killed themselves.

Noise and shouts outside.

"The door was blasted open and inside . . ."

"Hand grenades, weren't they?"

"Nothing but pulp left."

"Yes, he sent everyone out. Laid the eggs all around him, tied them together with a length of fuse, and lit the thing with a cigar."

The divisional veterinary, who had gone out to look for Hesse, came back and took his seat at the table. "He was recently married too," he said. "The son of a public prosecutor from Merseburg."

Vilshofen had heard the pistol shot and the explosion of the hand grenades, but he had paid no attention. What did it signify if one man shot himself and another found a more thoroughgoing way of eliminating himself? That was happening all around here, every hour; individuals and whole groups were doing it and the commander in chief's oral ban didn't amount to a row of pins. All that was on this side of the door, the rotting, collapsing door. But Vilshofen was already outside, at the gate, as it were; snow and night and horror were all around him, but he could also see the light of the resurrection dawning. The stony-faced general to whom Vilshofen was speaking had also scarcely noticed the shot and the explosion. He stood with his head tilted somewhat to one side, as if he were listening; he nodded once and his eyebrows twitched slightly, apparently to indicate agreement. He heard the rush of the waves; but the descending waters did not seem to touch or to refresh him.

"Of course this isn't any brand new discovery, Herr General," Vilshofen had said. (He was referring to the epithet the general had applied to the principal agent of the present disaster.) "We haven't forgotten all the facts yet. Frisch, Beck, Brauschitsch, Halder, Höppner at Moscow, Sponeck at Kerch —the whole long list of dismissed, demoted, condemned generals. But there's another fundamental fact to be considered. We, our caste of professional army officers, built golden bridges for this opportunist and spread carpets for him to walk on. And not only we but our colleagues in the coal and iron industries.

"Yes, sir, their schemes were new and old at the same time. All these projects for political dominion are nothing but copies of British, Spanish, and Portuguese originals from the fifteenth and eighteenth centuries; there is nothing original about them, nothing that grew up out of our own soil and our own souls. To that extent they're the ideas of a cheap climber. And the fact is that we, all of us—and I myself am no exception—believed in them. It took this nightmare of Stalingrad to open my eyes. Yes, sir, we've been fooled by him, all right."

This was the remark to which the general had responded with a nod of agreement. "And he was going to unite us to our people again, our people from whom we had become alienated. He had strapped them to the block, and we helped like the executioner who dons gloves for the solemn act. Even in madness there is an inner logic, and that logic has worked itself out upon us personally and individually. We builders of bridges, we spreaders of carpets, we executioners' assistants have ourselves become bridges and carpets for his foot to trample upon. The servants have become sacrifices; now we lie bound and without any will, any humanity of our own, no more than privates, a whole army of privates with no more to say than a stone in the road (if only the road led somewhere!), a worn, crushed stone on the road to nothingness. The express train races along without ties or rails and you, general, and I, also a general—both of us are nothing but connecting rods, universal joints, crankshafts, part and parcel of the screeching steel, when we ought to have our hands upon the throttle.

"And the vehicle is thundering along at full speed—past trees, telegraph poles, butts of houses, bleeding torsos, men with bandaged heads, suicides, women's hands clapped over tear-stained faces . . . and we ride and do not know where we are riding, what we are riding over, what is shrieking so loudly under the rims of our wheels. The Führer sits in the cab and cannot see, for the windshield has been made opaque by snow, dirt, bones, and the coagulated blood of the columns that gave one shriek of horror before they were run down. The Führer drives and you, general, and I, a general, know nothing, we see nothing, we are only rolling wheels crushing men and horses and steel beneath us.

"This is no nightmare; it is reality."

Vilshofen looked up. He was still in the cellar. At the table was a company of sallow faces. One lean one with his hand, a wedding ring on one finger, holding a large colored handkerchief and wiping the back of the head and the nape of the neck. A gnome's head, lined and furrowed, with large, flushed ears. Another face, somewhat pasty, somewhat sulky, with an expression of: Really, I've had enough of this. Delicate features with the look of a woman suffering from migraine. Then there were three gray, expressionless faces. This was the cellar, this was the gloomy haze to which Vilshofen returned.

During the First World War Vilshofen had seen the commanding general, then a captain, restore the shattered morale of his soldiers, had watched him clamber up out of the trench, stalk forward with artillery fire bursting all around him, and ask for a light for his cigarette, then politely thank the man who gave it to him. In his youth the general had staked his young life for the sake of being an example to his men. It was obvious that his old life was no longer of value to him and that he had not spoken up in order to save it. His declaration was no hole into which he was trying to crawl for shelter. Now he had sat down and was again silent, a very white, very old man.

"Not for him. I wouldn't think of it. No!" the general said once more, and again became immobile.

Vilshofen spoke again. "Gentlemen, it's perfectly clear that 'he' is nothing without the army the generals have lent him. What is needed now is a complete about face, and that doesn't

269

mean only about face, but: about face, march. That's it—drummers on the right wing. To your feet, march, march, march!"

Vilshofen's speech was all that the officers needed to bring them back to normal. All this talk was pure abracadabra to them, but it was exhilarating. Vennekohl still felt hollow, but after all you had to keep your chin up; he regained sufficient self-confidence to keep his monocle in his eye and stare at this "Vilshofen case" which was gradually proving to be highly interesting. Where'd the man get that way, talking about being "stung," Vennekohl thought. Gönnern, too, was thinking his own thoughts about Vilshofen. The man had always been a hothead, and with all the tension of the past few days and weeks, it was only natural that the bow, drawn too taut, would snap. A man of remarkable gifts; it was to be hoped he'd get a grip on himself again.

Vilshofen turned to the other commanding general who was candid and receptive; moreover, he had no reservations about Vilshofen personally. On the contrary, he considered Vilshofen a sympathetic personality and a pleasant companion. And, good God, things had come to such a pass that really strong language was certainly called for.

He and Vilshofen sat down at the end of the table.

"It's certainly true," the commanding general said. "He's a man who talks everything to tatters and carries everything too far."

"Not only words, but things and human beings as well, Herr General. Every piece of iron had to be forged into a cannon, a rifle barrel, a shell. Every scrap of leather, every thread of cloth, everything without exception had to serve one single purpose and one alone—shooting and being shot at. Total war. We knew better, but we believed him when he told us that only we Germans could do it."

"Unfortunately true, Vilshofen. I myself practically believed in miracles. There you were; there was such force in the man; his methods of sheer violence were so disconcerting, his successes so surprising. . . . Still and all, we must consider the fact that we always made trouble about it when orders from on top were completely crazy, like the time we were directed to brand the bodies of prisoners of war."

"And here too, as far as this military idiocy of Stalingrad was concerned, we protested emphatically," Gönnern interjected.

"No, we weren't blind, and in our sector of the front a 'decree from the top' was far from an absolute directive. Vilshofen, you've always been with the troops at the front and so you have no idea how often we've fought out the conflict between our moral sensibilities and our 'soldierly duty to obey.' "

"Conflict, rot! Supineness!" Vilshofen said sharply. "I am thinking of Voroponovo and of Döllwang's combat group. And if it were only just Döllwang's combat group, Gönnern."

"Yes, yes, it must be discussed," the commanding general said. "There has been inconceivable horror, and it hasn't been by accident. We ourselves are participants; we've ridden right into it."

"In our best moments we knew better," Vilshofen said, "but knowing is not acting. We knew that and we know it. At this very minute we know that Stalingrad is burning. And where it is now burning it has already burned. Snow, wood, hair, men —from the Volga to the Don is one vast stench of burning. And by this time we know. For protest is knowledge, general. And you, colonel, were explaining it a minute ago. Gönnern, you were just reading about it. Vennekohl, you too contributed your bit."

"How's that?"

"I mean that the road lies behind you, that you've left a trail."

"Is there an interpreter in the house?" Vennekohl asked in comic despair.

"We know that there is more to this than the stench of charring bones and frying human flesh. We no longer need read Mephistopheles' description of 'the city of fire forever flaming.' And as for finding 'the lads with straight and lads with crooked horn, the finest lot of devils ever *born*'—perhaps you, Gönnern and Vennekohl and Unschlicht, and I make no exception of myself, perhaps all we need to do is to look in the mirror." ("Not bad that," Vennekohl sneered, "I'm getting not to mind it. It's like he's the one that had the case of cognac and guzzled it all at one sitting.")

"As long as we thought we could keep our soup warm at the fire, we didn't crawl into a hole like this and philosophize about God and the world and humanity. We know and we knew. And once upon a time we too thought that if the rascal got on the horse's back he'd ride till it foundered. But we let the clumsy fellow ride up hill and down dale, over the rights of nations and individuals, over the honor of a soldier and all other kinds of honor; the orders for killing and burning were issued, and orders for holding out to the last man and the last cartridge, and those orders are still being carried out. For three days there have been no orders from Army Headquar-

271

ters. Corps is silent; for two days there have been no orders from corps headquarters. But still it goes on. More telephone calls, more red-tape, battle orders, counterattacks. Can you explain that to me, gentlemen?"

"Well, at least I've got to try. . . ." Vennekohl straightened up to his full height, dropped his casual, mocking dialect momentarily and articulated clearly: "A while back I believe I heard the phrase 'last spasm'. . . ."

"You heard rightly, Vennekohl."

"Yes, and blind cows, or were they horses? Well, I must say, if any of you want to put up with that and with all this crazy talk, you can. But I won't go along with you, do you understand, sir? And by the way, I'd like to know if you've got anything against counterattacks in general?"

"Yes, I do have something against counterattacks. I'm against them when they're carried out by a commander who spends his whole day sitting on a heap of dirt and scanning the sky for a plane to save him. I'm against counterattacks when the soldiers have been obtained by sifting the wounded and the dying out of the cellars. Stand up on the railroad embankment, General Vennekohl. A rather stiff way to go about it; still, that's dignity for you! But stop reducing men to pulp, and men who are no longer men, no longer soldiers, who are really nothing but blind horses, or blind cows if you like, their hide encrusted with sores, with shrunken udders, pustules, brittle bones. That's what your soldiers are like; that's what they looked like when they fell in to make their counterattack, Vennekohl. I went out to look at them."

"So, did you? Charming of you."

"You're forgetting yourself, Vilshofen. Really, this is going too far."

"I agree, that's pretty strong medicine."

"Medicine?—that's a rank insult. Our men, these frightful battles, epic battles, and every one of them a downright hero. And here someone comes along and talks about blind horses without udders. . . . Why . . ."

"For shame!"

"Shame!"

"Disgraceful!"

"It burns me up!"

"Why you . . ."

Vennekohl and Vilshofen appeared to be on the point of blows.

"Gentlemen, I must beg you . . ." the senior general inter-

272

vened. At any other time such a request would have produced instant silence; this time, however, the dispute continued.

"Vilshofen, you're carrying things too far," another of the generals could not refrain from shouting.

"Comparing German soldiers to cows!" Vennekohl growled once more.

"To old, sick, feeble cows ready for the slaughterhouse, sir. Strong, clean, healthy men of twenty and twenty-five turned into ruptured, swollen, trembling, one-legged creatures. And then to ferret these creatures out of the holes where they've crept off to die and to make them counterattack—does that strike you as decent, sir?"

"Gentlemen . . ." the general from the south interjected again.

"Permit me to explain what I mean. I am saying that the front and the headquarters are two worlds. Let us think back a little; it is not so long since we saw a corps headquarters in this area. Officers at their desks, well rested, bathed, shaved —a punctual, precise daily routine. Morning gymnastics, dress uniform at meals, the whole tone almost that of an officer's club. Riders on prancing horses in the streets, the neighing of horses in the bright morning air. I must say, we—I was standing with my adjutant, Latte—hadn't seen or heard anything like it for a long time. Just think back, Unschlicht; that was in December on a morning when the mist was billowing over the steppe. It was the end of December, between Christmas and New Year's; that means it was at the time the men on the west front were sleeping in the snow and passing blood in their urine and their stools. That morning we heard dogs barking and the thud of horses' hoofs, and then we saw appear out of the mist, cantering and trotting, the commanding general, followed by colonels, captains, and lieutenants. You, Unschlicht, were sitting beautifully in the saddle. Corps staff had organized a hunting party, a very late hunt, in more senses than one. Can't you imagine, gentlemen, that the man in the snow with his daily ration of a hundred grams of bread, suffering from strangury and dysentery—can't you imagine him so confused at first that he thought he was dead and watching a world of ghosts riding past in the mist. And let us remember that we celebrated Christmas and celebrated New Year's, that a commander's birthday or a new Oak Leaf Cluster always was an occasion for a simple gathering and for drinks. But at the same time, when a captain from the front lines wanted to celebrate a Knight's Cross, he couldn't dig up a single bottle of brandy. Yes, gentlemen, when I spoke of two worlds I did not pull the phrase out of the air. And to return to the matter at hand, I must say this: the measure of our suffering is full. Our torment is so terrible that it no longer matters to us if our sores are exposed to the public view. But even now you are still living your normal lives; you still have uniforms and changes of clothes in your suitcases; you still enjoy horse meat that a whole army has eaten itself to death on; up to this very minute you are still able to rest, to wash, to brush your teeth. Do you think it possible before the whole world—and don't forget that in spite of our ignorance and our blindness we are standing before the eyes of the world, here on this stage at Stalingrad—to present the spectacle of German soldiers attacking: limping, staggering figures can still be scared out of their holes by a general. Do you really think it is possible and permissible, gentlemen? It is shameful, disgraceful. It is such an abyss as Germany has never before fallen into, a disgrace such as no one has ever before imposed upon Germany."

"It is chaos; I saw it coming and I fought against it, but everything I said was spoken to the winds," the general from Gumrak said.

"Vilshofen," the other commanding general interposed, "I want to ask you a question. Whom do you mean by 'we' and who are the others you are talking to."

"Sir, you have many years as a front-line officer behind you. If you compare your past with your present, you will see the answer in the discrepancy between them. There is a gulf between the front and the leadership, gentlemen; you don't know what is going on and you haven't known all along. When we were still across the Don you, Unschlicht, were evacuating Verkhnaya Golubaya, and when we were defending the Golubaya heights and falling back step by step to the Don, you gentlemen evacuated the headquarters in Vertiachi and Peskovatka. Of course you had to evacuate, but that's not the point. All I am saying is that you don't know what it looked like when we followed in your tracks through the ashes and the dreary stench of Verkhnaya Golubaya, through the corpse-filled camp of starved Russian prisoners in Vertiachi and through the discarded plunder in the headquarters at Peskovatka. You don't know what it was like when we, decimated groups of us, established a Stalingrad west front under the sky on an open field in a blizzard, and then followed your tracks again through Dmitrevka, through Novo-Alexeyevka, through heaps of loot, dead cattle, abandoned matériel. The

Kasachi hills, Height 135, the five Scythian burial mounds have remained dots on the map to you—and I repeat, any other way is unthinkable; a headquarters can't set up its maps in the main battle line.

"You talk of heroism but you don't know how men were shattered, how men went to hell. You did it to them, gentlemen, with your defense lines that were nothing but empty theories. And you also do not know how the troops melted away under your hands. Orders for defense. Hold at any cost. You draw defense lines on your maps and dub them Violet or Sunflower; if only you had come up front some time and taken a look at your Violet and your Sunflower. What did they look like? What did the men look like? Had they any rations? Any ammunition? Cut off from the men as you were, you simply don't know. No wires, neither imaginary nor real, lead up front. Up front everything collapses, everything goes to hell. The rear issues orders. The front is a world of ruin. In the rear, physical and moral decay. And here you are reaching down into the sewers filled with tears and the pus of untreated wounds to fetch up your reserves. And that has been going on for weeks; starting from Kletskaya, for seventy-seven days.

"Think of the Stalingrad soldier, his patience, adaptability, tenacity, perseverance, his capacity for suffering, his silent enduring of sheer torture, his dutifulness, his ability to wait and to fight to the last. What heights of undemonstrative martial courage he has attained. And think finally of his faith, his unconditional faith which was his greatest glory and has become his greatest fault. What sort of monument will you erect for him, gentlemen, what inscription will you cut into the stone?

"For Führer, folk, and fatherland? But the Führer is written off; there is no longer any connection between the people and the insanity of this Führer—they had no voice in this war in the first place; and the fatherland has no frontier on the Volga to defend.

"Since the Führer is on the wrong track, his following has gone altogether astray. The commander, you tell me, is torn by inner conflict: on the one hand the enduring, patient, obedient troops and on the other the insane orders. If the commander obeys the orders he destroys his troops; if he does not obey them he finds himself standing before a wall that threatens to fall on him and destroy him. In that conflict our commanders have not taken the way of conscience, but the path of least resistance; they have obeyed, carried out the orders, and destroyed their troops.

"The soldier who escapes one disaster marches into the next; he moves over a road that is an unending succession of disasters. His shoulders are flayed, his backbone bent, his feet blistering lumps; he becomes a worn-out, rotten-lunged domestic animal, all the strength of his manhood gone. (Go through the Stalingrad cellars, gentlemen, and look around.) He becomes in reality the udderless, blind cow with soft, rotting bones ready to decay. And the slaughterer is here with his assistants, ready to club the poor creature on its moist nose and kick its swollen flanks to get it up on its feet again and drive it to the yard. I repeat, gentlemen, just take a look around in the cellars. . . . What inscription will you cut upon his monument, gentlemen?"

"Well, by God, all I hear is monument; the man's getting monotonous," Vennekohl muttered. But then came a sudden flash of lightning that was aimed directly at him.

" 'He died a soldier's death.' You can scarcely put that on his stone. There he was, the man who came out of the snow-pits on the west front of Stalingrad. After battling with his rifle, after an even tougher battle with his spade, he crawled, utterly exhausted, to the hospital, blood and excrement running down his leg. The doctor hardly examined him; he could smell death in the man; the dull eyes and the weepy voice were symptoms enough. The sick soldier was laid aside and died of dysentery. So. The men at Ilarinovski, on Height 135, at the Kasachi hills were killed by the enemy on the field of battle—you can say that of them. But the ones who were wounded on the eastern slopes and who were picked up and carried off—we met those men again at the dressing stations in Baburkin, in Dmitrevka, in Otorvanovka. And there, in Otorvanovka, the main defense line was established according to orders right in the middle of the dressing station which had not been evacuated. The battle passed over the wounded there; shell fragments showered down on them and the collapsing walls killed them. The order for that battle was carried out by a colonel named Vilshofen."

"But what are you getting at, Vilshofen?"

"We've had just about enough of this."

"Really, we have other and extremely serious matters to take care of."

"Damn right we have."

"Those men had to give up their lives; you, gentlemen, have to hear an accounting of their deaths. I want to make it clear that this manner of dying has nothing to do with our conception of a soldier's death in the fullness of his strength. Rather, such deaths result from panic, from totally mistaken conceptions of duty, complete breakdown of an organization. We can't blame it on the failure to reinforce or to supply by air. When this state of affairs first became apparent, when hunger marched and the growing number of deaths from exhaustion made it perfectly obvious, *then* we should have taken our own decision and overridden the madness of our superiors. But instead we remained instruments carrying out orders issued by the inmates of a madhouse, and we are, to this day. To this very day, Vennekohl."

"How's that?" Vennekohl snapped.

"Now the battle has reached the very door of this headquarters. And so men are scraped up, our of the garrison headquarters, out of the theater cellar, out of the Timoshenko cellar, no matter where they come from. I've already told you who these men are, what they've been through; you know they're half dead, you know how wretched they look, you know what pitiful creatures I've compared them to. And with such men a counterattack is started. Naturally, to get such men on their feet again, to make the thing work at all, a general is needed to go right along with them. . . ."

"This is too much for me, too much. I guess you've gone stark raving mad, Vilshofen!"

"You are not stark raving mad, General Vennekohl, but you issue the orders of a madman. You know Captain Tomas, don't you, sir?"

"Who?"

"Two days ago Captain Tomas lay in the cellar of the theater, suffering from a head wound. Formerly he was company commander in a tank regiment. A few hours ago he stood several hundred yards from here, under your orders, in command of an anti-air-craft battery; apparently you hadn't been able to locate a flak officer for this insane business."

"Well, what are you getting at?"

"There were three flak guns, one with a badly damaged sighting mechanism. Even Tomas, a tank captain, refused to use this gun . . ."

Vennekohl sprang to his feet, his face red and puffy.

"May I ask, Vennekohl, what answer you gave Captain Tomas?"

Vennekohl gurgled something inarticulate.

"I'll repeat your words. You answered: 'It must be used; you can just as well sight over the barrel.' What I would like to know is whether you have ever seen anything like that done at close range?"

Vennekohl opened and closed his mouth several times. Vilshofen continued: "You stated: 'This is our last extremity; whatever happens now is bound to happen, and it doesn't matter.' You know the result of the action, Vennekohl."

It could be plainly seen that Vennekohl did not know anything about the results.

"The battery accomplished nothing at all, Vennekohl. Since you apparently don't know what else happened, I'll tell you. All three guns were shot up—by tanks. The crews were all killed except for two men. Captain Tomas was carried off with a severe splinter wound in his leg."

General Vennekohl no longer stood swollen like a pouter pigeon. The burst of crimson vanished from his face; he turned gray. But he continued to hold himself erect and stiff.

"I should inform the rest of you that these three guns were all that was left of an entire battalion. At the Kasachi hills and up to sixteen days ago the battalion still had twelve 8.8 cm. guns left out of a total of thirty light flak guns and eight hundred and fifty men. Vennekohl, I offered you my hand before, and I knew what I was doing. Vilshofen at Otorvanovka, Gönnern at Voroponovo, Vennekohl in Stalingrad—we're all on the same level, gentlemen!"

"That ends everything, then."

"That breaks all ties of comradeship."

"I quite agree," said Vennekohl.

Lieutenant Colonel Unschlicht stood up, his bearing irreproachable, his forehead high and pale. He opened the door and closed it noiselessly behind him.

"But, gentlemen, do you want to imply that we aren't on the same level? We carried out the orders. In doing so, we destroyed the army. Under our leadership divisions were reduced to groups of pale, hollow-cheeked creatures and a march of divisions became a procession of wretches on their way to the slaughter house."

"Really now, I must ask you to leave, Vilshofen," the commanding general said.

"Yes, sir, I was already about to go, and I'm going now, sir," Vilshofen replied. He buttoned his coat and looked around for his rucksack. It was all terribly embarrassing and regrettable, Gönnern thought, but he was relieved. The others also sighed with relief. There was a general shuffling of chairs and a sudden babble of voices. Another package of cigars emerged and one of the officers lit one, after politely offering a cigar to a neighbor.

"What's the trouble now?" Gönnern irritably asked his adjutant, who had just come in.

"This lieutenant again, sir."

"What lieutenant?"

"A Lieutenant Lawkow."

"There's some excitable lieutenant here," Gönnern said, turning to the man beside him, "who says all hell is loose near the garrison headquarters and will we kindly withdraw our troops. And we haven't any troops there at all."

"That's what I told him, sir," the adjutant put in. "But he says the whole chain of command is so confused that nobody can make anything of it, so perhaps we do after all. . . ."

"But we simply don't have anything left. We have nothing but our command post."

At this point Vilshofen came back to the fray. He was now standing at the door, his rucksack slung over his shoulders. "Permit me one more question, gentlemen. Otherwise there will have been no point to our whole long conversation. I've noticed the tendency here to do nothing and to let things happen. To do nothing against ourselves either, I mean, not to lift our own hands against ourselves. . . ."

Good God, was that starting again! Really, this man Vilshofen is all the rope we need to hang ourselves. Maddening, but on the other hand it is true that the question hasn't been settled.

"Here is my question. Some time in the future, back in Germany, how do you imagine it—the captain of a great ship which went down with its entire crew, that captain walking along the sunlit street, the sole survivor. A huge ship, a huge crew, thousands of surviving wives of the drowned men, still greater numbers of the surviving children of those men. But the captain goes his way, sits down in a café, takes off his panama hat and orders a beer and a cigar. Do you think that is possible, gentlemen? Never has such a thing occurred; do you want to make this kind of captain an accepted fact of German life, an accepted idea to the German mind? What do you think it will be like when you are back in Germany some time, the sole surviving commanders of an entire army that was destroyed? How can you dare to desire life, unless you use your life to fight the man for whom you've done this bloody work? There was Hartmann; he died with his men when they were sacrificed. That is consistency. But if this same consistency is applied to the two dozen generals and the five thousand officers who are still alive, if these generals and officers also supply corpses, it will mean that the crime is crowned, irrevocably sealed. This crime is being carried through for the sake of a propaganda slogan that we all heard today on the Berlin radio: 'They died that Germany might live.'

"That is a lie, gentlemen. They died of every imaginable physical and mental ill, and some of those ills were not their own, but ours; and they died for a purpose that is only now becoming apparent. To put the black seal of apparent truth on that lie by our own deaths would be to give it wings and make of it a death for millions. You would have died that the crime might live and go on, that the cellars of Berlin, Hamburg, Bremen, Munich, and Nuremberg might be like the cellars of Stalingrad. You would have died so that in Germany, too, corpses might be piled up in the street like cordwood, so that in Germany, too, the crime and the wages of crime can be magnified a thousandfold. And that must not be! Guilty and half guilty, witting and unwitting, we have lived for crime and carried its banners to the four quarters of the globe; we have planted them two thousand miles from the German borders. But here, at the highest peak and just before Germany plunges into the lowest depths—for that is what Stalingrad is and as military men you know it, even if you cannot yet see the moral element—here, at this time, it would be worse than anything else to die for the crime and for the continuation of the criminal work.

"That is the situation, our own particular situation. And that situation makes logic of the illogical need to remain alive in spite of everything. You must accept the gift of life as a sentence to life. And do not forget that life is henceforth to be used to fight the man and the crime he has committed against Germany and the other nations.

"And so, gentlemen—LIVE!"

Slowly the door closed behind Vilshofen, slowly, as though it were being released with great deliberation, the latch rose and snapped back into its slot.

The man in the long truck driver's coat strode through the city of a hundred ravines. Under the snow lay a collapsed house, a broken-down car; under the snow lay stucco and columns and curving banisters; under the snow lay a mummy, its withered hand protruding. A bluish light flickered over the shapes, and through the windows of a tall building front the stars gleamed.

The man walked along the street. His way led down passage-ways through buildings, over courtyards, past long, silent walls that were no more than holes, row on row of empty window-openings. It was inconceivable that once upon a time there had been a sewage and water system here, stores, offices, theaters, restaurants, hospitals, lights in the streets. It was a dead city, buried under a rain of ashes a thousand years ago and just thrown up into the starlit night by some eruption beneath. The ground was still shaking, the ashes still trickling down. In this wasteland the man's footsteps were the only sign of life.

He reached a broad square, filled with mist from the ice-coated river. Rocket shells flashed in the mist like rows of street lamps, went out and rose again, white and flickering. Upon a hill of mist stood a burning house; a second burning building glowed deeper inside the fog; a third spat masses of black smoke that billowed up toward the sky. This third house was a corner building with three wings, the former garrison headquarters where all the wounded men pouring into Stalingrad had been collected. At the corner and to the right and left of the tall building a skirmish was in progress. Bursts from machine guns, exploding tank shells, and the sharp crackle of flak guns could be heard. The man crossed the square and plunged into the labyrinth of streets on the other side of it. Alleys dipped precipitously like boulder-strewn streams. At the bottom of these streets was the shore. Charred wooden houses, fences and gates gone, collapsed sheds, a railroad track, on the track locomotives with gaping bullet holes. This whole area was undermined by dugouts, cut by communication trenches, blockaded with walls of earth and rubble and barbed-wire entanglements. This area, on the shore of the great river, was the last ninth of the city which the attackers had never entered, never taken.

The man in the truck driver's coat tramped on through the city. He made a track through the deeply-drifted snow in a ravine, climbed the opposite slope, passed through more gates and by more columns, more towering chimneys, more wrecks of buildings, and more white fields. Through one ruin a gaunt Russian girl scurried like a mouse, picked up a piece of wood, and vanished into a hole.

Again he saw a garland of exploding shells stretching from stump to stump of buildings; then more façades with empty window openings, more towering chimneys, more splashing fountains of rubble and snow from mortar hits. The fire was directed against the massive black walls which had formerly been the building of the People's Commissariat for Internal Affairs. Adjoining this building was the city jail.

The man in the long coat left the city jail behind and walked toward the wall of gun flashes on the edge of Stalingrad. Where the wall showed a dark patch, he stepped through. In front of him stretched the broad steppe over which he had once come riding in a tank. Following the same path, he strode out into the white night.

Behind him lay the moon city with its craters, snow-filled holes, cracked and split asphalt, gutted stone structures, with its groaning cellars, with its endless row of caverns, street after street of them, filled with sick, sore, scarred men, with its Goethe and hymnals and cognac and the Spengler tossed on a rubbish heap.

Here was the scene of the lost battle, of the lost war, of the zenith of German power and the most crushing defeat in German military history. Here the German people had fallen to the lowest point, politically and morally, in their history. Where the need of the hour had been courageous defiance of the rulers, four and twenty generals had clicked their heels as one man; where revolt should have flared up in the masses of the soldiers, there had been nothing but physical and spiritual dissolution, apathy, a dumb dying without even a curse upon their lips. The man who walked in the snow and night carried within himself the vision of that fall into nothingness, that dissolution into shrieking atoms.

"Lord, how are mine adversaries increased. . . ."

This psalm had been set to music and was now being sung in the cellar on the edge of the city—not in the generals' room, but in the adjoining compartment. Hands with long fingers and knobby joints laid the flute which had accompanied the singing back into its satin-lined case and shut the lid. This was the first time Lieutenant Colonel Unschlicht had played the flute with his whole soul. Up to now playing the instrument had been something of an exercise of the will. But this time the melody had penetrated literally to the marrow of his bones. In this hour of need the instrument had become for him a means of expressing his innermost being. His care in replacing it in its case seemed perfectly proper, but the fact that he left the case behind him on the table and did not pack it into his rucksack might well have been taken as a warning sign. The other officers, a major in the engineers, the intendant of the corps, a captain and a lieutenant, had already shouldered their rucksacks and donned their fur caps. There was nothing more to say; it had all been discussed beforehand. Five men, five white faces.

"Very well, gentlemen."

Like thieves they stole out of the cellar, past the door to the common room, ascended the steep corridor, and went by the sentry outside. The sentry was startled when the lieutenant colonel's pallid face appeared suddenly at his side. He recovered and saluted properly, then stared dazedly at the five officers with their rucksacks.

Lieutenant Colonel Unschlicht led the way, keeping several paces ahead of the others. They passed through ravines and crossed the square where the garrison headquarters stood, its top stories swathed in smoke. They went on down to the slope overlooking the shore of the river and to the area near the Russian shore fortifications. Here they moved in Indian file out on to the river and walked down the center of the frozen stream, through drifting snow. The ice underfoot was irregular; crevices had formed and frozen together again; ice floes had jammed into humps. The sky appeared higher than it had ever been, and never had they seen such a multitude of brilliant stars. The city that ran for fifteen miles along the right bank of the Volga seemed as far away as the land to a sailor whose ship is skirting the seacoast; the howling tumult in the interior of the city did not reach them here. But when the artillery across the Volga rumbled for minutes as though a railroad train were passing and when the heavy shells crashed down upon the wounded city, then all the depths and abysses roared at once. Afterwards there was only the snow again, only the sky and the silence. The men lowered their heads against the wind and struggled on, step by step, over high drifts and broken lumps of ice.

A plane strewed flares, and earth and sky were transformed. The city was wiped away by the white light. The shore ceased to be a high, steep coastline towering up in the mist; the rows of hollow stone boxes were laid bare, the frozen tumult of this jungle-like toothpick world revealed. The light penetrated into every pore and every hole. Some of the white balls of light floated down over the river and hung there with teardrops of light streaming from them. Then the five men could only throw themselves down and bury their faces in the glittering whiteness of the snow. When the last drop of light had faded, when the sky arched above them again and the stars twinkled once more as though the ghostly light had not been at all, they got to their feet again and continued on downriver.

Again a cannon thundered on the opposite bank and again the sound was re-echoed a hundredfold. Again flares fell and the men lay prone. After three hours of this marching, during which under normal conditions they might have covered eight miles, they had traversed scarcely six. When the lieutenant colonel, who had kept a considerable distance ahead throughout the march, turned suddenly toward the shore, the others felt that it was too soon. They thought they should have gone on downriver until dawn, before cutting back to the west bank. However, they silently followed in the footprints of their leader. They reached the shore and climbed over the high embankment. In the snow were black traces of fire and the remains of charred wooden huts; then came a row of empty houses whose doors slammed to and fro in the wind. Amid this ghostly, incessant slamming of masterless doors rifle shots rang out.

What was the matter with the lieutenant colonel?

Even while they were on the ice in the middle of the river he had sometimes failed to lie flat under the light of flares, but had gone striding on through the snow, a solitary dark tower. As he stepped on to the shore he had shown no signs of fear that he might step on an anti-personnel or anti-tank mine, although he knew that a mine belt had been laid along the shore. And now too he walked forward without looking to the right or left, without taking any precautions.

Where were they? Whether they were still in South Tsaritsa or had already reached Yelshanka, they did not know. At any rate, they had stumbled into a battle sector again. An automatic gun was strewing shells. The four flattened out on the ground. The lieutenant colonel stalked stiffly on. It was then, with their faces pressed into the snow, their bodies aching with weariness from the walk over the ice, their heads ringing from the peals of exploding shells, that they understood. They looked up at the lieutenant colonel who was striding along in the flare of the gun like a tall, battered scarecrow, and they realized suddenly that he did not at all want to break out of the pocket. He was seeking something else, that was clear.

And at once the something else came.

The lieutenant colonel raised both arms and held them up for a period no longer than it took the four officers to blink. Then he staggered, fell backward, and lay stretched full length in the snow. The others lay where they were and heard his groans. It was up to the senior officer, the major, to crawl up to Unschlicht, and this he did. A rough splinter from an automatic gun shell had torn away half of the lieutenant colonel's face.

"Sir..."

Groans.

"Sir, can I do anything for you, sir?"

"Yes, what we agreed on when we set out."

When they set out they had agreed that if any of them were wounded on the way, the others would administer the *coup de grâce*. The major did not realize that he was groaning louder than the wounded man. He took out his service revolver.

"Sir, may I ask you one question, sir? Do you believe you will go to Heaven, sir?"

"Yes, I shall go to Heaven."

The report of a pistol resounded on the icy air. It was an hour before dawn, and that was the end of the attempt to break out of the pocket. The major, the intendant, the captain, and the lieutenant lay in a circle around the dead man. When the first light crept up from the Volga, they stood up. With raised hands they approached the nearest Russian sentry.

Black and massive, its walls a yard and a half thick, stood the building of the People's Commissariat for Internal Affairs, which the German soldiers called the GPU house. The structure had been bombed to shreds; the roofs had been swept away, the upper stories burned out, and bomb holes led like airshafts down to the lower rooms, which were long halls. The massive exterior walls afforded excellent protection against splinters and shielded the courtyard, which was as big as a drill ground, from direct fire.

In the courtyard stood a field kitchen which for days had been short of wood and water. Day and night a long queue of men stood before this field kitchen. Right behind it, along the path in the snow that led to the latrine, lay stiffly-frozen dead men, victims of shells from Russian mortars which were keeping this yard under fire.

The survivors of a tank corps, the remains of two motorized divisions and splinter groups from other units were quartered here; these men were maintaining a sort of defense line on the western edge of the city and had occupied firing points in the ruins round about. Altogether there were some two thousand men, and together with the masses of wounded and the occupants of the neighboring ruins, some five thousand men were collected in this area. The ordinary soldiers occupied the large rooms above-ground. The staffs, of which there were a great many, were underground in the long arched corridors of the jail cellars. Double guards were posted at the entrances to these cellar rooms and refused admittance to anyone not there on business.

In one of the jail cells, six paces long and two paces wide and about the height of a tall man, with a small barrel window, Major General Damme lived. Having lost his entire division, he had with him only his staff officers, who had taken quarters in adjoining cells. Twenty-four hours ago Damme had suddenly become a commander of troops again. The commander of the tank corps who had "gone to the front," that is to say, who was wandering around somewhere in this world of ruins, had given Damme deputy command of his corps.

Now Damme sat at the table, a telephone at his ear, engaged in a damnably unpleasant conversation. The person on the other end of the line was no less than the commander in chief of the Sixth Army.

"I've heard, Damme . . ." that was how the conversation had begun, "that you have been conducting negotiations with the Russians."

There was no denying it and the time had come to speak right out. "Yes, field marshal!" (He almost said 'Herr General.' The chief had been promoted just that day and since no word ever came from the army, there had been no official announcement of it.) "Yes, I personally conducted the negotiations with the Russians."

What did they want of him? For days Army had not been issuing orders; practically speaking, it had not been in command for a long time. The only word they had heard from the higher echelon for days had been: Hold! How could they hold when there were no arms left? What did Army want when for days it had been silent as the grave?

"The chief of staff informed me of this extremely serious matter, Damme."

Damme could well imagine that the chief of staff would have his hand in the affair. Even without the change in tone, the sudden sharpness that entered the almost plaintive voice, Damme could easily imagine that the commander's evil genius was sitting right opposite him, supervising the conversation.

"Now listen here, Damme. Your negotiations do not even affect your own division, but a unit belonging to someone

286

else which has been entrusted to you only temporarily. And still you have offered to surrender?"

"Yes, sir, I have. But I first called a meeting of all the officers of the troops entrusted to me. The officers were informed that steps were in progress to put an honorable end to the heroic struggle. Every one of them was asked individually: Is this agreeable to you? And every one of them stood up and replied: Yes. What else can we do; how can it possibly go on . . . ?"

"You know the order, Damme?"

"Yes, sir, I am familiar with the order, sir."

"Then it should be perfectly clear that negotiations are altogether out of the question. The order will be carried out. The order will be carried out punctually and to the end, sir."

The order from the Führer's headquarters read: "To the last cartridge." The supplementary army order read: "Enemy overtures for a parley are to be rejected by fire." Supplementary orders for commanders of troops who no longer had any troops and were left with only their staffs, read: "The headquarters must be defended." It was all perfectly clear—on paper, at least.

"But there is nothing left to eat, sir."

"I am aware of that."

"The wounded are no longer being cared for, sir."

"I am aware of that."

"The ring is shrinking all around. In the face of the Russian cannon—you don't need a telescope to be able to see them. . . ."

"I am aware of all that."

"And it's perfectly clear that we can no longer count on being relieved, sir."

"You know the order."

The conversation continued in this fashion. It had begun at half past eleven at night and was still going on at half past twelve. It lasted until nearly one in the morning, and for the last quarter hour the army chief of staff took over and thundered rudely and insultingly; he grew more and more offensive and at last launched into wild, frantic threats.

After it was over Damme ran his hand through his hair, and his hand came away wet. The order must be carried out —such an order, plain idiocy. Impossible! That's what it was, absolutely impossible. Sweating like a horse. Head empty, back cold, no appetite—this last was easiest to bear, with rations what they were. No interest in a game of bridge any longer; no interest in anything. In other days you would have taken a couple of cups of hot tea with a good shot or two of rum to them, covered yourself with blankets, and sweated it right out. But here, with this everlasting cannonade, this everlasting huddling in a damp cell, that everlasting little barred window before your eyes, those everlasting horrible scenes outside—no human being could endure it. It was, in one word, impossible.

So naturally, when a German captain, one of the men the Russians were sending back frequently now, had stepped in accompanied by a Russian major, he had of course sat down with the two of them and considered what was to be done. There must be a drop of brandy somewhere, damn it all, he had said to his interpreter, Wiedemann. No, none at all? Well, then, make a pot of coffee. But there was no coffee left either. Nothing to offer his guest, and outside the window they carried another man past and tossed him onto the pile of corpses. There you had it, and under such conditions plain common sense pointed the way. There was no need for lengthy deliberations, nothing to do but to put an honorable end to the heroic struggle, and that was precisely the formula they had agreed on. Everything had been arranged and the surrender had not yet taken place only because the Russian officer said he wanted to take in a few more troops at the same time, the Twenty-Ninth Motorized Division and whatever other scattered units were around here. And then had come this damned telephone call from the army and from that chief of staff.

Really, the whole thing was arrant idiocy. And all the while this firing kept on, all the while they kept dragging out dead men stiff as boards, all the while the racket in front of the field kitchen went on, and the whole thing was senseless, aimless. And he himself—his hair came out in handfuls when he touched it. His digestion was no longer functioning. How could it, without a drop of coffee or a cigar? He was getting into a state of total mental depression, was absolutely incapable of work. But something had to happen now; tomorrow was the appointed time. Tomorrow morning the men were to line up and surrender; that was his agreement with the Russian.

General Damme got up, opened the door, and called loudly down the long corridor for his interpreter. Wiedemann, who had already found out about the telephone conversation and had been conferring with the colonels and the other staff officers in the adjoining cell, came out at once. He had been waiting for this call and knew what was wanted of him. The colonels had already guessed what the general would do after the telephone conversation, and they had already made their decision: Then we will have to do it ourselves.

"Well, Wiedemann, I've been forbidden to surrender. We must inform the Russian officer. We must say that we are breaking off negotiations. Will you please undertake this mission?"

Damme sat down again in his empty cell after Wiedemann had left, and again sheer wretchedness stared down at him from all the walls. He stared at the wall in turn, and he too knew what was being discussed on the other side of the wall. And Damme thought: Well, the colonels will have to do it themselves.

The cellar of the theater was connected by an underground corridor with a number of cellars under the ruins of the Red Army House. In the various chambers of these cellars, which were known as the "Timoshenko cellars," was a whole underground village of wounded, and in the lowest quarter of it, swathed day and night in hot vapors, was Doctor Huth's operating room.

Huth was done in. His nerves were still stout; they had withstood everything, the roars of pain under the knife, the sight of men dying in agony and dying silently for seventy-seven days. In the steaming vapors from endless wounds Huth had shrunk away to skin and bones, but his hands had continued to labor untiringly, without trembling, as he fought against the evermounting tide of death. If a hundred patients had died after a successful operation, one of them, perhaps, had lived, and Huth tried to credit himself with this one. But now even the one could no longer live without the watery soup that, in addition to a hundred other miracles, had so far preserved his life. For days no rations whatever had been supplied to the men in the theater cellar. Therefore the doctor's incisions in living flesh, his sawing of living bones, the torment he inflicted in operating successfully, now merely prolonged the process of dying.

This conclusion was the end-product of a long chain of thought. Huth did not complete the incision he had begun to make in a man's thigh. He laid the scalpel back on the table, turned around, removed his oilcloth apron and hung it on a nail. After washing his hands and arms and putting on his jacket, he turned around once more and studied the man on the operating table. The body was not too muscular, but well formed; it gave signs of a vitality that, under other circumstances, would probably have sufficed for another half century.

The man was a young captain, and Huth recalled that he had had him here on the table a few days earlier, with a head wound. The captain drew breath. His lips, half parted from pain, quivered. His eyelids opened and his gray, still veiled eyes, stared unseeingly. Huth did not want to wait until the narcosis of pain vanished completely. He had the power to relieve this man instantly of all pain, to do to him what the system he served was doing on an organized, mass scale to the old, the sick, and the useless. But his mind reeled back from this thought. His scruples were not religious, but perhaps after all it was something fundamentally religious, an innate ethic, that kept him from such an act.

Viktor Huth fled up the stairs, leaving the wounded man on the table and the medical aides in the room. He reached the large vault where, man jammed up against man, with only narrow footpaths between the grounds, some seven or eight hundred wounded, sick, dying, and already dead men lay. Within two or at most three days this cellar would house no one but the dead, line upon line of them with greenish-hued abdomens, filthy brown faces, and dissolving eyes, giving off a more and more frightful reek of decay. But now death was still held at bay, shouted down by a polyphonic choir of powerful voices. Out of unendurable pain men screamed themselves into unconsciousness. The men who had been fed up to now and still had their strength, shouted their hunger. Feeble voices lisped prayers. A maddened torso that still had lungs with which to screech reared up and then fell down helplessly again.

A superhuman voice fed by batteries resounded through the room. This radio voice made the sufferers forget their pain for a time; it interrupted the act of dying, made raging men pause for breath, divided the cellar into two parties for and against it, for listening to it and for having it switched off.

"Turn it off, turn it off!" a chorus bawled.

"Louder, louder!" others shouted.

"Turn it off."

"Leave it on."

"That fat rat."

"That swollen belly."

"Should've kept his word."

"It's all his fault."

"Letting us starve."

And amid all this a man in fever screamed, "Water!" Another, frayed by pain, screamed, "Morphine!" Electric lights hung from the ceiling (that was the distinguishing feature of this cellar, which was under the direct charge of Army Head-quarters) and illuminated the upper half of the vaulted room; the lower part was quite dim. Among the ragged out-stretched and seated figures moved the two chaplains, Koog and Kalser, who had met again in this dungeon. Chaplain Koog listened to a last message from a dying man. Caplain Kalser murmured over another in whose throat the death rattle had already begun: "May he behold the Eternal Light." Doctor Huth leaned against the wall. He caught sight of the wounded captain whom he had left behind on the operating table. The captain had come up, dragging his wounded leg behind him. He collapsed to the floor beside the doctor.

"Doctor?"

"What can I do for you, captain? There's no sense to it; it will only mean it will take you longer to die."

"Then let it take longer, doctor. Please, doctor!"

"All right, stretch out your leg, but first listen."

"What is that?"

"Reich Marshal Göring."

And amid the screams and curses, the tumult of "turn it off" and "leave it on," came the suave tenor voice, and the chaplains, the doctor, and the captain listened.

"People's army . . . people's community . . . Germans together to the last . . . have broken with outmoded ideas . . . but, my comrades, they alone can fight who are passionately concerned. . . ."

"Who are passionately concerned, and let me not grow slack in thy struggle, my God," Chaplain Kalser prayed, and he closed a soldier's eyes. His own lids half shut, he looked around and caught sight of the next man who needed him. But there were so many, so many by now. Slowly he stood up, wearily walked a few paces, and knelt silently beside the next. Doctor Huth, thirty-four years old and looking like a mummy, was still alert; he noticed everything that was going on around him—the two chaplains, the dully brooding, the silently dying, and the considerable number who, in a surge of fury, consumed the last strength left in their hearts. He observed a paymaster's assistant who seemed youthful in spite of his sunken eyes and the constant quivering of his long fingers. He heard the orders a delirious tank lieutenant was shouting; they were orders such as would be given to men in a trench, and undoubtedly the lieutenant's last assignment had been as an infantry officer. Then he heard the captain beside him sobbing. He realized that the man was going off into a fit of compulsive weeping. "What's the matter, captain? I'll do it for you, but let's wait a bit."

Tomas wept at this moment, not from anxiety, but from a memory that had completely overwhelmed him. The last radio broadcast he had listened to had been the round-up at New Year's, and he had been terribly moved when the announcer from Königsberg had spoken. The recollection had lingered long in his mind, like sad, despairing music. For the Königsberg announcer was a girl and his fiancée, and he had heard her voice that night. Now, however, the voice was the Reich Marshal's tenor.

"Weltanschauung . . . weltanschauung . . . unshakable welt-anshauung . . . weltanschauung that our Führer has created. . . . What power there is in this weltanschauung . . . what blessing . . . duty of the leaders to be examples to the men. . . . What Herculean labors our Führer has performed . . . out of this pulp, this human pulp . . . to forge a nation hard as steel." This was followed by the sentence: *"A Führer who is the greatest German in history,"* but that sentence was not heard, it was drowned out in the shrieking, the wailing, the outcries of "Turn it off!" and the alternation, "Turn it off—leave it on." The tank lieutenant roared: "Bring up the ammunition. Speed up the firing over there. Stay prone, damn you, stay prone! Fire!" A top sergeant came down the steps with an armful of discarded sausages, large red sausages. "Tank Regiment 36," the sergeant called. Men of that regiment, who were lying in one corner, shouted as loud as they were able, "Over here, over here, sir." Everyone shouted, "Me too, me too, sir." The sausages caused a momentary commotion and were distributed in a moment. Those who received a portion gulped it down greedily. The others sat around, looked on, and afterwards fell back in exhaustion. The men who had eaten were also exhausted by the effort and lay down on their sides.

Above the unconscious and the helpless the Reich Marshal's voice floated. *"The icy Russian winter and the weakness of various leaders were additional difficulties to be overcome; here again the Führer directed everything, everywhere, and with his strength he held the Eastern Front. . . . Then came the day when for the first time German tank division infantry broke into the fortress of Stalingrad and took a firm hold on the Volga, the river that is Russia's fate."* (The entire cellar groaned.) *"The enemy is tough, but the German soldier has grown tougher . . . we have taken away the Russians' coal and iron, and without that they can no longer make armaments on a large scale. . . . Now we see them making a last effort, though admittedly a gigantic one . . . new divisions, others with their ranks refilled, but there are no new classes of soldiers; no, they must now take weary old men, sixteen-year-old children. . . ."*

"Old men! Children!" One man repeated the words at the top of his voice. The enlisted men howled. The officers sat hunched, teeth clenched under their bloody scraps of bandage. Then the groans stopped; the men gave way to sheer fury, bursting blood vessels, temperatures rising, the crack of a suicide's revolver.

The oily tenor droned on.

"Rising above all these gigantic battles like a mighty monument is Stalingrad, the struggle for Stalingrad. One day this will be recognized as the greatest battle in our history, a battle of heroes, the battle that is now being fought there by our infantry, engineers, artillerymen, flak gunners and every other man in that city, from the generals down to the last private. Those men are now fighting there against tremendously superior forces, fighting for every stone, for every foxhole, every trench, fighting and fighting, spent, exhausted, but still fighting. We have a mighty epic of an incomparable struggle, the struggle of the Nibelungs. They too stood to the last. . . ."

"So we're written off already!" one man shouted.

"Written off." The staggering thought swept through the cellar. They knew it, of course, but the fact that someone told them, shouted the words at them, was too much.

"That overstuffed pig stays where he's warm and comfortable."

"I'm no hero, I'm hungry."

"Hungry!"

"Funeral hymn."

"Turn it off, turn it off."

". . . this sacrifice, my comrades. If any of you are ever tempted to falter, think of the warriors of Stalingrad. . . . My soldiers, thousands of years have passed, and thousands of years ago in a tiny pass in Greece stood a tremendously brave and bold man with three hundred soldiers, Leonidas with his three hundred Spartans. The sky was darkened by the masses of arrows that rained upon them, and the three hundred did not waver, did not weaken. And then the last man fell . . . and now only the inscription stands: Wanderer, if you should come to Sparta, go tell the Spartans you found us lying here as the law bade us. . . . Some day men will read: If you come to

293

Germany, go tell the Germans you saw us lying in Stalingrad, as the law bade us. . . ."

"Help!"

It was a cry of utter distress. The high-pitched scream hung in the air. The cellar became once again the cellar of the theater, the quarters of the wounded. Men continued to die. The fearful waves of pain returned, surged over them all. Scarcely any of them heard the following sentences.

"To the individual soldier it does not matter whether he dies at Stalingrad, at Rshev, in Africa, or in the icy north. . . . There will always be gripers who complain about that. . . . When the soldier sets forth, he counts on the probability that he will not come back. And if he does come back, it's because he's had his luck with him. . . ." Scarcely anyone heard this sentences: *"Of course it is the Jew who is running things over there. We need only know the Jew with his Old Testament type of hatred. . . ."* Scarcely anyone heard: *"Who, I ask, is so God-forsaken that he refuses to see where our armies stand today? Do we not stand from the North Cape down to Africa and east to the Volga?"*

Few heard his lame apology:

"And why do we not take revenge, many of our comrades are asking. Do not forget, comrades, that it is a vast theater of war, that the tremendous might of the German Air Force is fighting in the south, fighting in the north, fighting in the east. . . ."

Here, at any rate, it was not fighting. The falling bombs were Russian bombs, and it was unlikely that old men and children were piloting the bombers. But few listened now; the Reich Marshal's voice floated along on the edge of the tumult. This cellar had been given up for lost, all of Stalingrad had been given up for lost—that was what the oily voice from Berlin made perfectly clear. And one man had cried out: *Help!* On the floor a man lay with blue face and foam on his lips. Against the wall leaned men whose muscles had totally atrophied; others were nothing but frameworks of bone. Some could not see, some had become totally deaf. And MP's trampled down the rows, looking into the faces of the sick, turning over the dying to make sure that they were not dissimulating. They actually found a few who could be propped up on their feet and taken along to fill the gaps of some unit. But above all the tumult rose this one mad, cracking voice. A man screamed out his soul, and in his cry for help was the appeal of the entire cellar.

Viktor Huth was still leaning against the wall. He was thinking about law and lawlessness. Any immoderate effort had to end in disaster, he thought. The march to the Volga (and they had intended to go on much farther, to the Ganges, on forever) had inevitably to terminate in a cellar like this. His eyes rested again on the young paymaster's assistant who sat opposite him, sunken-eyed and stony-faced, his only movement this continual spreading and closing of his fingers. The world is reflected in a drop of water, and this march to the east, undertaken out of no inner necessity and therefore wanton and lawless, was reflected in the athetoid muscular movements of the paymaster's assistant.

Suddenly, amid the screams, the howls, and the gasps of death, another sound intervened, the dull thud of the approaching end. A near-by shell hit made the whole massive vault shake and rumble. As the next artillery shell struck and the conscious men in the cellar held their breath, Huth stood up. He finished the operation on Captain Tomas; it was his last operation. Then he ran up the steps and into the street, past the sandbags and the barricade, and out into the glaring, floodlight square. The men at the 10.5 cm. howitzer and the military police at the entrance to the department store ruin were in a huddle and so itent on the shelling that Huth passed unchallenged through the gate and reached the door that led to the commander in chief's section of the cellar.

The theater cellar he had left was now shaken every few minutes by the shells striking near by, and the eight hundred wounded there breathed to the rhythm of the explosions.

The military police who guarded the ruin of the department store—a whole band of them with plump, ruddy faces—had instructions to demand identification from everyone who wished to enter, to find out where he came from and whom he wished to see. But these military policemen were no longer functioning too well. For the cellars of the ruin were not only occupied by Army Headquarters; they also housed the combat headquarters of a regiment and a battalion, and therefore the door was open for orderlies and messengers and all sorts of other persons with all sorts of missions, as well as those who pretended to have missions.

Shells from heavy artillery zoomed overhead. Near by, tank shells exploded. A flare hung over the yard, dripping droplets of light and illuminating every corner. The army staff, now in its fifth headquarters since the beginning of the encirclement, could no longer move; it was stuck fast right in the midst of the battle. The MP's fell prey to the same nervousness that filled the entire building; instead of examining every new arrival as attentively and warily as they usually did, they repeatedly glanced at the corners of the yard and at the dark tunnel of the entrance, as though they expected the Unknown to come leaping out at them at any moment.

Two colonels, a captain, and a medical lieutenant demanded admission at once. One colonel wanted to see the commander in chief, the other colonel was a member of the army staff, the captain had been ordered to report to the commander in chief's adjutant, the medical lieutenant was Viktor Huth.

An excited doctor, coatless and hatless, wanted to see the commander in chief of the army. At any other time this sort of request would have aroused a genial smile of amusement. But just now this doctor was merely one face in a group, one more figure in the phantasmagoria that was being produced without letup by the very pavement of the courtyard. A military policeman who seemed somewhat drunk said, "Come on, now, be good and get the hell out of here." But the next moment Huth and the entire group of military police and the others lay flat on their faces on the pavement, from which the snow had been swept away. A shell that had fallen into the yard exploded with a hiss and sent fragments slapping into the walls. Beside Huth lay the colonel from the army staff; he had heard Huth's request and when they stood up again he said, "Come along with me, lieutenant."

Accompanied by the colonel, Huth passed through the line of military police. The two officers who headed the MP's saluted the colonel. There were no doors; a dark tunnel opened out before them. A ramp led down into the cellar. Down below here it looked very much like the inside of a large garage. In the center was a broad hand-truck track; to the right and left were individual compartments supported by concrete posts and concrete arches overhead, and with windows along the exterior walls. About a third of these windows rose above ground level and were protected against shots by sandbags. These compartments were divided from the corridor by crude board partitions with rough doors in them. Lights were burning inside the rooms. The corridor was illuminated only when one of the doors stood open.

Lieutenant Huth stood close to the end of the ramp and waited for Colonel Carras who, after taking him in, had asked him to wait. Huth realized that he would scarcely have got in without assistance and that he would get no farther unless someone prepared the way for him. Therefore he stood and waited patiently, watching the ghostly dance that went on before his eyes. The corridor was a strange, dimly-lit alley chockfull of officers, orderlies, clerks, military policemen, and others who bustled back and forth among the rooms or sat on the floor along the walls. The scene was a familiar one to him; what was startling was the realization that the wave of decay, the wretched creatures seeking shelter, was already pouring into the very Headquarters of the Army.

The two officers who had come in with Huth knew their way about and had gone on. One of them, Colonel Steinle, who had seen his combat group destroyed at Yeshovka and was now quartered in the city jail, wanted to see the commander in chief. What he wanted was exactly what Huth wanted: capitulation.

The other officer, the captain, was General Vennekohl's adjutant. In Vennekohl's absence Army Headquarters had telephoned him and inquired: "How many decorations do you need, War Merit Crosses, German Crosses, Iron Crosses first class? Well, draw up a list and bring it here." The captain had come and went in to see the commander in chief's adjutant.

"Let me see your list. How many are there?"

It was a long list. The adjutant did not even glance at the names or the recommendations. He reached into a box under his cot and counted out the requested number of Iron Crosses. Vennekohl's adjutant did not know what to do with the heap of them. He found an old newspaper, folded it into a paper bag, and so went off with his supply of decorations.

Next door, in the operations officer's room, stood the operations officer and the army adjutant general. On the table stood a half-empty bottle of brandy, sliced pumpernickel breads wrapped in torn cellophane, packages of butter and cheese and a can of French sardines. The two officers were busy packing their rucksacks; they also gathered up the remains of their meal and packed that away. The operations officer opened the door slightly to see whether the coast was clear. They sent their orderlies to the exit with their rucksacks; then they themselves stole out. The route they had chosen for their attempt to break out of the ring was the way across the Volga. On the other bank of the Volga they intended to strike out toward the south until they came halfway to Astrakhan, then cross the Volga again and try to reach the German army in the Caucasus.

A few doors farther on sat the tailor of Roske's regiment. He had before him a pile of clothes, coats, field blouses, trousers, riding breeches—the whole wardrobe of Colonel Roske who only yesterday had been a regimental commander and who today, as the successor to General Hartmann, was now commander of Hartmann's infantry division—which no longer existed. As such, after a radio message to the High Command of the Armed Forces and a prompt reply, he had been promoted to the rank of general. The tailor was now hurrying to remove the colonel's insignia and sew on the shoulder boards, collar tables, gold buttons, and red trouser stripes of a general. The newly-promoted general came in and said, "Come on, forget it. It makes no difference whether I fall into a mass grave with a colonel's or a general's insignia."

Roske was playing host to the army, since the department store had formerly been General Hartmann's province. In that capacity the new general had his hands full. He had turned over to a major the direct command of the small remnant of his regiment which was now fighting in the streets that led to the square.

Colonel Steinle had passed through the first part of the underground alley, past the signal center, past the rooms of the signal regiment commander, the army surgeon, and General Roske. He now stood in front of the curtain that separated the end of the corridor from the main part of the cellar. Behind the curtain were the rooms of the commander in chief's immediate staff.

There was a burst of noise, a door was flung open, and before him stood the very person he had most wanted to avoid, the Sixth Army chief of staff.

"And where may you be going?" the chief of staff barked.

"I absolutely must see the commander in chief, sir."

"What do you mean, you must see him? No such thing. The field marshal has serious concerns; he has to work and must not be distrubed."

"Sir, it is serious concern for the army that has led me to take this step."

"I forbid you to see him; I will not let you come in here."

The curtain parted and a captain came out. "I beg your pardon for interrupting, sir, but it's urgent," he said to the chief of staff. The two stepped aside and the captain said: "A report, sir. The tank corps is capitulating."

"After I talked with Damme and after Damme gave his word? Impossible!"

"The message is not from Damme, sir, but from the commanding general. The commander of the tank corps has returned to his headquarters, sir."

The chief of staff stood rigid, with tense, oval face, gray hair, great staring eyes. In this moment of mounting fury his eyes changed color until they looked like opaque glass.

I! I can do everything, I understand everything, see through everything; the others are incompetent, unintelligent, stupid, and no one, no matter what his standing, has any call to make his own decisions. This was the chief of staff's attitude; Colonel Steinle and almost all the other officers were aware of it. The man was considered to have a very competent mind and a tremendous capacity for work, and it was true that he could get a tremendous amount of work out of others, Colonel Steinle thought. Even while he played cards his staff of orderlies could keep everyone around in breathless suspense. In short—the line officer reflected—the chief of staff was a typical general staff officer to whom no man was human unless he was on the general staff.

Steinle also observed that the chief of staff had completely forgotten him. And as the chief rushed into the orderly's room, snatched up the telephone, and shouted, "Connection," only to learn that the connection had not been broken, Colonel Steinle thrust the curtain aside and entered the part of the corridor which contained the offices of the chief of staff, the operations officer, the supply officer, the clerical staff, and the commander in chief.

In the orderly's room the chief of staff was still seeing red. He had not even heard the captain say that the report was not from General Damme, but from the legitimate commander of the tank corps. Therefore he roared into the telephone:

"I suppose you've gone insane, Damme. If I had had any inkling of it, Damme, I would have had you and your whole staff arrested. What's that, who . . . who are you . . . a lieutenant?"

Neither General Damme nor the commanding general was on the other end of the wire, but a lieutenant who politely repeated his message: "I have been ordered to inform you, sir, on behalf of the commander, that the tank corps is capitulating at this moment and that after delivering my message I am not to receive any reply. According to my orders, I must cut the telephone line, which I herewith do, sir."

"I'll have you shot, you and the whole staff, do you hear?"

But there was no one to hear. The lieutenant had in fact cut the wire. The chief of staff threw the receiver back on the table. An unhealthy flush rose to his face. He looked as if he were on the point of choking. He rushed out of the room, strode down the dark corridor up to the entrance and back, and grew even more furious as he stumbled over the men sitting on the floor.

Colonel Steinle went up to the door that bore the inscription, "Commander in Chief." The door was open and he entered. On a large round table stood coffee cups, but the room appeared deserted. Steinle was about to turn back when he noticed the half-parted curtain to a darkened adjoining room. There he suddenly caught sight of the field marshal. The room was not quite dark; it was illuminated by the pale light of radio tubes, and beside the radio sat the commander in chief, hands in his lap, hunched up, his profile toward the colonel.

The colonel mustered courage for a low-voiced: "Herr Field Marshal!"

The field marshal looked up and recognized him.

"Oh, it's you, Steinle? What news? Please sit down."

The field marshal came out of his den and sat down opposite the colonel. Steinle described the situation on the so-called front and the condition of the perishing troops. On one side of the table sat the officer who had seen the deaths of a thousand men he knew by name; facing him sat the high-ranking general staff officer who knew the members of his staff and his commanders, and no one else. For him, individual men existed only in multiples; they were moved hither and yon in masses, beginning with ten thousand, a hundred thousand, or three hundred thousand; they were advanced or retreated in the mind and on paper exclusively; they could be crossed off by the ten thousands and, in the particular case in question, by the hundred thousands. On the one side sat the man from the roaring battlefield who saw nothing behind him but smoke, snow, and dead bodies; on the other sat a man who ruled over that same battlefield, but for whom the smoke and tumult of downfall presented itself as markings on a clean map. Nevertheless, that man had foreseen the debacle at a distance, and had probably seen it coming sooner than the colonel. Not for nothing had he earned a striking reputation for correct, sober, objective, and often annoyingly pessimistic estimates of the situation. He was an old soldier; even during the First World War he had been on the general staff. Later he had been a teacher at the Military Academy; in this war he had been deputy chief of the general staff. He had proved himself an extraordinary aide and adviser in planning operations under commanders who then made the decisions. But then he had suddenly been given a command, an army, and had found himself required to make decisions on his own, and decisions of a magnitude that few other commanders had faced. That was one aspect of his predicament. The other was the chief of staff who had been assigned to him. In the normal course of events this man should have been his adviser; but the natural relationship had been inverted and the chief of staff had in practice seized actual power of command for himself.

Essentially, Colonel Steinle told the field marshal nothing new, and the reek of blood and decay around this officer of the line was calculated rather to repel than to attract the commander in chief. There was no need for him to see the disaster exemplified in the crude, individual cases. But he was well aware of the significance of his army's destruction, both for the present stage and the future course of the war; the whole picture lay spread out before his eyes like the pages of an open book. Therein he saw his special task: to transform the debacle into glory and the defeat into victory, to accomplish the impossible, if not in the real world and for this war, then in the world of illusion and as a preparatory step for the next war. At this moment, therefore, his only concern was to find out what grand gestures the dying army was still capable of making in order to provide the heroic example his superiors demanded, in order to stimulate men to a firmer dedication to this struggle for expansion and possession of the world. He personally had settled matters with himself and looked forward to death in the near future. The sacrifice of his life was required and accorded with the "example" his army had to provide. He had climbed the highest peak of his personal existence; now he had the highest mission to perform. And that mission was not assigned directly by the Führer nor directly from the hands of those who had reached out across the map of Europe for oil and ore. That mission was assigned to him directly by the *idea* he had served and which had raised him so high. In the First World War that idea had failed; it would lose in the Second World War as well (such was the defeated field marshal's estimate of the present situation). But his speculations went far afield and he felt sure that it would win at last in the Third World War.

The two failures could only be considered expeditions in search of loot. But if the third succeeded, the first two tries would then be stages on the road to world rule, and therein lay the glory. Blood, piles of brown corpses, the far-flung stench of decay—these did not matter compared to that future glory. So the field marshal, with both feet already in a vast grave, was looking forward to a still vaster grave in the future, one that would encompass whole nations.

But the question was, how should the army take its final step? And that, as a matter of fact, was not going quite according to schedule. "As a matter of fact that isn't quite the way I imagined it," the field marshal said. It was not quite the picture his chief of staff had drawn for him—the chief had generalized somewhat on Hartmann's case and had sent a radio message to Berlin: "Generals and privates are fighting shoulder to shoulder on the railroad embankment, with swords, bayonets, and spades." It was simply not so. The colonel explained to him that "Damme" was not an isolated case; that large and small units were surrendering everywhere along the edge of the city. For days, since Gorodishche and Gumrak, the lower officers had been refusing to execute orders which demanded more than the troops could give. Right now, Steinle said, that was the case everywhere in the front lines. A lieutenant would say to his captain, "I'm deserting now, I'm quitting, sir." And the captain would reply, "What do you mean? You can't quit." The lieutenant: "Nothing to eat any more." And he would go off with ten, twenty, or forty men.

"That is the picture of the front line at this time, sir."

"Yes, as a matter of fact it's quite, quite different from what I thought," the field marshal replied.

"There was that order for breaking out, sir. . . ."

"Oh yes, that unfortunate plan!"

The plan had been for the tank corps to cross the Volga and work its way eastward, for the infantry divisions to attempt to break out to the north, south, and west. The idea had been for a centrifugal dispersion of parts of the army in all directions. Army Headquarters had been forced to drop this plan.

"That order was based on a totally illusory conception of conditions and the infantry could not possibly sympathize with it, sir. The withdrawal of the order could not close the gap that has developed here between the troops and their command. That order contributed to the disintegration imposed by outward circumstances. And now the troops are dissolving, falling apart bit by bit, splintering. Chaos is upon us. Army Headquarters is silent. The troops are waiting for only one more order, for the order that will counter the chaos and initiate organic capitulation instead of anarchic surrender by groups."

"Capitulation is forbidden!" The field marshal repeated the formula that had been his sole word for so many days now. The left half of his face again began to twitch convulsively.

"But, sir, that means forcing further disintegration upon

the troops. Do you want things to come to the point where the men force their way into your bunker here? They'll come and shoot you right here. Do you wish to see a revolt start under the very eyes of the Russians, sir?"

"My dear Steinle!" The field marshal stood up and smiled knowingly. "It will never come to that, I assure you, Steinle. For the rest, thank you."

That was the colonel's dismissal. His mind reeling, he made his way back through the cellar. The field marshal, the theoretician, knows, he thought. He knows so much about what has been done to the men here that he knows he need no longer fear rebellion or any spark of activity from such men. Steinle had not realized it until he saw the sudden smile on the field marshal's face. He knows, he knows, Steinle thought again and again, he knows the men are completely burned out.

Colonel Carras had been to the headquarters of the Army High Command and he had been to the Führer's headquarters. He had seen the Führer, had had the privilege of clasping for a moment a disagreeable, lifeless hand. For this honor he was now to give up his life, to add the body of a Colonel Carras to all the other corpses in the rubble here. Spring would come again and the sun would shine once more. Colonel Schuster would still be sitting at his desk in the personnel department of the Army High Command and assigning specially delicate and honorable missions. He would meet Carras' widow in the street and note that she looked somewhat pale, but wonderfully elegant with her pallor and her black dress. At about that time, during the cleaning up here, a dusty skeleton would be pulled out of the ruins, loaded on a cart, and afterward dumped into a ravine on top of a large heap of other bones. "Go tell the Germans you saw us lying . . ." No thanks, no, not at all, thank you. Another matter if you could be the wanderer, if the specially honorable mission consisted in making the report. Then it might be a different matter.

Just what was this especially honorable mission of his anyway? Did it differ in any respects from that of the other five dozen odd officers who had been flown in? They had told the defenders of Stalingrad: On the way here we saw so many troops, in Schachty, Mariupol, Rostov; tank troops from Africa, infantry divisions from France, Yugoslavia, and Norway, white-painted tanks with tremendous guns, Belgian artillery horses with tremendous hindquarters. What was his mission but to sit in Army Headquarters here and needle the generals? But for that kind of work they might just as well have sent the night-club entertainers, Paul Hörbiger or Cläre Waldoff, into the pocket—and for all he cared the two of them might just as well be buried here. Why the devil should the morale builder be Colonel Carras, a man whose social graces were well known, who kept his bad moods to himself? Why the devil should he die here and die a true Spartan's death and be thoroughly, irrevocably dead and gone? It wouldn't do him any good after that fake fat Leonidas in Berlin had removed his false Spartan or Nibelung whiskers (the man got everything balled-up, didn't he?) and had forgotten all about it.

This business was serious, deadly serious.

Carras had been outside, had crossed the chalk-white, flood-lighted square at the risk of being killed by the rain of bread-and-sausage-filled bombs. A major stood there with the bleeding remnants of his regiment, holding the last entrance to the square. In at least one spot the Russians were already only four hundred yards from the Army Headquarters. Mortars were already shelling the yard. When he returned from his brief expedition he had had to throw himself flat on the pavement beside a young medical lieutenant. Of course the man was right—raising the white flag was the thing. That would make a fine ending for the epic they had dreamed up in Berlin. The wounded must not be allowed to die; it would be utterly senseless. And the death of unwounded Carras would also be utterly senseless. Therefore he had taken the man inside with him. He would support him, would get this affair over with, and then would accompany the doctor back to his cellar and help arrange the surrender there. Yes, that was the way it would have to work out. That was the sole light in this blackest night.

Carras had left Dr. Huth at the bottom of the ramp and hurried on through the cellar, through the crowd of people, the clerical quarters, the various staff officers' rooms. Then he had returned to his ray of light, the doctor, and told him they would have to be patient for a while; all the officers who counted were at the moment fearfully busy. They certainly were that. Not to mention the commander in chief, who was fearfully burdened and sat there like a wind-bent reed (Carras had caught a glimpse of him in passing). The chief of staff (Carras had opened the door and hastily closed it again) had been shouting ferociously into the telephone: "I'll have the whole staff shot at once from general down to lieutenant." The place was full of would-be escapers. The operations officer was skipping out, abandoning the army; the commander of the signal regiment was packing his rucksack; the commander of the reconnaissance company was leaving his radioman in the lurch. All of them were packing their rucksacks and secretly stealing off, some bound for the Volga and the Kirghizes, some intending to cross the Karpovka and go back to the Kalmucks. Nothing to do but cheer them on.

From behind the curtain emerged new oracular pronouncements. "It is not dishonorable to turn one's weapon against oneself." Result: the crack of pistols. "It is not dishonorable to attempt escape at the last moment." Result: rucksacks and knapsacks and even suitcases were being feverishly packed. "It is not dishonorable to be taken prisoner." This last oracle was bruited about, although it had not yet been verified and its authenticity was somewhat questionable, for up to this moment there had been a written order reading: "Negotiators are to be rejected by fire," and "Imprisonment means a painful death or rotting in Siberia." Moreover, the chief of staff was still raging through all the rooms, and wherever he caught sight of a rucksack there was a bitter row, and whenever anyone was found engaged in a tête-à-tête with a Russian it did him no good to cite the oracle of the cellar; he was promptly stood up against the wall. For this building the order that had been issued to all other headquarters was still in force: "The command post must be defended to the last cartridge." The few who were still disciplined did not go around spreading the words of the oracle; they hoarded hand grenades under their desks and in their sleeping bags. Carras had encountered a number of officers engaged in this edifying occupation—although some of them were only preparing for a rather exotic form of suicide. The orderly had assured him, however, that the chief of staff's office had not yet been turned into a munitions dump, let alone a citadel.

Carras returned to the chief of staff's anteroom and this time there was no need for him to peep in; he could hear the din through the closed door. In reply to his questioning glance the officer on guard explained that the tantrum was on account of some particularly stubborn lieutenant who was telephoning for the tenth or twentieth or thirtieth time. The lieutenant was insisting that headquarters order the troops battling in the vicinity of the garrison headquarters, who no longer knew who their commander was, to cease fighting.

The chief of staff came out of his room. He was white with

rage and saw no one. He strode forward, pushed the curtain aside, and roared down the length of the corridor to the MP sergeant on duty: "Sergeant, a detachment! Lawkow's the fellow's name, Lieutenant Lawkow. I'm making you responsible for this. Bring him here, I want to see him."

"He called the chief of staff a murderer," the officer informed Carras. Obviously this was again not the moment for Carras to talk to the chief of staff, especially since his business was on the same order; the theater cellar, like the garrison headquarters, was also a medical station.

Carras drifted on down the corridor, glancing into rooms where officers were at their meals. The army staff, after having moved five times, was poor as a church mouse. But Hartmann's division was on "home territory" here, still had provisions left, and tonight was the time for eating and drinking up everything that remained. The Army Headquarters officers who wanted to get in on the party would saunter through the rooms occupied by the "Hartmann men." On one such expedition Carras encountered his double. At any rate the other officers insisted that the commander of the army signal regiment was the spitting image of Carras. Naturally, it is always embarrassing to meet one's self eye to eye, so to speak, and particularly so when one's alter ego is at the moment doing something with a small army pistol. However, Carras's first interpretation proved wrong. The signal regiment commander snapped the safety catch on and stuck the pistol into his hip pocket. "Just imagine," he recounted, "I was going out to rustle up some breakfast for my men and found my adjutant with this thing in his hand again, safety catch off, already to go bang-bang and get it over with. Well, I've taken it away from him, but I don't know whether it will do any good. I can't keep after him all the time and stop him from playing with fire. I've got too many other patients, and after all I've got my own troubles at a time like this."

"Your adjutant is that big strapping fellow, isn't he?"

"Yes, he's the one, healthy as a horse. And imagine, he has a charming wife, married her in Belgrade just before the encirclement. She's the daughter of a rich businessman. And a fellow like that thinks of knocking himself off!"

"If I remember rightly your adjutant has been a regular whatdyacallit, a stalwart right along, hasn't he?"

"Oh yes, he's a stalwart all right. If I ever dropped a word about Hooth or Manstein, or expressed doubts or said that Operation Thunderclap was arrant nonsense, he'd jump with a 'But, sir, I must say, sir, your attitude is absolutely untenable.'

306

What a stalwart he was, one hundred per cent a believer. He believed the army communiqué was sacred, believed everything like a good pious soul. And now for the past five days he's been all broken up, sits with his head in his hands, muttering, 'So it's all lies, all fake, all phony.' He sits cursing and brooding about revenge. And just now I said to him, 'Please take down the Reich Marshal's speech in shorthand.' And all of a sudden he slammed the pen and pencil into a corner and rushed out, his face white as a sheet, and when I caught up with him I had to grab this thing here away from him. Things are breaking down, all right."

"And what are you yourself going to do?" Carras asked.

"And what are you yourself going to do?" his double retorted.

Both showed their teeth, both smiled. The signal commander said, "So we too have come to the parlor game that's all the rage here: Surrender—shoot myself? Surrender—shoot myself? Well, first of all I want to get some food for my men. For the rest: the order is, to the last cartridge!"

The chief of staff passed by. Both officers looked after him; then their eyes met. This time they did not smile at one another. Then the signal regiment commander said:

"Just imagine, a little while ago I was in to see him and reported: 'Sir, I hereby report that So-and-So and So-and-So have disappeared.' Naturally I expected him to blow his top. But instead he shook hands with me and said, 'Well, we can't help these things any more.' What do you think is behind this sudden excess of softheartedness?"

"I think his ranting is fake and I think his ostentatious calm is fake too," Carras said. But only as he said this, and watched the chief of staff striding down the corridor with an air of magnificent composure, did Carras realize that it was all sheer camouflage.

"To my mind the man has gone to pieces inside," the signal regiment commander said.

They parted. Colonel Carras hur.ied after the chief of staff, caught up with him in his office, and had a brief conversation with him. Then he rushed out and went up to Lieutenant Huth. "Doctor," he said, "I think it's time. I think they're ready for it now."

Huth looked up at Carras. He noticed now for the first time that the colonel had green eyes and that a green glow was spread over his entire face. It was no hallucination, although Huth knew he was ripe for hallucinations. The face was that of a cat in deep water, but in the shifting muscles of that face the doctor read a strong determination to remain alive in spite of everything. That, he felt, was a sound and healthy instinct which he could trust, and therefore he could entrust his business to this man. And his own business was a minor affair compared to the real business of the hour, compared to the decision the hour required. He did not feel himself important enough to demand such a decision. But he felt competent to ask for the capitulation of the theater cellar. It was all the more logical since for days it had theoretically been planned to leave the wounded behind if the army attempted to break out "centrifugally." He had come to demand that this plan be put into effect.

"Yes, sir, I am ready also."

Huth walked along beside Carras down the crowded cellar corridor. The curtain had been thrown back. Because Huth was accompanied by the colonel, the two MP's posted to the right and left of the curtain let him pass without question. He went by a clerical room and a stairway barricaded with sandbags and reached the door that led to the chief of staff's room. As Carras opened the door, heavy mortar-bomb hits rumbled down the corridor from the other side of the cellar. Huth and Carras crossed the anteroom and stood before the chief of staff.

The chief was sitting at his desk. He was a man with an energetic face and such gleaming eyes that Huth at first thought of drug addiction, then decided that this fixed gleam indicated a neurotic character and overstrain. A great surprise was in store, not for Huth, but for Carras, the officer on duty, and another officer, all three of whom had previously seen the chief explode with fury at the mention of the word capitulation and threaten to shoot any generals who suggested it. The chief of staff kept his eyes fixed on the doctor. His expression gave no hint of his thoughts. But he let the doctor talk, let him say things he would previously not have tolerated. Once he turned his head and listened to the now regular explosions of shells outside; then he looked attentively at the doctor again.

Huth finished what he had to say.

Then the chief said (and at this the other officers' surprise turned to uneasiness): "Please sit down, doctor, and give me a few minutes." Then the chief left the room, went to the commander in chief's adjutant, called in the army interpreter and exchanged a few words with him. He sent for Hartmann's successor, General Roske, and had a brief conversation with him also. Then he sent an officer into the adjoining ruined building to fetch the artillery commander whose sector included the Red Army House and the adjacent theater cellar. After that he went to the door of the field marshal's room. But he changed his mind and went away without entering.

This conversation between the chief of staff and the interpreter led not only to the surrender of the theater cellar, but to the surrender of the Army Headquarters at a time when the men all around were still dying, as they had been dying for the past seventy-seven days. For the men were still bound by the order: "To the last cartridge." And that order was never rescinded!

"The bulk of the wounded pouring into Stalingrad are to be collected at the central garrison headquarters and tended there," one of the last Army orders had read.

When Major Simmering with his procession of wounded men from Gumrak turned in at the wide gate and entered the yard, it was already growing dark. By the time Lieutenant Lawkow passed through the gate there were stars in the sky, the walls of the building rose blue against the night. The piles thrown up against the windows of the ground floor could be recognized for what they really were only by certain protruding parts and peculiar twists. This heap, six feet high, ran from the entrance to the corner of the yard and from the corner to the door of the wing; beyond the door it began again and ran on. Big as it was, the building was completely surrounded by corpses.

Major Simmering had stopped at the sight of it. The column of wounded men he was leading, except for those who were still outside in the street, also stopped. Without any command they stood still for a long time, arms dangling, heads and eyes wanting to turn away and unable to, forced to look down upon an outspread hand, a twisted leg, a gaping throat, white teeth in an open mouth. The "collected" wounded stood silently facing those who had been collected yesterday and had marched yesterday across this yard.

"Would you mind explaining, sergeant. . . ."

Major Simmering addressed a medical aide who held one end of a stretcher which he was handing to two other men standing at the top of the heap. On the stretcher lay another corpse.

"You see, sir . . ." the sergeant said, and waved his hand helplessly. The gesture implied: Don't waste your time here; once you get inside you won't need any explanation.

"Has the yard always looked like this, sergeant?"

"Nothing like it up to four days ago, sir. But burial is impossible because of the firing and the frozen ground. We were putting the bodies over there in the shed. Now the shed is filled right up to the roof. And more and more men keep pouring in here. The only work the medical company is doing is carrying out the dead, and we can't even cope with that any more."

That was the situation when Major Simmering arrived with his column of wounded.

When Lieutenant Lawkow arrived he was only one among many men who were coming to this place individually, from Stalingrad ravines, from dens in the ruins, from the vast desert of snow outside the city. All of them started back, horrified, at this heap of corpses on which the starlight lay like mist. But where else should they go—back to the holes, back to the snow? There darkness, solitude, and hunger had harried them. This was the place the "Army" had established for the wounded; here they hoped to receive at least some horse-meat soup, if nothing else. And so they disregarded the pile of corpses. That was something else; the men lying there had had ill luck. But they themselves were still standing on their own feet; they still had hope. And so they thronged to the door, and even though their shattered arms, broken bones, or wounded sides were so painful that they could not help screaming, still they pressed on and finally reached the interior of the building, reached at least the stairwell, if no farther for the present.

That was as far as Lieutenant Lawkow had got.

Major Buchner had also got that far when he brought Lieutenant Loose there. Although he could not fight his way through to a doctor, he found a technical sergeant of the medical company and brought him over to Loose. He saw to it that the sergeant had his lieutenant carried off before he left. Not until he was outside under the open sky did he hear the screeching that, inside the building, was so peculiar and so deafening, so incomprehensible that he could not be sure what it was. Were those human voices or did the building hold in captivity large birds, imprisoned in cage upon cage piled three stories high and in the three wings of the structure, birds that fluttered madly against the walls and fell back to the floor again as shattered, dark lumps with bleeding beaks and broken wings, able only to utter wild, inarticulate cries? What was it? Was it a vast aviary full of dying birds? Was it a stable, and stables piled upon stables, filled with burning horses who snorted, tore at their chains and thudded to the floor when they collapsed? Or were there thousands of human beings in there? Could they be human? When Buchner reached his troop of men outside in the street, the screeching, fluttering, and tramping was still in his ears, and when he again passed by the starlit heap he knew what was inside there: it was Death. And with this knowledge in his heart he had walked indifferently through the mortar fire and the gunfire, had walked silently, with unvarying pace, ahead of his men to the place where they had found the flour mill.

Lieutenant Loose was carried inside. No examination by a doctor was necessary. In this building there were only two categories of sick and wounded patients, the ambulants and those who could no longer walk. The sergeant could easily decide to which category a new man belonged. In Lieutenant Loose's case the ripped trouser leg and the shirt wrapped around the wound had hardened into a single bloody rag, so that the decision called for no racking of brains. The sergeant said, "Out in the corridor with him." The stretcher-bearers carried Loose out and set him down at the rear of the row. Lieutenant Loose, although he had fought in the war, lain in foxholes and mud, and grown accustomed to the rough tone of soldiers, was still a well-brought-up young man. Because he was, he waited quite a while. After a long time he asked one of the medical aides when he was going to be taken to the doctor. The man did not know. A while later Loose demanded that a doctor see him. No doctor came and he was not taken to one; but two medical aides came along, lifted his stretcher, and set him down again a short distance farther down the corridor. This was repeated several times. Behind him the row stretched out endlessly and Loose gradually moved forward. The corridor was very long, pitch-black, and intensely cold. Doors must be open somewhere; Lieutenant Loose insisted that the doors be closed. But nothing changed; it remained dark and cold and felt as though the wind from the open steppes were howling through the corridor. All that happened to him was that he was constantly moved a few places forward. He could not see the men who lay ahead or behind him. He heard calls and screams, but most of the men lay in numbed silence. Somewhere firing was going on; Loose heard that also. He was moved forward again, and suddenly he saw the end of the corridor. There was no door, no operating room; the corridor ended nowhere. Neither door nor window, but a square as high and wide as the corridor itself, and in and beyond this square was nothing but the sky. The sky with its fierce cold rushed through the corridor. What had happened to the men who had been moved up here before him? Now he realized suddenly that the stretcher-bearers had always come back with empty stretchers. Up front there was nothing but the hole and the starlit sky. What had become of the others? Lieutenant Loose was not unconscious, nor was he apathetic like most of the men here. Only a few hours ago he had been at the "Tartar Wall" and had crossed the airfield. His leg was shattered and he could not move, but otherwise he was a healthy man with freely-circulating blood and nerves intact. Here he lay, and some twenty or thirty men lay in front of him. Now he demanded: "Take me away from here. Carry me to a doctor or to another room. I won't stay here!" The bearers moved him another space and again vanished into the darkness. He was bound here; his smashed leg chained him to the spot. The sky, the howling wind, the cold—his nose and fingers were like ice. Then fear overwhelmed him. Lieutenant Loose began to shout, to roar. His screams were so loud, so piercing, that at other times the doctors and the entire medical company would have come running. But now his voice was only one in a Babel of screams and nothing happened.

Lieutenant Lawkow had also made his way into this building. He searched for the field kitchen and finally found it in one of the cellars. Clusters of soldiers clung to the stairway and he had to get past them. But he was small and agile and when he was cursed at he gave as good as he received, and so he finally reached the feed trough. He was given a cupful of hot water, the only nourishment that had been handed out here for days. Lawkow poured the hot water into his stomach. Then he wanted to sit down near the stove—in the first place because it was warm, and then because it was the best observation post; you never knew what was going to develop and it was just as well to be on hand if anything did. But the cellar was cleared out, and it did not help him in the least to take part in the "clearing." The MP's who were driving the men up the stairs threw him out with them. But still Lawkow was able to avoid the stairway; he slipped out into the corridor and roamed through the rooms of the cellar. "Roaming" is not the right word for it, however; rather, he clambered over bodies, squeezed through overcrowded chambers, and had to work his way everywhere step by step.

They were huge cellars, cavern upon cavern, and filled with an indescribable variety of men. Stragglers, officers, enlisted men, Croats, Italians, stable grooms, looters, construction troops—an assemblage of leaderless men. There were also some combat troops who had quarters here and had lined some of the rooms with machine guns. There was also the detachment of MP's which the garrison staff had left behind. There were Flemings and Walloons. There were also some sick men among the wounded, including some sick with dysentery who relieved themselves right where they were. These men were so weak that they could not stand on their feet. Officers sat among them or came along and stepped over these sick men. And since these officers had spent all their time at headquarters and up to now had not seen how dysenteric soldiers died, they were outraged at this "shameless conduct." These officers were here because they expected the place to surrender and wanted to be in on it. There was also a general in the cellar, an artillery commander without any staff or following at all. He was there for the same reason as the others, and he insisted on a cellar room for himself alone. However, the room was contested. A band of weary men bandaged with rags poured into the room and instantly took possession of it. Among the gray figures of the men from the front, who had sat down on the single bench, along the walls and on the floor, Lawkow saw the man with the red stripes on his long trousers; he saw a puffy face and heard spluttering ejaculations. But there was nothing of command in his protests. The men seeped in like viscous mud; there was nothing that could affect them. The general sank back on his chair with an air of resignation. Apparently he had decided to make the best of the intrusion; he seemed content that he was permitted to stay.

A group of soldiers excitedly surrounded a captain.

"Sir, there's a first lieutenant with us. He's been here for a week and this is the third time he's stolen our rations."

"Where have you yourselves got any rations?"

"Our platoon has been dissolved and the platoon commander distributed what was left."

The captain was the commander of the only combat troops stationed in the cellar. These men were wounded soldiers from a dissolved motorcycle platoon. The captain went in to see the lieutenant. The man looked scarcely different from the plaster wall, blackened by smoke from warming cans, against which he sat slumped.

"Lieutenant . . ." The lieutenant scarcely raised his head. "Can't you stand up? Are you wounded?" The lieutenant was

313

not. At this injunction he stood up. He was a tall fellow and very seedy-looking—not only in his dress. His name was Wedderkop—that was all the captain could get out of him. The man would not or could not say what unit he belonged to.

"The men say . . ."—"Yes, sir, I did."—"So you, an officer, have robbed the men!"—"If you wish to call it that, sir."—"Well, lieutenant, I suppose you still have a pistol."—"No, I don't need one."—"Well, my driver will bring you one. . . . You men go outside now," the captain said to the soldiers. "You can come back in two minutes."

The men cleared out of the room. The driver went into it and came out. The two minutes passed. The driver went in again and found that nothing had happened. This was repeated a second and third time. Each time the driver reported to the captain: "It isn't done yet." The fourth time it was done, but not quite as prescribed. A shot rang out, and Lawkow saw the driver replace his smoking pistol in its holster as he closed the door behind him. "All right, you can go back in," he said to the men standing around. Then he reported to his captain, "It's done, sir."

In these cellars Lieutenant Lawkow met an old acquaintance, the previous commander of his battalion, Captain Henkel, he who had vanished as suddenly as he appeared and had not been seen since. Henkel was in a state similar to Lieutenant Wedderkop's. "Why, my dear Lawkow," he said as soon as he caught sight of the pock-marked little lieutenant. "I'm so very glad to see you."

"I'm not glad at all."

"I still can't understand what led me to come to Stalingrad when I had a post that suited me perfectly with my printing squad in Kharkov and when I wasn't in the least ambitious and didn't at all want to command a battalion."

Lawkow turned away and moved on through the cellar.

There was a doctors' room, the operating room. In one corner lay a surgeon both of whose legs had gone black. The man knew perfectly well he was done for if gangrene developed. He lay smoking a cigarette and chatting with his neighbor about Göttingen, where they had both attended the university. The combat troop commander was assembling his men. Outside on the street an infantry engagement was going on; the flashes of rifles could be seen through a window blockaded by stones. A sergeant said good-bye to his captain. "If you ever get back to Vienna, sir, give my love to Kummitsch's widow." The captain called after him, "Don't do anything foolish, Kummitsch." But Lawkow saw the sergeant walk away with

the peculiar gait he already knew so well. This imminent suicide, Captain Henkel, that Lieutenant Wedderkop, a raw-boned
Dutchman, a general whom the common soldiers had long ago
nicknamed "Baron Milksop," rows of faces, corpses that you
stumbled over, stall upon stall, cavern upon cavern, a huge
circus, but without any of the glitter; everything gray in a gray
ring, floodlights extinguished, make-up worn off, all the glorious pantomime reduced to gestures of hopelessness, the slim
and lovely girl writhing with bellyache and soiling her sheets
—that was the cellar.

Major Simmering, when he came in, proved to be the high-
est-ranking officer among the doctors in the garrison headquarters. He went into the doctors' room and, since the medical major in charge of the place could not be reached, he asked
Captain Bäumler for a report on the situation. The rest of the
doctors were at various places throughout the building. Their
sole medical activity, Bäumler informed him, consisted in offering consolation, while the medical personnel were entirely
employed in carrying the dead out into the yard.

The remnants of several medical companies and some
twenty doctors had been assigned to this building. The numbers shifted because of deaths, departures, or new arrivals.
When Bäumler had arrived four days earlier more than a
thousand half-starved seriously wounded men lay in the building and had received no care or rations whatever. How many
there were at the moment he could not say. The house was
filled beyond belief. The wounded lay without shelter in the
corridors, on the stairways, and in the half-wrecked rooms
as high up as the third story. Moreover, the cellars were overcrowded, partly by a combat unit, partly by a large detachment
of military police, partly by refugees and stragglers. Up to
now there had been no fighting for the building itself. But in
the adjoining ruins there were troops and fighting was going
on there. Occasionally, too, a mortar or tank shell would strike
the building, pierce the thin partition walls, and kill a number
of men. There were no medical materials left at all and no
rations either.

Such was Captain Bäumler's report.

Major Simmering had Bäumler show him through the
building, starting with the cellar. He looked into the packed
rooms filled with stragglers, into the quarters of the military
police and the shelters of the combat troops. During this inspection he said nothing, merely shook his head. They went
on up the stairway. It was much like a packed subway esca-
lator and they had to weave their way through the crowd.

This crowd, however, was not standing, but sitting down with legs outstretched or drawn close to their bodies, their heads pillowed in their hands or drooping against their neighbors' shoulders, their eyes open or closed. Major Simmering went through all three stories. It was the same everywhere: the wounded, the dead, the diseased (typhus) lay among one another and on top of one another, groaning, gasping, dying. All were feverish and all wanted to drink, but the water had to be made by thawing snow and there was not enough. Delirious men roared. Men demanded that someone give them a pistol and somehow, from somewhere, they got one. Naked window openings yawned wide in the upper floors, and outside were the night and the stars. The occupants of the rooms tore up the floorboards, made fires, and huddled around them. The red glow attracted the fire of the enemy artillery. Whole rooms with all their occupants were blown up. The air was poisonous with sulfurous vapors from exploding shells. Major Simmering stepped up to one of the window openings and looked down at the street. Groups of hobbling, slow-moving figures could be seen approaching the building. The stream of wounded coming here in search of help had not yet ceased.

Major Simmering returned the way he had come. On the first floor he talked to several men of the medical company. Here he also met the medical major who was in charge of the building. The major—Simmering knew him from Berlin and had not seen him since—turned to him as though they had been standing in the same operating room for days. "I was just about to begin when a tank shell tore off my surgeon's hands, both hands," he said. With these words he vanished into the glare of the open fires, the smoke, and the sulfurous vapors. Simmering looked at Bäumler, who lowered his eyes.

"Well, captain, we must begin." They walked on. "But tell me, what kind of setup is this?" he asked as they stepped into the long corridor whose double doors—they reached from floor to ceiling—were wide open and held so by ropes. Apparently another set of doors must be open at the other end, for an icy current of air swept down the long tunnel, passing over the stretchers on which the patients lay.

"We don't know what else to do, sir, except to lay the hopelessly severe cases out here where they'll die swiftly and painlessly by freezing. That way we make room for the lightly-wounded men who are impatient."

"So this is the first aid you administer here?"

"The most humane thing to do, it seems to me, sir."

Both doctors returned to the cellar proper. Most of the

other doctors had meanwhile assembled in the doctors' room. Major Simmering addressed them. "As you know, gentlemen, the order against capitulation is still in force. But what we may do and what to my mind is most urgently necessary at this time is to identify this building by raising Red Cross flags. On the other hand this means that only wounded, sick, and medical personnel can remain under those flags. We must therefore clear the building of the combat troops, the military police, and all unwounded soldiers. That is our immediate and most important task and I want you to assist in carrying it out, gentlemen."

Lieutenant Lawkow observed a new wave of movement in the cellar.

On the one hand there was a new influx of men, and these were wounded only, men with stumps of limbs, with splits, with plaster casts that were weeks old and black as their faces. And on the other hand old inhabitants began moving out amid protests, expressions of regret, or with silent resignation. Among those being thrown out were persons like his Captain Henkel or the gentleman in civilian dress who insisted that he was not a soldier at all, but a railroad official, and that he had been brought here from Paris to be stationmaster of the Stalingrad railroad station.

"It's really a great pity and we all would have loved to see you at the railroad station in your red cap," said Lawkow who had begun assisting the doctors in the general bouncing operation. "But you must get out of here, really, sir, this isn't a railroad station."

"I wish to make a protest because I was not flown out."

"Right again, but this isn't the place for that either. You'd do best to hand your protest directly to the supreme commander of the Luftwaffe."

"Come, move on, pick up your suitcase," one of the MP's said. The military police were also helping to clear the cellar. Although Major Simmering had feared objections, the military police unit had surprisingly agreed to leave the building. They reasoned that they could not accept capture anyway; the civilian population knew them and their work too well, so that their only choice was to fight to the last cartridge. After a talk between the major and the captain in charge of the combat group, that unit too left in a body.

The clearing of the cellar was making progress. Roomful after roomful of men moved away, and the cleared spaces were instantly filled by the press of wounded men behind. But the whole action had been started several days too late. The firing upon the house intensified. The rumble of explosions could be heard far down in the cellar rooms. The fact that there was no firing from the building itself did not suffice. It would be necessary to make the near-by groups outside also cease firing. But to accomplish this an order from the commander of this sector of the city would be needed. Someone would have to go outside and try to communicate with him. Captain Bäumler had volunteered to do this; Lieutenant Lawkow offered to go along and assist.

The swarm of doctors had meanwhile reached the general's cellar compartment. Lawkow and Bäumler were curious to see how the affair would turn out and decided to wait for the general's departure. Apparently the general had no intention of giving up his quarters. Lawkow could not get very close; the door to this section of the cellar was besieged by soldiers. The MP's stood silently by without taking part. Inside a brisk squabble was going on between the doctors and the generals. Finally the doctors had to bring up their reserve in the shape of Major Simmering himself. Outside the soldiers chorused: "He won't do it, won't for the life of him. He wants to stay put." Then they began shouting the general's nickame: "Baron Milksop." Once again the earth shook and the foundations groaned. For a few seconds the men in the cellar stopped listening to the voices of the medical officer and the general. Then someone said: "At last, he's started to pack up."

One of the doctors came out of the room and said to Bäumler, "It really took some strong language."

Lawkow and Bäumler set out. They went upstairs and crossed the yard into the white, thunderous night.

An hour and a half later Lawkow returned alone. Bäumler had been killed by a burst of fire from somewhere. The stars were no longer visible. Out of the smoke and mist flashed the explosions of automatic guns. The garrison headquarters at the lower end of the square towered up out of a mount of mist: a huge stone head, horribly mutilated, smoke puffing out of its eyes. And the eyes were red. Lawkow came upon a flak gun and a line of riflemen who were firing. This line which was blockading the street was one of the many groups that were still fighting without knowing what they were fighting for or who their superiors were. They crouched behind ruins and fragments of walls because that was what they had always done when any activity showed up ahead, and they did not ask now any more than they ever had whether their sniping was bringing destruction down upon a huge building crammed with wounded. "Why are you bastards still out here?" Law-kow asked one group. "Where do you want us to be—inside there where we'll get nothing to eat and croak?" one of the men responded. And that was the sole explanation; they were here because as long as they constituted the front line they could count upon getting something to eat, and they knew that otherwise they would not be given a crumb. Here, too, of course, there was a captain for the group. He had received the order to hold the line and that was what he was doing, or trying to do. And over the captain was a colonel who could not be located. And over the colonel—that was where the confusion began. Neither Gönnern in his cellar nor Vennekohl in his ravine nor Damme in his jail cell would admit to having given the order, and none of them would rescind it.

By circling around the combat group Lawkow got into the garrison headquarters from the rear. He climbed through a window and then entered a long corridor where interminable rows of stretchers lay on the floor. The way was blocked by the wreckage of walls and still further blocked by a curtain of flaming beams. The glow of the fire flickered on the faces of the men on the stretchers, giving them a rosy, living appearance. Lawkow had to go back. He crawled through a hole into a room and through a tumbled, praying, and wailing mass of humanity, a mass that was nothing but a screeching bellows, a throng of suffocating lungs gasping for air. He reached a second room and could go no farther. He tried to turn around, but that was no longer possible. In his way were heads, arms, legs, smoke, the sense of imminent disaster. The beams of the ceiling were still holding, but no one knew how much longer they would hold. He could go no farther, not by his own strength. Now Lawkow too became nothing but a screaming lung, a thing tormented by pain, perhaps standing, perhaps head down. Perhaps the wave threw him against the ceiling and let him fall again. A long billow deposited him in the stairwell. That was where he was trying to go, so that he could descend into the cellar. But all of them wanted to get there now, not only the men from the first story, but those from the second as well. The stairway still went up that far—to the second story. But of the stairway itself—steps, railings, and landings—nothing could be seen. It was a fantastic garland winding upward, a shouting, singing, roaring garland built of bodies, bodies jammed fast, motionless, lifeless bodies. The garland was burning—it was a dangling Jacob's ladder, and from up-thrust arms, from heads, from hair, smoke rose. The man who was only a legless torso had as good a chance of reaching bottom as those who still possessed arms and legs. There was nothing for them to do but to let themselves fall, and this they did; they fell down the sloping stairway to the bottom or plunged through the air to the bottom, rebounding from the mass like grains of corn below the chute of a grain elevator. Arms and legs were no longer necessary; each man was a grain and fell upon the heap, to be thrust on, somewhere, perhaps even into the cellar, perhaps alive, perhaps dead.

Lawkow shouted, and then he stopped shouting. He choked and puffed smoke out through his mouth and nose; he flailed about with his one arm and both legs. A wave—of contorted faces, clawing hands, popping eyes, mouths full of bloody foam—cast him out into the corridor, the long corridor with the powerful current of air.

Now again he saw the curtain of burning beams, this time from the other side. And since anything was better than that hissing and spitting and biting and snatching, he tried to detach himself from the mob. He succeeded and plunged through the wall of fire. On the other side, he knew, it was quiet.

It was only a step through the flames, and there again were the stretchers and the faces of men whose sufferings were over. There was the large, open window through which he had climbed in. The sky beyond the window was foaming red. Now, as he retraced his steps, Lawkow saw that he had climbed in over a ramp of corpses.

He got outside the building again and returned to the flak gunners. He wanted to continue on to the telephone he had used earlier. But this proved to be unnecessary; a wire led directly to the shattered building before him. He went in, held the telephone mouthpiece to his lips, and with the burning, collapsing garrison headquarters before his eyes, he cried:

"General, it is too late now. I am reporting what I can see from where I stand. The walls are like glass, transparent. The building is a raging fire from top to bottom. The stuff pouring out of the splitting sides is not fish roe, but human beings. Everywhere, in all the rooms, on all the stairs, on the collapsing floors, men are screaming. I can see them, I can still feel the bite of their teeth in my hand, the scratches from their fingernails on my face. . . . That is a hospital in your command sector, general!"

The garrison headquarters burned down to the foundations. Flames shot out of all the windows, chunks of wall fell through the three stories and thudded against the arched ceiling of the cellar. On both flanks of the house combat troops retreated. Firing went on along the sides and at the rear; the smoking, burning façade and a part of the forward wing became Russian land once more. And at the front, all the hatchways to the cellars opened and men spewed forth out of holes, windows, cracks in the wall. Major Simmering with a troop of doctors and the surviving wounded and sick who could still walk, as well as a few who slid and crawled along the snow, reached the outside and their longed-for captivity.

"I will obey."

That phrase had transformed streets into avenues of death, houses into charnel houses, hospitals into battlefields; it had made the land between the Volga and the Don a vast land of death; it had reduced regiments and divisions to herds of hopeless cattle. But once, one time, that fearful phrase was not pronounced. At the point when the phrase no longer applied to the infantry, the captains and the line officers, when the top of the pyramid, the head of the military hierarchy was involved, when the phrase had to be applied personally to the head—it was not pronounced.

A man with a weary face seamed by thought and with the weary clerk's hand of a Prussian general staff officer, sat clutching his marshal's baton. The baton had been given to him so that the hand might clasp it in death. A dead field marshal on the Volga was required, after six billion Reichmarks had gone up in smoke, after two hundred thousand human lives had been squandered. The dead field marshal on the Volga was essential to complete the glory of the death march, to place the crown upon the pale brow of the destroyed army, to raise a beacon light upon the fields of snow so that a coming generation would be able to steer straight when it set out once more on a new march of conquest to the Volga. That was the idea, the command, the law which had settled firmly in the field marshal's brain and heart, which had become blood of his blood and flesh of his flesh.

The man was weary unto death and at the same time racked with restlessness. The twitching half of his face—the tic extended from his ear to his temple and forehead and down to his jaw—resembled at this moment the palm of a hand stretched out on a board and struggling in its last convulsions. And the great symbol for the future was destined to be this twitching face, rather than a dead marshal's hand clasped around a baton.

The fateful phrase that had caused the deaths of two hundred thousand men was not pronounced. The man sat behind a curtain in a darkened compartment in a cellar. Someone's hand had touched his door and then been withdrawn; and now he ought to stand up, walk down the cellar corridor, find his chief of staff and shout into the chief's ear the phrase that had not yet been pronounced, the phrase that would stop the negotiations. He must shout so that the words would resound from one end of the cellar to the other; he must cry out: "I will obey. The headquarters must be defended. To the last cartridge—that order applies to this building also!"

The man from whom this decision was expected stood up and groped his way down the dim corridor. He passed the chief of staff's room and entered the office of Roske, the divisional commander. "What is the situation, Roske?"

"Very grave, sir. The Russians are everywhere. The noose is tightening all around."

The man returned to his cubbyhole, sat there for a while in the dark, his head bowed, his hands resting slackly on his knees. Then he stretched out on the bed. He was a man who sought the counsel of history, particularly of military history, and in this decisive hour of his life he did not search in vain for a historical parallel. In November, 1918, at the end of the lost war, the Supreme Command of the Army had withdrawn General von Gündell after the general had already been appointed to head the Armistice Commission. Thus the Armistice Commission had been stripped of all military character. At that time a field marshal had said: "This is probably the first time in world history that political rather than military men are concluding an armistice. However, I am quite in accord with that, especially since the Supreme Commander no longer has the power to issue political directives."

The man who had lost the war refused to take the responsibility for the imminent national catastrophe. That was something a field marshal had done in November, 1918, at the end of a lost war. *Ergo*: in January, 1943, at the end of a great lost battle a field marshal could say: "I will have nothing to do with it." That same night his chief of staff was to declare that the field marshal insisted upon being considered a private person. Since it had once been possible, there was precedent for the second time. But this arrangement was not very satisfactory. The field marshal sat in the dark and his face twitched.

Meanwhile the affair took its course. The principal actors were the chief of staff of the army, the army interpreter, and the newly-promoted divisional commander, General Roske.

The department store was under fire by artillery and mortars for twenty minutes. The chief of staff had a conversation behind closed doors with the interpreter and General Roske. Then the interpreter and the general put on their fur coats and left the building. The chief of staff remained behind, straight and tall as a tree, his shoulders thrown back more than ever, his eyes if possible even more glittering. He issued orders, brief, unequivocal orders. Officers received them and passed them on.

"To all operations officers: burn papers.

"To all supply and administration officers: burn lists and account books.

"To all personnel officers: burn records.

"To all intelligence officers: burn, burn, burn."

The army signal officer also received an order:

"Order from the chief of staff. Destroy radio equipment. Destroy codes."

It was unequivocal enough, but the signal officer did not understand. He had expected something quite different, the order to fight and the tumult of hand-to-hand combat in the cellar rooms, and at the last the mine that would thoroughly and surely destroy the entire building, himself, and his radio equipment as well. He emerged from his room, wanting to check up on the order, and in the corridor he met ordnance officers, reserve officers, medical officers, veterinaries, administrative officers, and civilian officials, all of whom had received the same orders. Colonel Carras was there too, saying to some of them, "Don't worry your head about it. Burn the stuff; it's worthless now anyway." To the signal commander he said, "It's all right, go ahead and smash your place to pieces."

The building rumbled. Somewhere in the darkness of the corridors it sounded as though railroad trains were being shunted. The corridor filled with the smell of fire and with plaster dust. The lights went out in a number of rooms. Candles flickered up, hopeless little fireflies in a vast cavern.

Colonel Carras led the signal commander behind the curtain to show him something. There, between the chief of staff's room and the commander in chief's room, was a stairway leading up to the street. It had been barricaded up to the ceiling with sandbags which had frozen solidly together. Now a number of men were busy with crowbars, prying apart the sandbags to clear the stairs.

"The back stairs are being made ready for the guest!" Colonel Carras said.

The signal commander returned to his room and gathered his men around him. Before he began the destruction of his apparatus he radioed the group in Stalingrad North and transmitted the codes, so that this isolated group would now be in a position to communicate directly with the army group and the Army High Command. Then the papers were burned, the equipment and generator smashed. Once more a number of lights went out and more candles were lit. Silence settled over the building. The rumble of shunting trains at the ends of the cellar, the crash of breaking fragments, and the screaming explosions outside all ceased.

The bombardment had been halted.

Something else had happened. As the signal commander stepped out into the darkness dotted with fireflies, he sensed the change. As he caught sight of the apathetic men along the walls, covered with chalkdust but looking as though they had awakened after a sleep of a hundred years, he felt certain about it. Then he ran past the curtain into the corridor filled with staff members, with red stripes and uniforms of gold and silver, red and blue and green, like figures from an oriental bazaar. He succeeded in glancing into the commander in chief's room, and there he saw it, right before his eyes.

The guest had arrived.

What had happened was this:

The field marshal had not spoken the words. He had slept, at any rate retired to sleep. The chief of staff had acted, but not as the chief of staff of the army, for then he would have had to inform whatever units of the army he could reach of his changed decision. He had acted as might the landlord of any private house threatened with destruction. His two emissaries, the army interpreter and General Roske, had gone outside. They had crossed the courtyard and the passage and Roske had paused in the gateway. The square was dark; the floodlights had been turned out. In the sky above a transport plane hummed, circled, and seemed to wonder what to do with its load. Artillery continued to hack away at the front of the building. The interpreter, a Balt, hurried on. He reached a railroad underpass where a Russian tank stood. The hatch was open and a lieutenant was peering out of the hatch.

The interpreter called out to the Russian tank lieutenant. The Russian beckoned him to come closer. And the Russian-speaking German officer said to him: "Lieutenant, order the firing to stop. I have something big for you; it'll mean promotion and all the decorations you can imagine. You can come with me now and take the field marshal and the whole staff of the German army prisoner."

"*Shto-takoi?* What's that?" Promotion, decorations, field marshal—it was all a little too much at once and the interpreter had to repeat it. Then the lieutenant disappeared inside his tank, radioed to the rear and popped out again. This time it seemed a bit out of key to the interpreter; the lieutenant was much too casual about it.

"*Ladno,*" the lieutenant said. "All right."

Two more Russian officers and several machine gunners joined them and the interpreter led the way across the square. General Roske was still standing in the gateway. The fire had suddenly ceased. The general did not leave his cover, but he funneled his hands at his mouth and called out something in broken Russian to the approaching men. The Russians did not understand him. When they reached the doorway the general said in his feeble Russian that the Germans' big chief wanted to talk with the Russians' big chief.

The "big chief" of the troops in this sector, the twenty-one-year-old Ukrainian tank lieutenant, Fyodor Yelchenko, said, "*Ladno.*" And General Roske and the interpreter led the detachment across the yard, and then avoiding the ramp, showed them through a side entrance directly into the segment of the cellar that lay behind the curtain.

Now the signal officer and the other officers who had emerged from their compartments saw the group sitting around the commander in chief's round table: the tall, windburned adjutant to the commander in chief, General Roske, the interpreter, the Russian tank lieutenant, and two other Russian officers. The machine gunners stood in the background. The field marshal's compartment was lit only by the tubes of his radio set. The chief of staff went up to the curtain, stood at attention, and said: "I must report that the Russians are here." Without waiting for a reply, he dropped the curtain which he had momentarily lifted.

The men around the table negotiated, although there was not much to negotiate. The tank lieutenant declared that German soldiers and officers who laid down their arms would be treated in accordance with the ultimatum issued by Generals Voronov and Rokossovski. And outside in the corridor among the officers with their red stripes, their gold and silver shoulder boards, their collar patches, and their white camouflage cloaks, the laying down of arms was already in full swing. The officers tossed their pistols on a heap that grew higher and higher.

General Roske, the adjutant, and the interpreter stood up and, accompanied by the Russian tank lieutenant, entered the small adjoining compartment. The Russian looked around. It was a tiny .place; perhaps the night watchman of the department store had once lived here. In one corner the field marshal lay on a bed. He half sat up. He was fully dressed under the blanket and was wearing his decorations from the two wars.

The field marshal laid his revolver on the table and a small sword beside it. The Russian took the revolver, indicated the sword, and said: *"Nye nushno!"* The field marshal might keep his sword.

They then returned to the other room and sat down again. The chief of staff explained, the interpreter translating, that the field marshal insisted upon being considered a private person. The one condition he made was that he be driven away in a closed car, not led on foot through the city.

The surrender took its course.

From the smoking ruins of the garrison headquarters a few last survivors crawled and stumbled out; more emerged from the ruins in the vicinity, combat soldiers with blackened faces and flaming eyes. They raised the white flag and gathered around the large group of wounded and sick who stood in the middle of the square.

A few hundred yards away, at the square near the railroad station, there was still firing. The Russians fired and the Germans fired, rifles, machine guns, submachine guns. Across the square and from building to building there was a humming and buzzing as of hordes of infuriated, flaming insects. A number of tanks rolled up in wedge formation. The hatches opened and suddenly the firing ceased and silence rose up to a sky now turning milky. In the black window-openings where only a moment before guns had flamed, white rags now appeared. After the first man and the first group had ventured onto the square, others followed. And from other places gray streams of soldiers poured into the square, their hands raised, fur caps or pointed hats over their heads and ears, their heads bowed. Before long a cluster of some seven hundred German prisoners of war stood in this square.

Major Buchner awoke out of a roaring blackness. Before his eyes the features of his adjutant, Lieutenant Loose,

326

formed. But it was not Loose after all, it was Sergeant Januscheck. And Januscheck said: "We must get out of here, sir. The place is falling to pieces on top of us." All the others, his whole group, were there. Major Buchner started up and staggered out into the yard. The flour mill was burning. The storeroom was in flames. Burning wheat flew into the air like a rain of stars. There must be several hundred pounds of it. And he had received two and a half pounds of flour for his twenty-seven men—and had had to give up his last cigarettes for it. And now the flour was going up like a giant fireworks display and black flakes were raining down on him. The yard outside was dark with people. But no one wanted to venture out into the street. At the gate all movement halted. From behind came shouts: "What's the matter? You can see the street—are the Russians killing prisoners?"—"No, they're just lining them up."—"They're not killing the officers either, are they?"—"No, nothing's happening to the officers either." And then, driven partly by pressure from behind, a mob of soldiers rolled out into the street. Again perhaps four or five hundred prisoners of war lined up near the ruins.

Through the cellars and the ground floor of the wrecked jail came shouts of: "Come out, all of you, the Russians are here." And the Russians were there, standing in the middle of the yard. The doors flew open and officers and soldiers poured out.

A lieutenant colonel shouted: "I'll shoot down anyone who surrenders."

A colonel roared: "The defense goes on."

But the mass of the soldiers, close to two thousand of them, moved on, moved out of the building. The lieutenant colonel and the colonel were insignificant dots in this slow-moving procession.

Suddenly a 2 cm. flak gun began firing. The gun was protected by an earthen rampart. Men standing near by called out," The chief of the tank corps."

The chief of staff of the tank corps and several younger officers stood behind the gun, their faces contorted, and fired as fast as they could. The Russian mortar batteries again began shelling the square. Some of the Germans and some of the Russians were killed or wounded. "Kill the dogs, shoot them down," some men shouted. But the mass of the soldiers simply stood. They had already thrown away their arms and were too apathetic to do anything. What was the use of getting yourself killed at the last moment? Let the Russians take care of it. And the flak gun continued to hammer away, the Russians continued to fire. Once more a cry of madness rose to the sky, from two, three thousand throats. More and more throngs of men were still pouring into the square, all wanting to be taken prisoner. Minutes passed before the flak gun was silenced; more than twenty minutes passed before the Russian commander could have a wire brought up and resume communications with his mortar batteries, so that the Russian fire also stopped again. Here, in front of the jail, some five thousand soldiers and officers, including a number of colonels and generals, surrendered.

It was an hour before dawn.

At another place General Vennekohl sat in his bunker. All his men had left him; the Russians had already infiltrated the area and there was no sentry in front of his bunker. For hours he sat there weighing the question: Surrender—shoot myself? Then he heard cautious steps on the stairs that had been cut into the earth. A figure in a padded jacket, followed by a second, appeared; two broad Russian faces moved cautiously into the dugout. "Well, at last; that's fine," Vennekohl sighed with relief. But the Russians stared in astonishment at the German general. Obviously they had expected to find the bunker empty.

"Russki soldat?" Vennekohl asked.

"Nyet soldat," one of them replied. They were Russian civilians who had escaped from a German unit and had not planned upon taking a German general prisoner. Vennekohl was plunged once more into the tormenting question, although it was by now no longer a question, for to be taken prisoner he had only to wait, while to shoot himself required resolution, and it was just this that Vennekohl could not muster up at all.

So the capitulation began, without there having been any common decision to surrender and without any common procedure. Wherever there had been organized efforts and initiative on the part of line officers, as at the city jail, for example, they were opposed by staff officers, and the results were bloody massacres at the last moment. Some surrendered, some continued to fight, and both processes went on at the same time and in the same places, in inextricable confusion; often surrender and fighting took place in the same dugouts. The men who raised their hands on this night and clustered in gray masses were only the first thick drops of what later would become streaming rivulets and then a rushing torrent.

The sky turned gray and a white, icy mist rose over the land. Five tanks, painted white, rolled forward on a field of rubble surrounded by ruined buildings like a spacious circular stage. The tanks looked like torpedo boats in a white sea. A short-legged man with a big head and a small, stocky body suddenly found himself facing the silent semicircle of tanks. The night before he had promised his commanding general over the telephone that he would defend his command post. Now he had just come out of the commanding general's ravine, where only a moment ago he had reiterated his promise and they had shaken hands on it. He carried his carbine slung on his shoulder, as he had been doing the night before. Moreover, his belt was stuffed with cartridges. And here before him stood the five white tanks with their silent gun muzzles raised, and at the entrance to his bunker stood a detachment of Red Army soldiers. This was the same as or similar to the desperate situation in which the entire army had been involved for days. Telephone calls and personal conversations, clasped hands, a last greeting and a final promise—what else was there to do but raise the carbine and bang away at the group of Red Army soldiers and the tanks? Nothing to stop you from shooting and getting yourself killed. But it was sheer madness and not reasonable behavior, not for a commander of an infantry division and a consultant of the Military History Section in the Army High Command. And, after all, you were no longer young enough for that kind of attitude and that kind of crazy conduct; you were much too worn out and dulled. General Gönnern did not touch the strap of his carbine. With an expression of desperate resolve and a somewhat automatic gait he covered the twelve paces back to his bunker. The Red Army soldiers grinned and let him pass. The general reached the bottom of the steps. He opened the top button of his collar, pressed his hand firmly against his throat and breathed deeply. Below everyone was standing, in the center of the group the two white-haired commanding generals. Gönnern did not address them at all; he spoke in the singular and what he said might have been addressed to any one of them, or to himself. "Well, sir," he said, "the Russians are outside." This they already knew, and Gönnern could read in their eyes that they too had already made their decision. A moment of silence passed; then Gönnern turned on his heel. He mounted the steps again, looked at the Red Army men, and picked out an officer from among them. "Officer," he said, "there are three generals down here who wish to surrender."

At this same time, four hundred yards away, among the ruins of the Aviation Academy, General Geest occupied a bunker defended by men in snowholes who were still firing. General Geest, his yellow, bony face under a steel helmet, his chin propped in his fists, sat staring at the hard tabletop. A figure at the door momentarily blocked the snowy light from outside. It was his adjutant, Major von Bauske.

"This is the time, sir. I would suggest doing it now," Bauske said.

"Don't start that again, Bauske. You know the commander in chief's order. He has forbidden suicide."

"I am going to do it, sir."

"I am not, and if you insist on it, please don't do it here in the bunker."

A few minutes later Geest went to the door and looked out into the milky world. He saw his adjutant again, a hand grenade in outstretched hand. Geest turned abruptly, went back into his bunker, and resumed his earlier posture. Again a shadow fell across the table. It was Bauske again. He had not done it, and now Geest became sentimental. It was partly the hour; the air was in motion and there was a solemnity about this gray morning. Geest gripped Baron von Bauske's hand and said, "This is your greatest victory, Bauske, the conquest of yourself. And for this . . ." He stooped to his desk drawer, opened it, and took out an Iron Cross, First Class (in special circumstances a divisional commander may confer this decoration upon members of his staff). He pinned the cross to Bauske's breast. "For this, Bauske, for this!" Bauske was, after all, an excellent and brave officer, deserving in other respects.

A few minutes later—the men in the snowpits were still firing and attracting Russian fire—General Geest saw Bauske lying in the snow with a bullet through his head.

A moment afterward Geest caught sight of General Vennekohl passing by, escorted by a detachment of Russian soldiers. At this Geest called to the Russians and he, with the remainder of his staff and the sixty men who were left of his division, surrendered.

Vennekohl, Geest, Gönnern, and the two commanding generals had surrendered close to the edge of the city. They were led back through Stalingrad to the headquarters of the Russian army on the banks of the Volga, and as they passed they were seen by hordes of German soldiers who also surrendered when they realized what was afoot.

Dawn had come. With the day the icy mists of the Volga began surging through the tall skeletons of stone and the miles of windowless streets. Until this city was reached, it had all been an extravagance and a Herculean jest, a procession with fireworks, hunts, and human sacrifices, a gory sightseeing tour through many countries, a Ship of Fools setting out for the unknown under an imbecile captain. Only at the finish, on the last stretch of the way, had the participants realized that they themselves were the fat steer with gilded horns and adorned with colorful ribbons which was being led to the slaughter. Up to now it had not been serious; now the great reversal began. *"Dust thou art, and unto dust shalt thou return."*

The first day of the sore pilgrimage began.

The cellars erupted, and from them men poured into the mist, men with rag-wrapped feet, men in hooded coats, in service coats, in overcoats, in rags; lice-ridden, scabby, starved, covered with sores and wounds, one with a blanket, another with a crudely-tied bundle, another with nothing at all in his hand. Gray face beside gray face jammed whole blocks of the city.

From the Volga a "T 34" pushed its way up a ravine through piles of corpses, sending fragments of bodies flying to both sides. And the men who stood near were too weary to raise their hands and wipe the bits of flesh from their faces. At a field kitchen that had been set up in the street one man got himself ten portions and lay down and died, and those who had got nothing because of him later broke down on the march and died; but the men who marched on paid no attention either to the one or the others.

And then, from the "Square of the Fallen," came a procession of a hundred-odd men in heavy coats with fur collars, with big fur caps on their heads, fleece-lined camouflage cloaks over all, and warm boots on their feet. Their faces showed nervous strain, but no sign of physical distress. After them came soldiers carrying dufflebags, knapsacks, suitcases. And the long line of dirty gray men stood there with leaden arms dangling. It was impossible to tell from their eyes what the men were thinking or whether they were thinking at all.

From cellars, from holes in the ground and hiding places in the rubble, from sewer pipes and ruined buildings and ravines, an endless stream of new faces rose up, gathered in gray hordes, and waited to be marched away. There was no need for these soldiers to strew ashes on their heads. They were "done for," in their legs, their brains, their gut, their hearts. They were without a past, without a future. The march to the Volga could not be considered a past, nor was it the basis for a future. These people were done for, burned out, dust and ashes.

A lane opened in the avenue of misery. An automobile blew its horn and the men with empty hands and without rations for their journey, stepped aside. The automobile came from the same direction as the procession of staff officers. It was a closed car, but the windows were clear and to the person inside the faces in the street passed by like a line of smoke, one streak of smoke on either side of the road. In the front seat of the car sat two Red Army soldiers; in back was a Russian officer, and beside him a tall man with a face like that on a commemorative medal. At this moment the left half of this face, ordinarily marked with a defect like a spot of scab on a handsome, well-shaped apple, was not twitching —so heavy had been the burden that had fallen from this man that now, in this passing moment, he felt wonderfully light.

Before him were the faces of the soldiers whom he was leaving without a last order of the day, without a farewell, without thanks. These beaten hordes were certainly not fit subjects for conversation. The man in the car knew all about the dysentery, typhus, and starvation that had afflicted his army; the whole picture had been presented to him in figures. But the figures had not shown that refuse pails from the operating rooms had been stolen, that the refuse pits from the surgeries had been opened and the contents eaten. There were no paragraphs in the situation reports for that sort of thing; he had seen nothing of it on paper and therefore he had scarcely any conception of the present state of his army —a state in which a single word, especially if it spoke of hidden food, could arouse delusions and drive hundreds of men into active madness. Thus he could not understand the curious zeal of certain men on a shed roof. He did see that they were rolling dead men off the roof, but his imagination refused to grasp the possibility that among those puppetlike stiff bundles there were also living wounded men. Such an idea was altogether impossible. In any case, that screaming, gesticulating, and altogether odd band of men on the roof could not provide a subject for conversation between a captured German field marshal and the Russian officer accompanying him. There was that T 34—and undoubtedly that Russian tank, like the Russian submachine gun, the German Messerschmitt, and the Czech Bren gun would someday be reckoned the finest productions of their kind to come out of the war. But that, too, was not a suitable subject; it would inevitably have led the conversation around to military matters, which he must avoid.

But at last he had his subject. He saw a Red Army man rolling a cigarette for a German "Landser." The Russian soldier's tobacco, *makhorka!* "That is something that has always interested me, Mr. Polkovnik," the field marshal said. "This soldier's tobacco of yours, which you call *makhorka*. Does it actually contain nicotine like real tobacco?"—"Anyway our soldiers smoke it by preference, *Herr Feldmarschall;* they wouldn't exchange it for real tobacco. As far as I know it does contain nicotine."—"Of course, it probably would; otherwise how would it induce that pleasant stimulation, that sense of general well-being, which the soldiers obviously get from *makhorka,* just as they would from real tobacco. By the way, what do the plants look like, Mr. Polkovnik?"

It was a rich subject and could be spun out for a long time.

Outside the automobile windows more and more groups of soldiers in tattered uniforms, with hollow faces, limping along with the aid of sticks, their feet wrapped in scraps of burlap, moved through the snow. No quartermasters, no supply troops had prepared even the most pitiful straw pallets for them. No one had thought of them at all; in the whole army only the MP's and the courts-martial had functioned to the last minute—ordering and carrying out executions. And the field marshal rode by, chatting about a plant with verticillate leaves.

The Führer was far away and could not see these gray hordes of soldiers who were more crushed and more miserable than the defeated and miserable grenadiers of Kolin and Kunersdorf. This Führer was the man on the long arm of the lever (and, to boot, a man of straw). The army, encircled and isolated, had been thrown back upon its own resources like a solitary ship in mid-ocean, and it was the commander in chief of this army who had carried out the command of doom. The chief of staff of the army cannot be made the villain-in-chief. This scoundrel is not difficult to understand; as a Nazi within the framework of the Prussian general staff he was no more than a figure of momentary interest, an experimental life-form, so to speak, which after scarcely ten years proved to be incapable of survival. It was not the blood-thirsty Nazi general, but the tall man with the cameo-like face who had personally gone through two wars and who represented a tradition reaching back to Rossbach and Leuthen, it was this man who already envisioned a third world war, who here guaranteed consistency in policy, even if the policy were insane. It was he who placed the nimbus of historical tradition around an army's death sentence.

The idea of world rule had made a slow start amid the conditions of a small Central European state. It had grown out of the sweat of oppressed subjects, out of the atmosphere of the barracks, had faced its first decision on a world scale, and had failed. Monstrously puffed up and supported by a totally unscrupulous contempt for human beings and human lives, it had started on its course a second time. And after a tremendous initial leap it was falling again, on a theater of war that covered a whole continent. It had laid on a battlefield the bones of two hundred thousand men. A whole country was in mourning, a whole nation stripped of its power: helpless workers, farmers without rights on their own farms, the middle classes declassed and hiding in the ruins of their bombed property. And here, amid this great shambles on the Volga, a hemiatrophia developed on the face of a field marshal. It had happened the night before, a sign of great excitement and the expression of a dilemma. Within him was the commandment to accept death, and on the surface was his own skin. And in a flash of logic he broke through two centuries of dense clouds. Sacrifice is conceivable, he realized suddenly, only when it is done for the sake of one's own soil, for the preservation of one's own people. But it was impossible to try to glorify an unsuccessful marauding expedition by making an idealistic sacrifice. It was absurd, it was grotesque. This lightning flash of insight illuminated the battlefield where two hundred thousand corpses lay, and it lighted the field marshal's way over the dark bridge.

And now in the sedan the private person with the finely-cut features sat chatting about the Russian soldier's tobacco. "So the flowers of this plant are usually white or red but occasionally yellow? Aha, now I see, Mr. Polkovnik. It must be the common loosestrife of the family of Lythraceae. We have it in Germany too; there are over twenty varieties. Very interesting indeed. . . ."

The field marshal continued to chat about *makhorka.*

Outside were soldiers, the chaff of the threshed army, empty husks of what had once been living forms. And they began to move like a heap of chaff blown along at the touch of the wind. A shuffling along on invisible feet, a flowing movement, incredibly slow, away from the Volga, toward the west.

334

No hand was raised to salute the marshal. No one cried "Heil!"

The parade of beaten soldiers moved along the road toward Gumrak, dipped into a ravine, and bobbed up again on the other side. It wound on, a long gray thread—ten, twenty, thirty thousand men, half of what was left of the army, while the other half was still being hacked to bits, showered with steel, blown into the air. For it was still not enough! Their German mothers had borne them for this last fantastic fluttering under the bright winter sky. Their commander had received the radio codes from the southern group and also the copy of the Reich Marshal's speech. Iron and flames and dust were still raging through the factory yards and the windowless sheds where the commander's men lay. The copy of the speech had been the last straw. In a fury he had radioed the Führer's headquarters: "Request no premature funeral sermons." But an hour later he had sent the stipulated message declaring that he would fight to the last man. This was the formula that had been coined to describe the army's last spasms, but now that the army command had fallen silent without even issuing a last order or a last greeting, this formula was nothing but a rhetorical flourish. A large number of troop commanders could no longer sympathize with any such final bit of stage-acting. A group of old colonels pointed out to their commander the insanity of his behavior, and one of these graybeards got down on his knees and pleaded with the commander to put an end to the slaughter of the men. Finally, the troops to both sides of the factory area refused to be carried on to destruction any longer. At the "Tennis Racket" and at the bread factory the soldiers laid down their arms and let the Russian tanks roll through right up to the doors of the staff headquarters. Before long another twenty thousand soldiers and officers, including the commander of the north group, his chief of staff, and seven generals, were taken prisoner, and the procession flowing westward gathered recruits in the evening and on the following morning.

There were now forty-five thousand men streaming along the road. Forty-five thousand men, and the last crumb of bread had been consumed, the last roll of bandage used up, the last pint of gasoline expended or blown up. There was no transportation; all the personnel carriers, trucks, ambulances, command cars, and tractors had been driven until they could go no longer or had been blown up. Army Headquarters had foreseen only the grave for its men, and it had run the army economy accordingly. These thousands of men had been yielded up to death. Dysentery, typhus, and plague marched with them. The possibility of marching these stricken soldiers to the west, opening the German front, and turning them over to the men who were responsible for their condition—this idea had to be dropped. Not a man, with the exception of the staff officers, would have survived the two hundred and fifty miles and reached the German lines alive.

Russia had to absorb this living chaos.

Forty-five thousand men here and, together with the German soldiers who had been captured earlier, there were ninety-one thousand men—a vast mass that suddenly had to be cared for, supplied, and transported. The Russians' own pockets were empty. The villages of the steppe had been leveled to the ground. The cattle on the farms had all been slaughtered. The railroad lines had been destroyed. The only usable railroads lay beyond the former Russians lines. The procession of prisoners moved toward Kotluban; they would have to travel that far on foot. The Russians chose Gumrak as the destination for the first stage in the journey. In order to equip this improvised reception center, the Russian front troops contributed part of their provisions, their doctors, their medical corps men, and medical supplies. But the bulk of the prisoners moved along at a speed of half a mile an hour and took two days to cover a distance which normally should have been done in five hours.

At evening the icy mist rose again, and not only from the Volga; it seethed up out of all the ravines, the very breath of the snow-covered landscape. The marchers reached Krutaya Balka, the comparatively shallow ravine with its grim tributary gorges. Over the wooden bridge, from which the plank flooring had been partly removed and the holes stuffed with horse bones and frozen snow, the procession moved: fleshless, exhausted creatures wrapped in coats and rags, now a large group, now a small one, now a pair whose heads drooped and who clung to one another for support. Then a man pulling another along on a sled. Then a column in loose formation. More and more of them, an endless stream, men shuffling, stumbling, slipping, getting up again and going on; more and more, like smoke from a moving train.

The march had begun while the sun stood high in the sky. But earlier there had been nothing here but the white wasteland of snow. And at that time, before the prisoners reached this ravine, a solitary man had crossed the bridge in the morning mist. He had paused in the middle of the bridge and looked down. Below he had seen a dead horse and a dying fire. Around the embers four men had been huddling, looking like ruffled birds with their coats and their shelter halves powdered with drifted snow. The man in the long truck driver's coat had called down to them: "Hey you, down there, what are you doing here? Why don't you rejoin your troops; what are you waiting for here?"

"For the end!" one of them had replied.

The voice had sounded familiar to him. He had gone down to them and then he had seen that the man who had answered was Sergeant Gnotke. Gnotke had shaken the coat off his back, stood up, and said "Colonel, sir," (colonel or general, it really didn't matter any longer) "there's no sense in it any more. Once I thought it was enough to keep alive whatever happened, and that helped me to keep going. But now I'm not even sure that's true any more, and that's bad."

"Very bad, a terrible situation," Vilshofen had replied, and he had looked at the others.

"This is Private Altenhuden; he can't get up any more," Gnotke had explained. "And this is Private Franz Schiele; he can't stand up either." Altenhuden, whom Vilshofen knew, looked as he always had; his face was peaceful and of a delicate blue hue. Franz Schiele, whom Vilshofen did not know, had the same calm, delicate blue features. "And this is Matthias Gimpf; he's asleep now and when he wakes up he talks about snow and marching prisoners."

"Well, let's sit down."

And Vilshofen and Gnotke sat down.

"A very difficult situation, not one that a man can get out of alone," Vilshofen had taken up the thread of the conversation and the thread of his thoughts. It couldn't be done alone. You could not take a step alone. One didn't come into the world alone, and if one went out of it alone, one became nothing but carrion lying under the open sky.

"It can't be done alone, Gnotke."

"No, it can't." None knew this as well as Gnotke. There sat Gimpf—up to his shoulders in snow, his forehead burning, his lips parching. Gimpf had long been testimony to Gnotke's fear of being alone. "But we were not alone," Gnotke went on, and the reproach in those words had not escaped Vilshofen, nor had he been unaffected by that reproach.

"No, we were not alone. We knew that a comrade lay beside us, that behind us . . ." But there the tangle began. Up front there were the men with the rifles, side by side. Behind were the commanders, the staffs, the supply troops. Still farther behind: the division, the corps, the army, the Army High

337

Command, the High Command of the Armed Forces, the Führer and Supreme Commander. And from the bottom to the top it had to be one current, one will, one fate, and this pyramid was to be the embodiment of the people's strength, the executor of the people's will, the guardian of the people's destiny.

It was all clear, clear as crystal. . . .

But in reality the only clarity—and considerable pain—was in the eyes of this man of fifty as they regarded the weather-beaten soldier's face of Gnotke and the two blue death masks and the perspiring, flushed face of the fevered Gimpf. Clear too was the flashing, crystalline sky, for time had passed and time was still passing, and Vilshofen's bright, open eyes were obviously the eyes of a sleeping man.

He awoke again.

The army moving on millions of nailed boots up to the glittering apex, from bottom to top the clear embodiment of the people's soul—so he took up his thought where he had left it. All clear, all transparent . . . except that at the moment he was sitting in a ravine, that opposite sat a man with his hands buried in the wide sleeves of his coat, opposite another who was going under at the moment without making any attempt to keep afloat, and still another already setting forth on the great voyage, and opposite were also two blue stones that were already at the bottom of the deep sea. And above was the bridge over which gray endless lines of living creatures were moving, larvae without eyes or with eyes fixed on the ground, thousands and tens of thousands of feet. And these were no longer stout grenadier boots. On the line went, leaving an unending, slimy trail. And suddenly, while the army here was already no more than thick mud trickling along, a cannonade shattered the sky, black clouds of smoke rolled up from North Stalingrad, and another three thousand, four thousand men fell. That certainly was not the will of the people, not this superfluous cannonade and not these creatures crawling over the bridge and not these men transformed into blue corpses. Many, many things could not be the will of the people.

And it was no longer transparent; it was becoming opaque.

This time, when weariness overwhelmed him again, Vilshofen slept with closed eyes. But his thoughts wound deviously on, and the sky continued to rumble; the procession on the bridge went on and there was a bustling near him. Gimpf was talking in his delirium and Gnotke was trying to soothe him.

The soul of the people had certainly not crawled fifteen hundred miles to this Krutaya Balka. The shuffling of feet on the bridge up there and the state of affairs down here below the bridge had no connection with any kind of soul. It at most had something to do with the Army Propaganda Section. The divisions, corps, armies, the High Command and the OKW, the Führer—that whole gigantic pyramid was no expression of the popular will. Wretched German people, you built cities, built cathedrals, placed free tillers on a free soil, reached lofty heights in art, in science, in law, in language. You evolved the Hansa, evolved guilds, evolved free crafts, found manifold modes of expression for your nature. Your military organization can only be considered one aspect of your being, one department of your complex social constitution. That department expanded, grew all-powerful, swallowed up everything else. It broke down all dikes and flooded over the boundaries of other countries, and the tiller had to leave his soil, the workman his work, the priest his parish, the teacher his pupils, the youth his companions, the husband his wife; the people ceased to exist as a people and became nothing but fuel for the monstrous, smoking mountain; the individual became nothing but wood, peat, fuel oil, and finally a black flake spewed up out of the flames.

Such were the dozing thoughts of a man who had once been a student of philosophy before he entered the army in the First World War, who had remained an army officer, had served in the foreign and intelligence branches of the armed forces and who in 1939 had set out to make the impossible possible.

Another man in that ravine, Matthias Gimpf, was also dozing—murmuring to himself, gesticulating. Caught up in his dream, he would sometimes glance up, recognize his comrade Gnotke, then lose himself in fearful, snowy night. Gimpf's nostrils and lips were black from dried mucus and from his stertorous breathing. His face was a deep red, but it was free of the spots that covered his throat and chest; these he had exposed to the cold air. Gnotke put snow in his mouth; then, when Gimpf complained about a violent headache, Gnotke held a snow-cooled hand to his burning forehead.

Gimpf had spoken out at last and was no longer a puzzle to Gnotke. In his delirious spells and also in his intervals of consciousness he had talked about everything. Gnotke now knew where he had lost his grasp on reality—on the road from Vyazma to Smolensk one moonless, snowy night.

Gnotke heard it again, and Vilshofen, now wide awake, heard it too.

". . . Two kids with their fur caps and little mittens like clumsy little puppies . . . must have been about four years old.

They straggled behind and fell and couldn't get up again. Captain Steinmetz ordered the kids shot and Sergeant Leopold carried out the order. . . . After that there were three more and I carried out the order. . . . Captain Steinmetz gave the order about the caps and we took the prisoners' caps away. . . ."

The hoarse voice rattled on ". . . Frightful weather, cold, wind, snow . . . they stood packed like sardines in the factory. . . ."

Vilshofen opened his eyes again. The ravine was smoking, the tributary gorges were smoking; everywhere hoarfrost had settled and dense mist rose up to the sky. The evening star hung beside the bridge like a light on an anchored ship, a pallid spot in the mist. Voices could be heard on the bridge; the damp air carried the sound like a telephone wire. Words in Russian: *"Tashchitye saboi!* Lug him along!" Words in German: "He's done for, he can't make it, we can't make it either."

Tramping, shuffling, weary scraping of feet. One man fell flat and remained on the ground. His whimpering died away in silence. More words: "Chaplain . . . you have something in your knapsack, don't you!" —"Nothing but last messages. But here, in my coat pocket, there's one more package of hardtack. . . ." And then, the voice dying away at the end of the bridge: "So. That will have to last. Till Gumrak."

Murmured words, tapping of feet twenty, thirty yards away. The mist conducted sound, but that was not the strangest part of it. It was quiet, incomprehensibly quiet. For seventy-seven, for a hundred days, for two hundred days from the Mius, day and night had been shattered by the thunder of tanks, of cannon, of Stukas. And now everything was still. It could not be grasped, could scarcely be endured. The earth, the sky silent and no sounds in the mist but coughing.

A hoarse sentence was spoken by the sick man below the bridge. "We threw the caps away, out into the snow."

"Why out into the snow?" Vilshofen asked.

"Then they ran and wanted to get them back, and then we fired."

"Who ran?"

"The Russians," Gnotke replied.

"What is he talking about?" Vilshofen asked.

"He was one in a detachment of guards and he's talking about a column of prisoners who were being moved from Vyazma to Smolensk. . . ." Gimpf opened his eyes again; it was one of those intervals when he came out of his delirium.

His expression changed; the light of reason appeared in his eyes. He recognized his former commander.

"Were you there, Gimpf?" Vilshofen asked.

"Tell the colonel what you couldn't do and the real reason you were sent to the penal battalion," Gnotke said.

"I was in the guards detachment at Camp 271 in Vyazma," Gimpf murmured.

"Tell him about the shipment of prisoners to Smolensk and how many there were."

"Fifteen thousand."

"How many reached Smolensk?"

"Two thousand."

"And what happened to the rest?" Vilshofen had sat up abruptly and leaned his face close to the sick man.

"Left on the way . . ." Gimpf murmured.

"On the way? And what were you saying before about children with fur caps and little mittens?"

"They died on the way, the soldiers, the women, the children . . . and those three clumsy little ones, those three too. . . ."

"Thirteen thousand! Gimpf, Gimpf!" Vilshofen gripped his arm. But Gimpf's face contorted, the whites of his eyes filled with blood. His mind was obscured again. Black foam rose to his lips and he gurgled incoherent words: "Captain Steinmetz. . . . No cartridges left. . . . With the spade. . . . Oh, oh . . . snow . . ."

Feet shuffling in the snow—the blue face of the dead soldier Schiele—the face of the dead soldier Altenhuden—Gnotke bending over the writhing Gimpf.

The silence of death. The catastrophe. . . .

Not only a military catastrophe, not only the wrong lines drawn on a strategic map, not only mistakes in columns of figures. . . . Three children, four years old. . . . How do three murdered children weigh in the balance? And, fearful thought . . . there are not only these three children, there is not only Vyazma. . . .

How heavy is the guilt?

How does the dead Stalingrad army weigh in the balance, how much does this ghostly procession of prisoners weigh? What else must be laid upon the scales? Can guilt be weighed? How can it be weighed?

Children shot, women shot, old men, helpless prisoners shot —according to orders, "as the law provides." What sort of law is that? Is it a law of nature, of reason, of metaphysics, of

341

human intercourse? Is it a law dedicated to preserving the interests of all? What is its origin, who passed it?

Is it the law of the German people, the same people who brought forth a Guttenberg, a Matthias Grünewald, a Martin Luther, a Beethoven, an Immanuel Kant? Is it the law of a creative people living by the fruits of its own creations?

Did the German people have no other political face to show the world?

What a contorted countenance! A peasant boy from old peasant stock in Sauerland, from an ancient culture, with red spots on his neck, his hair damp, his eyes rolling, black foam bubbling on his lips, the gasping breath stinking. But the contortion did not lie therein. The catastrophe was not only a military catastrophe, the collapse not only a physical collapse. It was not only the typhus foam on the lips that counted. German people, what madness is being sweated away here, and whose madness!

Matthias Gimpf died, having not yet begun to live. His life had come to a dead stop in deep powdery snow on the road from Vyazma to Smolensk. He had never been able to come away from that road, from the face of a child who could not understand how it could suddenly become a motherless wolf's cub that was made to sink down in the snow, a child that could not understand how a being with a human face could drive it to such a fate. He had never been able to escape the face of that child. The eyes of the Russian child and the large gray eyes of his mother in Sauerland asked one and the same question, and it could not be answered. A lightless night, footsteps in the snow, footsteps here and footsteps there, and he died. The dying was hard, was a shrieking of the entire body and a spewing out of heated smoke, was slumping back in the snow again and pouring sweat and choked words, was convulsion and vomiting where there was no more to vomit. It took a long time for him to die; death came piecemeal. The last was a twitching movement of his left foot. That was the slightly frostbitten foot which had given Gnotke so much concern for many weeks. And Vilshofen now stared at this foot, or rather at the fur-lined boot which had once been his own, which he had given Gnotke and which was now on the dead man's foot.

"We must endure, Gnotke," Vilshofen said after a while.

Gnotke's eyes also rested on the foot, which had now ceased to twitch. He looked up at the bridge for a moment, then turned to Vilshofen and examined the gaunt face, deeply hollowed under the cheekbones, and the prominent nose and large eyes.

A conversation began between this soldier who was now altogether alone and who could not see his way any further, and the general who wanted to fight his way on through snow and chaos, through error, crime, and the fearful fate that had been brought on by obscure powers. Vilshofen could not help re-examining his role once more. As a good officer, he realized, as one who had himself lain in the dirt up front, who had shared his cigarettes and bread and other things with the men, his role had been a more significant one than that of the bad officers. Not the uncomradely ones, not the officers who flew out of the pocket, not the ones who thought only of saving their own skins and whom the soldiers did not trust, but he who had the confidence of his men, *he* had led those men to destruction.

This, then, had to be admitted: that all moral and ethical qualities were necessarily tainted, necessarily produced what was contrary to themselves, if the possessor of those qualities carried out orders and obeyed a law which was not *the* law, but simply rules set up by a conspiracy of asocial owners who wanted to own more and more, to secure more coal, iron, and soil for themselves, who wanted to feather their own nests.

At the edge of the bridge a man lay, screaming his soul out into the night. The column moved past him and no one paid any attention to him or his screams. Once again a Russian voice said, *"Tashchitye saboi,"* and again there were laments and mutters, "We can't make it ourselves." Then curses and an order in Russian; the fallen soldier was picked up and carried along, though perhaps he would be set down again after a while. And here sat a man who had carried another along for weeks, who had put his own boots on the man. In this place, where men were run over by fleeing columns of trucks, where the wounded and the feeble and presumably some who still had their strength were left behind in the snow, whole truckloads of them, where entire hospitals were permitted to go up in smoke —in this place such behavior had been rare. That was the moral fiber that counted, and now a man like that who had already gone through a thousand hells was ready to give up.

"There sits Altenhuden," Gnotke said. "Only yesterday he said he must fix the gate at home; the hinge is rusted through, he said. And there sits Schiele; he has a daughter and no one else in his family, and he said he would have to draw the balance from his savings account so that his daughter wouldn't lose the property she inherited from her mother. If I'd had to listen to that kind of thing a few years ago I would have taken a chair and hit them on their heads. Then I was a storm trooper, you see, and everything I didn't understand seemed like crap to me, and suspicious besides. Now here they sit and I'm not altogether free of blame for their sitting here, nor for Gimpf's lying here in the snow. Well, now I'm sitting here too and here I'll stay. I'm through, I've had enough."

The hordes marched over the bridge, from noon to midnight. The mist had sunk away, had crawled back into the ravines out of which it had arisen. A bridge stretching from one bank of snow to another, and the bridge itself was of snow. Above arched a starry sky and below the bridge flowed a pallid stream. Those who noticed the group of figures in the ravine below the bridge scarcely registered the sight. If one of the Russian guards happened to see them, he assumed that they were a group of frozen men like the many who lined both sides of the road.

Defeat was the defeat of every individual too. Limbs numb, souls dumb, the creatures that marched across the bridge were the burned-out slag of the lost battle. And generals were there who already knew and even spoke of the war as lost. And this man here (Vilshofen looked at Gnotke who sat hunched up, his head resting on his crossed arms) had experienced defeat much farther back. By now Vilshofen knew enough about him to know that he had dropped out of the storm troops by 1934. At Moscow he had been virtually crossed off for the second time. Only sheer strength, like a weed's, only some primal force had enabled him to go through the trials that had awaited him. Through it all he had remained a man, understood the Altenhudens, the Schieles, the Gimpfs at his side; he was a man whose roots stretched out to those around him, and out of these roots he had drawn strength. He felt responsible for the dark destinies of others and knew the harm he had once done when he too fought in the streets. He had retraced his steps to the source of the German disease. The generals were against the Führer because he was losing the war; this man was against the Führer because he had begun the war and because, ten years earlier, he had already begun a war against the German people and had misued the people for aims hostile to its own interests. That was one difference; it constituted, at any rate, a fundamentally different stage of perception. And therefore this man here with that bony face of his that had risen afresh out of hunger and fire was a grain of the salt of the earth. The deceived, beaten, hopeless, stunned nation needed him if it were ever to return to itself, if it were ever to rise again.

"Gnotke!" Vilshofen said.

Gnotke raised his head again and listened. He realized that the man who was speaking to him was also a beaten man. He too was sore and flayed by thought. And if only he had spoken so a bare two weeks ago, a Captain Döllwang, a Lieutenant Latte, a Private Liebich, Fell, Liebsch, Kalbach, Stüve, and hundreds of others would still be alive. And if he had spoken so earlier still, an entire tank regiment would have heard him and perhaps have acted accordingly. But Gnotke listened anyhow. And it was true, he himself had said that it was enough to keep alive under all circumstances. And it was also true that you had to know what you were living for. Now this colonel was like a lantern-bearer lighting the way through darkness. What was it about himself, Gnotke wondered, that this man was insisting on having him for company?

"There sits Altenhuden and there sits Schiele." This time it was Vilshofen who said it. "Broken gates, rusty hinges; all Germany is broken and mothers' bequests have been lost more than once over. There are so many there who are orphaned, so many who are aimless, so many who are neglected. And there is so much that has to be made good, rebuilt. Don't you think, Gnotke, that every hand will be necessary and every head as well?"

"I imagine so. But—I've got to say it once and for all, sir. I come from the penal battalion, sir. That means, from the lowest of the low. . . ."

"I don't exactly come from the highest of the high, but still I've been a part of the staff command, and the burden of blame is naturally a good deal heavier on me than on a soldier from the penal battalion."

"You mean for the lost battle, sir?"

"During these nights in Stalingrad I've been thinking of a good many other things besides the disaster on the battlefield. When I speak of blame now, I mean our guilt toward our people who have been led astray and whose physical existence is menaced, if they are not already altogether lost. And that has to be made up for!"

"Oh, I see. . . ."

"What do you see?"

"I suppose you are thinking of the next war, sir."

345

"No, Gnotke. In the first place, the weapons were the wrong ones. And in the second place the blow was aimed in the wrong direction. Our failures at home and our guilt have produced even greater failures and greater guilt toward the outside world. To my mind it is not our business to interfere in Europe and the whole wide world; above all we have to restore order, straighten things out at home."

"Oh, I see, the Black Reichswehr, political murder and that sort of thing. We had that in Pomerania. And the Feme and the SA, too, and then the SA had to be killed. We've had it all."

"Good God, Gnotke. Every man must be able to breathe freely, to be master in his own house, to keep and to consume what he produces with his own hands. That is, putting it crudely, the kind of order we have to create."

"Yes, I've heard that story before, too."

"Good God, all the figures of speech used up, all words twisted, no faith left, nothing left, everything burned down to charred stumps! . . ."

It was a strange conversation between a general and a common soldier, but the hour was an extraordinary one. Two frozen faces of dead men and a third twisted corpse were the witnesses. Low-flying fog surrounded the group. Across the bridge marched what had once been an élite army. The sky was high and cold, dotted with twinkling stars. Air suffused with death; the scenery of a theater of war just before the curtain descends.

Two faces. The general and the gravedigger, not general and gravedigger any longer, but two defeated men. How could these two work together? There had been fighting and destruction, and if the fighting had not been necessary, if it had been criminal, what values could arise out of the defeat? Vast sorrows had been poured out into the snow, and was nothing to remain, nothing? . . . It would not do for the defeated to join their comrades in defeat for another "crusade" such as this had been. For it had been nothing but a march through the blood of other peoples; it had meant only the crucifixion of their own people. Was it to be repeated again and again, endlessly?

"Look, Gnotke, beyond this abandoned battlefield and beyond this lost war gleam new battlefields and future theaters of war."

"I've had enough of that."

"So have I."

"I don't know, sir, how we two can team up."

346

"That's just what we have to find out; that's what counts."

That was what counted, that was what this pair had to do beneath the falling curtain, that was what they tried to clarify. It was not the end of the tragedy, but it was the close of an act.

Now, the morning and evening mists, the sky with its stars, and for the second time white fog billowed up out of all the ravines. All the fields were still and sparrows twittered on the rubble heaps in the shattered villages. Another evening came and another morning; the sun rose again out of the frozen Volga, wheeled on above the gables and stone chimneys and the roofless skeletal buildings of ruined Stalingrad, traveled high above the cracked white mirror of the Volga Steppe, rolled downhill toward the Rossoshka heights and toward the Don and in setting, cast a fiery glow over the fields and hills of the Don Basin. And wherever the sun's rays struck, from the Volga to the Don and far and wide over all the villages of the Don Steppe, lay silence.

Through snow and silence the procession moved; day and night it crawled over the wide white bowl rimmed by the Volga hills and the Rossoshka heights. From Central Stalingrad across the airport and on over Krutaya Balka, on across the flat steppe and over the railroad embankment, along the railroad embankment to Gumrak and then on through the Don Steppe toward Kotluban it crept; and from North Stalingrad through Gorodishche and Alexandrovka and then likewise defiling into the Don Steppe toward Kotluban, where there was land that the war had not destroyed and a railroad that could receive the river of men.

Snow and silence. And in the deserted villages the sparrows twittered and on the steppe black clusters of crows rose up from the heaps of corpses and with wings beating heavily flew over the slowly-moving groups of stumbling men. The march passed stretches of road marked by horses' bones stuck upright in the snow. And sometimes figures in torn German trench coats would emerge out of the mist and stand staring with feverish eyes at the marchers. Most of the prisoners scarcely looked up at them, and when one would finally call to the others and invite them to join the line, the watchers would reply in hollow voices that they had to defend their positions, and they would vanish again into the mist.

During the brief rests on the march the men piled into dugouts, face against face and leg against leg, the few cots piled with clusters of men. When the men lying in top bunks broke through they did not get up, even if those underneath were being crushed and killed. Those for whom there was no room in the dugouts stood outside in the glistening night, much the way a circle of calves will stand in summer with their heads close together for protection from the cruel sun of the steppe.

On they moved at a speed of half a mile an hour.

A steppe settlement rose out of the plain on the horizon. When they came up to it they saw that it was nothing but a vast park of shattered and plundered vehicles standing side by side, wheel against wheel, roof against roof, trucks, personnel carriers, jeeps, and busses. Those who wanted to collapse against the walls of a truck or crawl underneath one, never to rise again, were not prevented. The road descended into a ravine which was a graveyard of tanks, cannon, and flak guns and a feeding station for swarms of black crows. On the other side of the ravine the road rose again to the level plain. Feet slipped and slid down the road along which they had once moved in flight. Panic had once surged along this road, men had been run over and trampled into the snow, and over these bodies wheels had passed again. Now the icy coating of the road was a mosaic of heads, hands, and faces over which the feet of the marchers tramped. They moved on through Gumrak, past the railroad station filled with frozen corpses, past the dozen sidings on which stood freight cars filled with frozen corpses. Beneath the snow some of the markings on these cars could be read: *Deutsche Reichsbahn Düsseldorf* or *Deutsche Reichbahn Hannover;* and others like *France, Belge, Danmark, Rsecsposolita Polska, Eesti, Magyarorszag, Romania, Hellenike Demokratia, Jugoslavia.* But no rag-wrapped foot flinched as it marched over this "Mosaic" road, stepping on a flattened-out face. The gigantic cemetery of vehicles reminded no one of the triumphal advance; the tank graveyard in the ravine did not awaken memories of the army that had been lost in the course of the advance; the corpse-filled freight cars with their markings from every land did not arouse thoughts of the vast graveyard of nations the army had left in its trail or of the slave empire it had intended to build.

There were a few men here and there who were still capable of thought. When Major Holmers marched past the railroad cars and deciphered the chalkwhite letters *Eesti* and *Romania* he reflected that export goods had once been shipped to Hamburg in these same cars, naphtha and lead and corn and raisins. When Major Simmering passed the railroad station and saw, beside a huge pile of amputated arms and legs, the armless and legless bodies, he turned his face away. Doctor Huth, who was marching at his side, expressed his thought: "Help is not always help." When it is in the service of a crime, help itself becomes a crime, Simmering finished the thought without speaking. When Major Buchner, who had been tramping along in a half doze, glanced up and saw 8.8 cm. flak guns, scattered crates of ammunition, and snow-covered fragments of dead men, he said to himself: All the expostulating over the telephone was useless. I should have turned the guns around, shot everything I had at the Tulevoy ravine, and blasted the whole crazy staff at headquarters there. That would have been one way out, and if nothing else it would have shortened the murderous business. Little Lieutenant Lawkow, as he passed a group of bunkers south of Stalingradski and saw piles of smashed crates and empty tin cans, reflected that this was what it had looked like when the staffs skipped out. They calculated rightly that everything was going up in the air anyhow, whether or not they provided leadership, and so they cleared out and we idiots stayed and defended our position. What a crazy business; we marched to war against "the Rothschilds and Ballins and Bleichröders and the whole international fraternity of corrupters of the people." And finally here on the Volga we had the whole gang of corrupters right with us, all tricked out in their red stripes and their monocles, and a worse sink of corruption than this mob the world has never seen.

But there were few who had such thoughts, few who had any thoughts at all. The overwhelming mass of the men crawled along. This army had been an élite army and the majority of the soldiers had been recruited from rural districts, not from the cities. These farm boys had been cut off from their native environment and soil even before the war, in the "labor service" and premilitary training. The infantrymen among them had traveled on foot more than fifteen hundred miles and their intestines were, as autopsies later demonstrated, without coils and rubbed smooth as glass ribbons. Their inner organs as well as their muscular structure had been deformed. Now they had reached bottom. It was as though their souls had fluttered out of their bodies as the cannon roared for the last time, and the silence through which they marched was the silence of the grave. They shuffled on with frozen feet or frozen toes, with faces gnawed by frost, some without ears, some without noses. The corporal's chevrons and the sergeant's braid had been for them insignia of rank in the sole imaginable order of things. When the meaning of these insignia vanished, the whole world of order fell apart. They shuffled on, and it was exceptional if a hand reached out to steady a stumbling comrade. It was altogether out of the question that a last crust of bread would be shared. The whole was sick and the cells were sick, and interrelationships no longer existed. The organism had disintegrated into its juices, into blood and mucus, yellow gall and black gall, and each individual as well was in process of disintegration. Only one step separated him from it; he clung with only one hand to the vessel of life. And many let go; their will to live had been used up in the endless journey and in the thunder of battles from the Carpathians to the Volga.

Chaos had been ordered, and this was it.

The gray tide reached the Don plain, poured on along the railroad line to Kotluban. Freight cars stood at various places along the line, and these cars took in the defeated army and carried it along from there. But the end was not yet. The excrement that poured out of the toilets of the cars and froze the color of blood in lumps between the tracks, betrayed the guest that rode with these maimed hordes.

This procession had left behind it on the march and on the railroad as well a host of dead who died from wounds, from white and red dysentery, from typhus and from psychic paralysis. The names of these dead are written in snow. But there are other graves, those of Russian doctors, medical aides, and nurses who accompanied the defeated army and found death on the way. These graves count: they are written in the book of humanity. On the first stage of the journey, up to the first reception camp, there were forty-two of these graves.

A whole nation led astray, dispersed, breaking across frontiers, following the unfurled banner of madness, spreading out over the map of Europe, over the valleys and forests and fields and seas, and in this inhuman effort itself ground to scrap, pulverized. . . .

That nation, from deepest darkness, must be led to the brink of a new day, must not become a color blotted out from the palette of the nations, a note no longer sounded by the orchestra of the world. For this all men who are of good will must hold out their hands to one another, and find a common road that is still passable.

This it was that that the two men in Krutaya Balka had been discussing. Small wonder that it had appeared so difficult, though they spoke a common language, for the gulf was very deep, the roads all blocked, words all misused, good faith all spent.

A wind arose, an icy wind from the snowy wastelands of the East. But the sun shone over all the land from the Pamir and Lake Balkash, from the Aral Sea to the Volga, and the air was filled with a diamond brightness, and so the wind held the first hint of spring as it hummed through the hollow factories, towering ruins, and cracked walls of Stalingrad. It swept on over the cratered and trench-scarred plains, over piles of wrecked tanks, over wheels and guns. And there was nothing in the sky, no more whine of motors, no more geysers of earth and smoke, nothing but the musical sighing of the wind. The earth was void, and from Central Stalingrad through Gumrak and on to the villages of the Don Steppe ran the broad track of many feet, a long line, the fate line of a nation.

In the Krutaya Balka, where three bodies rested beneath a rough mound of snow, another track led up the ravine and across the white field until it entered and was lost in the broad trail of the marching army.

It was the track of two men walking side by side.

YOU WILL ALSO WANT TO READ THESE
EXCITING WAR STORIES
FROM BERKLEY

ESCAPE FROM COLDITZ
   by P. R. Reid   (S1761—75¢)

MEN AT WAR
   ed. by Ernest Hemingway   (Z2121—$1.25)

ROMMEL, THE DESERT FOX
   by Desmond Young   (N1651—95¢)

THE THEORY AND PRACTICE OF HELL
   by Eugen Kogon   (N1621—95¢)

PACIFIC WAR DIARY
   by James J. Fahey   (Z2308—$1.25)

THE BRASS RING
   by Bill Mauldin   (Z2309—$1.25)

Send for a *free* list of all our books in print

These books are available at your local newsstand, or send price indicated plus 15¢ per copy to cover mailing costs to Berkley Publishing Corporation, 200 Madison Avenue, New York, N.Y. 10016.